Praise for

"The strong hero in Jimmy and the snappy
dialogue between him and Sheri draw the
read
betw
story
turning

—*RT Book Reviews* on *Lone Wolf Standing*

"Cassidy creates strong conflict and tension. An
intricate plot, sympathetic characters and hot
chemistry between Debra and Trey make this a
great read."

—*RT Book Reviews* on *Her Secret, His Duty*

"Cassidy just keeps getting better."

—*RT Book Reviews*

"Carla Cassidy has done a good job of
portraying the fragility but resilience
of the survivor and the detailed work of
investigation… Crime fans will get hold of
Deadman's Bluff and be determined to solve the
mystery by themselves."

—*Fresh Fiction*

"A terrific, enthralling addition to [Cassidy's]
Cowboy Café series."

—*Goodreads* on *Cowboy with a Cause*

Carla Cassidy is an award-winning and *New York Times* bestselling author who has written more than fifty novels for Harlequin. In 1995, she won Best Silhouette Romance from *RT Book Reviews* for *Anything for Danny*. In 1998, she also won a Career Achievement Award for Best Innovative Series from *RT Book Reviews*. Carla believes the only thing better than curling up with a good book to read is sitting down at the computer with a good story to write. Visit her online at carlacassidybooks.com.

Look for more books by Carla Cassidy in Harlequin Romantic Suspense—the ultimate destination for heart-racing romance and high-stakes suspense! There are four new Harlequin Romantic Suspense titles available every month. Check one out today!

New York Times Bestselling Author

CARLA CASSIDY

Snowbound with the Bodyguard

and

The Cowboy's Secret Twins

HARLEQUIN® ROMANTIC SUSPENSE CLASSICS

ISBN-13: 978-0-373-60667-2

Snowbound with the Bodyguard and The Cowboy's Secret Twins

Copyright © 2014 by Harlequin Books S.A.

The publisher acknowledges the copyright holder of the individual works as follows:

Snowbound with the Bodyguard
Copyright © 2008 by Carla Bracale

The Cowboy's Secret Twins
Copyright © 2009 by Carla Bracale

Recycling programs
for this product may
not exist in your area.

Printed in U.S.A.

CONTENTS

SNOWBOUND WITH THE BODYGUARD   7

THE COWBOY'S SECRET TWINS   233

SNOWBOUND WITH
THE BODYGUARD

Prologue

"**O**rder up." Smiley Smith, owner and short-order cook at Smiley's Café, banged the small bell on the counter to punctuate his words.

Janette Black wiped her hands on her cheerful red-and-white apron, then walked over to retrieve the Thursday special.

She grabbed the plate and served it to the man seated at the long counter. "Here you go, Walter." She smiled at the old man who came in every Thursday afternoon regular as clockwork for Smiley's meatloaf.

"Thank you, honey. Can I bother you for another cup of coffee?" Walter offered her a sweet smile.

"For you, Walter, it's no bother." She turned around and went to get the coffeepot, grateful that the lunch rush was over and she only had two more hours in her shift. Then she could go home and snuggle her little boy and visit with Nana until it was time for her to be back here first thing in the morning.

"How's that grandmother of yours?" Walter asked as she poured his coffee.

Janette's heart warmed at thoughts of her grandmother. "She's okay. We have her heart condition under control. She tires easily, but she's doing just fine."

Walter laughed. "She's a corker, that one. It will take more than a couple of strokes to keep her down."

As Janette began to wipe down the countertop, she smiled. Her grandmother wasn't just a corker, she was the woman who had raised Janette from the time she was three and the woman who was now helping Janette raise her little boy. Nana's last stroke had been nearly a year ago, but she had astounded the doctors with her recovery.

Janette was just giving the shiny surface a final swipe when the tinkle of the bell over the front door indicated another diner arriving.

She looked up and her blood froze. There were three of them, all wearing the khaki uniforms of law enforcement. Sheriff Brandon Sinclair led the way, swaggering in followed by two of his trusted deputies.

There were only two cafés in Sandstone, Oklahoma, and she'd chosen to work at Smiley's because the other place, Lacy's, was where Sinclair and his men usually ate their lunch.

Sheriff Sinclair surveyed the café like a king overseeing his domain, his ice-blue eyes narrowing just a touch as his gaze landed on Janette.

Take a table, she mentally begged. If they sat at the table, then Heidi, Janette's coworker, would wait on them. Janette had spent the past year of her life doing everything possible to avoid contact with the sheriff.

As he and his deputies headed toward the counter, her stomach bucked with a touch of nausea and her heart began to beat the rhythm of panic.

She couldn't lose it. Not here. Not now. She refused to let him know how he affected her, knowing that he would relish her fear.

He's just another customer, she told herself as the three seated themselves at the counter. "Can I take your orders?" she asked, surprised to hear her voice cool and collected despite all the emotions that quivered inside her.

"Coffee," Sinclair said. "What kind of pie is good today?"

"Apple," Janette replied tersely, then added, "the apple is always good."

"Then let's make it coffee and pie for all of us," Sinclair said.

Janette nodded and turned to get the coffeepot. She could do this. As long as she didn't look at him too long, as long as she didn't get close enough to smell his cologne. She had a feeling if she got a whiff of that cheap, cloying smell she might vomit.

She filled their cups, trying to ignore the way Sinclair's eyes lingered on her breasts. Her throat tightened and her heart banged harder against her ribs.

"Never guess what I heard through the grapevine," Sinclair said to his deputies.

"What's that, Sheriff?" Deputy Jed Billet asked.

"I heard that Janette has a little baby boy. What is he, about five months old, Janette?" Sinclair gazed at her knowingly.

She turned to get their pie, her hands trembling as she opened the display case that held the desserts. He knew. Dear God, he knew.

"Gonna be tough, being a single parent," Deputy Westin said.

As she placed the pie in front of Sinclair he reared back on the stool. "A boy. There's something special about a boy, don't you think so, Jed? I mean, I love my three little girls, but I always dreamed about how great it would be to have a son. Unfortunately, all my wife could pop was girls. Still, a boy needs a father, don't you agree?"

A roar went off in Janette's head. She had to escape. She had to take her son and leave Sandstone because she knew what evil Sheriff Brandon Sinclair was capable of, and as long as she remained in Sandstone he had the power to do whatever he wanted to do.

If he decided he wanted her baby boy, she knew he'd find a way to get him.

Chapter 1

"I'm sorry, ma'am, but I just got word that the bus isn't coming."

Janette blinked and stared up at the man in charge of the Cotter Creek bus station. She straightened in her chair as she realized she must have dozed off. She wrapped her arms around her still sleeping son and gazed at the man with confusion.

"Excuse me?" she said.

"The bus. It's not coming. It's been held up by weather."

"By weather?" Dulled by sleep, she stared at him as if he were speaking a foreign language.

He nodded. "Ice." He pointed out the window. Janette followed his finger and gasped in surprise as she saw the icy pellets falling from the sky. The ground was already covered with at least an inch.

Where had it come from? When she'd arrived at the bus station two hours ago the skies had been thick with gray clouds, but there hadn't been a hint of snow. Of course the last thing on her mind when she'd left Sandstone had been the weather forecast.

She looked back at the man and tried to swallow against the sense of panic that had been with her since she'd packed her bags and left Sandstone that afternoon. A friend of her grandmother's had driven her the thirty miles to Cotter Creek, where a bus to Kansas City ran every other day. It was supposed to run today.

"Will it be here tomorrow?" she asked.

"Depends if the weathermen are right or wrong. They say we're in for a blizzard, but they're wrong more often than they're right." He shrugged his skinny shoulders and pulled a stocking cap over his head. "You best get settled in someplace for the night. I've got to close down here. Check back in the morning and I'll know more about the schedule." He was obviously in a hurry, tapping his heel as he looked at her expectantly.

"Of course." She stood, grateful that Sammy still slept in his sling against her chest. She didn't want to show how scared she was, didn't want to do anything that might draw unnecessary attention to herself.

She'd find a pay phone, call the nearest motel and get a room for the night. Hopefully she'd still have time to get as far away from Sandstone as possible before Brandon Sinclair even knew she'd left the small town.

She grabbed the handle of her large suitcase and

draped the diaper bag over her shoulder, still groggy from the unexpected catnap.

She was barely out the door before the bus station, little more than a shack, was locked up behind her. The ice that fell had coated the sidewalk and created shiny surfaces on everything else in sight. Under different circumstances she might have found it beautiful.

With Sammy safely snuggled beneath her wool coat, she looked up and down the street. She didn't know Cotter Creek well. Perhaps there was a bed-and-breakfast someplace nearby where she could spend the night.

A new disquiet soared through her as she eyed the deserted streets. It was just after six but it was as if the entire town had packed their bags and left. There wasn't a person or a car on the street.

She should have asked to use the phone in the bus station. She should have asked the man where she could get a room for the night. But the nap had dulled her senses, and he'd hurried her out too fast for her to think clearly.

The sight of a phone booth in the distance rallied her spirits. Cotter Creek was near a major highway, and that meant there had to be a motel somewhere nearby.

Pulling the suitcase behind her, she hurried as fast as the slick concrete would allow toward the phone booth, feeling as if luck was on her side as she spied the small phone book hanging on a hook just inside the door.

She stepped into the booth and closed the door behind her, grateful to be out of the cold wind and stinging ice. With cold fingers she thumbed through the book until she found the page with the motel listings. Make that one listing. The Cotter Creek Motel.

Digging change from her purse, she felt Sammy stir as if the rapid beating of her heart disturbed his sleep. She drew a deep breath to steady her nerves.

She'd wanted to get as far away as possible as quickly as possible from Sandstone and Brandon Sinclair. Okay, so she couldn't get on the bus tonight. She'd cool her heels in a motel room and catch the bus the next day. Although she hated to part with a dime of the money that was neatly folded and tucked into a side pocket in her purse, she really didn't have a choice.

She *had* to get out of town tomorrow. Thirty miles was far too close to the devil and his minions. She wouldn't be satisfied until she was a thousand miles away. Once she got settled in a new town, she'd send for Nana and the three of them would build a new life where Brandon Sinclair couldn't bother them.

She dropped the change into the slot and punched in the number for the Cotter Creek Motel. A man answered on the third ring. "No room at the inn," he said.

"Is this the Cotter Creek Motel?" she asked, her hand tightening on the receiver.

"Yeah, but if you're looking for a room, we're full up. They've shut the highway down up north and I've got a houseful of travelers. I've even rented out my sofa in the lobby." He sounded positively gleeful. "Sorry." He hung up.

Janette held the receiver for a long moment, her heart pumping with panic once again. She hung up and frantically thumbed through the skinny phone book, looking for a listing of a bed-and-breakfast, a rental room, anywhere she could get a warm bed for the night. There was nothing.

She wanted to call her grandmother and ask her what to do. Where to go. But she'd only worry Nana, and that was the last thing she wanted to do.

Besides, Janette was an adult. She had to handle this. She was twenty-four years old and a mother, and the most important thing in her life at the moment was little Sammy. She had to get him someplace safe and warm.

She leaned her head against the cold glass of the booth and watched as the ice began to turn to snow and pick up in intensity. What was she going to do? She and Sammy couldn't spend the night out in the elements.

Desperation filled her and she felt a panic attack coming on. The palms of her hands grew slick with sweat as her throat seemed to constrict. She closed her eyes and drew in deep breaths, forcing the attack away. She didn't have time to be weak now. Sammy needed her, and she needed to get him someplace safe for the night.

She opened her eyes once again. The clouds and ice were creating an early twilight. She straightened as she saw a light shining from a window of one of the store-fronts in the next block.

Where there was light there might be somebody who could direct her to a place for the night. She checked to make sure her coat was securely fastened to keep Sammy as warm as possible, pulled up her hood and tied it beneath her chin, then stepped out of the phone booth and into the wind that had begun to howl with fierce intensity.

She kept her gaze focused on the light, a beacon of hope. It didn't take long for her gloveless fingers to turn numb and her cheeks to burn with the cold. Ice pellets pinged on the sidewalk and her bare skin.

She walked slowly, carefully, not wanting to fall on the slick walkways. Before she reached the radiating light, she saw the shingle that hung above the doorway. West Protective Services.

She knew that name. She frowned thoughtfully, then remembered. There had been an article in the paper not too long ago, a human interest story about the family who owned and operated a bodyguard business. The article had described the family as honorable, trustworthy people who put their lives on the line for their clients.

If she remembered the article correctly, they had been instrumental in cleaning up Cotter Creek when a development company had tried to take ranch land and had hired people to kill the ranchers.

You have to trust somebody, a little voice whispered in her head. She had no other choice. Once again she felt her throat closing up, a quickening of her heart and a sense of doom that portended one of her panic attacks.

Not giving herself a chance to second-guess her decision, she started for the door. She reached for the door handle just as a man barreled out and into her.

He bumped her with just enough force to cause her to lose her footing on the slippery sidewalk. She felt herself careening backward, but before she could fall, two big strong hands grabbed hold of her shoulders and steadied her.

"Sorry. Are you all right?" His deep voice was nearly carried away by the wind.

She looked up into the greenest eyes she'd ever seen. In an instant she assessed him. Shockingly good-looking, bold features, tall, with broad shoulders beneath a thigh-length black coat. He looked at her as if she were an apparition blown from the North Pole.

She had no idea if she could trust this man or not. Under any other circumstances she would never ask a stranger, particularly a man, for help. But she was out of options. "Please…I need help."

All Dalton West wanted was to get home and out of the snow. He'd been absorbed in paperwork and hadn't noticed the weather until he'd gotten up to stretch and had realized the forecasted storm was upon them. He'd hurriedly shut down the computer and turned off the coffeepot, his only goal to get to his nearby apartment. The last thing he wanted was to be snowed in at the office.

But with this woman looking at him with eyes the color of a summer Oklahoma sky, eyes that were filled with both desperation and wariness, he reopened the office door and ushered her inside. She swept past him, pulling a large suitcase behind her as she entered.

As he stepped back inside she turned to face him. "I…you protect people, right?"

He nodded, wondering what she was doing out in the snow. "That's my job."

"I want to hire you for the night…to protect me."

"Protect you from who?" he asked.

She gave a nervous laugh. "Not who…what. I need you to protect me from the weather. I arrived here in Cotter Creek a couple of hours ago to catch the bus, but it seems the bus isn't coming this evening. I need a place to stay for the night, but the motel is all booked up." At that moment the sound of a crying baby came from beneath her coat.

She unfastened the buttons to reveal a tiny boy in a blue coat. Dalton didn't know much about babies, but the little guy looked to be only a couple of months old. As his blue eyes landed on Dalton, he grinned and bounced in his sling.

"This is my son, Sammy, and I'm uh…Jane Craig. I was hoping you could find us a room or something for the night," she said. "I can pay you for your trouble."

There had been just enough hesitation before she spoke her name that Dalton sensed she was lying. She had a pretty face, heart-shaped with those big blue eyes and pale eyebrows that arched perfectly above them. Her trembling full lips were a faint shade of blue, indicating to him that she had already been outside too long.

Why would she lie about her name? Or had he just imagined that moment of hesitation? Business had been slow enough lately that maybe he was looking for mystery where there was none.

"I'm Dalton West," he replied, then frowned and looked out the window where the blowing snow was creating almost whiteout conditions. He could think of several places he might be able to get her a bed for the night, but none of them were within walking distance, and nobody in their right mind was going to get in a car to come and pick her up.

There was really only one alternative, and it wasn't one that made him a happy man. "Look, I have an apartment two blocks from here. You can stay there for the night and I'll bunk downstairs with my landlord."

It was obvious from the expression on her face that she didn't like the idea. Dalton raked a hand through his hair and tamped down an edge of impatience. He certainly could understand her reticence. She was a young woman alone with a baby and he was a virtual stranger. In her circumstances he wouldn't be thrilled by his suggestion.

"Oh, no...I couldn't," she began.

"Look, Jane. I'm a bodyguard by profession. I make a living protecting people. You'll be safe for the night. Besides, I don't know what else to tell you. We're out of options." His glance went back out the window, then he looked back at her. "And we need to get going before we can't get out of here."

She hesitated another minute. "I'll hire you for the night to protect me. We'll keep it a business deal."

"Fine. You can write me a check when we get to my place." It was obvious to Dalton that she couldn't afford their usual fee. Her coat was worn and her shoes looked old. This was not a woman rolling in dough.

As she rebuttoned her coat to protect her son from the elements, he grabbed hold of her suitcase.

They stepped back out into the howling wind and stinging snow, and Dalton fought the impulse to take her by the elbow to help her keep her balance on the slick sidewalk. There was something about her posture, something about the look in her eyes that warned him she would not appreciate it.

The howling wind made conversation next to impossible so they trudged side by side in silence, heads bent against the mix of ice and snow falling from the sky.

It was difficult to pull the suitcase on its wheels through the thick snow that blanketed the ground. Instead Dalton picked it up by the handle to increase their pace.

The two-block walk seemed to take an eternity. He breathed a sigh of relief as they turned off Main onto Maple Street. He could barely see just ahead the white two-story house with the wraparound porch he called home.

Normally, Dalton didn't mind being snowed in for a day or two. He was a solitary man who enjoyed being alone, but it looked as if at least for the short-term he'd be spending his snow time with his landlord, George.

When they reached the house he motioned toward the staircase that led up the outside. His apartment was the top floor. She went up the stairs before him as he hefted the heavy suitcase up stair by stair.

At the top he unlocked the door, then opened it and gestured her inside. He followed just after her, flipping on the interior light and welcoming the warmth the place offered.

He turned to look at her. Her lips were now completely blue and she trembled almost uncontrollably. "Let's get out of these wet coats and shoes," he said.

The whole scene felt a little surreal. The snow outside, a mysterious woman and baby…it was like the setup of some ridiculous movie.

He unbuttoned his coat and watched her do the same. Her gaze didn't meet his but rather swept around the room like a rabbit hunting for a safe burrow.

He followed her gaze, taking in the place he'd called home for the past two years. When George's wife had died five years ago, the old man had renovated the house with this apartment upstairs. It was a way for him to keep his house and not feel so alone.

The apartment was roomy, with a nice-sized living room, a small but fully functioning kitchen, a half bath off the laundry room and a large bedroom with a full bathroom. Dalton had furnished it in a minimalist, functional style. But as he saw it through another's eyes he realized it was a cold space, with little personality.

He frowned and took her coat from her to hang in the small utility room off the kitchen. "Make yourself comfortable," he said and gestured to the sofa. "I'm just going to put these wet things in the other room."

He left her there, hung the wet coats on hangers to dry, then returned to find her still standing in the center of the room, rubbing the baby's back as he once again slept.

"Where were you headed?" he asked.

She jumped at the sound of his voice, as if she'd momentarily forgotten he was there. "Uh, Kansas City. I was going to visit my sister."

Again he had a gut feeling she wasn't telling him the truth. She refused to hold his gaze and even though the room was warm, her lips trembled slightly. And he realized she wasn't cold. She was afraid.

"Look, why don't we just get you settled in. The kitchen is there." He pointed to the doorway. "If you want anything to eat feel free to help yourself. I'll just go change the sheets on the bed then I'll be out of your hair." He started toward the bedroom but stopped as she called his name.

"If you just tell me where the sheets are, I'll change the bed. And I need to pay you."

"The sheets are on the bottom shelf in the bathroom, and it really isn't necessary for you to give me any money."

"Yes, it is," she countered, and her chin rose with a show of stubbornness. "It's important we keep this a business transaction."

"Fine," he replied. He named a nominal fee and watched as she opened her purse and carefully withdrew the amount in cash. "I'll just get a few things together then I'll head downstairs," he said as he took the money from her. He shoved the bills into his pocket, then grabbed her suitcase and wheeled it into his bedroom. He gathered a small overnight bag, then returned to the living room where she still stood in the center of the room, as if frozen in place.

"You should find everything you need for the night, but if you need anything you can't find, I'll write down my cell phone number and leave it on the kitchen table."

She gave an imperceptible nod of her head. "I... Thank you for this. I wasn't sure what I was going to do."

"You'll be fine here for the night and we'll sort things out in the morning."

"Thank you again," she said, then disappeared into the bedroom and closed the door behind her. He heard the click of the lock being turned.

Dalton stared at the closed door for a long moment. His family would probably tell him he was crazy for allowing a stranger to take up residence in his place even for one night. But they hadn't seen the vulnerability, the sheer desperation that clung to her closer than her coat.

Besides, what was she going to do? Tuck his television under one arm, her son under the other and run out into a blizzard? There was nothing here for her to steal that wasn't insured. He didn't know if he believed that she'd told him her real name or her destination, but he knew for sure that she'd needed someplace warm and safe and she'd found it here.

He went into the kitchen and wrote his cell phone number on a sheet of paper and left it on the small oak table. Then he wrote his own home phone number down and returned to the bedroom door and knocked. She opened the door, her eyes wide and wary.

"I just wanted to let you know there's leftover roast beef in the refrigerator if you get hungry and there's extra blankets on the shelf in the closet if you need them. If you need to call your sister to let her know where you are, here's the phone number." He held out the slip of paper.

"Thank you, I'm sure we'll be fine." One hand snaked out to take the piece of paper from him. "I guess I'll see you in the morning." She closed the door again but not before Dalton saw something flash in her other hand, something silver like a blade.

A knife?

Every instinct he owned shot to high alert. He'd been trained to look for trouble, and he had a horrible feeling he'd just invited trouble into his home.

Well, he couldn't do anything about it now. He headed for the interior staircase that led downstairs to George's living quarters.

He would have to face it—her—in the morning.

Chapter 2

She saw the red lights flashing in her rearview mirror and glanced down at her speedometer. Damn. It looked like she was going to get a speeding ticket.

She supposed she was lucky that she hadn't gotten one before now. Two nights a week she'd been making the twenty-five mile drive from Sandstone to a local community college, taking classes to eventually take the GED test. She always drove too fast on this particular stretch of deserted highway.

Pulling over to the side of the road, she wondered how many extra hours she'd have to work to pay for this particular mistake. As if money wasn't already tight enough.

Glancing in her rearview mirror once again she saw the patrol car pull to a stop just behind her. The *flashing red light went off, as did the headlights. As the driver's door opened she recognized Sheriff Brandon Sinclair getting out of the car.*

She fumbled in her schoolbag for her license as he approached the side of her car. She rolled down her window and offered him a small smile. "Sheriff Sinclair," she said.

"Turn off your lights and get out of the car," he told her.

She frowned, but didn't think about not doing as he asked. As she got out of the car Sheriff Sinclair smiled. "Well, well, don't we look all sexy in that little skirt," he said, and there was something in his eyes that made her suddenly afraid.

Janette awoke with a gasp, heart pounding as she sat up and stared wildly around the unfamiliar room. The large mahogany dresser and the navy overstuffed chair weren't hers. She wasn't in her room. Where was she?

Then she remembered. She was in Cotter Creek, in Dalton West's bedroom. Sammy slept peacefully next to her on the king-sized bed. She lay back down and shoved the last memories of her nightmare away.

The large bed had been a luxury after years of sleeping on a twin in her tiny bedroom in the trailer where she lived with Nana. Despite the luxury, sleep had been a long time coming. She'd jumped and tensed at each moan and groan of the unfamiliar house. Even when she had finally fallen asleep, it had been a night of unrelenting nightmares.

Surely by noon or so the streets would be cleared of

whatever snow had fallen overnight and the bus would finally arrive. It had to come today. She needed to get as far away from here as possible.

When the streets are cleared, he'll come looking for you, the little voice whispered in her head. She felt like a fish in the bottom of a barrel, far too close, far too easily caught.

She'd left the bedroom only once during the night, to make a bottle for Sammy. Knowing that he would probably sleep for another hour or so, she got out of bed and headed for the adjoining bathroom. She wanted to be dressed and ready to leave as soon as possible.

It wasn't until she stood beneath a hot spray of water that she thought of the man who had allowed her into his home. In another lifetime, under different circumstances, she might find herself attracted to him. He was certainly easy to look at, with that thick dark hair and those gorgeous green eyes.

He reminded her of another man—a man who had not been quite as handsome but had devastated her, bitterly disappointed her at the time she'd needed him most.

She didn't need a man in her life. She and Sammy and Nana would be fine. All she had to do was get out of this town and decide where they would all begin a new life, far away from the reaches of Sheriff Brandon Sinclair.

After showering she wrapped herself in one of the large fluffy towels and walked over to the window for her first look outside.

She gasped as she saw that the storm hadn't passed

by but instead seemed to be sitting right on top of the little town of Cotter Creek. It was impossible to discern street from sidewalk. Snow had transformed the earth into an alien landscape where nothing looked as it was supposed to.

There weren't just a couple of inches on the ground, there was at least a foot and a half and it was still falling from the gray, heavy sky.

Janette knew someplace in the back of her mind that it was beautiful, that the world looked like a winter wonderland, but all she could think was that the snow was a disaster, big fat fluffy flakes of doom falling from the sky.

Trapped. She was trapped there, and the only faint comfort was that if she were trapped by the weather, then so was Sheriff Brandon Sinclair.

She turned away from the window and crouched on the plush rug to open her big suitcase. The first thing she saw inside was the bright red book bag she'd thrown in at the last minute. Inside were the books she'd bought to study for her GED and the tape recorder she'd used in class.

It had been more than a year since she'd opened the bag that now represented not only the dream she'd once had for herself of getting more education, but also the worst night of her life.

She hadn't opened the bag since the night she'd been pulled over for a speeding ticket, and she didn't open it now. She set it on the floor and dug out a pair of jeans and her favorite blue sweater. She didn't have a lot of choices as she'd packed only a minimum of clothes for herself. Most of the suitcase contents were cans of powdered formula, cereal and diapers and clothing for Sammy.

Once she was dressed and had brushed out her long, wet hair, she eyed the phone on the nightstand. She should call Nana and let her know what was going on. The old woman would worry if she didn't hear from Janette. Thank goodness the call wasn't long distance, Janette thought as she punched in her grandmother's number.

Nana answered on the second ring and Janette pressed the phone to her ear as if to get closer to her grandmother. "Nana, it's me."

"Janette, honey, where are you?" Nana asked. "Did you get off before this storm?"

"No, I'm still in Cotter Creek."

"At the motel?" Nana asked.

"The motel was already full by the time I found out the bus wasn't coming. The snow was coming down and I didn't know what to do, but then I saw a light on in the West Protective Services office." Janette twisted the phone cord around her little finger. "I hired Dalton West to be my bodyguard and he brought me to his apartment for the night."

"Are you safe there?" Nana asked, her voice filled with concern.

Janette considered the question. "Yes, I think I'm safe," she finally replied. It was odd, but having survived the night she did feel safe.

"I've heard about those Wests," Nana said. "Supposed to be good solid men. I'm just grateful that you and that precious little boy are away from here and not out in this storm someplace."

Janette glanced toward the window and frowned. "It looks like I'm going to be stuck here for a while." She twisted the phone cord more tightly around her finger. "Has anyone been by to ask about me?"

"Nobody, honey. The storm moved in and nobody is going anywhere at the moment. Don't you worry none. He'll never know from me where you went and by the time he makes his way here to ask questions you'll be far out of his reach."

"Let me give you the phone number here, just in case you need to reach me." Janette read the number off the piece of paper Dalton had given her the night before. "I'll call you when I'm about to board the bus. Maybe they'll get the streets cleared by tomorrow."

"You just take care of yourself and Sammy. Don't worry about things here. I got my friends at the trailer park to take care of me and I'll be fine as long as I know you're fine."

Janette unraveled the cord from her finger. How she wished she could crawl through the phone line and feel her grandmother's loving arms around her, to go back to a time when she didn't know about fear, about evil.

Afraid that she might cry if she remained on the phone much longer, she quickly said goodbye then hung up. Checking to make sure that Sammy was still sleeping soundly, she arranged the bed pillows on either side of him then walked to the bedroom door.

She hesitated before turning the knob to step out of the room. She'd told Nana she was safe, and at the moment she *felt* fairly safe, but she'd also been unaware of any danger on the night Sheriff Sinclair had pulled her over on the side of the road.

As much as she'd love to stay holed up in the bedroom until the bus pulled in, that was impossible. She hadn't eaten since lunch the day before and her stomach was protesting its neglect in loud angry growls.

The scent of freshly brewed coffee greeted her as she opened the bedroom door, letting her know she was no longer alone in the apartment.

Energy surged through her as all her senses went on high alert. Her feet whispered against the living-room rug as she moved toward the kitchen.

She hesitated in the doorway. Dalton stood at the stove with his back to her. A white, long-sleeved jersey clung across his broad shoulders and worn jeans hugged the length of his legs. He was barefoot and his hair was rumpled like he'd just crawled out of bed.

A sizzling noise was quickly followed by a whiff of bacon and Janette felt the nerves in her stomach calm. It was hard to be frightened of a barefoot man frying bacon.

She must have made some sort of sound for he whirled around to look at her. "Good morning," he said. "There's coffee in the pot if you're interested."

"I'm interested," she replied.

He gestured to the coffeemaker on the counter. "Cups are in the cabinet above."

She walked over to the cabinet, retrieved a cup, then poured herself some coffee. She carried it to the table and sat, unsure what else to do.

Dalton turned back around to flip the bacon. Janette was aware of a tension in the air, the tension of two strangers sharing space.

"It looks like you're going to be stuck here for at least another day or two," he said.

"Maybe I could find another place to go to," she offered.

Once again he turned around to face her. "It would take me half the day to shovel enough snow just to open the outside door. Trust me, nobody is going anywhere today." A muscle in his jaw tensed, letting her know that he wasn't particularly happy about the unforeseen circumstances.

"I'm sorry about all this," she said. He'd never know just how sorry she was that she was stuck here in Cotter Creek.

"We'll just have to deal with it," he replied, then turned his back on her once again.

Taking a sip of her coffee, she had a vision of Brandon Sinclair tunneling his way through the snow to find her. She mentally shook the thought out of her head.

Once again she stared at Dalton's back. He was a fine-looking man and so far he'd been nothing but honorable. He made a living protecting people. Maybe she could tell him. Maybe she could tell him the truth. The thought of telling somebody and having them believe her was wonderful.

"How about an omelet?" he asked. "I'm making myself one and can split it with you."

She felt bad, that this man was not only having to share his personal space but also his food. Still, she was starving and it seemed silly to refuse. "That sounds good," she agreed.

Once again she sipped her coffee, watching as he prepared the ingredients for the omelet. "Is there anything I can do to help?" she asked.

"No thanks, I'm used to doing things my way," he replied.

"Tell me about this business of yours. I read an article not too long ago about West Protective Services. If I remember correctly it's a family business, right?"

He nodded. His tousled hair made him appear less daunting than he had the night before. "It was started by my father, Red West. Eventually all of us started working for the business."

"All of you?"

"I've got four brothers and a sister. Joshua is the youngest and he just got married to Savannah, who owns the local newspaper. Then there's Clay, who met his wife when he was on assignment in California. They have a little girl, Gracie. There's Tanner, the oldest. He and his wife, Anna, just had a baby."

Janette felt herself relaxing as he talked. Not only did he have a nice, deep voice that was soothing, but it was obvious from the affection in his voice as he spoke that the West family was a close one. It was easier to trust a man who loved his family.

"Then there's Meredith. She recently moved to Kansas City with her fiancé, Chase. She and Chase are planning on coming back here in March to get married. Finally there's Zack. He doesn't work for the family business anymore. He married Katie, the woman who lived next door to our family, and he's the sheriff of Cotter Creek."

Any hope she might have entertained of being truthful with Dalton West crashed and burned. *He's the sheriff of Cotter Creek.* The words echoed inside her head.

There were only thirty miles between Cotter Creek and Sandstone. There was no reason for her not to believe that Brandon Sinclair and Zack West were not only acquaintances but also perhaps friends. She had no idea how far-reaching the good-old-boy network was in the state of Oklahoma.

One thing was clear. For as long as she was stuck in this apartment, she couldn't tell Dalton the truth. Her very life and the life of her son might depend on her keeping her secrets.

At that moment, as if he'd awakened and sensed his mother's despair, Sammy began to cry from the bedroom.

Dalton drew a deep breath as "Jane" hurriedly left the kitchen to get her son. He was exhausted, having spent the night on George's tiny sofa after hours of listening to George talk. And the old man could definitely talk.

He'd already been feeling a little irritable when he'd climbed the inside staircase back to his apartment. As if spending an evening with George hadn't been enough, he was now stuck in his apartment with a stranger, a woman whom, he had to admit, stirred something inside him just by being there. A woman who'd had a knife in her hand the night before.

Could he really blame her for wielding a knife? After all, as much as she was a stranger to him, he was a stranger to her. She'd had no idea what kind of a man he was, what she'd been walking into when she'd entered his apartment.

He cut the omelet in half and placed it on two plates, then added the bacon and put the plates on the table.

She couldn't know that he was a solitary man who didn't particularly enjoy sharing his space, his world, with anyone. Even though he found her amazingly attractive, all he wanted was for her and her son to move on.

She returned to the kitchen, her son and a bottle in one arm and a box of powdered cereal in the other. "I need to make some cereal for Sammy. Do you have a small bowl I can use?"

Dalton got out the bowl, then watched as she tried to maneuver with the wiggly baby in her arms. "You want me to hold him while you get that ready?" he asked reluctantly. He didn't particularly like kids, had only thought about having a couple once, a long time ago, but it had been nothing more than a foolish dream.

"Thanks." She smiled at him for the first time, a real, open genuine smile that unexpectedly shot a flash of heat through his stomach.

As she offered the baby to him, Sammy seemed to vibrate with excitement and offered Dalton a wide, drooling grin. As soon as Dalton had him in his arms, Sammy reached up and grabbed hold of his nose, then laughed as if finding the West nose vastly amusing.

"He likes you," Jane observed as she measured out the rice cereal and added warm formula.

"You sound surprised," Dalton replied.

"I am. He's usually not good with strangers, especially men."

"What about his father?" Dalton asked as she stirred the cereal, then set the bowl on the table.

Her eyes darkened. "His father isn't in our life." To his relief she took the baby back and sat at the table.

For the next few minutes they sat in silence. She alternately fed Sammy and herself while Dalton ate his breakfast.

Sammy laughed and smiled at Dalton every time Dalton looked at him. He had to admit, the kid was cute with his tuft of dark hair and blue eyes. Dalton finished eating before Jane, or whatever her real name was. "Do you need to call your sister in St. Louis to tell her you've been delayed?"

"I already did," she replied.

Dalton stared at her. She'd told him the night before that she was on her way to visit her sister in Kansas City. Women interested him, but a woman with secrets definitely intrigued him.

He didn't call her on her slip, but instead leaned back in his chair and watched as she finished feeding Sammy. He didn't want to be intrigued by her. He wanted the snow to melt quickly and her and her cute baby to move along on their way to wherever. However, the weather report that morning hadn't been exactly favorable for her to make a quick escape out of his house.

Taking a sip of his coffee, he gazed out the window

where the snow still fell in buckets. At least she didn't seem to be a chatterer. She didn't expect him to entertain her with lively conversation.

Silence had always been Dalton's friend. Growing up in a household with a rambunctious bunch of siblings had made him appreciate his solitary life now. Odd that he suddenly found the silence strangely stifling.

"We're lucky we still have power," he finally said to break that uncomfortable silence. "The news report this morning said that half the town is without power and phone service."

"That's terrible," she exclaimed.

"Most folks around this area are prepared for situations like this. They have wood-burning fireplaces or generators that will be cranked up. We Oklahoma people are solid stock and know how to deal with an emergency."

She frowned. "I certainly wasn't prepared for this particular emergency."

"According to the weather report I heard the snow is supposed to end by nightfall. If that happens, then first thing in the morning the locals will get out and clear the streets."

"It can't happen fast enough for me," she replied. She looked up from Sammy, her blue eyes dark and troubled. "I'm sorry I can't get out of your hair right now. I know when you offered me a place to stay last night you had no idea that I'd still be here today."

Dalton shrugged. "We'll just have to make the best of it."

"I just hope if they get the streets cleared in the

morning then the bus comes tomorrow afternoon." There was a thrum of desperation in her voice.

"Surely your sister will understand the delay."

"Of course." She averted her gaze from his and focused on her son in her arms. "I'm just anxious to get gone."

"Is this a vacation trip?"

She kept her gaze firmly on her son. "Yes. It's been a long time since I've seen my sister and she hasn't met Sammy, so I thought it would be nice to take a trip to visit her. I suppose it was foolish to plan a trip in late January. But babies are only babies a short time."

She was rambling, and it was Dalton's experience that people who rambled were usually hiding something. She seemed to realize what she was doing for she suddenly clamped her lips closed and frowned.

Getting up from the table she started to grab for her plate. "I'll take care of that," he said.

She gave him a grateful nod, then once again disappeared from the kitchen. Dalton remained seated at the table. He sipped his coffee and looked out the window. Although he stared at the snow, his mind was filled with those blue eyes of hers.

At thirty-three years old, Dalton had worked the family business for twelve years. He'd spent that time studying people, and the assessments he made of those people sometimes made the difference between life and death.

Jane Craig was lying. He'd seen it in those impossibly blue eyes of hers. Secrets and lies. There had been something in her eyes that had looked not only like quiet desperation, but also screaming fear.

His mind whirled with all kinds of possibilities. Who in their right mind planned a bus trip in the Midwest in January? Especially with an infant? He could write off the appearance of the knife the night before as a wary woman in the home of a stranger. But what was she doing with a wicked-looking knife like that in the first place?

Secrets and lies. What he was suddenly eager to find out was whether her secrets and lies could be the difference between life and death, and whether the snowy conditions had suddenly made him a player in a drama he wasn't prepared to face.

Sheriff Brandon Sinclair stared out the window and silently cursed the snow. He'd been in a foul mood since the day before, when he'd gone back to the diner to have a little chat with Janette and discovered she'd up and quit her job, just like that.

He'd been on his way to the little rattrap trailer where she lived with her grandmother when a six-car accident just outside of town had required his immediate attention. By the time he'd finished up, the ice had begun to fall in earnest.

He tried to ignore the sound of his three daughters playing in the middle of their living-room floor. He hadn't thought about Janette Black since the night they'd had sex over a year ago.

Then yesterday morning he'd heard the rumor that she had a little baby boy, a rumor that had been confirmed when he'd spoken with her at lunch.

Since that moment, he couldn't get her—or more

precisely the boy—out of his mind. *His son.* He knew in his gut that the kid was his.

"Brandon, honey, your breakfast is waiting," Brandon's wife, Sherrilyn, spoke from someplace behind him.

He grunted but didn't turn around. Sherrilyn was a good woman. She'd come into the marriage not only crazy about him, but with the kind of respectability and a trust fund that Brandon had desired. She kept the large house neat and tidy, tried to anticipate his needs before he knew them and was an adequate if boring bedmate.

She loved being the sheriff's wife, and while Brandon was feared and respected by the community, Sherrilyn was loved for her charity work and big heart.

But, when it came to giving Brandon what he'd wanted most in life, she'd failed miserably, pumping out three girl babies instead of the boy he desperately wanted.

"Mommy, Susan won't share," Elena, his youngest, whined from the living room. She was always whining about something. Girls whined. Girls cried, and he had three of the whiniest, weepiest girls in the county.

He narrowed his gaze as he turned away from the window and headed for the kitchen. As soon as the snow stopped, he'd get that boy. He didn't much care what he had to do, but eventually that little boy would be living with him, being raised by him. Boys needed their daddies, and if the only way to get that kid was over Janette Black's dead body, well then that could be arranged, too.

Chapter 3

Janette stayed in the bedroom with Sammy for most of the morning. She played peekaboo with him, laughing as he grinned and squealed at her antics. When he started to get sleepy, she picked him up in her arms and sat in the chair near the window, rocking and singing softly to him until he fell asleep.

She placed her lips against Sammy's downy hair, drawing in the sweet baby scent of him. He was her heart, this little boy. Before his birth she had loved him, but nothing had prepared her for the depth of her love for him now.

Her heart squeezed as she thought of the threat that felt ominously close, a threat to this baby and their future together. She would do whatever it took to keep him safe and away from the man who was his biological father. She shoved aside thoughts of Sinclair, unwilling to allow the chill that thoughts of him always produced to consume her.

She was conscious of the sounds of Dalton in the next room. It was a good thing he'd told her about his family before she'd confessed what was really going on.

She should have known it wouldn't be safe to tell him the truth. Bodyguards probably had to work closely with law enforcement officials. For all she knew, Brandon Sinclair could be a drinking buddy of the entire West clan.

When Sammy was sleeping soundly, she gently laid him in the middle of the big bed and tucked the pillows around him to stop him from rolling anywhere. She stood for a long moment staring down at the baby who owned all of her heart.

She would do whatever it took to keep Brandon Sinclair away from Sammy. She would run to the ends of the earth, hide for the rest of her life if that's what it took.

You're nothing but trailer trash, Janette. Nobody is going to believe you if you ever tell. Those were the last words she'd heard from Sinclair that night on the highway. He hadn't spoken to her again or even looked at her until yesterday in the café when he'd told her he knew she had a son.

She'd tried to be so careful during her pregnancy. Thankfully she'd gained little weight and had been able to hide her condition until her eighth month. It was only then that she'd told the people who'd noticed that she was pregnant that she'd had a fling with a man passing through town. Because she believed Sinclair—nobody would ever believe her if she told the truth.

Tired of being cooped up, she finally left the bedroom and entered the living room, where Dalton sat in a chair reading a book as a saxophone wailed the blues from the stereo. She wasn't concerned about the noise waking Sammy. From the time he'd been born he had slept like the dead, undisturbed by loud noises.

Dalton looked up and nodded at her. "Are you ready for lunch?" he asked and closed his book.

"No, thanks. I'm fine." She gestured to the book on his lap. "Please, don't let me interrupt you."

"You aren't. It isn't a very good book, anyway."

She glanced to the overflowing bookcase against one wall. "You must read a lot."

"I enjoy reading," he agreed. His piercing green eyes seemed to peer directly inside her. "What about you? Are you a reader?"

She sat on the edge of the sofa. "I'd like to be, but there never seems to be enough time. Between taking care of Sammy and my job there aren't many hours left in the day."

"What kind of job do you have?"

"Right now I'm a waitress, but that's not what I want to do for the rest of my life." She hesitated a moment, then continued, "I had to drop out of high school my junior year because my nana…my grandma got sick, so the first thing I need to do is get my GED."

She wasn't sure why she told him this. It was more information than he'd asked for and she was certain he didn't care what her future plans might be.

Those direct green eyes of his held her gaze. "Your grandmother is important in your life?"

"Definitely. She raised me. It was just me and her, and of course my sister," she hurriedly added. She'd never been a liar, and the lies she now found herself spouting bothered her more than a little bit.

"What about your parents? Where are they?"

"Who knows? I never knew my father and when I was three my mother dropped me off at Nana's house and we never heard from her again. Nana told me she was a troubled woman with drug problems. I think she's probably dead by now."

Janette had long ago made peace with the fact that her mother had been unable to parent her. At least she'd been unselfish enough to put her in Nana's care, where she'd been loved and looked after.

"I'm sorry to hear that," he said, and she was surprised by the touch of empathy she heard in his deep voice. "My mother was murdered when I was just a boy."

"That's horrible," she exclaimed.

He shrugged. "You deal with the bumps life throws you." He stood suddenly, as if to end the conversation of that particular topic. "Are you sure you aren't ready for some lunch? I'm going to make a sandwich."

"I guess I could eat a sandwich," she agreed and got up to follow him into the kitchen. Once again she found herself sitting at the table while he fixed the meal. "I need to give you more money," she said. "You're feeding me and everything. I feel terrible about all this."

He smiled then, and the power of his smile shot a

wave of heat through her. It was the heat of a woman intensely aware of an attractive man. It shocked her, but she embraced it, for it was something she hadn't felt for a very long time, something she'd thought Brandon Sinclair had killed.

"I think I can manage to feed one slender woman for a couple of days without declaring bankruptcy," he said.

She returned his smile. "I just want you to know that I appreciate it." She glanced toward the window where the snow appeared to be slowing down. Surely by tomorrow she could leave.

She gazed back at Dalton. "So, I guess your dad raised you, then? It must have been quite a challenge, considering how many of you there were."

Once again he grinned, transfusing his rather stern features with an unexpected warmth. "Ah, Dad had a secret weapon. He hired a cantankerous old cowhand as a housekeeper. Smokey Johnson not only threatened to beat our butts if we got out of line, he followed through on his threats often enough to make us take him seriously."

Despite his words it was obvious he held a lot of affection for the cowhand turned parental figure in his life. For the first time since she'd stepped out of the bus station yesterday evening, some of the tension that had coiled inside her eased.

"Ham and cheese okay?" he asked.

"Perfect. Is there anything I can do to help?"

"Nah, sit tight. I can handle it. Besides, if you work as a waitress I doubt you get too many people offering to wait on you."

She laughed. "That's the truth." He smelled nice, like minty soap and a touch of sandalwood, and she felt herself relax just a little bit more.

"Is your sister older or younger than you?"

The question came out of left field but reminded her that she couldn't let her guard down for a minute. "Older," she said. "Why?"

"Just curious." He walked over to the table with their lunch plates. "What would you like to drink? I can offer you milk, water or a soda."

"Milk would be nice."

He rejoined her at the table a moment later with two tall glasses of milk. For the next few minutes they ate in silence. "From what you told me earlier it sounds like all of your brothers and your sister are married and having kids. Why aren't you married?" she asked to break the uncomfortable quiet.

A flash of darkness momentarily chased across his green eyes. "I guess after growing up with a houseful of people I've discovered in my adult years that I enjoy my solitude," he replied. "I like living alone and not having to answer to anyone and have no plans to ever get married."

He took a drink of his milk, then continued, "What about you? I'm assuming things didn't work out with you and the baby's father?"

She looked down at her sandwich and pulled off part of the crust. "No, we tried to make it work. He's a great guy and everything, but we just weren't good together." She looked at Dalton once again and forced a small smile to her lips. "But thankfully we have managed to remain good friends."

How she wished this were true. How she wished that Sammy's father was a good man who could help her instill the right qualities in their son instead of a monster who would taint the innocence of the little boy.

Dalton leaned back in his chair and studied her. "You're a pretty woman. I'm sure you won't have any problems finding some special guy to share your life."

There was nothing in his voice to indicate he was flirting with her in any way, but she touched a strand of her hair self-consciously. She hadn't felt pretty in a very long time and she was surprised to discover that his comment soothed a wound she hadn't realized she possessed.

"I'm in no hurry at the moment to make any commitment to anyone," she replied. "I just want to be able to take care of my son and myself."

At that moment the phone rang, jolting every nerve in Janette's body. What if it was Dalton's brother, the sheriff? What if Dalton mentioned that he had a young woman and a baby staying with him?

What if Sinclair had already begun the search for her and had contacted Dalton's brother? Horrible scenarios went off in her head, mini-movies of doom.

As Dalton started to rise to answer, she grabbed him by the forearm and held tight. Her heart beat so hard, so fast she wondered if he could hear it. "Please, please don't tell anyone I'm here."

His eyes pierced her with a sharpness that was almost

painful. He didn't answer but instead pulled his arm out of her grasp and walked over to the phone.

"Hello?" he said, his gaze never leaving Janette. "Yeah, hi, Dad. I was just eating lunch."

As Dalton continued his conversation, he never broke eye contact with Janette. The tension that had dissipated earlier crashed back through her, twisting in her gut like a deadly Oklahoma tornado.

His voice remained pleasant as he carried on his conversation with his father. When he finally hung up he returned to the table and reached out to grab her forearm as she had done his.

"Now, Jane," he said, his voice deceptively calm. "You want to tell me just what the hell is going on?"

Dalton stared at the woman and tried to ignore how fragile, how warm, her slender arm felt beneath his grasp. Her stunning blue eyes were wide and darted around the room as if seeking somewhere to run, to escape. She tried to pull her arm free from his grip but he held tight, just as she had a moment earlier.

"Talk to me," he said. "Tell me why you don't want me to mention to anyone that you're here."

This close he could smell the scent of her, clean with a touch of honeysuckle fragrance. She closed her eyes and he couldn't help but notice the length of her eyelashes. She tried to pull away from him again and this time he let her go.

She wrapped her arms around herself as if she were cold and looked at him. "I'm sorry. I lied to you before." She looked down at the table.

He frowned. "Lied about what?"

She got up as if she wanted as much distance from him as possible, but he had a feeling that what she was really doing was giving herself time to think. He wasn't at all sure he was going to believe anything that fell out of her mouth at this point.

Moving to stand next to the window, she turned to face him. "I lied about Sammy's father. He isn't a nice man. He…he used to beat me. He was abusive and I needed to get away."

There was a tremble in her voice, a timbre of fear that made him want to believe her. "You think he's looking for you?"

Again she wrapped her arms around her middle. "You can bet on it. And if he finds me he'll hurt me. He might hurt Sammy."

"That's not going to happen here," Dalton said firmly. He offered her a smile. "After all, you've hired me as your personal bodyguard and I promise you I'm damned good at what I do."

She didn't return his smile and that, along with the darkness in her eyes, made him believe her. "Is that why you carry a knife?" he asked.

She raised a pale eyebrow. "How do you know about that?"

"I saw it last night when you opened the bedroom door."

She returned to the table and sat, her gaze going out the window. "I won't let him hurt me again." She looked back at Dalton and there was a hard glint in her eyes.

"I just want to get out of here. Once I get to my sister's I'll be just fine."

"What's this guy's name?" Dalton asked.

"What difference does it make?"

He shrugged. "Just curious. I know most of the families in this area. Just thought I might know him."

She blinked once...twice. "His name is Billy Johnson. I doubt if you know him. He's not from around here. His family is from someplace back east."

Once again he had the feeling she wasn't being completely honest with him. Did he care? If he were smart he would stop asking questions now. In the next day or two she wouldn't be his problem.

"I'd better go check on Sammy," she said and rose from the table.

He watched her hurry away, unable to stop himself from noticing how the worn jeans fit snugly across her shapely butt. He was acutely aware of the fact that physically he was attracted to her, but that didn't mean he wanted to be pulled into her life drama.

He got up from the table, carried their lunch dishes to the sink and began to rinse them. As he worked, his thoughts drifted to his last assignment.

It had been over a year since Dalton had worked a case as a bodyguard. Her name had been Mary Mason, she'd lived in Tulsa and she, too, had been the victim of domestic violence. He'd worked for her for almost four months, guarding her between the time she'd filed for divorce and the divorce proceeding itself, which had been expedited by a judge sympathetic to her situation.

Mary had known the statistics, that in these kinds of

cases the most dangerous time for an abused wife was in the weeks prior to the divorce.

In those four months, he'd fallen head over heels in love with her and she had appeared to feel the same way about him. They had forged a bond that he thought would last the rest of their lives. They'd made plans for a wedding after her divorce, laughing as they created a fantasy event fit for a king and a queen.

It wasn't until the day after the divorce proceedings that the fantasy exploded. Mary told him she needed some time to regroup, that he should return to his home in Cotter Creek and give her a little time alone.

He'd understood the request, had encouraged it, so certain was he that they would be together. He'd called her often, they'd emailed, but after only a month he'd received a Dear John letter. She'd fallen in love with another man. They were getting married. Dalton had made a wonderful temporary hero, but that's all he had been.

He scowled as he put the dishes in the dishwasher. The whole thing had left a bad taste in his mouth, a heartache that had been long in healing. Since that time he'd worked the office, answering the phones and keeping the books. He preferred dealing with paperwork instead of people.

Footsteps sounded on the inside staircase that led from George's place upstairs to Dalton's. A moment later, a knock sounded on the back kitchen door.

Jane might not want anyone to know she was here, but it was already too late to keep that piece of information from his landlord.

George would have thought it damned odd that Dalton wanted to sleep on his sofa if Dalton hadn't told the old man that he'd given harbor from the storm to a young woman and her baby.

He opened the door to see George wearing hot pads on his hands and carrying a fresh pie. "Had some canned apples and thought it was a good day for some pie and coffee." He swept past Dalton and into the kitchen, where he deposited the pie on the table. "So, how about making us some coffee to go with this work of art." He pulled out a chair and sat.

Dalton grinned. "Feeling a little cabin fever, George?" He got a pot of coffee ready to brew.

"I hate being cooped up. You know me, Dalton, I'm a social kind of man. Sitting and listening to my own thoughts bores me to death. Where's your houseguest?"

At that moment Jane appeared in the doorway with Sammy in her arms. She froze at the sight of George. "Jane, this is my landlord, George, from downstairs," Dalton said.

George popped up from the chair and walked over to where she stood. "Jane, nice to meet you. And who is this little fellow?"

Sammy took one look at George's big, silly grin and screwed up his face. He wailed as if George were the devil himself and burrowed closer to Jane's chest.

"Oh my." George quickly stepped back.

"I'm sorry," Jane said. "He's hungry. I was just going to fix him a bottle."

Dalton realized she not only held the boy in her arms, but also juggled a bottle and a can of powdered formula mix, as well. Short of putting Sammy on the floor, it was going to be next to impossible for her to hold him and make the bottle.

"Want me to take him?" he asked and gestured to the crying child.

She shot him a grateful look. "If you don't mind. It will just take me a minute to get this ready."

He nodded and took Sammy from her. Almost immediately Sammy not only stopped crying but grinned at Dalton as if the two were best buds.

"Would you look at that?" George exclaimed. "That boy is plum crazy about you."

"He'll be a lot crazier about that bottle," Dalton replied, grateful a moment later when Jane took her son back. She sat at the table, Sammy in her arms sucking on his bottle with obvious contentment.

"George brought up a freshly baked apple pie," Dalton said as he got out coffee mugs from the cabinet.

"Hmm, that sounds good. Apple is my favorite." She offered George a tentative smile.

"My missus, God rest her soul, loved my apple pies. Always told me if God served pie in heaven, then he'd be serving mine," George replied. "Guess this snowstorm took you by surprise."

"Definitely," she agreed.

George could talk, and that's what he did for the next hour. Sammy finished his bottle and fell asleep. Dalton sat and sipped his coffee as George entertained Jane with colorful descriptions of people in town, humorous stories of his misspent youth and his fifty-year marriage to the woman who had owned his heart since he was sixteen.

Dalton had heard the stories before. What he found far more interesting than George's conversation was watching Jane interact with the old man.

As she listened to George, she looked relaxed. Her long blond hair was so soft-looking, so shiny, it made a man want to reach out and touch it, coil it around his fingers, feel it dance across his chest. The first time she laughed aloud, Dalton was shocked by the pleasure that swept through him. She had a great laugh, one that would easily evoke smiles in others.

Although she visited with George in general terms, he noticed that she gave nothing of herself. She didn't mention family or friends, didn't speak of her hometown or her job.

Irritated with these kinds of thoughts, he got up to pour himself another cup of coffee, then returned to the table. He didn't want to think about how sweet she smelled or how her lips were just full enough to tempt a man.

She'd given no indication that she might be up for a short, reckless affair to pass the time until she got on the bus out of town. And the last thing he wanted was any kind of emotional entanglement with any woman. She'd be gone soon, and that was that.

It was just after three when George finally got up from the table. "It's been a real pleasure," he said and smiled at Jane. "There's nothing nicer than spending a snowy afternoon in the company of a beautiful woman. Unfortunately, at my age, a good nap is also a pleasant way to spend the afternoon, and I'm past due mine."

She offered him a sunny smile. "Thank you for the

pie, George. Your wife was right. It was the best I've ever eaten," she replied.

George beamed as if kissed by an angel.

"George, have you mentioned to anyone that I'm here?" Jane asked.

"Can't say I have." George scratched the top of his head. "Haven't talked to anyone except Dalton since this storm moved in."

"I would appreciate it if you wouldn't mention it to anyone." She flashed him a bright smile. "I'm kind of hiding out from somebody."

George's eyes lit up. "Ah, a woman of mystery. Your secret is safe with me." He started to turn to head out the way he had come, but paused and pointed to the window. "Would you look at that?"

Both Dalton and Jane looked through the window where the snow had finally stopped and the sun peeked out from behind the last lingering gray clouds.

Chapter 4

"You think the bus will run tomorrow?" Janette asked Dalton. The three of them were in the living room, having just eaten supper. He was seated in the chair and she was on the sofa. Sammy was gurgling happily from a blanket on the floor.

"Doubtful," he replied.

For the past hour they'd heard the sounds of plows starting the storm cleanup and each grind of gears had been like music to her ears. She just hoped and prayed she got out of there before Sheriff Brandon Sinclair somehow discovered where she was.

"Although most of the locals who have plows will be out and have our streets cleaned, it will probably be at least another day or so before the highways are completely cleared and the bus can show up." He gazed at her curiously. "Surely you can't be afraid that your boy-friend will find you here. You didn't know you were going to be here, so how could he know?"

"Logically, I know that, but emotionally, I just have this terrible need to get out of town, to get as far away as possible," she replied. "I just want to stay safe."

"I told you that you'd be safe here," he said. "When that bus comes, I'll personally see you safely aboard and in the meantime nobody is going to harm you while you're in my home."

A new burst of gratitude filled her. She'd taken a terrible chance coming into the home of a stranger, but Dalton had proven himself to be nothing other than a good, honorable man. She leaned back on the sofa. "So, what do you do when you aren't bodyguarding?" she asked. She'd been in his home for twenty-four hours but didn't really know anything about him.

"I mentioned before I like to read, and when the weather's nice I do a little work at the family ranch."

"Family ranch?" She could easily imagine him, long legs astride a powerful horse, a cowboy hat pulled down low over his brow.

"My dad has a huge ranch north of town. It's be-come something of a family compound. My brother Tanner has a house on the property, and Clay and his wife, Libby, have been talking about building there."

"Hmm, that sounds nice. It must be wonderful to have such a close, loving family unit. I used to wonder what it would be like to have a whole mess of siblings."

He laughed, a deep low sound that warmed her. "Be-lieve me, it's not as wonderful as it sounds. You wait in line for the bathroom, you wait to be served at the table, you share everything you're given and there's incessant noise."

She searched his features. "But there must have been something wonderful in it."

He frowned, the gesture doing nothing to detract from his handsomeness. His gaze drifted to the window and he stared out for a long moment before answering. When he looked back at her the deep lines in his face had softened.

"I suppose there was something wonderful about it," he said as if conceding a huge point. "I definitely never felt lonely and I knew my family always had my back when I got into trouble."

"And did you do that often?" she asked. "Get into trouble?"

His eyes gleamed with a hint of mischief. "Probably more than my share, although nothing serious. What about you? Were you a wild child or one of those Goody Two-shoes who always played by the rules?"

It was the first conversation they'd had where she didn't feel on edge, wasn't afraid of screwing up the lies she'd already told with new lies. Maybe she was feeling more relaxed because the snowplows sounded like imminent escape.

"I was in-between," she said. "I'm sure my grandmother would tell you that I had some wild moments and like your Smokey, she didn't hesitate to burn my butt if I needed it. But I never broke any laws or anything like that."

"That's a relief. I wouldn't want to be harboring a criminal in my house," he said, his green eyes teasing.

She returned his smile. In different circumstances she had a feeling it would have been easy to like Dalton... really like him. Although he seemed reserved, when he smiled at her she wanted to break through that reserve and get to the heart of the man.

But she couldn't afford to be attracted to him. As soon as the streets were cleared she'd be out of his apartment and as far away from Cotter Creek as she could get.

This was nothing more than a temporary respite from the drama that her life had become on the afternoon that Sheriff Brandon Sinclair had walked into the café.

"I'll bet you spend a lot of time with your family," she said.

"Not really. Oh, we get together for the usual holidays, but most of the time I'm perfectly satisfied alone."

"Still, I imagine it's a good feeling to know that they're there if you need them," she replied.

Sammy cooed like a dove as he found his own fingers, his legs kicking with happiness. She watched Dalton as his gaze went to her son. Dalton looked back at her. "You've got a tough road ahead of you."

"What do you mean?"

"A single mother, no father in the picture and you mentioned that you don't have your GED yet. You've got an uphill battle ahead of you."

"I know," she agreed, suddenly sober as she gazed down at Sammy. "I might have grown up poor in a trailer park, but I'm going to make something of myself so that Sammy has everything he needs." She heard the angry resolve in her own voice, a resolve that had strengthened when Sinclair had told her that she was nothing but trailer trash and nobody would believe her if she told what he'd done.

"There's nothing wrong with being poor, or growing up in a trailer park," Dalton said softly.

She smiled. "Spoken like a man who has never known what it's like to be poor."

"You're right," he conceded. "I was lucky never to have to worry about finances. The bodyguard business pays well and we all share in the profits of both the business and the ranch."

"Did you always want to be a bodyguard?"

"When I was ten I wanted to be a rodeo clown," he said. "When I was twelve I wanted to be an astronaut, then a treasure hunter and a gold miner."

She laughed. "For me it was a movie star, a ballerina then a princess." She sobered. "It never entered my mind that in reality I'd be an abused woman on the run with a small baby."

"Your sister will take you in?"

"Of course," she replied around the lump of fear that swelled in her throat. She had no idea where she was going, no idea what she'd find when she arrived. Her only support system was a sixty-eight-year-old woman with a bad heart.

Dalton ran a hand through his thick dark hair, not breaking eye contact with her. "Why do I get the feeling that you aren't telling me everything?"

"I don't know what you're talking about," she said

and looked down at Sammy, who had begun to fuss. "I'd better get him a bottle," she said as she got up from the sofa.

It was a relief to escape those piercing, intelligent eyes of his. She didn't know what he saw that made him think she was keeping secrets, but there was no way she could tell him the truth. And in any case, it didn't matter. She would be gone soon enough.

She fixed Sammy his bottle, then picked him up off the floor. "I think I'm going to go ahead and call it a night," she said.

He nodded. "Unless it will freak you out entirely, I'm planning on sleeping here on the sofa tonight. I like George a lot, but his sofa is small and last night he kept me up until long after midnight telling me stories I'd heard a dozen times before."

She was surprised to realize the idea didn't freak her out. She trusted him to remain the perfect gentleman he'd already been. "Would you rather stay in your own bed? Sammy and I could bunk in here," she offered.

"No, I'll be just fine. Good night, Jane," he said.

She wished she could hear her real name on his lips, but fear still ruled her decisions, including the decision to tell him little white lies, as much as she hated it. "Good night, Dalton."

Even though it was relatively early, Janette breathed a sigh of exhaustion as she got ready for bed. It was hard work watching every word that fell from her mouth and being careful not to say too much or too little.

When she was in her nightgown she moved to the window and stared outside. The street in front of Dalton's had been plowed, leaving piles of snow on either side that glistened in the streetlights.

The sooner she got on the bus the better she'd feel, but escaping this part of the country certainly didn't ease the fear that was a constant inside her.

She might escape Sinclair but then she'd have to face settling into a new place, finding work and taking care of Sammy *and* earning enough money to send for Nana. Dalton was right. She had a tough road ahead of her.

Sammy finished his bottle, and she sang softly to him until he fell asleep. It took her longer to sleep and when she finally succumbed, the dream began almost immediately.

"Well, well, don't we look all sexy in that little skirt," Sinclair said, and there was something in his eyes that made her suddenly afraid.

Janette held out her driver's license, but he didn't take it from her. Instead those cold, blue eyes of his swept leisurely down her body. "You were going awfully fast. You doing drugs?"

"I don't do drugs, Sheriff," she exclaimed.

"I'm going to have to frisk you to make sure you have nothing illegal on you." He stepped closer to her and she smelled the scent of him, a stale sweat odor mingling with an overly sweet cologne.

Unconsciously she took a step backward, heart pounding painfully hard. He narrowed his eyes. "Don't you fight me, girl. I'll have you in handcuffs so fast your pretty little head will spin." He grinned. *"Or maybe I'll just have to shoot you for resisting."* And then he put his hands on her.

Hands. Everywhere on her. And hot breath on her face. And in her dream she did something she hadn't been able to do that night.

She screamed.

The scream pulled Dalton from a dream of a naked Jane in his bed. He shot upright on the sofa, for a moment not knowing what it was that had awakened him. Then it came again, a scream of such terror it raised the hairs on his arms, on the nape of his neck.

Jane!

He stumbled from the sofa and into the bedroom, adrenaline surging and heart pounding. He flipped on the overhead light and instantly realized Jane was in the middle of a nightmare. She thrashed on the bed, flailing her arms and legs as if fighting for her life.

Sammy cried out, too, and his eyes fluttered open, but he settled back to sleep, as if accustomed to his mother having bad dreams. "Jane," Dalton called softly.

She moaned, whipping her head from side to side, but she didn't open her eyes. He approached her, trying not to notice that the sheets had slipped down to her waist and the pale blue silk nightgown she wore did little to hide her full breasts.

The fight or flight adrenaline that had filled him at the sound of her scream now transformed to another kind of energy as a surge of desire struck him mid-section.

"Jane," he said again as he moved closer to the edge of the bed. Still she didn't respond. He was going to have to touch that soft-looking pale skin and he knew he was going to find it far too pleasant.

"Jane, wake up. You're having a nightmare." He leaned over and took her by the shoulders.

Her eyelids snapped open and she looked at him, wildness in the depths of her eyes. She stared at him and the wildness left as recognition struck. She released a little gasp and to his surprise launched herself out of the bed and into his embrace.

She trembled in his arms and sobbed silently into the crook of his neck. He tentatively slid a hand down the cool material that covered her back. "Shh, it was just a dream," he said softly.

It would be easier to comfort her if he wasn't bare-chested, if he wasn't so intensely aware of every point where her bare skin made contact with his.

She raised her face to look at him. Her eyes were misty with tears but her full lips parted as if in invitation or some kind of strange desperation.

He didn't think about kissing her ahead of time. He didn't consciously plan to. It just happened. One minute he was gazing at her face and the next minute his mouth covered hers. He didn't just kiss her, she kissed him back, her mouth opening against his as he pulled her closer to him.

The kiss lasted only a second or two, then she pulled away from him, a horrified look on her face. "I'm sorry," she said, her cheeks blossoming with high color.

"No...I'm sorry," he replied stiffly. "You were screaming and obviously having a nightmare and I...I just meant to wake you."

She released a breathless, embarrassed laugh. "I'm definitely awake."

"Then I'll just…uh…let you go back to sleep." Dalton backed out of the room, afraid that if he remained another minute longer he'd want to kiss her again.

What was he doing? he wondered as he threw himself back on the sofa. Every nerve in his body was electrified, every muscle tense. His response to that kiss stunned him. He knew virtually nothing about Jane Craig except that her skin had been soft as silk and her lips had been hot and willing.

It was possible by tomorrow she'd be gone. It was even more certain that he didn't want to be involved with her. He didn't want to know what she dreamed about, he didn't want to share his life with her in any way, shape or form. It had been wrong to kiss her, because all he could think about now was how much he wanted to kiss her again.

He fell asleep dreaming of the sweet heat of her mouth and awakened the next morning stiff and sore from the night on the sofa. He got up, nearly tripping over Sammy's diaper bag on the floor. He swallowed a curse.

By the time he'd made coffee, some of the stiffness of his muscles had begun to ease, as had his foul mood. He sat at the table, his hands wrapped around a mug of fresh brew. Even though it wasn't quite seven o'clock he could hear the sounds of plows already at work.

Maybe the bus would come this afternoon, he thought. That would be a good thing. He could see Jane and Sammy to the bus stop, wish them well on their way, then return to his solitary life without temptation. And Jane Craig had become a definite temptation.

He still sat at the table with thoughts of Jane when a knock sounded on his door. He jumped up from the table and hurried to answer. He pulled open the door to see his brother Zack standing on his landing, his gloved hands holding a shovel.

"Hey, bro, just thought I'd check in to see if you survived the storm. I just finished clearing off the driveway and your car and thought you might have a hot cup of coffee for me."

Dalton held the door tightly. *Please, please don't tell anyone I'm here.* Jane's words pounded in his head as he stared at his brother. "You didn't have to do that," he said. "And you don't want to come in here, Zack," he finally said. "I've got the flu, been throwing up off and on all night."

Zack frowned and took a step backward as if to avoid any germs floating in the air between them. "You need anything? We've about got all the major roads cleared in town and some of the stores are opening this morning."

"Nah, I'm fine. I just think I might be contagious so it wouldn't be a good idea for you to come inside, but I really appreciate you cleaning off the driveway. I'm sure George appreciates it, too. I'd love for you to come in, but I'm really not feeling well." Dalton couldn't tell if Zack believed him or not but he breathed a sigh of relief as Zack backed down the stairs, promising to check in on him later.

Dalton closed the door, hating the fact that he'd lied to his brother for reasons he didn't quite understand. If

Jane's abusive ex-boyfriend had somehow tracked her to Cotter Creek, then why on earth would it matter if the local sheriff knew about it?

He turned to see Jane standing in the bedroom doorway, Sammy in her arms. "Thank you," she said.

"Don't thank me. I'm not happy about lying to my family." He walked back into the kitchen, aware of her following just behind him.

When he saw that she was about to prepare a bottle for Sammy, he held out his hands to take the kid from her arms. As always, Sammy looked delighted to see him. He launched himself into Dalton's arms with a big grin that lit up his entire little face.

"Is this kid ever in a bad mood?" Dalton asked as he sat in a chair. Sammy smelled like baby powder and lotion, a pleasant scent that reminded Dalton of dreams half-forgotten and abandoned.

"Rarely," she replied, moving to the sink. As she stood with her back to him he couldn't help but notice again the tight fit of her worn jeans across her butt. She had a great butt. Besides the jeans she wore a pink sweater that hugged her slender curves and complemented her blond coloring.

She fixed the bottle, then took Sammy from his arms and sat in the chair next to his, her hair falling softly around her shoulders. "If the streets are clear enough maybe it would be best if I found someplace else to go until the bus runs again."

She looked so small, so utterly vulnerable, and at that moment Sammy smiled at him around his bottle's nipple, the gesture sending a stream of formula down the side of his mouth.

"That isn't necessary," he replied. "Zack just told me the streets are practically clear, so I imagine that the bus will run tomorrow."

"Good." She held his gaze. "About last night..."

"You had a nightmare. I comforted you. That's all there was to it." He got up to pour himself another cup of coffee. "You want some breakfast? I was thinking maybe I'd make a stack of pancakes."

"You don't have to go to all that trouble for me," she protested.

He grinned at her. "I'm more than willing to go to that kind of trouble for me."

She returned his smile. "Well, in that case pancakes sound wonderful."

Breakfast was pleasant. Sammy entertained with coos and grins as his mother and Dalton ate pancakes and talked. The conversation was marked with a new easiness that he suspected came from the fact that they both saw the end of their confinement together.

She made him laugh as she shared with him funny stories about her grandmother. He noticed that in none of the stories did she mention the older sister she was supposedly on her way to visit, but he didn't call her on it. Instead he simply enjoyed the way her eyes sparkled as she spoke of the old woman who had raised her.

She might not have graduated high school, but she was smart as a whip. She argued politics with him and spoke easily of current affairs. He had a feeling she would do well no matter what path she chose in life.

The rest of the day passed pleasantly. As Sammy took a late-afternoon nap, Dalton and Jane sat at the table and played poker with toothpicks as chips.

"You're one heck of a bluffer," he said after she'd won her third pot.

She laughed. "If you think I'm good, you should play with Nana. She's the ultimate poker player in the family. In fact, she gets together once a week with some of the other ladies in the trailer park and they tell everyone they're playing bridge, but they really play poker."

He laughed, but his laughter was cut short by a knock on his door. "Sit tight. I'll get rid of whoever it is." She cast him a grateful look as he got up from the table.

It was probably one of his other brothers coming to check in on him. He'd have to play the sick card again. Hopefully he could bluff as well as Jane when it came to fooling his family members.

He pulled open the door to see a burly, dark-haired man he'd never seen before standing there. He wore the khaki pants and coat of law enforcement. "Yes?"

"Dalton West?"

"Yeah, I'm Dalton."

"I'm Sheriff Brandon Sinclair from over in Sandstone. I hate to bother you, but I'm looking for a woman named Janette Black. She's traveling with a baby and I have reason to believe she might have come here." His gaze went over Dalton's shoulder, as if trying to see inside the apartment.

Dalton tensed but offered the man a frown of confusion. "There's no woman or baby here," he said. "What makes you think she'd come to me? I've never heard of this Janette Black before." That part, at least, was true. But it didn't take a rocket scientist to know that Jane was really Janette.

"She stole money from the café where she worked and when we went to find her just before the storm hit we discovered more serious crimes. Her grandmother has been murdered and Janette is a person of interest. Your name and phone number were on a piece of paper next to the old woman's bed, so we thought maybe she'd come here."

"Sorry, I'm afraid I can't help you." Dalton's head whirled with the information Sheriff Sinclair had just given him. What in the hell was going on?

Sinclair studied him for a long moment, then held out a card. "If you see her, or if she tries to make contact with you, give me a call. She's dangerous, Mr. West. She needs to be behind bars."

"I'll keep that in mind," Dalton said. He murmured a goodbye, then closed his door. He waited until he heard the sound of the sheriff's boots going back down the stairs, then he went into the kitchen.

Janette sat at the table, her face devoid of all color. As she stared at him a deep, wrenching sob ripped from the back of her throat. "He killed Nana. First he raped me, and now he's killed Nana," she cried.

She jumped up from the chair. "I'm—I'm going to be sick." She ran for the bathroom as Sammy began to cry.

Chapter 5

Janette stood in the bathroom fighting not only an all-encompassing grief, but wave after wave of nausea, as well. Just hearing his deep voice had made her ill. Knowing he'd been on the other side of the door had sickened her.

He'd found her.

He'd said he found a notepad with Dalton's name and number next to Nana's bed. There was no way Nana would have willingly given him that information. Oh God, she must have died trying to protect Janette and Sammy.

Blinded by her tears, she leaned weakly against the wall and wondered if it were possible to die of grief. She felt as if she were dying. Her heart felt as if it might explode at any moment.

Nana was dead.

Nana was dead.

Never again would Janette feel Nana's arms around her, never again would she see the old woman's eyes shining with love, her wrinkled face wreathed with laughter.

And Janette was wanted for her murder. That's how he would get Sammy. He'd see her tried for a murder she hadn't committed. She'd spend the rest of her life in prison, and Brandon Sinclair would have her precious boy. And her nana, the woman who had meant the world to her, was dead.

"Janette?" Dalton knocked on the door.

She sucked in air, trying to staunch the deep sobs that ripped through her. She didn't want to face him, was afraid that he might believe all the horrible things that Sinclair had said. And if he did believe Sinclair, there was nothing to stop him from contacting the lawman and letting him know she was here.

"Janette, come on out. We need to talk." His voice held a quiet command.

She grabbed a handful of tissues and wiped at her eyes, at her nose, then tossed the tissues into the trash. But she was reluctant to open the door, afraid to face him. What if she told him the truth and he didn't believe her? She didn't think she could handle it.

"Janette, you can't stay in there all night."

He was right. She couldn't stay in the bathroom. She opened the door. He no longer held Sammy, but as she stepped out of the bathroom Dalton opened his arms to her. She walked into them as tears of rich, raw grief began to flow again.

His strong arms surrounded her, and they felt like shelter from a world that had been terrifying for a very long time. She cried into the front of his shirt, wondering how she was going to survive without Nana's loving support.

After several minutes, Dalton released her and led her to the sofa. Sammy was once again on his blanket on the floor, staring up at the ceiling as if fascinated by the patterns the late-afternoon sunshine made as it drifted through the window.

Dalton sat next to her, his features inscrutable. "The truth, Janette. I need to know the whole truth," he said softly. "You said *he* raped you. Were you talking about your old boyfriend?"

She had two choices. Continue with the lies she'd told him, or tell the truth about everything. Her heart banged against her ribs. "No." The word whispered out of her on a wave of despair. She knew it was time to tell the truth. She had nothing to lose now and she wanted— needed—Dalton to know.

She grabbed a strand of her hair and twisted it around her finger. "There is no ex-boyfriend. The man who raped me, the man who killed my grandmother, is Sheriff Brandon Sinclair."

Dalton's eyes narrowed and he drew in a quick breath of surprise. "I think maybe you need to start at the beginning and tell me everything."

She leaned back against the plump sofa cushion and closed her eyes, fighting the overwhelming grief that still reached out to smother her in its clutches. She opened her eyes and gazed down at Sammy, who in the midst of her heartbreak had fallen asleep.

Looking at Dalton, she fought against the tears and drew a deep, steadying breath. The beginning. "It happened one night when I was driving home from the classes I was taking to study for my GED. They took place at a community college about twenty-five miles from where I lived in Sandstone."

She rose from the sofa, unable to sit as she fought against the panic that remembering that night always brought. It was a panic that constricted her lungs, closed up the back of her throat and quickened her heartbeat. It was the fear of having to remember and the additional stress of wondering if Dalton would believe her.

"Janette." He reached out and took her hand. Holding it firmly he drew her back on the sofa next to him. "It's okay, you're safe for now." He didn't let go of her hand. It was as if he knew she needed support, something to cling to as she went back to that horrible night.

She nodded and swallowed hard. "The highway between the community college and Sandstone is pretty deserted after dark. I was about halfway between the college and home when I saw the lights of a patrol car in my rearview mirror. I knew I was speeding so I pulled over to the side of the road, figuring I was about to get a ticket."

She paused and drew another deep breath, trying to still the frantic beat of her heart. Dalton squeezed her hand, as if to give her strength and she desperately needed it. She needed all the strength he could give her to get through the rest of it.

"I thought something was odd when he told me to turn off my headlights and get out of the car. He told me I had been speeding and asked if I was doing drugs. I've never touched drugs in my life," she stated emphatically.

Dalton nodded, his expression giving nothing away of his inner thoughts. "Had you had run-ins with him before that night?"

"Never," she replied. "I'd seen him around town, on the streets, but he'd never spoken to me before, never even noticed me that I knew of."

"What happened next?" he asked.

A trembling began deep inside her. It was as if all the warmth of the room had been sucked out and an arctic chill had taken over the world. Tears blurred her vision once again and she blinked them away, angry that after all this time the memory of what happened still had the power to make her cry.

"He told me he needed to frisk me and he warned me that he'd hate to have to shoot me for resisting." She looked down at Dalton's hand around hers, unable to look him in the eyes.

"He raped me there on the side of the road." The words didn't begin to describe the horror, the violation of that night.

Her nose filled with the sweaty, ugly scent of Sinclair. Her skin wanted to crawl off her body as she thought of the way he'd touched her, the sounds he'd made as he pushed himself against her. "I won't bore you with all the ugly details."

She pulled her hand from Dalton's, afraid he could feel the ugliness inside her. She couldn't look at him, was afraid to see disbelief in his eyes. She'd fall completely to pieces if she saw doubt or condemnation there.

"What happened after?" His voice was soft, as if he understood the emotions blackening her soul. Thank God he didn't press her for any of the details of the rape itself, for she'd shoved those particular memories deep inside her in a place where she wouldn't easily retrieve them.

She looked up into those warm green eyes of his. "Nothing," she said simply. She forced a smile of dark humor. "I guess I should be grateful that at least I didn't get a speeding ticket." The smile faltered and fell away as tears once again burned at her eyes.

He raised a dark eyebrow. "You didn't tell anyone?"

She leaned back and stared at a point just over his shoulder. "Who was I going to tell? I couldn't exactly report the crime to the sheriff." There was more than a touch of bitterness in her voice.

She shook her head. "I didn't tell anyone. I didn't want to tell Nana because I thought it might destroy her. It wasn't until I realized I was pregnant that I finally told Nana and the man I'd been seeing at the time." A shaft of pain stabbed through her. "He asked me what I'd been wearing that night, implying that it was somehow my fault. Needless to say that was the end of that relationship."

"And you're sure Sheriff Sinclair is Sammy's biological father?" There was a faint note of apology in his voice.

She wanted to be offended by the question, but realized Dalton really didn't know anything about her. It was a fair question, she supposed.

"I'm positive. The guy I was seeing at the time…we hadn't…you know, been intimate." Her cheeks burned and she kept her gaze averted from his.

"So, you realized you were pregnant. What happened then?"

She looked at him once again. It was impossible to read him. She had no idea if he believed her or not, couldn't get a sense of anything that might be flowing through his head.

"The last thing I wanted was for Brandon Sinclair to know that I was pregnant. I managed to hide my condition from everyone until late in the pregnancy, then I told people who noticed that I'd had a fling with a salesman passing through town." She gazed down at Sammy. "As far as I was concerned Brandon Sinclair had no right to know about my condition. From the very beginning Sammy was my baby and nobody else's."

"So, he didn't know anything about Sammy."

"I didn't think he knew until three days ago when he walked into the café where I worked." She told him about Sinclair and his deputies coming in and the sheriff asking her about her son.

"There was something in his eyes, something in the things he was saying that let me know I had to take Sammy and run and so that's what I did. I didn't steal anything from the café, but the moment the sheriff left, I told Smiley, the owner, that I didn't feel well. I also told him I wasn't happy working there and I was quitting, then I went home."

She paused a moment to draw a deep breath then continued, "Nana agreed that I needed to take Sammy and leave town, get as far away as possible from Sheriff Sinclair. One of Nana's friends drove me here to catch the bus. Our plan was that I'd get settled someplace far away from Oklahoma, then I'd send for Nana and we'd start building a new life together." Grief once again rocked through her and new tears burned at her eyes as she thought of her grandmother.

Dalton studied her, a tiny frown furrowing the area in the center of his forehead. "After that night of the rape, did he continue to bother you? To threaten you in any way?"

She shook her head. "No. Of course, I went out of my way to avoid him. I kept my pregnancy pretty well hidden, too. The few times we did run into each other, it was as if nothing had ever happened. He'd look right through me, as if he had no memory of what he'd done."

She wrapped her arms around herself, fighting a new chill. A bitter laugh escaped her. "Who was I going to report it to?" she said more to herself than to him. "Who was I going to tell about the rape? The sheriff? His deputies? Brandon Sinclair owns Sandstone."

Leaning forward she stared at the wall just over Dalton's shoulder. "Everyone is afraid of him. He'll get Smiley, my boss at the café, to agree that I stole money. He'll get anyone in town to say anything whether it's true or not, because nobody wants to get on his bad side. Besides, when he was done with me he reminded me that I was nothing but trailer trash and nobody would ever believe my word over his."

"I believe you."

Those three words, so simply spoken, wove a strand of warmth around her heart. She hadn't realized how badly she'd wanted to hear somebody other than her nana say them. She began to cry again.

Dalton pulled her against his broad chest as her tears flowed once again. He believed her. Dalton, better than anyone, knew that a gold badge of law enforcement could hide a sick, twisted soul.

There was no way she could fake the grief she felt for her grandmother and there was no way she could have manufactured the trauma she'd exhibited as she'd told him about the rape.

He tightened his arms around her. There was a special place in hell for men who raped women, and a place beyond hell for men in authority who abused women.

Janette's tears finally ebbed and she raised her head and looked at him, the blue of her eyes dark with tortured sorrow. "I just can't believe she's gone," she said, her voice hoarse with emotion. "I just talked to her yesterday morning."

"Yesterday morning?" Dalton frowned, the sheriff's words replaying in his mind. "You spoke to your grandmother yesterday morning?"

She nodded and moved out of his embrace. She wiped at her cheeks and tucked a strand of her shiny hair behind her ear. "I called her from here to let her know that I was stuck here because of the storm."

"But according to what Sheriff Sinclair told me, he found her dead before the storm moved in."

Janette blinked in confusion. "But that's impossible." Her tears disappeared as a tenuous hope shone from her eyes. "He lied. And if she wasn't dead when he said she was, maybe she isn't dead at all. Maybe he just said that to get you to turn me over to him." She jumped up from the sofa and headed to the cordless phone on the end table.

Dalton leaned forward and watched her. As she punched in numbers she looked small and fragile, and the thought of a man touching her, taking her with force filled him with a simmering rage.

He watched her face as she gripped the phone receiver tightly against her ear. The hope that had momentarily lit her eyes faded.

"Nobody answered," she said as she hung up. "Even the answering machine didn't pick up." Her eyes grew shiny with tears once again.

"Is there anyone else you can call to see what's going on?"

"Nana's friend, Nancy." She quickly punched in the number. "She lives next door to Nana at the trailer park. She'll know what's going on. Nancy," she said into the phone. "It's me."

Myriad expressions played across her face as she listened to the voice on the other end of the line. "Oh, God, is she…" Tears once again fell from Janette's eyes but she offered him a tremulous smile.

"Nana, are you all right?"

As she said these words a knot of tension eased in

his chest. Either she was a better actress than Meryl Streep or she was now talking to the grandmother she'd thought murdered.

"Does he know where you are now?" Janette asked. "Are you sure you'll be okay?" She paused and listened for several minutes, then continued, "We're fine and hopefully tomorrow we'll be on the bus. Don't worry, Nana, everything is going to be okay. I love you, too. I'll stay in touch."

Janette hung up the phone and stared at Dalton, her eyes once again haunted with fear. "She's alive, thank God." She returned to the sofa. He saw the tremor that went through her body, but when she gazed at him he realized it was anger shining from her eyes, not fear.

"What's happened?" he asked.

"Yesterday morning Nana braved the snow to go to Nancy's and have coffee. She was there for about two hours. When she got home she had the feeling somebody had been in her trailer. She didn't find anything out of place or missing so she chalked it up to her imagination. Then last night she was feeling lonely and unsettled, so she went back to Nancy's to play some cards and spend the night. During the night her trailer was set on fire."

Shock filled Dalton at her words.

"Thank God she wasn't home. He meant to kill her, Dalton." Janette's hands clenched into fists at her sides. "He meant to kill her and blame me so he can see me in prison. Then he'll be free to claim Sammy."

They both looked at the sleeping child on the floor. A weary resignation filled him. He'd offered her safe harbor from a snowstorm but now it appeared that the storm in her life had nothing to do with the weather outside. And he had a feeling whether he wanted it or not, her storm had become his.

"Why don't we get something to eat? It's past dinnertime and I think we both could use something warm in our bellies." He got up from the sofa and she followed him into the kitchen. "Grilled cheese and soup?" he asked and pointed her to the table.

She shrugged, as if it didn't matter what he offered her. He opened a can of tomato soup and poured it into a saucepan, then when he had it warming up he prepared the grilled cheese for the awaiting skillet. As he worked, she stared out the window where darkness had begun to fall.

He had to admit that there was something about her that touched him, that called on protective instincts he'd thought had been lost when he'd lost Mary.

"It must have been a tough decision to have the baby under the circumstances," he said. "A lot of women would have chosen a different option."

"I thought about an abortion," she replied. "But, to be honest it was just a passing thought. It might be an option for a lot of women, but it wasn't for me. I was easily able to separate the innocent baby from the monster who had raped me."

She smiled then, the first smile he'd seen from her since the appearance of Brandon Sinclair on his doorstep. It was like sunshine breaking through chill wintry clouds. "Sammy is the best of me and there hasn't been a single minute that I've regretted my decision to give him life."

That's mother love, he thought. That fierce, shining emotion he saw in Janette's eyes, that was what he'd lost when his mother had been murdered. Dalton rarely thought about the mother he couldn't remember, but a shaft of unexpected grief stabbed him now.

"It was a sheriff who murdered my mother twenty-five years ago," he said. Her eyes widened as she stared at him. "The sheriff of Cotter Creek, Jim Ramsey. He was arrested a couple of months ago when he stalked my sister."

"Why? Why did he kill your mother?"

Dalton stirred the soup, then placed the first two sandwiches into the skillet. "He said he loved her, but it wasn't love, it was a sick, twisted obsession. He approached her one night on the highway and told her he loved her, that he wanted her to leave my dad, and when she refused he lost it and strangled her."

He didn't miss the parallel in what had happened to his mother and what had happened to Janette. Men they should have been able to trust had accosted both on a lonely stretch of highway. The only difference was, Janette had survived and his mother had not.

"Oh, Dalton, I'm so sorry."

He nodded and swallowed around the unexpected lump of emotion that rose up in his throat. "It was a long time ago. She was a wonderful, loving person."

"And your father never remarried?"

Dalton flipped the sandwiches. "No, never even looked at another woman. He and my mom were true soul mates and when she was gone he never showed any interest in pursuing a relationship with anyone else."

"From what my grandmother told me, my mother wasn't even sure who my father was." Her gaze went back to the window again and when she looked back at Dalton a tiny frown furrowed her forehead. "Why would he tell you that I'd killed Nana?"

Dalton took up the grilled cheese sandwiches and placed them on two separate plates. "If he burned down her trailer last night it's possible he doesn't know she isn't dead. If he puts out the word that you're wanted for questioning in a murder case, then you're going to have trouble hiding out. He can get law enforcement officials in every county keeping an eye out for you."

He set the plates on the table then went back to grab the two bowls of soup. "If you're trying to cheer me up, it isn't working," she said dryly.

She placed her spoon in her bowl, but didn't begin to eat. Instead, she looked back out the window, where night had completely fallen. "Do you think he believed you when you told him you didn't know me, that I wasn't here?"

Dalton followed her gaze to the window and a tight knot of tension formed in his chest. "I have a feeling we'll know before the bus shows up in town."

Brandon raised his collar against the stiff wind that blew from the north. He stood across the street from Dalton West's place, eyes trained on the upper windows. She was in there. He smelled her, the trailer trash tramp who was trying to keep his son from him.

He'd known that she'd blown town, had taken his son and left Sandstone. A visit to her grandmother's house yesterday had given him his clue. The old lady wasn't home but he'd gotten inside and taken a look around. The minute he'd seen the name and phone number on the nightstand, he knew in his gut that he was on her trail.

It was obvious from the condition of the small bedroom in the trailer that Janette had packed up and left. Clothes were thrown helter-skelter and there wasn't a baby article to be found except for the crib, which was stripped of bedding.

He'd been enraged. He'd gone back to his office, researched to find out what he could about Dalton West, then late last night had returned to the trailer and set it on fire. He considered the death of Janette's grandmother collateral damage. He hadn't yet gotten the official report of the fire from their fire chief, but he knew the man would write up whatever Brandon told him to.

With the old woman dead and Janette wanted as a suspect in an arson-murder case, she'd find it difficult to get out of Cotter Creek. She was a wanted woman, and if he put a reward on her head, she wouldn't be able to show her face anywhere.

He'd known he'd find Janette, and he had. He narrowed his eyes as he watched the windows. Even though Dalton West had told him he'd never heard of Janette Black, that there was no woman with a baby inside his place, Brandon knew he'd lied.

The sheriff had done his homework. He knew Dalton West was a bachelor who lived alone. But he'd watched the silhouettes move back and forth in front of those windows and knew the professional bodyguard wasn't alone. And if that wasn't enough, when Dalton had opened the door and Brandon had gotten a glimpse inside, he'd seen a diaper bag on the living-room floor, a diaper bag with the same blue teddy bear print that had decorated one area of one of the small bedrooms in the trailer.

She was in there, and there was no way she was going to escape him. One Oklahoma bodyguard wasn't going to stand in the way of Brandon Sinclair getting exactly what he wanted.

Chapter 6

The cough woke Dalton. An irritating cough that pulled him groggily from his sleep. His eyes burned as he sat up on the sofa and realized the air was filled with the acrid scent of smoke.

Fear shoved aside the last of his sleepiness as he grabbed his gun off the coffee table where he'd placed it before going to sleep the night before.

He turned on the lamp next to the sofa and gasped as he saw the dark smoke that swirled in the room. Fire! They had to get out.

Maybe George had forgotten to turn off a stove burner and something had caught flame. Dalton didn't give much thought to what caused the smoke, he just knew he needed to get Janette and Sammy out, for the smoke appeared to be thickening by the second. Fire could be dangerous, but smoke was just as deadly.

He pulled on his boots, then grabbed a coat, his cell phone and car keys and hurried into the bedroom where Sammy and Janette were asleep. He turned on the overhead light and Janette stirred, but didn't awaken.

"Janette." He walked over to the bed and shook her shoulder with a sense of urgency. A spasm of coughing overtook him as she opened her eyes. "We need to get out of here," he finally managed to gasp.

She didn't ask questions, obviously aware of the imminent danger that whirled and darkened the room despite the overhead light. "I'll get your coat," he said. "Just grab what you need."

As Dalton raced back through the kitchen into the small utility room where he'd hung her coat the night she'd arrived, he felt no heat beneath his feet, heard no ominous crackle of flames. But that didn't mean they weren't in danger.

She met him at the bedroom door, pulling her suitcase behind her and Sammy in her arms with a blanket over his head. He thought about telling her to forget the suitcase, but realized the case contained all the possessions she and Sammy had left in the world.

He grabbed the suitcase from her and motioned her toward the door that led to the interior staircase. He needed to make sure George got out as well.

Before he opened the stairwell door he felt the wood, wanting to make sure it wasn't hot, that deadly flames weren't already attempting to burn through. The door radiated no heat so he opened it and motioned for her to precede him down the stairs.

The smoke wasn't as intense in the staircase, and still he could feel no heat radiating from any of the walls. But where there was smoke, there had to be a fire.

They hit the landing to the first floor and Dalton entered George's area of the house. "Wait here," he said to Janette as he raced through George's living room and down the hallway to the bedroom where the old man slept.

It took him only minutes to rouse George from sleep and get his coat and shoes on him, then together they all made their way to the front door.

It wasn't until they opened the front door to get out that Dalton's brain fully kicked into high gear. "Wait," he said urgently before Janette ran outside.

His mind whirled with suppositions. Brandon Sinclair had burned down Janette's grandmother's place. This evening he'd come to ask if Janette was here. Was it possible Sinclair hadn't believed Dalton when he'd said he didn't know Janette? Was it out of the question that he'd set a fire to try to smoke her out?

"Janette, my truck is in the driveway. I'm going out first and when I get outside you run for the truck. George, you come out after Janette." He released the lock on his gun, knowing he might have to provide cover for her if Sinclair was outside.

He knew by the look in Janette's eyes that she perceived his thoughts, realized the potential for danger. She gripped Sammy more tightly against her as George took the suitcase from her hand.

"Problems?" George asked.

"Possibly," Dalton replied. George nodded and straightened his thin, sloped shoulders.

Dalton went out the door, gun drawn, and with every sense he possessed on high alert. The night held the eerie silence that snow-cover produced, a preternatural calm that could be deceptive.

Snow crunched beneath his boots as he stepped onto the front porch. The cold air stabbed his lungs as he drew deep, even breaths. He looked both directions, seeing nothing amiss but unwilling to trust that the night shadows held nothing dangerous.

He took several more steps, then turned back to the house, noting dark smoke rolling out of a partially opened basement window. Had George left it open? The old man had a workshop downstairs where he did some woodworking. Had he left his wood-burning tool on, and somehow it had caught fire?

His heart pounded as adrenaline continued to pump through him. He had no idea how big a fire might be burning there, but it was apparent he needed to get the others out of the house as soon as possible.

Looking around once again he saw nothing that indicated any danger. He walked back up to the door and motioned for Janette to follow him as he tried to watch every direction around them.

The gunshot came from the left, the bullet whizzing by Janette's head as she screamed in terror. Dalton's body slammed her to the ground, and he hoped that in the process Sammy wasn't hurt.

"Get down, George," he yelled at the old man, who

had just stepped off the porch. George dove into a snow-bank with the agility of a man one-fourth his age.

Another gunshot exploded in the quiet of the night and the snow next to where Dalton and Janette lay kicked up. The shots had come from the direction of a large oak tree in the distance. Janette screamed again and Sammy's cries added to the melee.

Dalton's heart crashed against his ribs and he thought he could feel Janette's heartbeat through their coats. "I'm going to roll off you and start firing. When I do, run like hell to the truck and get inside. Stay down." He fumbled in his pocket for his keys and gave them to her. "And if anything happens to me, drive away and don't look back."

He didn't give her time to protest or accept, he rolled off her and began firing at the tree. At the same time he heard the sound of a siren in the distance and knew that somebody had heard the shots and called for help.

When he saw that Janette was safely in the truck, he stopped firing and waited to see if there would be an answering volley.

Nothing.

For a long moment he remained where he was, not moving, but listening…waiting…wondering if the threat still existed or not.

He got up into a crouch as the siren grew louder. Still no answering shots. He had a feeling the shooter had run at the first sound of the siren. He hurried to the driver's side of the truck and was surprised to see George come burrowing up from the snowdrift and running to throw the suitcase in the back of the truck bed.

Dalton had just backed out of the driveway when Zack's patrol car came screaming to a halt. "Get down," he ordered Janette. She bent so she wasn't visible and Dalton was grateful that at the moment Sammy wasn't wailing. He rolled down his window as Zack rolled down his.

"Call the fire department, and see to George," Dalton said. "I'll be in touch." As Zack yelled a protest, Dalton pulled out onto the street and sped away from his brother, the house and the quiet, solitary life he'd led.

Thankfully, Janette remained silent as he headed out of town and kept a watchful eye on the street behind him for anyone that might be following.

He needed to think.

Zack was a newly elected sheriff and aware of everyone's eyes on him. After the disgrace of Jim Ramsey, the last sheriff of Cotter Creek, Zack was proving himself to be a strictly by-the-book kind of lawman.

Dalton believed in rules, but sometimes rules had to be bent, even broken, and he wasn't convinced that Zack would see things his way.

If Brandon Sinclair had an arrest warrant for Janette, then Dalton feared his brother would feel it necessary to turn her over to him. He wouldn't want to put himself in the middle of a problem that wasn't his, especially in bucking the authority of a fellow sheriff.

"Where are we going?" Janette asked, finally breaking the tense silence in the truck as they left the town of Cotter Creek behind.

"A place where you'll be safe until we can figure things out," he replied.

Besides, if he did decide to confide in Zack, what could he tell him? That a strange woman had shown up on his doorstep and had initially lied about everything, but finally had told him a story that he believed?

Zack would ask for cold hard facts and Dalton had none. He couldn't prove that Brandon Sinclair had set the fire tonight or fired the shots. No doubt Sinclair hadn't used his service weapon; ballistics would probably lead to a dead end. He couldn't prove that Janette hadn't stolen money from her employer, although he could attest to the fact that she hadn't been anywhere near that trailer when it had gone up in flames. Unless Sinclair screwed around with the reported date of the fire.

He didn't want to put his brother in the untenable position of having to choose between doing his job or supporting Dalton's decision to break the law by hiding Janette.

He'd talk to Zack, tell him who he thought was responsible for both the fire tonight and the gunfire, but he wouldn't tell Zack where Janette was hidden away. He wouldn't give her over to Zack, who might find himself with no alternative than to turn her over to Sinclair.

He cast a quick glance at the woman in the passenger seat. She bounced Sammy in her arms and asked no more questions about where they were going or what they were going to do.

She trusted him.

After two snowbound days together, she trusted that he was taking her someplace where she'd be safe. It shocked him, awed him, and if he were to admit the truth to himself, it scared him more than just a little bit. She was placing not only her life, but also the life of her little boy directly in his hands.

He clenched the steering wheel tightly. He hadn't signed on for this, had simply offered a woman and her baby shelter from the storm. A tiny spark of anger filled him. He didn't want this responsibility. Since the debacle with Mary he'd consciously backed away from being involved with anyone, even his family. He didn't want anyone depending on him, needing him.

He didn't want the responsibility, but now that he had it, he couldn't turn his back. Janette had been trapped by the storm, and now he was trapped by her circumstances.

Janette thought she might be in a mild state of shock. She couldn't process the fire, the gunshots and now a drive down narrow, slick roads with darkness all around.

She should be terrified, but she wasn't. She was beyond terror and instead felt only a weary resignation, a stunning knowledge that she was no longer in control of her own life.

She glanced at Dalton. In the faint illumination from the dashboard his handsome features looked grim and more than a little bit dangerous. She could only imagine what was going through his mind right now.

Because of his kindness to a stranger, his home had been set on fire, he'd been shot at and he was now making a dash over the snow-slick roads to a safe place.

"I'm so sorry I got you involved in all this," she said. "All I wanted to do was leave town."

His knuckles turned white on the steering wheel as she felt the back end of the truck slide out. She caught her breath, then relaxed as he skillfully steered into the skid and straightened out the truck.

"I know," he replied. "We'll talk when we get where we're going."

That comment effectively staunched any other conversation she might have wanted to have. She cuddled Sammy closer against her and stared out the passenger window, where no lights from houses broke the darkness of the night.

He seemed to have a plan and she was grateful, because she had none. She couldn't return to his apartment because it was obvious Sinclair knew she was there. She felt terrible that she'd now placed Dalton in a horrible position. If he didn't turn her over to the sheriff, then he was breaking the law and could face even uglier repercussions of his own.

She'd like to be able to tell him just to drop her off somewhere, that she'd figure things out on her own. But that wasn't an option either. She couldn't go back to Sandstone and she couldn't get out of Cotter Creek. She was in a horrible state of limbo, with Brandon Sinclair like a hound dog sniffing her scent.

She sat straighter in the seat as Dalton turned off the main road and through an iron gate. He doused his headlights as they approached a large ranch-style home.

"That's my dad's place," he said as they drove past

the sprawling one-story house. "It would be better if nobody knows you're here on the property."

That explained him dousing the truck lights. They entered a pasture area and he threw the gears into four-wheel drive as they hit the thicker snow where no plows had been.

They passed another house where lights shone from several windows. "That's my brother Tanner and his wife's place," Dalton said.

Still they didn't stop. Once they'd passed the second house Dalton turned the truck headlights back on. There were other tracks in the snow. In one area it looked as if several trucks or cars had made figure eights.

An area of thick woods was on their right, mostly evergreen trees, which she assumed provided windbreaks. Eventually Dalton turned through a small break in the trees and pulled to a halt in front of a small cabin. Trees completely surrounded it, tall evergreens that made it impossible to see the place unless you were right on top of it.

"Who lives here?" she asked, nerves jumping in her stomach.

"For now, you do," he said as he shut off the engine. "At one time or another, I think all of my brothers have lived here for short periods, but for the last couple of months it's been empty. You should be safe here."

She *should* have been safe on the road between her home and the community college. She *should* have been safe in Dalton's apartment. She couldn't afford to take her safety for granted anymore.

"Come on, let's get you inside and settled," he said as he opened his truck door.

Janette got out of the truck and stared at the cabin. There was nothing welcoming about it. Illuminated only by the faint cast of the moon filtering through the trees, it looked dark and cold and forbidding.

She tightened her grip on Sammy as she followed Dalton up the stairs to the front door. He used a key to unlock it, then pushed it open, flipped on a switch that lit a small table lamp and ushered her inside.

The sense of welcome that had been absent from the exterior was present inside. Plump throw pillows covered a dark-green sofa, and a rocking chair sat next to the fireplace. The wood floor gleamed with richness except where it was covered by braided rugs.

"It's nothing fancy," Dalton said as he wheeled the dial of the thermostat on the wall. "There's a bedroom and bath and a small kitchen." He turned to face her. "We're deep enough in the woods that no one should see the lights, but I won't light a fire. I don't want smoke from the chimney to draw any curious people."

He motioned her to follow him into the small kitchen, where he opened cabinets to show her a stockpile of canned goods. "There's enough here to hold you for a night or two."

"You're not staying?" She tried to keep the fear out of her voice but didn't quite succeed.

"I've got to get back to town and check on George and talk to my brother."

"What are you going to tell him?" She studied his features, wondering if he'd decide to give her up, that this was all trouble he hadn't bargained to take on and he was finished with her and her mess.

He swiped a hand through his thick dark hair and leaned against the wall, his expression unreadable. "I don't know for sure. I'm still sorting out things in my head. But I promise you I won't tell him you're here."

He shoved off from the wall. "Things are pretty dusty in here, but there's fresh bedding in one of the dresser drawers in the bedroom, and it won't take long for the furnace to warm things up."

"I'm sure we'll be fine," she replied, although she wasn't sure of anything. She wanted to tell him not to leave her, that she needed him to hold her, to wrap her in his strong arms and make her feel safe.

She couldn't remember the last time she'd truly felt safe. On second thought, yes, she did remember. It had been the night of her bad dream when he had held her and soothed away her fear.

He walked over to the doorway that led off the kitchen and flipped on the light to illuminate a small bedroom with a double bed and a long dresser. "It's late. You should try to get some sleep. There's a phone in the living room. I'm assuming you don't have a cell phone."

"Where I come from cell phones are a luxury, not a necessity."

He nodded and headed for the front door. "You've got my cell phone number. If you need anything don't hesitate to call."

She followed him to the front door, nerves jangling inside as she watched him go out to the truck then return with her suitcase, which George had thrown into the back at the last minute.

"Will you be back later tonight?" she asked.

His green eyes narrowed intently. "I don't know. I can't make any promises. For sure I'll try to be back here sometime tomorrow. Is there anything you need for Sammy?"

"It depends on how long we're here. If it's for too much longer I'm going to need some more diapers." A sense of urgency swept through her. "Surely the bus will run tomorrow and I can get on it and away from here."

He stared at her for a long moment, and she had a feeling he wanted to say something to her, something she might not want to hear. Instead he turned toward the door. "I'll see you sometime tomorrow."

And with that he was gone.

Sammy slept soundly as she laid him on the sofa with pillows surrounding him while she went into the bedroom to make up the bed.

The last thing on her mind was sleep. Restless energy filled her, coupled with a simmering sense of terror that was unrelenting.

Was Sinclair still in Cotter Creek? Those gunshots tonight were intended to kill her. Had his intention been to kill them all, then pluck Sammy from her dead arms?

She now recognized that Sinclair would do anything to get Sammy. The man was insane. Was it truly about him wanting a son, or was it more than that?

Maybe he was angry that she'd left town and was afraid that once she was out of Sandstone, she'd feel safe enough to talk about what he'd done to her. It was impossible to know the man's mind. A chill washed over her, and it had nothing to do with the coolness of the room.

Once the bed was made she placed Sammy in the middle, then walked back into the living room, knowing that sleep would be a long time coming.

She stood at the living-room window and stared out into the darkness of night, her thoughts going to the man who had just left.

Smelling the scent of his pleasant cologne, which lingered in the air, she wrapped her arms around her middle and tried not to allow herself to wish for a life different than the one she'd been handed.

The memory of that single kiss she'd shared with Dalton warmed the chilled places inside her. What would it be like to kiss him longer, harder? What would it be like to lie naked in his arms, to make love with him?

She hadn't been with any man since the night of her rape, but she knew how good lovemaking could be if it was between two people who cared about each other. When she was twenty-one she'd had a relationship with a man that had lasted almost a year. They had enjoyed a healthy sex life for the last three months of their time together.

Although that relationship had ended, she was grateful now that she'd had it. It would have been terrible to know nothing about sex except those horrid minutes on the side of the road with Sinclair.

She could care for a man like Dalton West, a man who not only stole a bit of her breath away whenever she looked at him, but also radiated the strength and assurance of a good man.

Turning away from the window she released a deep sigh. The last thing she needed to be thinking of was indulging in an affair with Dalton. She was an uneducated woman with a son who was the product of rape. What made her think a man like Dalton West would ever want anything to do with her?

What she'd better figure out instead was how she was going to stay one step ahead of a demented man who wanted to take the only thing she cared about, a man who would stop at nothing to get what he wanted.

Chapter 7

Zack's patrol car was still in front of George's place when Dalton pulled into the driveway. He'd spent the entire drive back from the cabin trying to figure out exactly what he intended to tell his brother.

His first priority was to protect Janette, but equally as important was his desire to protect his brother. He refused to put Zack in a position where he had to choose between doing the right thing and handing Janette over to Brandon Sinclair, or doing the wrong thing and jeopardizing the job he loved.

He got out of his car, aware that he was about to walk a very fine line. George's front door was open, and when Dalton walked in Zack greeted him with a deep frown of frustration.

"It's about time you showed up. You want to tell me

what's going on?" Zack asked. "A fire of suspicious origins and gunshots, and I can't get George here to tell me anything."

George sat on his sofa, his arms folded across his chest and a stubborn glint in his brown eyes. "I can't tell you what I don't know," he exclaimed fervently. "I don't know how those rags started on fire in my basement and I sure as hell don't have a clue who shot at us when we ran out of the house."

"How much damage did the fire do?" Dalton asked, stalling for time.

"Thank God it was more smoke than flame," George replied. "Burned up a couple of boxes I had stored down there, but nothing too serious."

"Good." Dalton turned to his brother. "Why don't you and I go up to my place and let George get some sleep? He's not used to this much excitement in the middle of the night."

"You got that right," George exclaimed.

Zack nodded, his jaw muscle knotted with obvious frustration. Dalton told George good-night, then together he and Zack went upstairs.

Once in Dalton's living room Zack sat on the edge of the sofa and stared at his brother. "Now talk," he demanded. "I need some answers from somebody and as far as I can tell you're the only one around here who might have them."

Dalton remained standing. "Earlier this evening Sheriff Brandon Sinclair from Sandstone knocked on my door and told me he was looking for a woman wanted for theft and questioning in a murder case and had reason to believe she had come to me. I told him I didn't know the woman, but I don't think he believed me."

Zack frowned. "Why would he think this woman would come to you?"

"I don't know. He said something about finding my name and number in the trailer where this woman lives."

Zack watched him intently. "And you don't know this woman. What's her name?"

"According to Sinclair, her name is Janette Black, and, no, I don't know her. I can't imagine why she would have had my name and phone number."

"So, what? What does Sinclair have to do with the fire and the gunplay that took place here tonight?"

Dalton shrugged. "All I can tell you is that he was here asking about a woman named Janette Black. I told him I'd never heard of her and she certainly wasn't here, then he left. Hours later I woke up to smoke filling the house and I ran downstairs and woke up George. We ran out the front door and somebody started shooting at us."

Zack's frown deepened. "Why would Sinclair do something like that?"

"I don't know. All I can tell you is what happened," Dalton replied. The most difficult thing he'd ever done was hold his brother's gaze while he knew he wasn't telling the whole truth.

"Was the shooter targeting both you and George?"

"No, just me," Dalton answered. "I returned fire, jumped into my truck and that's when you got here."

"Handy that you just happened to have your gun with you when you ran out of the house."

"Dad always taught us to be prepared for anything," Dalton replied easily. "And to be honest, something about Sinclair didn't sit quite right with me. Call it instinct."

"Where have you been for the last hour?" Zack asked, watching Dalton intently.

"Driving…making sure nobody was following me." Although the lie fell effortlessly from his lips, he hated the way it felt inside. "I wanted to draw any danger there might be away from this house and George, but I didn't see anyone following me."

Zack frowned again. "This just doesn't make any sense. Why would Brandon Sinclair do something like this? I know Brandon. We've met for beers a couple of times. He's always seemed like a stand-up guy to me."

"If you're investigating the shooting and the fire, I recommend you start the investigation by checking Mr. Stand-up Guy's alibi," Dalton countered lightly.

"Is there some history here that I don't know anything about? Have you and Brandon had run-ins before?"

"Definitely not. I'd never met the man before he showed up on my doorstep earlier this evening."

"You having problems with anyone else? Are you working on something that I don't know about? Something to do with West Protective Services?"

"Nothing."

Zack stood, obviously as frustrated as he had been when Dalton had arrived. "I don't know, bro. I get the feeling you're not telling me everything."

"Believe me, when I figure out what's going on you'll be one of the first to know," Dalton promised.

Zack headed for the door. "You want me to put one of my deputies on the house? Keep an eye on things for the rest of the night?"

Dalton shook his head. "I have a feeling the excitement is over for the night." With Janette out of the apartment there was no reason for Brandon Sinclair to come calling again. And if he did, Dalton would be ready.

"You'll let me know if you think of anything else?"

"Of course," Dalton said. He watched as his brother opened the door and started to step outside, then paused and turned back to look at Dalton.

"Must have been a fast moving bug," he said.

"Excuse me?" Dalton frowned in confusion.

"The flu. You seem to be feeling much better now." Zack had a knowing glint in his eyes.

"I am. Must have been a twenty-four-hour bug that ran its course." Dalton hoped his cheeks weren't dark with the color of the lie.

Zack held his gaze for a long moment. "Dalton, you'd tell me if you were in trouble, right?" This time there was no frustration on Zack's features, only the deep concern of a brother.

Dalton wanted to tell him everything, but before he could do that he needed to talk to Janette. "I'm fine, really," he said, but he could tell his words did nothing to assure his brother.

Zack disappeared out the door. Dalton breathed a huge sigh of relief and sat on the edge of the sofa where Zack had been only seconds before.

It was obvious that George had stayed true to his word and hadn't breathed a word to Zack about Janette and Sammy being there.

A glance at the clock let Dalton know it was almost four. The last thing on his mind was sleep. He dropped his head into his hands and tried to make sense of everything that had gone down, everything he hadn't told his brother.

If he were smart, he would have told Zack everything. Zack would have probably honored whatever arrest warrant Sinclair had and turned Janette over. Then she would have been out of Dalton's life. He wouldn't feel responsible for her.

Zack would tell him that he was making decisions based on something other than his brain. Was that what he was doing? Was he allowing Janette's beautiful blue eyes and the memory of the hot kiss they'd shared to twist his logic?

Was it possible she and Sinclair had indulged in an affair, one that had gone bad? Was she the kind of woman to take money from her workplace? Make up a story about rape?

No. Even though he'd only known her for a brief time, he knew she wasn't that kind of woman. Granted, he couldn't deny that he felt a strong sense of physical attraction to her, but that didn't mean he didn't believe what she'd told him. That couldn't take away the likelihood that tonight Brandon Sinclair had set a fire, then had tried to kill them both. Those weren't the actions of a man who had nothing to hide.

Dalton had no doubt that the sheriff was behind what

had happened. But knowing and proving were two different things and until he had proof, he wasn't going to tell his brother anything. He stretched out on the sofa and listened to the quiet.

He should be thrilled. He finally had his place to himself again. He was blessedly alone, just the way he liked it. No fuzzy baby, no soft female voice singing lullabies. So why did it suddenly seem far too quiet?

She thought she might scream. It was too quiet. Janette sat at the kitchen table in the little cabin sipping a cup of hot tea. It was just after eight, but there was no morning sun shining through the windows. The skies were as gray as her mood.

Sinclair knew she was in Cotter Creek. He'd be looking for her. He also knew she'd been with Dalton, so he'd be watching Dalton's every move, waiting to see if Dalton eventually led him to her. How long would it take before he'd think that she might be holed up on the West property?

She wrapped her hands around the mug, seeking the warmth to banish the chill inside her. The short night had seemed to last forever. Sleep had been impossible even though she'd eventually gotten into bed and tried to rest.

Her mind had whirled, trying to process the events that had brought her to the small cabin, and each thought was tinged with an underlying fear. Would *he* find her there? Would *he* somehow be able to ferret out where Dalton had stashed her? She was all alone, without a weapon except the knife she carried.

She'd finally gotten up and retrieved her knife from her purse, then had slid it beneath her pillow where it would be in easy reach should she need it. The night had held sounds that made her jump and had kept sleep at bay.

Releasing a deep weary sigh, she gazed out the window and took another sip of her tea. Would Sinclair be watching the bus stop, ready to pounce if she so much as showed her face?

How was she ever going to get out of town? Out of Dalton's life? Certainly he'd made it clear on more than one occasion that he didn't want to be responsible for anyone, that he preferred a life lived alone.

He probably couldn't wait to get her on her way. How long before he tired of this…of her? And when he got tired of the hassle, of the drama, it was possible he'd turn her in to Sinclair.

He wouldn't do that, the little voice inside her head protested. If he intended to do that he would have done so when the sheriff showed up on his doorstep.

The morning passed with her feeding and playing with Sammy and her thoughts alternating between worst and best case scenarios. After lunch when she put Sammy down for his nap and stretched out on the bed next to him, she wondered when Dalton would show up.

What if he never showed up? What if Sinclair murdered him? Her heart began to pound at the very idea. A new grief tore through her as she thought of the possibility.

Stop it, she commanded herself. Dalton had proven the night before that he was more than capable of taking care of himself. He was far too strong, too smart to get taken by surprise.

She must have fallen asleep, for the banging on the front door shot her up to a sitting position as her heart crashed against her ribs.

Who was at the door? It couldn't be Dalton. He had a key. Had Sinclair found her? Was he out there now waiting for her to come to the door? She pulled her knife from beneath her pillow and gripped it tightly in her hand.

She slid out of bed and crept to the doorway, unable to see the front door from her vantage point. Her throat narrowed as her breathing came in half-panicked gasps. There was a phone in the living room, but she couldn't get to it without the person at the front door seeing her.

Once again the sounds of a fist against the door filled the cabin. "Janette, open the door. Dalton sent me." It was a female voice and some of Janette's panic dissipated.

Still clutching the knife, afraid of a trick, she walked cautiously to the door. Peering out she saw a woman with shoulder-length riotous red hair standing on the porch, a grocery bag in her arms.

Janette unlocked the front door and pulled it open only an inch, just enough to see the friendly brown eyes of the woman. "Who are you?" she asked.

"I'm Savannah—Savannah West—and I have some groceries for you."

Janette opened the door and Savannah flew past her on a burst of cold air and with enough energy to light up the entire cabin. Janette relocked the front door then hurriedly followed Savannah into the kitchen.

"I hope you're planning on peeling an apple," Savannah said dryly and looked pointedly at the knife still clutched in Janette's hand.

A blush warmed Janette's cheeks as she set the knife down on the counter. "So, you're Dalton's sister? I'm sorry, but I can't remember the names of everyone even though he mentioned them."

"Sister-in-law," Savannah said as she began to take items out of the bag. "I'm married to Joshua, the youngest of the bunch."

"Is Dalton not coming?"

"Maybe later. He was worried about being followed so he called me." Savannah's brown eyes radiated sympathy. "He told me what's going on and asked for my help. Don't worry, I won't tell anybody you're here." She pulled a package of disposable diapers from the bag. "Is your baby sleeping?"

Janette nodded. "So what exactly did Dalton tell you?"

"That you were in trouble, that he was keeping you hidden here until you both can figure out the next step. You want to put these in the freezer or refrigerator or wherever you want them?" She pulled out two small packages of hamburger and a wrapper of deli meat.

"How about you make a pot of coffee while I finish unloading these things," Savannah suggested. "Then we can have a nice chat."

Janette readily complied, grateful to have somebody

to talk to, somebody to break up the silence that had plagued her since Dalton had left.

Within minutes the groceries were put away and the two women sat at the table with fresh coffee. "I'm so grateful to have somebody to talk to," Janette said. "The silence was really starting to get to me."

Savannah smiled. "Joshua would tell you that silence never bothers me. If I don't have anyone to talk to then I'm perfectly satisfied to talk to myself."

Janette returned her smile, deciding at that moment that she liked Savannah West. "How long have you been married?"

"Only three months. We're practically newlyweds, but at the moment he's off in New York. He flew up last week to do a job for a friend and should be coming home sometime later this week. I can't wait for him to get back to me."

For the next few minutes Savannah told her about leaving Arizona and settling in Cotter Creek. She'd met her husband-to-be when a mutual friend of theirs had been murdered and the two had put their heads together to investigate a land scandal taking place in the small town.

"Are the West men all so...so..."

"Handsome? Strong? Stubborn?" Savannah laughed. "All of the above. They're good people, the whole West clan." She sobered. "You can trust Dalton. He's quiet and reserved, but he's a good man."

Janette nodded. "Are you a stay-at-home wife?"

"Heavens, no. I bought the local newspaper not long

ago and most days I'm either writing news stories or editing to get out the daily newspaper."

"I appreciate you taking time off to come here."

"I'd do anything for Dalton, for any of the Wests, but I have to admit I was also curious when he explained everything to me. Consider it my reporter nose for news."

Janette shot up straighter in her chair, heartbeat quickening. "But you can't print anything. I don't want any of this to get out. If you even breathe a word of this to anyone you could put my life, my son's life, in danger."

"Relax," Savannah said. "I'm one of those rare birds, a reporter with ethics. I would never do anything to put you and your son at risk. But, I do have a few questions to ask you."

Tension twisted Janette's stomach. "Questions about what?"

"About Brandon Sinclair."

Janette got up from the table to pour herself another cup of coffee. "Why would you want to know anything about him?" She remained standing by the counter, certain that she didn't want to have this conversation.

"Because I intend to do a little investigative reporting on my own and see what I can find out about this creep," Savannah said.

Janette returned to sit at the table. She set her cup to the side and grabbed one of Savannah's hands. "Please, please don't do that. If he finds out you're asking questions about him, he'll hurt you."

Savannah squeezed Janette's hand and offered her a reassuring smile. "Believe me, the last thing I want is for Brandon Sinclair to have me in his sights." She released Janette's hand. "I'm very good at what I do and he'll never know I'm gathering facts about him."

"Why would you even want to get involved in all this?" Janette asked.

Savannah leaned back in her chair, her brown eyes contemplative. "From everything I've ever heard about sexual predators, they don't just indulge their ugly impulses once then never do it again. My guess is that you probably weren't the first victim of Brandon Sinclair and you won't be the last."

"I'm sure you're right," Janette said softly.

Savannah leaned forward. "You know something about another victim? Have you heard rumors? Sandstone is a very small town, surely somebody whispered something about the good sheriff."

Janette shook her head. "I never heard anything specific, but I suspected that one of the waitresses I worked with at the café might have had a run-in with Sheriff Sinclair."

"What made you suspect that?"

Janette reached back in her memory to the painful days just after her rape. She'd spent the days trying to act normal, trying to pretend that the terrible violation hadn't taken place. But she'd been desperate to talk to somebody, to anybody.

"Right after it happened to me, I asked Alicia if she'd ever been pulled over for a speeding ticket by Sheriff Sinclair. She said no, but there was an expression in her eyes that made me think she was lying. When I pressed her about it she told me to back off and the next day she quit the job."

"You said her name was Alicia. Alicia what?"

"Alicia Patterson, but she won't tell you anything. Everyone in Sandstone is afraid of him," Janette exclaimed and her throat tightened up a bit. She felt as if things were spinning out of control.

Savannah offered her a reassuring smile. "Too bad for him I'm not from Sandstone."

"Please, don't do this for me."

"I'm not," she replied easily. "I'm doing it for every young woman who lives in Sandstone and the surrounding areas." She finished her coffee and stood. "Don't worry, I know how to be invisible when I need to be and somebody needs to step up. I want to get the goods on this guy and put him away."

"I just want to *get* away," Janette said, more to herself than to Savannah.

She walked Savannah to the front door and on impulse gave her a hug. "Thank you for the groceries and for the talk."

Savannah pulled her hood up and opened the door. "I'm sure we'll see each other again."

Janette watched from the doorway as Savannah got into her car and pulled away. She closed and locked the door and leaned her head against the wood.

Somebody needs to step up.

Sammy began to cry from the bedroom, having awakened from his nap. She hurried into the room and his tears instantly transformed into a watery grin. She picked him up and cuddled him close.

Somebody needs to step up.

"Not me," she whispered. With the weight of her son in her arms, she fought back tears. "Not me," she said more forcefully.

Chapter 8

It was dusk when Dalton pulled up to the cabin. It had been a long tense day. He'd spent most of the day in his apartment, staring out the window, watching for Sinclair and thinking.

He'd set in motion a quiet investigation into Sinclair, enlisting both Savannah and his brother Tanner's aid. As the eldest of the brood, Tanner was not only the most levelheaded of the bunch, but also a whiz with computers.

By morning Tanner would know everything there was to know about Brandon Sinclair. He'd know where he shopped, where he ate, how much he had in his bank account and if there had ever been a complaint filed against the man.

He hadn't told Tanner anything about Janette and

Sammy. He'd only said that he was doing a favor for a friend and needed to keep it quiet, especially from Zack.

What had surprised him more than anything during the day was how he'd noticed Janette and Sammy's absence. The quiet of his apartment had never bothered him before, rather he'd relished it. But, today, the quiet hadn't felt good. It had felt lonely. And that had irritated him.

As he shut off his truck engine, the front door opened and she stepped just outside and greeted him with a beautiful smile. Tension instantly built inside him. She looked gorgeous in a pair of jeans and a lavender sweatshirt, and her bright smile only added to her beauty.

He got out and walked to the back of the truck, picked up an oversized wooden cradle, then carried it toward where she stood.

"I thought Sammy might be able to use this while you're here," he said as she held open the door to allow him inside. He set the cradle on the living-room floor. "I know the bed in the bedroom is pretty small, especially by the time you surround Sammy with pillows. I figured this would be more comfortable for both of you."

She knelt down next to the cradle and looked up at him, those Oklahoma sky-blue eyes of hers shining brightly as she ran her hand over the rich wood. "It's beautiful. Where did you get it?"

"It was packed in a shed. It hasn't been used since Joshua was a baby."

"So it's a family heirloom."

"Yeah, I guess." The cabin smelled of lemon furniture polish and that evocative scent of honeysuckle.

"You've been cleaning," he observed, noting that all the furniture gleamed with a new sheen.

She stood. "I got bored and found some furniture polish under the kitchen sink."

"Sammy sleeping?"

"I just put him down." She ran a loving hand over the cradle once again. "I think I'll clean this up and move him into it."

As she disappeared into the kitchen, Dalton sat on the sofa. She was in a good mood now, but he had a feeling she wouldn't be in such a good mood when he told her what was on his mind.

She returned with the bottle of furniture polish and a rag and sat on the floor to begin the cleanup on the cradle. "I like your sister-in-law," she said as she worked.

"I know you didn't want me to tell anyone, but I knew I might need some help since Sinclair might be watching my place."

She looked at him worriedly. "Do you think he was watching when you left tonight?"

Dalton shook his head. "He's back in Sandstone."

"How do you know that?"

"I called his office and he answered the phone." Dalton leaned back against the sofa cushions. "He can't stay in Cotter Creek all day and night. He has a job and a family in Sandstone. He can't spend every waking hour hunting you down."

"Thank God for small favors, right?"

It took her only minutes to finish cleaning off the cradle. She folded several thick bath towels into the bottom of it, making a nice soft mattress for Sammy.

She left to get Sammy and Dalton drew a deep breath. Her scent eddied in the air and evoked memories of that single kiss they had shared, a kiss he wouldn't mind repeating even though he knew he was all kinds of a fool to even think about it.

Sammy didn't stir from his sleep as she gently laid him in the cradle and covered him with another towel. She stood and smiled down at him, her smile so soft, so loving, Dalton felt it in the center of his chest.

"You want some coffee or something?" she asked.

"No, I'm fine. But I would like to talk to you." He sat on the sofa and patted the space next to him.

She eyed him warily but sat, close enough that he could smell her fragrance, but not close enough to touch in any way. "Talk about what?" Her eyes were darker blue than they had been moments before.

"About bringing Brandon Sinclair to justice." He leaned back against the cushion. "I know the special prosecutor in Oklahoma City. His name is Trent Cummings and it's his job to prosecute elected officials, like sheriffs, who break the law. I intend to contact him about Sinclair."

She nodded slowly, her expression guarded. "Good. Somebody needs to stop him before he hurts more women."

"What we need if we're going to stop him is cold hard evidence and that's where you come in."

Her eyes narrowed slightly. "I don't have any evidence," she protested. Her entire body tensed and she appeared to shrink back from him, becoming smaller and looking more vulnerable.

"You are the evidence," he said, trying not to be affected by her obvious discomfort. "You and Sammy, especially Sammy. His DNA confirms that Sinclair is his father."

Her eyes flashed darkly. "But that doesn't prove he raped me. That just proves we had sex." Her voice was an octave higher than usual and she jumped up from the sofa as if unable to stand sitting next to him another minute longer. "Don't you see? He'll just tell everyone we had an affair. Nobody will ever take my word over his. He's the 'good and noble' sheriff and I'm 'uneducated trailer trash.' Nobody will believe me."

Her chest heaved and her hands clenched into fists at her sides. "Stop saying you're uneducated trailer trash," he said with more than a touch of irritation. "That might be Brandon Sinclair's definition of you, but it sure isn't mine."

"Have you forgotten that he probably has an arrest warrant for me?"

"No, I haven't forgotten," he said. "But he can't make a murder charge stick without a dead body, and we both know your nana is alive and well."

"He can still arrest me on theft charges, or maybe arson, or whatever he decides to conjure up."

"And he tried to kill us last night. He needs to be stopped."

Her eyes flashed once again. "And we can't prove that it was him who set the fire or shot at us last night. And you can bet he's already got a solid alibi set up for the time of the shooting."

She drew a deep breath and her hands slowly unclenched. "Look, I appreciate what you're trying to do, but I just want to get out of here. I intend to be on the next bus out of town, with or without your help."

"And you intend to spend the rest of your life looking over your shoulder? Wondering if and when he's going to find you? Wouldn't you rather stand and fight and stop him from raping other women?"

Her eyes filled with the sheen of tears. "Please, don't ask me to stay."

"But that's exactly what I'm asking of you," he said softly. "Stay and fight. Help us put him away." He stood to face her.

"It's so easy for you to ask that of me." For the first time a hint of anger deepened her voice and hardened her eyes. "You've probably never had to face anything alone. You have this great big wonderful family to support you in whatever decisions you make. You've never been poor and powerless and all alone."

Her anger rose with each word that left her mouth. "It's easy for you because if things go badly you lose nothing. You go back to your quiet, solitary life and never think about me or Sammy again."

"That's not true," he protested. He had a feeling no matter what happened here and now, it was going to be a very long time before he could forget Janette and her little boy.

He took two steps toward her. "Janette, you won't be alone in this. I'll be right by your side. I've got my brother Tanner checking into Sinclair's background. Savannah is going to try to touch base with the waitress you said might have been another victim."

She backed away from him, tears once again shining in her eyes, but he pressed on. "Don't you want to stand up and put this man behind bars where he belongs? Wouldn't you sleep better at night if you knew he wasn't someplace out on the streets? Maybe hunting you down?"

"You and your sister-in-law and brother can do whatever you think is right, but I intend to be on the first bus out of here." She flew into the bedroom and closed the door after her.

Dalton released a sigh of frustration. He understood her fear, sympathized with it, but he knew she was their best chance in taking down Brandon Sinclair. And he was determined to do just that.

Janette sat on the edge of the bed, her entire body trembling with emotion. Fear, regret and a burning shame all coursed through her.

Somebody needs to step up.

The words haunted her, playing and replaying in her mind like the refrain from an irritating melody that refused to be forgotten.

Somebody needs to step up.

She closed her eyes as a vision of Alicia Patterson filled her head. She remembered vividly the whisper of horror that had filled her eyes when Janette had asked her if she'd ever been pulled over by Sheriff Sinclair. She'd recognized that horror because she'd lived it and it had become an unwanted part of her.

Rubbing her temple where a headache had begun to pound, she tried to banish the vision of Alicia from her mind but it refused to completely go away. How many others had there been? How many more would there be?

He needed to be stopped.

Somebody needs to step up.

None of the women who had been abused by Sinclair were likely to look for a way to bring him to justice. They would feel the same hopeless helplessness that she'd felt. Stuck in a town where the sheriff was king, it was impossible for a mere vulnerable isolated woman to stand up against him.

But she was no longer in Sandstone. She was one step ahead of those women, for she'd already escaped the evil king's kingdom. And she wasn't all alone. She had Dalton standing beside her.

Do the right thing, that little voice whispered in her head. She'd tried to live her life always choosing to do the right thing. When Nana had gotten sick, the right thing for Janette to do had been to quit school to take care of her. When she'd discovered she was pregnant, for her, making the choice to give Sammy life had been the right thing to do.

And stopping Sheriff Brandon Sinclair from preying on any other women was the right thing to do. She got up from the bed, a bone-weariness weighing down her feet as she walked back to the door.

The idea of what she was about to agree to terrified her, but for the first time since that horrible night on the deserted highway, a rage began to build inside her.

Brandon Sinclair had not only raped her. He'd also tried to kill Nana, and last night had tried to shoot an innocent man. It hadn't been safe before this moment to get angry, because while she'd been a resident in Sandstone, anger had been an emotion she couldn't afford.

As she swung open the door and walked back into the living room, the anger flowed, rich and thick and righteous through her veins. Dalton sat on the sofa, but he stood when she came back into the room.

"All right," she said, her voice trembling with the raw emotion. "I'll stick around. I'll talk to your special prosecutor. I'll do whatever it takes to destroy Sinclair, but I have a few requests of my own."

"Like what?" Dalton sat back down and she joined him on the sofa.

"I want Nana out of Sandstone. Sooner or later he is going to find out that she didn't burn up in that trailer. He'll find her, and we can't let that happen."

Dalton nodded. "We can pick her up and bring her here."

She would have loved to have her nana here in this little cabin with her, but she shook her head. "No, I don't want her here. I want her someplace where she'll be safe if this goes bad."

Dalton frowned thoughtfully. "West Protective Services owns a safe house in Kansas City. We could set her up there for the time being," Dalton said. "I can make arrangements with my sister, Meredith, to meet her plane and get her settled in."

"I have one other thing to ask of you." The pounding in her head intensified and she raised a hand to press her cold fingers against her temple. The anger that had filled her dissipated, usurped by a new well of grief.

"What?" he asked, his voice a soft caress. "What else do you need?"

She closed her eyes for a moment and a picture of Sammy's little face filled her head, his downy dark hair above laughing blue eyes and that grin of his that had the capacity to melt her heart.

She opened her eyes and stared at Dalton with intensity. "If something happens to me, if I end up in jail or worse, you have to promise me that you'll take Sammy. You'll hide him where Sinclair will never get hold of him." She reached out and grabbed hold of Dalton's forearm. "You have to promise me that you'll keep him safe, that you'll never allow that man to get custody of him."

Dalton took her hand between his, surrounding her cold fingers with warmth. "Nothing is going to happen to you. You're going to be fine, and you and Sammy are going to have a wonderful life with your nana."

"But you can't promise that."

His eyes darkened slightly. "No, I can't promise that," he admitted. "We'll do everything we can to make sure that all of you are safe. I know how difficult this decision is for you, and I know it probably doesn't matter to you, but I'm proud of you and admire your courage."

She realized it did matter to her, that she cared about what he thought of her. She cared more than she thought possible, but she wasn't satisfied yet. "You have to promise me that you'll take care of Sammy if something happens to me. That's the only way I can go forward with this."

The gravity of his expression let her know he

wouldn't take this vow lightly. "Okay, I promise," he replied.

She was surprised by the depth of relief that flooded through her. At least she wouldn't have to worry about Sammy ending up with Sinclair.

"So, what happens now?" she asked. His hands no longer warmed the chill that resided deep inside her.

"First thing in the morning I'll call Trent and we'll set up a meeting with him, then I'll make arrangements to get your nana out of Sandstone. We'll see what Savannah and Tanner found out about Sinclair and hope that they can get us something to help make a case."

"Are you going to tell Zack about all this?" she asked.

He frowned. "Not until we have some solid evidence to present to him."

"I know how much you don't like keeping secrets from him."

He nodded. "That's true, but in this particular case I think it's necessary."

A new cold wind blew through her. "He'll know. Somehow Sinclair will find out that we're plotting against him. That's going to make him more dangerous than ever."

"Then we'll just have to be careful." He reached up and tucked a strand of her hair behind her ear.

At the moment she felt his gentle touch, she knew that she wanted to make love with him. She wanted… *needed* to make love with him in order to banish the memory of Sinclair's hands on her, his breath hot and sour on her face.

She knew it was crazy, that Dalton West was only

a temporary man in her life. Eventually this would all be over and he'd get back to his uncomplicated private life and hopefully she'd get on with her life.

She wasn't fool enough to think that there might be a future with him. Nature had blown her into his life and danger kept her bound to him. But once the snow was gone and the danger had passed, it would be over.

But there was tonight and she felt the need for his warmth, for his gentleness. She felt the need for him. Even as her desire swelled inside her, she was suffused with doubt.

Would he even want her? Certainly she'd tasted hot desire in the single kiss they'd shared. Had that been a momentary flare of madness, or was it reflective of the fact that he might be attracted to her?

"You've gotten quiet. What are you thinking?" he asked.

She breathed in deeply and looked into his beautiful green eyes. Her mouth suddenly felt dry and a trembling began deep within her. "I think maybe I'd like some coffee after all," she said and jumped up off the sofa.

Don't be a fool, a voice whispered inside her head as she went into the kitchen. *Making love with Dalton wouldn't make things better. It would only make things worse when she had to tell him goodbye.*

As she fixed the coffee, he came into the kitchen and sat at the table. She was acutely aware of his presence, as if the very thought of making love with him had fine-tuned every one of her senses.

Once the coffee was dripping into the carafe, she joined him at the table. "I don't want to talk about Brandon Sinclair anymore," she said. "I don't even want to think about him. Tell me more about your family. Fill my head with something good and positive."

And he did. As they drank coffee he talked to her about his brothers and sister, sharing childhood memories that made her laugh, sharing moments that made her more than a little bit envious of the close-knit West clan.

Darkness fell, and as he finished his coffee he stood. Dread swooped through her. She knew he was preparing to leave.

"I should get back to town," he said.

She got up from the table, as well. "You could stay here for the night." She swallowed, her mouth once again too dry. "With Sammy in his new cradle, the bed is big enough for both of us." She held her breath.

His eyes flared wider and filled with a heat that swept over her, through her. "I'm not sure that's a good idea."

Emboldened by the look in his eyes, she stepped closer to him. "Why not?" Her heartbeat raced in her chest, this time not with fear, but with something even more primal.

"Because I don't think I can sleep in the same bed as you." His voice was deeper than usual.

"I don't kick and I don't think I snore." She took another step toward him.

"That wouldn't be the problem," he replied.

"Then what is the problem?" She stood so close to him she could feel his body heat radiate toward her, could see the gold flecks that gave depth to his green eyes.

"The problem is that it's been a long time since I've been with a woman and I find you incredibly attractive."

His words gave her permission to take a final step toward him. She now touched him, her breasts against the hard width of his chest. "And I find you incredibly attractive." She raised her hands to his shoulders and leaned into him, her face raised.

She saw the kiss in his eyes before he lowered his head to deliver it. When his lips took hers a fiery heat flooded through her veins and she welcomed it, welcomed him with open mouth.

He wrapped his arms around her and pulled her close…closer still. His arms felt like safety, like security, and she reveled in the sensations that coursed through her.

His tongue swirled with hers, creating a fire of want inside her. She knew exactly what to expect, a night of passion satisfied and nothing more. At this moment it was enough.

When he broke the kiss she took his hand and led him into the bedroom. Although she didn't think it possible, her heartbeat raced even faster. She wanted this. She wanted him. But, she couldn't ignore a tiny sliver of disquiet that raised its ugly head.

The last time she'd had sex it had been a violent, terror-filled event, and she wanted none of that experience to bleed over into this time with Dalton.

When they reached the bedroom he once again took

her into his arms and kissed her. The kiss was long and deep, and as he kissed her his hands caressed her back.

She loved the feel of his hard chest, his firm thighs and his obvious arousal against her. He held her tight, but not so tight that she felt captive…helpless.

This time when the kiss ended, her fingers trembled as she unbuttoned his shirt. He stood motionless, as if holding his breath as she pulled the shirt from his chest.

Only then did he move away from her. He walked to the side of the bed and placed his gun, his cell phone and his wallet on the nightstand, then turned to face her. "Are you sure about this?" His voice vibrated with tension.

Instead of answering him with words, she pulled her sweatshirt off over her head and dropped it to the floor beside her.

His eyes glowed in the semidarkness of the room and her breath caught in her throat as his hands moved to the waist of his jeans and he unfastened the button fly.

As he took off his jeans she did the same. Then, with only the aid of the moonlight filtering through the window, they got into the bed.

Instantly he pulled her back into his arms as his lips found hers once again. His delicious skin warmed hers as his mouth took possession of her lips.

It felt right. It felt good, and it didn't matter what tomorrow would bring. Whatever happened, wherever she ended up building her life, she'd have the memory of this kind and good man to carry with her.

They lay side by side facing each other and his lips left hers and rained nipping kisses down her neck to the hollow of her throat. She tangled her fingers in his thick hair as his hands caressed her breasts through the thin material of her bra.

It didn't take long before she wanted to feel the palm of his hands against her naked breasts. She reached behind her and unfastened her bra, loving the deep moan that escaped him as she tossed it to the floor. Within minutes the last of their clothing was gone and their touches grew more intimate.

It wasn't until he moved on top of her that the first stir of panic closed her throat.

His breath was warm against her neck, his body not surrounding her so much as imprisoning her. Just like before.

Hot breath.

Hard body.

Trapped.

She squeezed her eyes tightly closed, fighting the overwhelming sense of dread, trying to catch her breath as the panic fired higher inside her. This wasn't Sinclair, and they weren't on the side of the road. There was no gun pressed to her throat, no reason for her heart to pound so painfully hard.

Dalton seemed unaware of the torment that had unexpectedly stolen passion and exchanged it for dark flashbacks to the worst night of her life. As he kissed her neck, she fought the scream that worked up from the depths of her.

He was suffocating her, his weight oppressive and scary. She couldn't move, had lost control. She couldn't breathe. Unable to stand it another minute she shoved against his chest. "I'm sorry. I can't do this. Please, get off me. Get off me!"

He instantly rolled to the side of her as she burst into tears.

Chapter 9

"I'm sorry. I'm so sorry," Janette cried into the pillow next to Dalton.

"It's okay," he said even as he fought to get control of himself. "It's all right, Janette. We don't have to do anything you don't want to do." Tentatively he reached out and touched her back, trying to comfort but afraid of frightening her.

It was obvious what had just happened, and his heart clenched with her pain. Brandon Sinclair should be stood before a firing squad for what he'd done to her, for the scars he'd left behind.

She didn't move away from his touch so he continued to rub her back and tell her it was okay. He tried not to notice the sexy curve of her back or the sweet scent that emanated from her warm skin.

Slowly her tears dried, but she still kept her face buried in the pillow, as if afraid to turn over and look at him.

"Janette, I'm not mad. Come on, turn over and look at me."

"How can you not be mad? Women who do what I just did to you are called a terrible name."

"There's a difference between women who get off on the power of playing a man and a woman who is suffering post-traumatic stress. I promise you I'm not mad."

She finally rolled over, the sheet clutched to her chest as she faced him. He leaned up on one elbow and smiled down at her. "It's okay, really."

She reached a hand up and touched the underside of his jaw. "How did you get to be such a nice man, Dalton West?"

"Trust me, at the moment I'm not feeling like such a nice guy. I'd like to find Brandon Sinclair and torture him slowly for a very long time." He started to roll out of the bed but she caught him by the arm.

"Don't go," she said softly. "Can't we just lay here and talk for a little while?"

She had no idea what she was asking of him. Blood still surged thick and hot through his veins. He was a man, not a saint, but maybe if he didn't touch her again he could stand remaining next to her.

He rolled over just long enough to turn on the lamp on the nightstand, then turned back to face her.

"Would it help to talk about that night?" he asked gently.

"No. I was doing fine until you got on top of me."

Her cheeks turned pink and she averted her gaze from his. "It wasn't until then that I had a flashback. With you on top of me I felt trapped…like I was suffocating…like I did that night with Sinclair."

"That will teach me to try to be in control," he said with a forced lightness.

She looked at him. "Maybe if I stay in control it will be okay. I mean, my head and my heart want to make love with you, it was just in that last minute that everything went wrong."

"Maybe we should both just try to get some sleep," he countered. He wasn't sure he could go through the same thing again and not get relief. His body still ached with the need she'd wrought inside him.

He tensed as she reached over and stroked a hand across his chest. Instantly desire fired through him. Her fingers curled in his chest hair, then uncurled and moved down lower.

As she wrapped her fingers around him more intimately he hissed in a breath. She was trying to kill him with pleasure. "Janette," he said, the word more a plea than a protest as he'd intended.

"Just…just let me," she replied, her voice husky and deep.

Dalton had always been an active participant when he made love to a woman, but as she stroked him he remained on his back, not moving to touch her in any way.

She leaned forward and pressed her lips against his chest, and that coupled with her warm hand surrounding him nearly undid him. He hung on to control by a thread.

She moved her lips up his chest to capture his in a fiery kiss. Her breathing increased, and when she raised her head to look at him he saw the glaze of want in her eyes.

The most difficult thing he'd ever done was to remain passive. He wanted to reach up for her, take her into his arms. He wanted to taste her skin, feel the soft weight of her breasts, but he remained unmoving, allowing her to stay in total control.

Her naked body gleamed in the lamplight and her blond hair glistened as it fell forward, the tips trailing across his chest in added torment.

Her nipples were out and he fought the impulse to lean up and capture one in his mouth. Although he wanted to touch her, there was something unbelievably erotic in allowing her to make love to him on her own terms.

It wasn't until she moved to get on top of him that he finally spoke. "There's a condom in my wallet," he managed to gasp.

She left him just long enough to open his wallet and retrieve the foil packet inside. She opened the packet and rolled the protection into place. He moaned with pleasure as she eased onto him, her sleek legs on either side.

He closed his eyes, knowing that if he continued to look at her he'd lose control too quickly. Her warmth gripped him tight as she rocked against him.

Her breaths came in quick pants and when he looked at her again her eyes were tightly closed and an expression of intense bliss shone on her features.

She moved faster and then she gasped and cried out his name. That was all it took. Dalton's release came in an explosion that rocked him to his very core. It was only then that he touched her. He cupped her face with his hands and drew her down for a kiss.

She melted against him, her body warm against his, her lips sweet and yielding. When they finished kissing she rolled off him and to her back.

"Thank you," she said softly.

A small burst of laughter escaped him. "Don't thank me. That was absolutely amazing." He rolled off the bed. "Don't move, I'll be right back."

He padded into the bathroom to clean up. Once alone, he thought about what had just happened and the fact that it shouldn't have.

She was getting to him. Oh, but she was getting into places inside him that he hadn't allowed anyone in for a very long time. And that scared him. That scared the hell out of him.

This situation...*she* was temporary. He'd sworn to himself that he would never again put himself in the position to help heal a woman so she could move on and fall in love with another man.

He'd sworn to himself he'd never again be a temporary hero for any woman, and yet wasn't that exactly his role in this case? If he were smart he'd go back into the bedroom, get dressed and get the hell away from her.

But the moment he reentered the bedroom, all thoughts of leaving fled his head. She gave him that smile of hers, the one bright enough to light up the room, and patted the empty side of the bed.

"I hope you aren't one of those men who fall immediately to sleep after sex," she said.

No, he was the type of man who felt the need to run
for the door and escape. Not exactly the actions of a
gentleman. He slid back beneath the sheets.

"Are you accustomed to men who fall asleep after
sex?" he asked teasingly.

She plumped the pillows behind her head and sat
up, the sheet clutched modestly at her neck. "I've only
had one real long-term relationship and, yes, he used
to fall asleep."

He rolled over on his side to face her and propped
himself up on his elbow. "Is that why you aren't with
him anymore?"

She grinned, looking incredibly sexy with her hair
tousled and her full lips still slightly swollen from his
kisses. "No. He worked as a rehab nurse and I met him
when Nana needed rehabilitation after her stroke. We
dated for almost a year." She pulled her knees up to her
chest and wrapped her arms around them, her features
contemplative. "He got a job offer from a hospital in
Indianapolis and moved there."

"He didn't ask you to go with him?"

"No. I think he knew I wouldn't go, that I couldn't
leave Nana. It wasn't a great love affair. It was pleasant
and nice while it lasted, but after he was gone I realized
I wasn't deeply, madly in love with him."

"And that's important to you? To be deeply, madly
in love?" he asked.

She flashed him that brilliant smile of hers. "Of

course. I think it's what every woman wants, among other things."

"And what other things do you want?" He tried to tell himself that he really didn't care, that he was just trying to hold up his end of the conversation. But deep inside he knew that wasn't true. He wanted to know her desires, her wants, the very dreams that drove her.

"A home, security. I want a job that I love and to be able to provide Sammy with things and opportunities I didn't have. I want to be able to afford to order pizza whenever I want it. Oh, yeah, and world peace."

He laughed and she unclasped her hands from around her knees and stretched out on her side facing him. "Now tell me about the women in your past."

"There's nothing to tell. I've had a few relationships, but nothing too serious. I've told you before, I like living alone, being alone." He needed to remind himself as much as her of this fact.

At that moment Sammy began to cry from the living room. He watched as she slid from the bed, grabbed a robe from the nearby chair and pulled it on. "I'll be right back. Don't go away."

As she left the room Dalton rolled on his back and stared up at the ceiling. The feeling returned—the need to run, to escape. Not just from Janette, but from the whole situation. He'd talked her into agreeing to stick around, to help them bring Brandon Sinclair to justice.

The man was dangerous and until they could get the evidence they needed to put him behind bars, he was a threat to Janette's very life.

He felt fairly confident having her here at the cabin.

Deep on West property, the cabin was known only by a few. The ranch hands would certainly notice a stranger wandering the property and would demand an explanation of his presence.

Still, if anything happened to her or to Sammy, Dalton would feel responsible for the rest of his life. He hoped he hadn't made a mistake in talking her into staying and fighting, because it could be a mistake with deadly consequences.

Janette stopped in the kitchen to fix Sammy a bottle and carried it into the living room. The minute he saw her he stopped fussing. He'd drink this bottle then would sleep through the night.

She changed his diaper, then carried him back into the bedroom and sat on the edge of the bed to give him the bottle. She was conscious of Dalton's gaze on her as she looked down at her son. "He makes me want to be better than I am," she said. She looked at Dalton. "That's what kids do for you." Sammy grinned at Dalton around the bottle nipple, as if punctuating her sentence.

For a few minutes they were silent, the only sound Sammy greedily drinking his formula. Janette's head was filled with myriad emotions. Love for her son tangled with an underlying fear of what lay ahead and, as she cast a surreptitious glance to Dalton, other less easily defined emotions rose up inside her.

Certainly gratitude filled her heart, not just for what he'd done in taking her in and keeping her safe, but also for allowing her to reclaim a piece of herself, a piece she'd thought forever broken.

"You gave me back my life tonight," she said to Dalton.

He raised a dark eyebrow. "Don't you think that's a little dramatic?"

"No, I don't," she countered. "I didn't think I'd ever be able to experience joy in lovemaking again. I thought my experience with Sinclair had destroyed that part of me. You showed me tonight that he didn't."

She frowned thoughtfully, remembering those moments of sudden panic when Dalton had moved on top of her. "I know it's going to take time before all the trauma of Sinclair is gone, but tonight definitely went a long way in my healing process."

"You'll be fine," he assured her. "Someday you'll find the man who can give you all the things you want from life."

She smiled. "I don't need a man to give me all the things I want. I intend to go out and get them. But, it would be nice to have somebody to share it all with."

She looked back down at Sammy. She had the feeling Dalton had said what he had to remind her that he wasn't the man for her. He didn't have to bother.

Even though she realized her heart was getting hopelessly involved with him, she knew better than to expect a happy ending. He'd made his position perfectly clear and she didn't expect that to change.

"Once Sinclair is in jail, do you intend to return to Sandstone?" he asked.

"To be honest, I haven't had enough time to think about it." She glanced back down at Sammy. The trailer they'd called home was gone. "There's really nothing left for us there except bad memories. If you're putting Nana in a safe place in Kansas City, then maybe that's the place where we should start over."

Sammy had fallen back to sleep, his bottle empty and his belly full. "You want me to bring the cradle in here?" Dalton asked.

"Do you mind?"

He got up and pulled on his briefs, then left the room. As he exited, she couldn't help the flutter of heat that swept through her at the sight of his near-nakedness. He had a physique that most men would envy and most women would want. And she wanted him again.

It surprised her, the healthy burst of lust that filled her. She hadn't thought about sex in over a year, but one time with Dalton and suddenly her head was filled with lustful thoughts.

And there was nothing more sexy than a man in briefs carrying a cradle, she thought as he returned to the room. He set the cradle on the floor on her side of the bed, then got back beneath the sheets.

She got up and put Sammy back into the cradle, then got back into bed next to Dalton. He turned off the lamp and the room was plunged into darkness with just a faint cast of moonlight dancing shadows on the walls.

Closing her eyes, she tried not to think about what she'd agreed to do by staying here. Even if the bus pulled up in Cotter Creek tomorrow, she wouldn't get on it.

A sliver of fear iced through her, chilling her to her bones. What if the special prosecutor didn't believe her story? Right now Sinclair could be manufacturing all kinds of evidence against her. He could bully anyone in town to say anything he wanted about her.

She fought the impulse to lean over and take Sammy from the cradle and hold him in her arms. She wanted to hold him tight, kiss his cheeks and smell his baby sweetness, because she had no idea if a time would come in the future when he'd be lost to her forever.

Dalton awoke first and found his arms filled with a warm, sleeping Janette. They were spoon fashion, him curled around her slender back. He drew in the scent of her, that floral perfume that enticed him.

It was only now, in this moment with her body warm against his and his defenses not erected that he could admit to himself that he'd grown to care about her more than he'd ever thought he'd care about a woman again in his life.

It was late. He could tell by the cast of the sun shining through the window that he'd slept longer than he'd intended. Of course, he hadn't drifted off to sleep until the wee hours of the morning.

He'd spent much of the night listening to Janette breathing peacefully in sleep and worrying about the decision he'd encouraged her to make. He now contemplated what he needed to accomplish that day because it was easier to focus on that rather than the feelings he had for Janette.

He needed to call Trent Cummings, the special prosecutor, and see when he could get the man out here to meet with Janette. He also needed to make arrangements to get Nana out of Sandstone and to the safe house in Kansas City.

Hopefully they could connect with Trent in the next day or so and get things rolling. He closed his eyes and breathed in Janette's scent.

In many ways she amazed him. He'd expected her to fight him about staying and seeking justice, he'd expected her to demand he put her on the next bus out of town. The fact that she'd agreed to stand and fight against Brandon Sinclair instead of running showed him the immense inner strength she possessed.

He knew he wasn't only getting too close to her, but she was getting too close to him, as well. Their relationship, such as it was, was built on forced proximity and circumstances beyond their control.

It had nothing to do with reality. He was a temporary measure of safety in her life, just as he'd been in Mary's. He rolled away from Janette and off the bed, glad that he didn't awaken her in the process.

He grabbed his clothes from the floor and padded into the bathroom. Minutes later, standing beneath a hot shower, he tried not to think about how her long legs had felt when she'd straddled him, how hot her mouth had been against his skin.

Brandon Sinclair had left scars inside her that would take time to heal, but Dalton felt certain that eventually Janette would be able to have a loving, passionate relationship with a special man.

He frowned, irritated by the fact that he didn't like the idea of Janette making love with another man.

By the time he was out of the shower and dressed,

Janette was up and making coffee in the kitchen. Clad in her pink robe, she looked soft and utterly feminine and a renewed burst of desire hit Dalton hard in the stomach.

"I've got to get back to town," he said gruffly.

"Surely you can stay long enough to have coffee and some breakfast," she replied. "I was just going to make some scrambled eggs and toast."

"Okay," he conceded. "I've got a lot to do today. And you need to call your nana and tell her what's going on." He sat at the table. "I'll call you later with details and we can set up getting her moved as soon as possible."

"Good, that will make me feel better." She poured him a cup of coffee, set it in front of him then returned to the counter where she put two slices of bread into the toaster, then began to crack eggs into an awaiting bowl. Sammy began to fuss from the bedroom.

"Want me to get him?" Dalton asked, figuring he needed to go back in the bedroom to get his wallet and gun, anyway.

"Thanks, I'd appreciate it."

The minute Dalton entered the room, Sammy stopped his fussing and began to coo, as if attempting to tell Dalton something very important.

Dalton grabbed his wallet and shoved it into his back pocket, then tucked the gun into the back of his waist-band and picked up the little boy.

Sammy wiggled in his arms and flung out a hand that promptly latched on Dalton's nose. "Hey, little buddy," Dalton whispered. "That's my nose." Sammy smiled in delight and Dalton's heart moved. This little boy had no idea that he was in the center of a storm, a storm that had the potential to see his mother either in jail or dead.

I can't let that happen, Dalton told himself. He had to summon every skill he possessed as a bodyguard in order to keep Janette safe until this was all over and she could begin a new life in whatever city she chose.

He carried Sammy back into the kitchen where Janette had already fixed a bottle for the little guy. As Dalton sat once again at the table with Sammy in his lap, she held the bottle out to him. "Do you mind?"

Dalton took the bottle and gave it to Sammy, who sucked greedily on the nipple. His innocent little blue eyes stared up at Dalton with intense concentration.

Dalton was shocked to realize if he wasn't careful Sammy would steal his heart completely and make him remember all the old dreams that he'd once possessed.

He refused to entertain those dreams again, especially with Janette and her son in a starring role. That would only lead to a new heartache and he wasn't interested.

By the time they finished breakfast it was after nine o'clock. With Sammy on a blanket in the living room, Dalton picked up the phone and dialed the number for the special prosecutor's office in Oklahoma City.

It took him nearly fifteen minutes, but he was finally connected to his old friend Trent. He quickly explained the situation and was disappointed in Trent's reply.

"I definitely want to pursue this and talk to your friend, but there's no way I can get to Cotter Creek for at least a week. I'm in the middle of something here that I'm hoping to tie up in the next week to ten days."

Dalton frowned. He'd hoped to get Trent here a lot sooner…like the next day at the latest. "You'll call me if you get free sooner?"

"Definitely." The two men spoke for a few more minutes, then Dalton hung up.

"Is he coming?" Janette asked hopefully.

"Not for a week to ten days."

A look of panic swept over her features. "So long? What happens in the meantime?"

A new burst of tension twisted Dalton's guts. "In the meantime we can only hope that Brandon Sinclair doesn't discover where you are. You know how to shoot a gun?"

Her eyes widened. "No. Why?"

He pulled his gun from his waistband. "I'd feel better if I left this here with you."

"I wouldn't," she said flatly. She leaned back against the sofa, a troubled expression on her face. "As much as I hate him, as much as I fear him, I'm not sure I could shoot him." She looked from the gun to Dalton. "I don't know if I could really pull the trigger and kill somebody."

Dalton tucked the gun back into his waistband. He knew that a gun was only as effective as the person who held it. "Maybe I should have Tanner or one of my other brothers keep an eye on you."

"No, please. I feel safe here. There's no way Sinclair can know about this cabin and I'd rather nobody else know I'm here. It's been my experience that the more people keeping a secret, the more difficult the secret is to keep."

Dalton nodded, his head whirling. "When I get back to town I'm going to rent a room at the motel and I'll have one of my brothers sit on it. Maybe we can catch Sinclair breaking the law and put him behind bars before Trent ever gets here. If nothing else the ruse of the empty room might keep Sinclair focused on the idea that you're there."

"I'm all for any plan that keeps him as far away from me as possible," she replied.

"I'd better get moving," he said.

She got up and walked with him to the door and he fought the impulse to lean down and capture her lips before he left. Minutes later, as he headed back toward town, he could only hope that he could keep Brandon Sinclair at bay until Trent arrived in town.

Chapter 10

It snowed again late that afternoon and Dalton called Janette to tell her not only would the weather make it impossible for anyone to get to Nana, but also he wouldn't be coming to the cabin that night.

She was bitterly disappointed with the length of time it would take before she could talk to Trent Cummings, with the damnable winter weather that complicated everything, but more importantly with the fact that she wouldn't have Dalton's company for the evening.

Falling asleep the night before with him lying next to her had been heavenly. The very sound of his even breathing had made her feel safe and warm. Watching him give Sammy his morning bottle had stirred a wistful hope that she knew could only lead to disappointment.

For just a moment, as she'd scrambled eggs and Dalton had held Sammy in his arms, she'd wanted this life with him to last forever. With each moment she spent in Dalton's company it was getting easier and easier to imagine what life with him would be like.

And that was dangerous. Dozens of times he'd said in one way or another that he wasn't interested in a relationship. He had no desire to be a husband or a father. It was a shame, because she thought he would be wonderful at both.

She now stood at the living-room window and watched the snow falling in big fat flakes. She hoped it didn't snow too much. She didn't like the idea of being snowed in here all alone.

Sammy was taking a nap, the cabin was silent and she was restless, filled with an uneasy sense of impending doom. "It's just the snow," she said aloud, hoping the sound of her own voice would soothe her. It didn't.

But she knew what would make her feel better. She walked over to the sofa, curled up in one corner and picked up the telephone. She punched in Nancy's number, and the older woman answered on the second ring. "Nancy, it's me. May I speak to Nana?"

When Nana's voice came across the line Janette fought against a swell of emotion that momentarily clogged her throat. She hadn't spoken to her grandmother since the night Sinclair had shown up on Dalton's doorstep, and she realized now that she had so much to tell her.

"Are you still at Dalton West's apartment?" Nana asked.

"No, I'm in a little cabin on the West property." She explained about the sheriff showing up, about the fire and subsequent shooting.

"Nana, I'm not leaving. I've decided to stand and fight him."

There was a long moment of stunned silence. "You know I've always supported you in every decision you've made," Nana said. "And I'm proud of you for wanting to fight him, to bring him to justice. But, I'd be lying if I told you this is what I want for you. I'm scared for you, for Sammy. Are you sure you're making the right decision?"

Janette wanted to laugh. Was she sure? Definitely not. She was filled with trepidation and doubts. But despite her fear and doubts she was committed to doing what was right.

"Of course I'm nervous and afraid. But Dalton believes me. He believes my story and he knows a special prosecutor who handles cases like this. Nana, I don't want to spend the rest of my life looking over my shoulder, afraid that Sinclair will find me, will find us. I want him to pay for what he did to me."

A swell of anger tightened her chest. "Nana, I'm not sure I'll ever be whole if I don't do this."

"Baby, if this is what you need to do, then do it. You know I'll stand right beside you," Nana replied.

For the next few minutes Janette explained to her grandmother about moving to the safe house in Kansas City. "I'm not doing that," Nana argued with a touch of her legendary stubbornness. "I'm perfectly fine here with Nancy and I'm not going to go anywhere unless you're with me."

"But, Nana, I'd feel so much better if I knew for certain you were safe."

"Don't you worry about me none," she said. "I've got so many friends in this trailer park, that man will never be able to find me."

Janette wasn't surprised by her grandmother's vehemence in remaining where she was. She'd had a feeling she'd never be able to talk her into going to Kansas City.

"Janette, honey. I'll leave Sandstone when this is all over and the three of us can go someplace new, if that's what you want. But, in the meantime I'm staying put right here where I'm at least close enough to you to get to you in a half an hour."

"Somehow I had a feeling you'd say something like that," Janette said dryly.

"Do you trust this man? This Dalton West?"

"With my very life," Janette responded without a second thought. "More important, I trust him with Sammy's life."

"Then that's good enough for me."

"He's a wonderful man, Nana. He's smart and kind. He can make me laugh and he makes me feel smart and pretty."

"Don't you go getting your heart all twisted up in this," Nana warned softly. "Dalton is helping you bring a bad man to justice, but that doesn't mean he's making a place for you in his life."

"I'm aware of that." Hadn't she spent most of the morning reminding herself of that very fact?

The two talked for a few more minutes then finally Janette said goodbye and hung up. *Don't you go getting your heart all twisted up in this.* Nana's words whirled around and around in Janette's head.

It was too late for the warning. She got up from the sofa and walked once again to the window to stare out at the falling snow. Her heart was already twisted up with Dalton.

She wasn't sure how it had happened, that in the space of so few days her heart could get so tangled up. But she knew she was precariously close to falling completely and irrevocably in love with Dalton West.

She drew a deep sigh. This cabin was so isolated. She'd never known such darkness as that which came with nightfall here. Last night there had been the faint illumination of the moon. But tonight, with the clouds, there would be no moonlight, no star shine, just deep, impenetrable darkness. If Sinclair somehow found her here, nobody would even hear her scream.

Releasing another tense sigh, she stepped away from the window and paced the length of the living room. The evening stretched out before her, empty and lonely.

The living room had a television but Janette had never been much of a TV watcher. She thought about waking up Sammy, but decided that was the height of selfishness, to wake up her infant son because she was lonely and bored.

Maybe it was time for her to get out her book bag and do a little studying. She didn't intend to work as a waitress for the rest of her life, and the best way to get ahead was to get that GED.

She went into the bedroom and opened her suitcase. For several long moments she simply stared at the red book bag. She remembered vividly the last time she'd carried it out of the building where she'd been taking the classes.

Proud. She'd been so proud of herself for taking her future in her hands, for making the effort to change her life for the better. Now as she stared at the book bag all she could think about was what had happened on her way home that night.

As she carried the bag to the kitchen table she realized Sheriff Sinclair hadn't just raped her body that night on the side of the road. He'd also raped her mind. He'd taken all her insecurities and thrown them in her face, telling her she was poor, stupid trailer trash.

Janette refused to allow Brandon Sinclair to define her. She'd been his victim for a brief period of time, but she wasn't a victim anymore.

With a new burst of determination she reached into the book bag and withdrew her notebook, a study guide and her mini-tape recorder.

She punched the rewind button on the tape recorder then opened the study guide to find the page she'd last worked on. She'd loved school and it didn't take her long to become totally absorbed in the work.

It was long after dark when she decided to fix herself a cup of tea. She punched on the tape recorder to hear the last lecture that she'd taped, then got up to heat some water for the tea.

"The United States constitution consists of a pre-amble, seven articles and twenty-six amendments." A pleasant female voice filled the room. Mrs. Rebecca Winstead had been the woman working to help adults achieve their GED. The last class Janette had attended had been going over the constitution.

"Over the next couple of nights we're going to be talking about the components that make up the document that is the supreme law of the land."

As Janette made her cup of tea, she listened to the tape, trying to absorb everything that might be important when she eventually took her test.

She carried her cup of tea to the table and at that moment Sammy awakened. She hurried into the bedroom. "Hey, little man." She picked up the smiling, wiggling boy and placed him on the bed to change his diaper. "Did you have a nice little nap?" she asked and efficiently took care of the wet diaper, replacing it with a clean one.

"Turn off your lights and get out of the car." The deep male voice boomed and Janette froze.

Sinclair. His familiar voice shot a stabbing panic through her. He was here! He'd found her! Wildly she looked around the room, trying to remember where she'd put her knife.

"Well, well, don't we look all sexy in that little skirt?"

She frowned, picked up Sammy and stepped back into the kitchen. The hated voice came from the small recorder in the center of the table.

She stared at the tiny machine as it continued to play the sounds of that night…the sounds of her rape. Somehow when she had reached into her book bag that night to retrieve her driver's license, she must have hit the record button.

Tears streamed down her cheeks as she hugged Sammy close.

They were tears of sorrow, for the innocent girl she'd been and tears of happiness because the tape was evidence, solid evidence that would put Brandon Sinclair behind bars for a very long time.

She started for the phone to call Dalton, to tell him the news, but halfway to the phone she changed her mind. She'd tell him tomorrow when he was here. It would be her surprise.

"We've got him, Sammy," she whispered, and for the first time since this all began, hope filled her up.

Dalton sat in the West Protective Services office and stared out the window. The snow that had fallen the day before hadn't been enough to create anything but minor problems and Main Street of Cotter Creek was back in business.

He'd called Janette first thing that morning to tell her he'd try to get to the cabin that evening. He'd come into the office in an attempt to keep his schedule as normal as possible. He didn't want anyone noticing that he was acting out of character until they had Brandon Sinclair in Trent Cummings' custody.

A room at the motel was now rented in his name and his brother Clay was sitting on it, watching for Sinclair to make a move. He'd told his brother only the minimum of information and that if he saw a man resembling the good sheriff trying to get into the room, he was to call Zack and Dalton.

He leaned back in his chair and frowned. He'd rather be at the cabin. He'd rather be with Janette and Sammy than sitting here wondering where Sinclair was now and what he might be doing.

Drumming his fingers against the desktop, he fought against a feeling of impending catastrophe. He had no idea why the disquiet roared so loudly in his head. He had a plan, he'd set it in motion and all they had to do was keep Janette hidden until Trent arrived in town.

Unless Sinclair knew the specific location of the cabin, Dalton couldn't imagine how he would find it, find her. Everything was under control, and yet he couldn't stop the worry that whispered through him. He wished Janette would have agreed to keep his gun. He wished she would have told him she was a sharp-shooter in another lifetime.

It was just after noon when the door opened and Zack walked in. Following at his heels was Brandon Sinclair. Dalton narrowed his eyes.

If he'd been a dog his hackles would have risen. As it was, every muscle in his body tensed. He nodded to his brother but didn't get up from behind the desk.

"Dalton, I understand you and Sheriff Sinclair have met," Zack said. Dalton merely nodded.

Sinclair cleared his throat and stepped closer, a flyer in his hand. "I've been passing out these photos of the woman I've been looking for. Maybe you've seen her around town."

Brandon Sinclair had the eyes of a predator, ice-cold, and as he looked at Dalton they were filled with a silent challenge.

Dalton took the flyer from him, gave it a cursory glance then tossed it on the desk in front of him. "Sorry, haven't seen her."

"She's a bad one, Mr. West. I told your brother here, Janette Black is a danger to anyone she gets close to. I want to get her into custody before she harms anyone."

Dalton raised an eyebrow. "I thought you told me the other night that she had already hurt somebody. Didn't you tell me she'd killed her grandmother?"

Red splotches appeared in Brandon's cheeks. "We don't know for certain what's happened to her grandmother. Initially we thought she was in the fire that destroyed the trailer where she and Janette lived, but our investigation turned up no bodies."

"Then what exactly is it she's wanted for?" Dalton held Sinclair's gaze intently.

"She's wanted on a number of charges. Theft and drug trafficking for starters. There's also been a number of home invasions recently and we think she was involved in those."

"She's just a regular one woman crime spree," Dalton replied. Zack shot him a sharp glance. "Look, I told you the other night I hadn't seen her, and nothing has changed, so if you'll excuse me I've got work to do." He pointedly turned his chair to face the computer, effectively dismissing both his brother and Sinclair.

"I've got to get the rest of these flyers handed out," Sinclair said to Zack.

As the two men left the office Dalton picked up the

flyer. The photo of Janette looked like a typical school photo. She looked younger and her hair was shorter. She'd said she'd had to quit high school her junior year. If he were to guess, this was probably the last school picture she'd had taken.

He still held the photo when the door opened and Zack came back in. He set the flyer aside. "I figured you'd be back."

Zack sat in the chair opposite the desk and studied his brother. "You want to tell me what's going on?"

"What makes you think anything is going on?" Dalton countered.

Zack's dark eyebrows pulled together in a frown and he leaned forward and thumped a finger in the center of the flyer. "You know something about this, about her. I know you do."

"What makes you think that?"

"Because I'm your brother, Dalton. I know when you're lying. Look, you don't want to put yourself in the middle between a lawman and a criminal. If you know anything about the whereabouts of this woman you need to tell me now."

"I've got nothing to tell you." Dalton leaned back in his chair. He hated lying to Zack, but until they connected with Trent Cummings he wasn't willing to share anything with his brother. As much as he didn't want to be between a lawman and his criminal, he didn't want Zack to be in the middle of a lawman and his own brother.

Zack leaned back in his chair and expelled a deep

sigh, his gaze still on Dalton. "What's up with you lately?"

Dalton frowned. "What are you talking about?"

"It seems like for the last six months or more you've withdrawn from all of us, withdrawn from life. You stay holed up either in here or at your apartment. You don't visit anyone, you don't date. You don't share anything of yourself with anyone."

"When did you get to be Dr. Phil?" Dalton asked with more than a touch of irritation.

"If I were Dr. Phil, I'd not only be able to point out the problem, but I'd also have an idea what had caused it."

"There's no problem," Dalton replied emphatically. "I like being alone. Why is that an issue?"

Zack raked a hand through his dark hair. "I guess it's not, if that's the life you choose." He stood and started for the door, but before he reached it he turned back to face Dalton. "Dad said he's seen your truck passing by the house a couple of times in the last couple of days."

"I've been staying off and on at the cabin. George is doing a little remodeling work."

Zack held his gaze for another long minute, then turned and left the office. The moment he was gone Dalton picked up the phone and called Emmett Treadwall, a local handyman and made arrangements for him to paint Dalton's apartment immediately. He then called George to let him know that the apartment was going to be painted. Covering tracks, covering his lies.

Maybe he should have confided in Zack, but without

any real evidence to damn Sinclair, he just wasn't sure what his brother would be forced to do.

In just a matter of days it would all be over. Hopefully Trent would believe Janette enough to start a full-blown investigation that would lead to Sinclair's arrest. Then Janette and her grandmother and little Sammy would begin a new life someplace where there were no reminders of the horror she'd experienced.

Temporary. All of this was temporary. Another week or so and she'd be gone. Once again he picked up the flyer and stared at her picture.

He'd been irritated the night of the snowstorm, irritated that even for a single night he had to share his space, accommodate somebody else's needs. He'd told himself he was living a solitary life, but maybe it was in reality a selfish life.

He tossed the picture aside and frowned, not wanting to chase that thought any further. Just a couple more days, then he could get back to his own life.

What he didn't understand was why that particular thought didn't hold much appeal.

Chapter 11

She was waiting for him at the door when he pulled up in front of the cabin just after seven. Knowing that Sinclair was in town, he'd driven around for an hour before coming here, making sure that he wasn't being followed.

The sight of her with Sammy in her arms warmed his heart despite his need to remain emotionally distant. As he approached, Sammy wiggled with delight, arms flailing as if to reach for him.

There was no way to maintain any kind of distance from an almost six-month-old baby. Dalton took the little boy from her arms as he stepped through the door. "Hey, buddy," he said, then smiled at Janette. "I think you've got a heartbreaker on your hands."

She laughed. She looked brighter, happier than he'd

ever seen her and a thrum of tension wound tight in his gut. He wanted her. God help him but he wanted her again. Even knowing that in a matter of days she'd be out of his life, even knowing that he could only be a temporary fixture in her life, he wanted her.

She grabbed him by the arm and pulled him toward the kitchen. "I hope you haven't eaten yet. I made a meatloaf and I've got a wonderful surprise."

"I haven't eaten and what's the surprise?"

"Let's have dinner first, then I'll tell you."

"Sounds good. And I have some news, too," he said.

He stepped into the kitchen and looked around in surprise. The table was set and in the center were two tall candles and a bottle of wine. He shifted Sammy from one arm to the other. "Where did all this come from?" he asked.

"I called Savannah. She did me a favor and picked up some things from the store and brought them out this afternoon." She took Sammy from his arms. "Sit. I'm just going to put him down, then I'll be right back to serve the meal."

As she disappeared into the bedroom Dalton sat at the table. The candles gave off a pleasant glow and their vanilla fragrance mingled with the scent of the meatloaf. And beneath it all he could smell the scent of Janette, the honeysuckle that now reminded him of making love with her.

He could get used to this, coming home from work to her and Sammy. He steeled himself against the very thought, against the sense of homecoming that had filled him the moment he'd seen her and Sammy at the front door waiting for him.

She came back into the room a few minutes later, the glow of happiness still lighting her features. "You look unusually happy tonight," he said.

"I am." She went directly to the oven and pulled out a meatloaf surrounded by potatoes. "First of all, I cooked Smiley's special meatloaf. Even people who profess to hate meatloaf love Smiley's recipe." She set the dish on the table. "Secondly, there's nothing better than candlelight to put a woman in a good mood. And third, I can't wait to tell you about my really big surprise. But first, we eat."

From the refrigerator she pulled out a salad, then joined him at the table. "And how was your day?"

He opened the bottle of wine and filled their glasses, then began to fill his plate. "Boring," he said, "except for the visit I got from Sinclair and Zack." One of her pale eyebrows danced upward. "Sinclair has been passing around flyers in town with your picture on it."

"Where did he get a picture of me?" She passed him the salad bowl.

"Looked like an old school photo. Did anyone else in town see you besides me?"

"The guy at the bus station was the only person I saw, and if Sinclair asks him any questions all he'll be able to say is that he saw me the night of the storm but didn't know where I went."

Dalton nodded. "I do have some good news."

"What's that?"

"I got a call from Trent today. He was able to wind

things up sooner than he expected in Oklahoma City so he's planning on coming to Cotter Creek sometime late tomorrow afternoon. As soon as he arrives in town I'll drive him out here to hear your story."

Her blue eyes held his steadily. "So this could all be over by tomorrow night."

"That's right. If everything goes well, Sinclair could be in custody as early as tomorrow night." He looked at her curiously. "Why don't you look pleased with that news?"

"Oh, I am pleased," she quickly said, then frowned, a charming little wrinkle appearing between her brows. "I was just thinking that I need to figure out what happens next."

"When you get your GED, what are your plans then?"

She took a sip of the wine, the set her glass back on the table. "I'd like to get a job that pays well enough that I can help support Nana and Sammy and also pay for college night classes. Eventually I'd like to be a teacher."

"An admirable profession. Is that something you've always wanted to do?"

She grinned at him. "Only after I'd finally given up my desire to be a princess."

He laughed and for the next few minutes they ate and exchanged small talk. Again Dalton was struck not only by her beauty, but by her intelligence and sense of humor, as well. Whenever she finally got settled in someplace she would have no problems dating and would eventually find a man who didn't want to live without her.

After they'd eaten they cleared the table and cleaned

up the kitchen. Despite his desire to the contrary, every bump of their shoulders, every brush of their hands as they worked side by side, sent sizzling electricity through him.

"Now are you going to tell me the secret that has you so excited?" he asked.

She poured them each another glass of wine, handed him his then pointed him toward the living room. "Go make yourself comfortable and I'll be right back." She disappeared into the bedroom.

Dalton carried both his wine and hers to the living room and sank down on the sofa, his curiosity piqued. A moment later she came into the living room carrying a red book bag.

"This is the bag I carried back and forth to the GED classes I was taking," she said as she set it on the coffee table. "I hadn't opened it since that night with Sinclair. Yesterday afternoon I decided maybe it was time to pull out the books and start studying again."

She sat next to him on the sofa and took out the books that were inside, then pulled out a small tape recorder. "I used to tape the classes so if I got confused about something or felt I missed something I could listen to the class as many times as I needed to."

He nodded, wondering where she was going with this. He reached out for his wineglass and took a sip, aware of a palpable tension radiating from her. He set his glass down and frowned. "Are you okay?" She was staring at the tape recorder as if it were a coiled rattlesnake getting ready to strike.

She looked up at him and smiled, a beatific smile

that shot a new ripple of desire through him. "I'm better than okay. Anyway, that night I had the book bag next to me in the car when Sinclair pulled me over. The best way to explain all this is this." She leaned forward and pushed the play button on the recorder.

"Turn off your lights and get out of the car."

Dalton nearly fell off the sofa as Brandon Sinclair's deep voice boomed from the recorder.

"Well, well, don't we look all sexy in that little skirt."

As the tape played, a sickness welled up inside Dalton as he heard the sheriff bully Janette. It was only when he heard Janette whimper from the tape and say no that he leaned forward and shut off the recorder. He couldn't stand to hear the rest. He didn't want to hear the sounds of her being taken against her will.

For a long moment they were both silent. Dalton stared at the tape recorder with a vague nausea rolling around in his stomach.

"I didn't know I had it until yesterday," Janette said, her voice seeming to come from far away as it penetrated the veil of rage that had descended over him. "I must have accidentally hit the on button when I went into the book bag to get my license."

She reached out and took one of his hands between hers. "The whole thing is on tape. We've got him, Dalton. It's not just my word against his. There's no way he can dispute what's on that tape."

Dalton stared at her. Although intellectually he'd understood that she'd been raped, that whimper he'd heard coming from the tape, the terror-filled protest that she'd released, moved it from intelligent knowledge to emotional sickness.

He wanted to kill for her. He wanted to weep for her. Her strength awed him…humbled him. He squeezed her hand, fighting for words.

"Dalton?" Her soft voice pierced the haze that had fallen over him. "Are you all right?"

He let go of her hand and instead pulled her into an embrace. She laid her head on his shoulder and he stroked the silk of her hair. "I'm just sorry. So damned sorry." Tears burned at his eyes.

"It's okay. I'm okay, especially now that I know he is going to pay for what he did." She looked up at Dalton and he saw that there were no shadows in her eyes, no pain of any kind. Instead her eyes sparkled with hope, with a new kind of peace.

As he held her gaze her mouth opened slightly and she leaned forward. He intended a soft, gentle kiss of healing, but the moment his mouth claimed hers and her tongue swirled with his the kiss became something much different.

Her arms curled around his neck as her kiss grew hot and demanding. He knew they were going to make love again, tasted it in her kiss, felt it in the willing way she filled his arms.

He told himself he didn't want to, that it would do nothing but complicate his conflicting emotions where she was concerned. But as she snaked her hand beneath his shirt and caressed his chest, he was helpless against the onslaught of sensations her touch evoked.

In all probability she would be out of this cabin, out

of his life within the next two days. But at the moment she was warm in his arms and he allowed good sense to be swallowed by desire, knowing that it would only make it more difficult when the time came to tell her goodbye.

A quiet desperation simmered inside Janette as she kissed Dalton. It was the desperation of a woman who had fallen in love with the wrong man.

She kissed him with all the heart, all the soul she possessed, needing to take the memory of this last chance to be in his arms with her when she left.

Her fingers danced across the warmth of his broad chest as their kiss grew more frantic, more needy. She broke the kiss only long enough to pull her sweatshirt over her head, then to draw him down to the floor.

"I want you, Dalton," she said fervently.

"I want you, too." He ripped his shirt over his head and tossed it aside, then stood and took off his jeans. While he was doing that Janette finished undressing, then when they were both naked, she lay back on the rug and beckoned him back into her arms.

He lay beside her, his gaze as hot as his hands as he caressed the length of her. His lips followed the path of his hands, nipping lightly at the base of her throat then kissing the fullness of one breast. A moan escaped her lips as rivulets of pleasure swept over her.

She knew this would be the last time she'd make love with him and she wanted to capture his taste and his touch in her memory. She knew his strength and his belief in her would sustain her through whatever her future held.

When she reached down to wrap her hand around his hardness, he released a low deep moan that only increased her excitement.

She hadn't realized that as a woman she'd been dead until Dalton had brought her back to life. Gratitude mingled with love, intensifying this moment in time with him.

They caressed each other as if they'd been making love together for years, with easy, sure movements that evoked the most intense sensations.

As he touched her intimately the build began, a rising wave of pleasure so intense she thought she'd go mad with it. And when the peak came, she cried out his name, trembling as the release swept her away.

She knew he was waiting for her to take the lead as she had the last time they'd made love. But she didn't want the lead. She parted her legs and motioned for him to get on top.

He hesitated, his eyes glowing and the muscles in his neck strained. "Are you sure?"

"I'm sure."

He moved on top of her and she waited for the panic to strike. The scent of him surrounded her, clean and with that touch of sandalwood she found so attractive.

He didn't take her, but instead held himself above her, as if waiting to see if she'd freak out. She realized at that moment that she wasn't going to freak, that her trust in Dalton was so complete, all she wanted was to be surrounded by him.

She pulled him closer and as he eased into her, there was no thought of anything but him. His mouth sought hers as his hips moved against her. She clung to him, loving the feel of his broad back beneath her fingers, wanting to urge him deeper into her.

He moved faster, faster still, his lips leaving hers as their breaths mingled in quick pants. When he stiffened against her she wanted to cry, because she was free of the specter of Brandon Sinclair, because she loved Dalton West.

He moved his upper body off of hers and stared at her in the waning light. "We didn't use protection."

"Don't worry, I'm on the pill. After...what happened, I wanted to make sure that if I ever got pregnant again, it would be my decision." His statement was a jolt back to reality. He was worried because he didn't want a baby. He didn't want a wife. There was no happy ending here with him.

She scooted out from beneath him. "I'll be right back. I'm going to take a quick shower." She left the living room and went into the bathroom and a moment later stepped beneath a warm spray of water.

Although she'd been with Dalton less than a week, the love she felt for him was deeper and stronger than anything she'd ever felt for any man. And visualizing a future with him was just as silly as visualizing herself a princess or a ballerina.

The door to the shower opened and Dalton peeked in. "Mind some company? I'm great at washing backs."

She smiled at him and stepped aside to allow him entry into the small shower. Even knowing that loving him was a study in futility, there was no way to guard her heart against him.

Twenty minutes later he was dressed and she sat at the kitchen table in her robe. "The next time you see me I'll have Trent with me," he said as he pulled on his coat. "I'll call you tomorrow and let you know what time we'll be here. Meanwhile, I'll fill in Zack and play the tape for him."

She nodded and stood to walk him to the door. She was glad he wasn't spending the night. Sleeping in his arms would only make things more difficult.

When they reached the front door he turned, drew her into his arms and smiled down at her. "Just think, by tomorrow night this will all be over. You can move on with your life and not be afraid of Brandon Sinclair any longer."

"It's truly over, isn't it?"

He nodded, his eyes suddenly dark. "You and your nana and Sammy are going to have a wonderful life." He kissed her on her brow, then released her and walked out.

She stood at the door and watched as he got into his truck. It was over. Tomorrow night she would tell her story to a man who had the power to bring Sheriff Sinclair to justice. With the tape, it was no longer a question of she said, he said. There was enough evidence to put him behind bars.

She should be feeling euphoric, but instead an unexpected chill walked up her spine. Twenty-four hours, she told herself. That's all she had to get through. Another twenty-four hours and it would all be over.

* * *

He knew where she was, and it wasn't in the motel room that had been rented by Dalton West. Brandon lay in bed next to his sleeping wife, his mind whirling. He'd thought Janette might have been moved to the West property, then had dismissed the idea as being too obvious.

A headache that afternoon had given him the information he needed. He'd been standing in front of the pain relief medications in the grocery store when he'd heard a woman asking about baby formula in the next aisle.

A glance around the corner had let him know it was Savannah West. He'd done his research on the West clan and knew she didn't have a baby.

He'd paid for his medicine, taken two of the gel-coated tablets, then had gotten into his car and waited for Savannah to emerge from the store.

A few minutes later she'd come out with a basket of groceries, then had gotten into her car and driven off. Thank God, he had driven his personal car that day instead of his official car. It had been easy to follow her as she headed north of town.

When she'd turned onto the West property, he'd known Janette was there. He'd returned to Sandstone to plot and plan.

Damn the bitch for leaving Sandstone, for thinking she could escape him. And damn Dalton West for sticking his nose where it didn't belong.

He didn't just want that kid, he wanted Janette Black

dead, dead so she couldn't talk, dead so she couldn't cause him any more problems.

She'd probably already told Dalton a tale, but he could easily deny that he'd done anything wrong. Okay, he'd had sex with her, but that didn't make him a criminal. He'd tell Dalton that they'd had a brief affair, that the sex had been consensual.

He smiled in the darkness of the room. By this time tomorrow night his life would be back to normal. Janette would be dead and, eventually, after all the red tape was through, that boy would be his.

Chapter 12

It snowed again the next afternoon. Janette stood at the window and stared at the fat flakes falling from the sky. She hoped it didn't snow enough to postpone Trent Cummings's arrival in Cotter Creek.

She was ready to get it over with, needed to get on with her life away from Dalton. He'd crawled too deeply into her heart. He'd made her wish for things that would never come true.

It was time to go, while she still had her dignity. She had a life to build for her, for Sammy and for Nana. She moved from the window and to the kitchen table where a cup of tea was growing cold.

Sammy was napping and she had spent much of the time after lunch trying to decide if they should go back to Sandstone or move to a whole new city.

When Sinclair was arrested the whole story would come out and Janette wasn't sure she wanted to be known around the small town as the woman the sheriff had raped. Still, Nana had a support system in Sandstone and she would miss her friends desperately if they chose to locate someplace else.

The trailer had been insured, so there would be some money from the insurance company that might be enough to buy another mobile home and place it on the lot where the old one had been.

Once again her gaze shot out the window where the snow seemed to have picked up in intensity. She couldn't wait for spring. She ached for budding flowers and greening grass and a sun of healing warmth.

Where would she be in the spring? At the moment Tucson sounded like a great idea.

She'd called Nana earlier to let her know that by the end of the evening, the nightmare should be over. She'd mentioned to the older woman that, if all went well, she hoped Nana could get a ride to Cotter Creek in the morning and meet Janette at the motel. They'd figure out what to do from there.

She took a sip of the lukewarm tea and frowned thoughtfully. Maybe she should turn on the television and see if they were under any sort of snow watch or warning.

That's just what she needed, another blizzard moving in that put her life on hold for another week or so. What worried her most with each day that passed was the fear that Sinclair would eventually figure out where she was.

Even if he thought she was on the West property,

she was comforted by the fact that the cabin was so well hidden. And surely if a stranger were wandering the West land, somebody would notice, a ranch hand or one of the Wests themselves.

She finished her tea, then went into the living room and sat on the sofa trying to decide if she should call Nana or not. Before she'd made up her mind the phone rang.

It was Dalton, and at the sound of his deep, familiar voice she sank back against the cushions and squeezed the receiver closer to her ear.

"Hi," he said. "How are things there?"

"Okay. I've just been watching it snow. I used to love the snow, but lately it seems like all it does is complicate things. Did you meet with Zack, and have you heard from Trent? Is the snow going to postpone his arrival?"

"I tried to reach Zack, but he got called to an accident and didn't get back last night. I've left a message for him to get in touch ASAP. And I spoke to Trent just a few minutes ago," Dalton said. "He can't get away from Oklahoma City until about three this afternoon. That would put him here after six and he promised me that the weather wouldn't interfere except that it might take him longer to make the trip."

"Thank God, because I'm ready to get this over with," she said.

"Yeah, it's past time we both got on with our normal lives," he said.

She knew he didn't mean the words to hurt, but somehow they did. They reminded her that she was really nothing more than an inconvenience in his life.

Oh, he might have enjoyed their lovemaking. After all, he was a man, but just because he'd liked having sex with her didn't mean he felt any kind of emotional attachment to her.

"That's what I've been doing all morning. Trying to figure out where I want to pick up the pieces of my life and start again."

"You aren't going back to Sandstone?" he asked.

She twisted the phone cord around her finger. "I don't know. I'm sure Nana would be pleased if I decided that we were going to stay there, but I'm not sure that's where I want to be. After tonight everyone in town will know that Brandon Sinclair raped me. I'm not sure I want to raise my son someplace where people know that information."

"What are you going to tell Sammy about his father?"

"Eventually the truth, but I want him to hear it from me, not from some kid down the block or some whispers in a store. I'll choose the right time and place to tell him about his father. Maybe by that time there will be a man in my life, a man in Sammy's who will fill any void he might feel."

There was a long moment of silence. "I hope so," he finally said.

"Any sign of Sinclair today?" she asked.

"Haven't seen or heard from him all day. I did hear from my brother Tanner. I'd had him working on a background check of Sinclair and unfortunately it turned up nothing."

"Did you expect it to turn up anything?" she asked.

"I figured it was worth a try, but no, I guess not. Savannah has tried to make contact with that waitress you spoke to her about, but so far she hasn't had any luck."

"None of that matters now," she replied. "We have Sammy and we have the tape and we have me. That's all we need to put him in prison. Do you have the tape in a safe place?" He'd taken the tape player with him the night before when he'd left.

"It's in the safe here in the office," he said.

She twisted the phone cord more tightly around her finger, vaguely wondering in the back of her head why nobody had replaced the phone with a newer cordless model. "What happens after tonight? Once I tell my story to Trent?"

"Hopefully Trent will be able to get a judge to issue an arrest warrant, then we'll have my brother Zack pick him up." He paused a moment, then continued, "Janette, I know you aren't sure what your next move might be, but I want you to know that you're free to stay in the cabin as long as you need to until you figure out where you're going to go."

"Thanks, but I'm planning on having Nana meet me at the motel here in town tomorrow afternoon so if you can just take me there tomorrow, I'll be fine." She couldn't stay here, not in the place where she'd realized her love for him.

"Have you checked with the motel to make sure they have a room?" he asked.

"I intend to do that as soon as we hang up."

"If they don't have any available rooms, I have one

rented there in my name. You could stay in it as long as you want or need."

"I'll play it by ear," she said.

They spoke for a few more minutes then hung up. She got up from the sofa and walked back to the window where the snow was still falling in small flakes.

What she really wanted he couldn't give her. Two wishes filled her heart. The first was that Brandon Sinclair would pay for what he'd done to her, and that was going to happen. The second wish was that Dalton West would love her enough to want to leave behind his solitary life and spend his future with her and Sammy.

She supposed she should be happy with fifty percent of her wishes being fulfilled, but just as Brandon Sinclair had left an indelible mark on her soul, Dalton had left a very different, but equally powerful mark there.

Brandon Sinclair was a lucky man. Dalton shut off the tape player and got up from his desk, fighting a raw aching grief and a rage so great it threatened to consume him. Sinclair was lucky in that he wasn't around for Dalton to put his fist in his face. He wasn't around to be introduced to the explosive rage that Dalton barely managed to contain.

He'd decided to listen to the tape in its entirety before Trent Cummings arrived. He'd known Trent would want to hear it and Dalton hadn't wanted to be blindsided by unexpected emotion in front of the special prosecutor.

And he had been surprised by the depth of his emotion as he'd listened to Janette's rape at the hands of Brandon Sinclair.

She'd never screamed. Although the rape had been brutal and there had been moments when he'd wanted to scream for her, she'd never screamed. But she'd said no. Fourteen times, she'd said the word. Twelve times she'd pled with him to stop.

Dalton slammed his palm against the doorjamb, needing to vent some of the rage that clawed through him. He was sorry he'd heard the tape, but much more sorry that Janette had experienced the ordeal.

How strong she was, how utterly amazing. A survivor, not a victim. A woman who had decided not to run but rather to face her abuser even when she'd known the stakes were so high.

He would make certain her bravery counted. He wouldn't rest until Sinclair was in jail, serving hell time for his crimes. It was the least he could do for Janette before he told her goodbye.

He stared out the window where the snow was once again falling. It had snowed off and on all day. Thank God Trent had called him a little while ago and told him he was half an hour outside of Cotter Creek and should arrive within the next forty-five minutes. It would be after dark by the time they got to the cabin.

He had fallen in love with her. The thought came out of nowhere and hit him hard in the gut, taking his breath half away.

He'd made the same mistake he'd made with Mary. He'd gotten too close, allowed himself to get too involved. Only this time it was worse. The depth of his emotion for Janette was so much greater than anything he'd ever felt for Mary. He'd opened his heart not just to Janette, but to Sammy, as well, and when they left they'd take a huge piece of him with them.

And they would leave and he wouldn't try to stop them. He knew the drill. He'd been an important part of her life for a brief time, but he'd never been meant to have a permanent place there. She was in transition, had come to him in the middle of a storm, but the storm would pass and she'd move on.

He moved away from the window and returned to his desk where the small tape recorder awaited the arrival of Trent. Again his heart clenched as he thought of what Janette had endured.

She deserved happiness and he knew without a doubt she'd find it. She'd build a wonderful life for herself, her son and her grandmother. She was strong and beautiful and eventually she'd find a man who wanted to share his life with her.

He knew she'd grown close to him, but that was only because she'd had to be dependent on him for a brief time. Once she got back her independence and was no longer ruled by fear, she'd recognize what she thought was love for him was actually gratitude.

Apparently that was his place in life, to protect and serve, to help heal vulnerable women, then let them go to find happiness elsewhere. He'd thought he was happy alone, believed that his life was exactly the way he wanted it.

He realized he'd been fooling himself. He was a man meant for a family. The days that Janette and Sammy had shared his space had made him recognize that he didn't want to live a solitary life.

He wanted laughter. He wanted love. He wanted somebody to share his life with, somebody to kiss goodnight. Maybe eventually he'd find that special somebody. But in the meantime he just had to figure out how to tell Janette goodbye.

Brandon pulled the collar of the white parka closer around his neck and narrowed his gaze. A half an hour ago, when he'd parked his car, he'd cursed the falling snow, but now he welcomed it as he crept closer to the sprawling West house.

It had been a day of frustration. His presence had been required in Sandstone for a meeting with the mayor of the small town. During the meeting, which had seemed to last an eternity, all Brandon could think about was finding Janette and shutting her up for good.

Finally, at five that evening, he'd told his wife he would be gone all night on a stakeout and had left the small town. He'd come prepared. Not only was he wearing white ski pants and the white parka that would allow him to blend in to the surroundings, but he also had another unregistered, throwaway gun and a high beam flashlight.

Now all he had to do was find her, and it was reasonable to assume that she was somewhere on the West property. He'd driven in earlier, holding his breath as he'd coasted past the main house with his lights off. He'd parked behind an old shed and now was headed toward the house where he knew the patriarch, Red West, had raised his family.

Before the night was over, he'd search every structure on the West land, scour every inch of the place in an effort to find her.

He approached the main house, where light danced out the windows. The illumination would make it easy for him to peer inside.

The wind howled like a banshee and sliced at any area of skin that was exposed. Snow crunched underfoot and he cursed beneath his breath, irritated with the weather, but more irritated by the very existence of Janette Black.

His heart beat fast as he eased up to one of the lit windows and looked inside. It was the kitchen of the house and there were two people there, an old man and woman. That would be Smokey Johnson and his new wife, Kathy.

Brandon had done his research. He knew that the old cowhand had married the retired FBI agent a month before and the two shared the house with Red West.

There was no sign of the bitch he sought in the kitchen, so he moved on to the next lighted window. In the living room an older man was in a recliner with a book open on his lap. He was asleep, and Brandon assumed the man was Red West.

So where was Janette?

He wasn't a stupid man. He knew that if the right people listened to her, she had the potential to screw up his life. He couldn't let that happen.

He moved from window to window, fighting a swell of frustration that nearly blinded him. Patience, he told himself. He needed patience. At any minute she might walk into the living room, or go into the kitchen to get something to eat or drink. Once she showed herself to him, it would all be over.

It didn't bother him that she might be in a house filled with others. Three old people were not going to stop him from getting what he wanted.

It took him twenty minutes or so before he decided to move on. He knew that Red's oldest son, Tanner, had a house somewhere on the property. Maybe Dalton had stashed Janette there.

The snow was coming down more heavily now. Already his footprints around the house were disappearing, covered by the new layer of snow. That was fine with him. Hopefully by the time the dead were found the weather would have destroyed any evidence the authorities might try to find.

He'd had chains put on his car tires, so hopefully when it was time to leave the snow wouldn't impede his escape. He got into the car and pulled forward, seeking the house where Tanner lived.

He continued to drive without headlights, using the pasture fences as guidelines to stay on the road, until he spied the next house. His deadly intent burned inside him, warming him despite the plunging temperatures and the icy wind that blew from the north.

A half an hour later his frustration was a gnawing beast inside him. As far as he could tell there was nobody home in Tanner's two-story house.

He returned to his car. Maybe she was in that motel room that Dalton had rented. Maybe he'd done the expected, thinking that Brandon would think it too obvious. He *had* thought it was too obvious and had made the decision to stay away from there.

Dammit. He'd been so certain she was here. In his mind there was no other logical place for her to be. He drove further into the property and came to a house under construction. Brandon had heard that Clay West was in the process of building a home, and this was probably it. It had been framed, but the walls weren't up. Janette couldn't be hiding there.

He knew he should head back to Sandstone before the snow got so deep that even chains wouldn't allow forward movement. But he kept creeping forward, unwilling to give up the hunt.

He had just decided to head back to Sandstone when he saw it…a faint light glimmering among a grove of evergreen trees.

Where there was light, there was a source of that light. New energy filled him as he parked the car, got out and moved as quickly as a streak of moonlight over the snow.

He saw the cabin nestled among the trees and he knew she was there. He also knew there was no way Janette Black was going to survive this night.

Chapter 13

Janette paced the living-room floor as she waited to tell her story to Trent Cummings. Dalton had called a few minutes before and told her Trent had arrived in Cotter Creek and they would be leaving the West Protective Services office within the hour.

She had a feeling the hour would be spent discussing her case with Trent and listening to the tape that had captured Sinclair's crime against her.

She was glad Dalton was playing it for Trent in his office. She hoped to never hear it again unless it was at Brandon Sinclair's trial.

It was strange. She was at the end of this particular journey in her life, but she didn't feel the expected relief she'd thought tonight would bring. An uneasiness filled her.

She thought it was because tomorrow she'd have to face the rest of her life—a life without Dalton. On impulse she went over to the sofa and picked up the phone. She punched in the number that would connect her to her grandmother.

Nancy answered on the second ring and immediately put Janette's grandmother on the phone. "Honey, how are you doing?" Nana asked. To Janette's surprise she began to cry. "Janette, what's wrong?" Nana asked urgently.

"Nothing...nothing's wrong," Janette managed to say. She swiped the tears from her cheeks and warbled an uneasy laugh. "I don't even know why I'm crying. Dalton is supposed to be here anytime with the prosecutor, and it looks like things are finally at an end."

"Then maybe those tears are ones of relief and hopefully a little bit of closure," Nana replied.

"Maybe," Janette agreed, but she knew where the tears were formed. They were created in her heart as she thought of never seeing Dalton again.

"Nancy's brother is driving me into town tomorrow afternoon," Nana continued. "I'll be at the motel by three or so."

"Good. I thought we'd stay a day or two and talk about where we go from here," Janette said.

"Janette, I want you to know that I don't want you making decisions with me in mind. I want you to build a life for you and that precious little boy of yours. Nancy has told me I can live here with her. I don't want you thinking you have to provide for me. I'm an old woman at the end of my life and you're a young woman, a new mother with your life ahead of you. Reach for all the happiness you can grab, honey. You deserve it."

They spoke for another few minutes then hung up. Janette got up from the sofa and walked to the doorway of the bedroom to stare at Sammy sleeping in the beautiful cradle.

Once again she felt the burn of tears in her eyes. Maybe it was just the relief of knowing it was all finally over. She could let go of the fear that had been with her every day since the rape. She'd never again have to look over her shoulder and be afraid that Brandon Sinclair was just behind her, ready to wreak havoc in her life.

She turned away from the doorway and instead paced the kitchen, thinking about her conversation with Nana. Even though Nana had said she could live with Nancy, had insisted that Janette think only of herself and Sammy, Janette knew Nana would miss them desperately if Janette chose to leave her behind.

And to tell the truth, she didn't want to leave her behind. There was no question that Janette's life would be easier with Nana in it. While she worked and went back to school, somebody would have to watch Sammy, and Nana was the one person she trusted to take care of her little boy.

She didn't just need Nana in her life, she wanted the old woman to play a major role there. Wherever she went, she wanted Nana to go with her.

Maybe Kansas City was a good place to start again, she thought as she drifted into the living room. There would be plenty of job opportunities there and community colleges galore. She and Nana could make a decision tomorrow at the motel.

Reach for all the happiness you can grab, Nana had told her. If she were to reach for what she truly wanted, she'd grab Dalton West and never let him go.

She'd build a life with him that others would envy. They'd share their lives during the days and share their passion for each other during the nights. He'd be the one who would teach Sammy how to be a man, and Sammy would grow up to be strong and morally decent and good.

It was a wonderful fantasy, but it had nothing to do with reality. She glanced at the clock on the top of the television. After seven. Where were Dalton and Trent? It had been well over an hour since Dalton had called.

She moved back to the front window and peered out. It was still snowing, more heavily than it had all day. She hoped the weather didn't hold up Dalton and Trent too long. She wanted tonight to be done and tomorrow to begin. She needed to get away from this cabin, away from thoughts of Dalton and what might have been.

She started to turn away from the window when, from the corner of her eye, she saw movement. It was just a flash, a blur of something, but fear spiked through her and she backed away from the window with a small gasp.

Although she hadn't gotten a real look at whatever was moving outside, the impression that burned in her head was that it had been far too big to be an animal. It had been big enough to be a man.

Dalton or Trent wouldn't be walking around outside,

and if it was one of the Wests, surely they'd knock on the door to find out who was staying in the cabin.

It could only be one person.

Brandon Sinclair.

Somehow he'd found her. Her heart beat so fast she couldn't catch her breath for a long moment. The back of her throat closed up as panic took over.

He was here!

She couldn't think, couldn't move. It was as if the cold of the night had moved inside and frozen her in place. *Nobody will hear you scream.* The words pounded in her head. She was so isolated that when Sinclair got inside the cabin, as he killed her then stole her son, nobody would hear her cries.

"No." The word of protest broke her inertia. No, she wasn't going to allow that to happen, at least not without a fight.

She raced to the phone and picked it up. No dial tone greeted her. The line was dead. If she needed any further evidence that Sinclair was somewhere outside, the dead phone was it. He'd made certain she couldn't call for help.

As she left the living room and hurried into the bedroom, a fist slammed against the locked front door. "Janette, open the door. We need to talk." His deep voice held the authority and confidence of his position.

Inside the bedroom Janette fumbled beneath her pillow and pulled out the knife she'd carried since the night of her rape. The knock came again, this time harder against the wood of the door.

"Janette, open the door or I'll break it down. We have official business to discuss."

Frantically she looked around the small bedroom, seeking a weapon or an escape route. Her gaze landed on the window. She raced to it and threw it open. Frigid air blew in, chilling the last of any warmth that might have been left in her body. With trembling fingers she removed the screen.

Where were Dalton and Trent? She needed them here now. As she picked up the sleeping Sammy and wrapped him tightly in the towel she'd used as an extra blanket, she heard a crash at the front door and knew Sinclair was breaking it down.

She couldn't stand and fight him, knew that she'd never stand a chance against him. There was only one possible means of escape, and that was out into the snowstorm.

Holding Sammy tight against her, she went out the window, the icy cold and snow stinging every inch of her bare skin. Someplace in the back of her mind she knew it wouldn't take long for her to die of exposure. She wore no coat, no hat and no snow boots. She was clad in only a T-shirt, a pair of jeans and a pair of thin cotton slippers. But that couldn't be helped now.

As she began to run away from the cabin, away from Brandon Sinclair, the snow continued to fall like beautiful white death from the sky.

Behind her she heard the crash and a roar and knew that Sinclair had gotten inside. A sob ripped through her as she ran, knowing that she'd rather die in the snow than at the hands of the man who had raped her.

* * *

Dalton hung up the phone and tried to squash the worry that roared through him. "The phone's dead," he told Trent, who stood at the West Protective Services front door.

"Maybe the storm blew down a line," Trent offered.

"Maybe," Dalton said, but wasn't sure he believed it. A thrum of disquiet kicked up inside as he grabbed his truck keys off the desk. He hadn't talked to Zack yet, which didn't help his mood. "Let's get out of here. We need to get to the cabin."

Together the two men left the office and got into Dalton's truck. They had spent the past hour with Dalton filling in his old friend about the particulars of the case. Trent had heard the tape and had also listened to Dalton's suspicions that it had been Sinclair who had set the fire and fired the shots the night Dalton had moved her to the cabin.

Trent's expression had grown more grim with each word that Dalton spoke about Sinclair. Dalton knew there was nothing Trent loved more than putting away bad guys who masqueraded as good guys.

Dalton tried to ignore the uneasiness that coursed through him as he started the truck engine. She'd never not answered the phone before.

He attempted to tamp down the anxiety as he turned on the wipers to swipe at the snow that had gathered on the windshield.

"You're sure she'll testify?" Trent asked as Dalton backed out of his parking space.

"She'll do whatever she needs to do to make sure Sinclair goes to prison."

"The tape is good evidence, but could be easily disputed without her testimony," Trent said thoughtfully.

"She's solid," Dalton said. "She's come too far now to back down. She wants Sinclair behind bars far more than you or I do."

"I'm not sure that's possible," Trent said as he narrowed his eyes. "There's nothing I love more than putting a crooked lawman behind bars. Sinclair is a disgrace to the men and women who put their lives on the line every day for the good of their communities."

"I wish I would have seen him the night of the fire," Dalton said. "Then we could get him for attempted murder."

"We'll get him," Trent replied. "And I'll see to it that he's put away for as long as possible."

The street was slick and Dalton had to keep his speed at a minimum. As he drove he fumbled for his cell phone and punched in the number for the cabin. The phone rang and rang and rang. He clicked off, his apprehension exploding into full-blown fear.

"No answer?" Trent asked, his handsome features lit by the dashboard light.

Dalton shook his head. "I've got to admit, I'm worried." That was the understatement of the day.

He opened the cell phone again and quickly punched in a new number. "My brother Tanner lives close to the cabin where Janette is. He can get there quicker than we can." He sighed in frustration as Tanner's phone went directly to voice mail.

Tossing his cell phone to the seat between them, Dalton tightened his grip on the steering wheel and stepped on the gas.

Janette was in trouble and it was his fault. The knowledge thundered in his head. He should have insisted she keep a gun with her, he should have made other arrangements for her. Jesus, he should have done something different to assure that Sinclair wouldn't find her.

Dammit, what had made him think that she'd be safe in the cabin all alone? He hadn't believed that Sinclair would be able to find her there, but apparently he'd underestimated the sheriff.

The snow made visibility difficult and Dalton felt the spin and slide of the tires on the slick road beneath them. The wind howled and buffeted the truck and he silently cursed the conditions that kept him from going as fast as he wanted to go.

Let her be okay. Don't let anything happen to her. Dalton's brain said the words over and over again, his heart pounding so loud in his ears he wondered if Trent could hear it.

Trent braced himself with a hand on the dash as the back of the truck spun out. Dalton quickly corrected the spin, the panic inside him nearly unbearable. But it wasn't the panic of nearly losing control of the vehicle, it was the sheer terror that had loosened itself inside him for Janette and Sammy.

"You going to kill us before we get there?" Trent finally said with a touch of dry humor.

"I'm trying not to." Dalton eased up on the gas,

knowing that if they wrecked there was no way they could be any help at all.

His cell rang. He picked up the phone and checked the I.D. Zack, finally. "Zack, I need you to meet me at the cabin immediately."

"What's going on?" Zack asked.

"You know that woman Sheriff Sinclair was looking for? Janette Black?"

"What about her?"

He didn't bother trying to fill in Zack on the tape and details. "I've got her at the cabin and I think she's in big trouble." As Dalton spoke those words aloud, his heart squeezed so tight in his chest he momentarily felt light-headed. "Hurry, Zack."

Zack hung up and Dalton tossed the phone aside again, hoping and praying that there was a logical explanation for Janette not answering his calls, hoping and praying that she and Sammy were just fine and Brandon Sinclair was nowhere in the area.

The snow was both a blessing and a curse. As Janette ran from the cabin, she was glad that the heavy snowfall would make it more difficult for Sinclair to see her.

The curse was that it hadn't taken long for her feet to become chunks of ice, causing her to stumble more than once as she ran blindly into the night.

Sammy had awakened and fussed against her, and she tried to soothe him as she ran, afraid that if he began to wail Sinclair would hear and would be able to pinpoint her exact location.

Her breaths came in painful pants, the cold air stabbing her lungs with each intake of air. Her bare hands ached, as did her face where the icy flakes of snow clung to her lashes, her lips and her cheeks.

Somehow in the space of a dozen footsteps she'd become disoriented. She was no longer sure she was going in the right direction to find help and with each step she took she grew more exhausted.

Eventually the cold disappeared and instead she became numb, feeling nothing but the screaming in her head. And that scream intensified when she turned and saw the beam of a high-powered flashlight just behind her.

He was coming! A sob ripped from her throat as she stumbled forward. The snow and the darkness of the night couldn't hide her if his high beam fell on her.

The flashlight swiped from side to side, and she knew at the moment he didn't see her, didn't know that she was so close.

Exhaustion pulled at her, but she forced herself to move on. She wasn't so worried about her own safety, but for Sammy's. She had to keep him safe from the man who had fathered him.

She pushed herself forward, putting one numb foot in front of the other in an effort to escape. She could hear him now, the swish of his pant legs as his thighs rubbed together, and her heart pounded so hard, so fast, she wondered if she were having a heart attack.

At least if she died she knew Dalton would somehow, someway get Sammy. Even if Brandon Sinclair plucked Sammy from her dead arms, she was confident it would only be a temporary thing. Because she trusted Dalton.

Because she knew he'd fight for her son if she couldn't fight for him herself.

Cold.

She was so cold. It was becoming more difficult to put one foot in front of the other. She just wanted to lie down and sleep and dream of Dalton and what might have been.

She knew that was the cold talking and so she pushed herself forward. Half-blinded by the snow, she nearly crashed into the small shed. All she could think about was getting out of the snow before her legs stopped moving altogether.

Sammy had become an unbearable weight in her arms and no matter how close she held him to her chest, she knew he must be feeling the sting of the cold.

Without conscious thought, she opened the shed door and went inside, then shoved the door shut behind her. Without the aid of a light she couldn't see what the shed contained. All she knew was the blessing of being out of the howling wind and the icy air. She'd take a minute and catch her breath, warm herself just a bit before leaving the structure and continuing to run.

It wasn't until she heard Sinclair roar her name from just outside the shed that she realized what she'd done. She'd run herself into a dead end, a blind alley. The only way out was back through the door she'd entered and on the other side of that door was death.

Chapter 14

The mind was a strange thing. In the flash of a moment it could process enough impressions and instincts to make a man sick. Dalton was definitely sick as his brain not only worked to wrap around the grim possibility that Sheriff Sinclair had found Janette, but also highlighted every mistake he'd made as her bodyguard.

And he'd made plenty.

"I shouldn't have left her out there all alone." He spoke one of his biggest mistakes aloud.

"You did what you thought was right at the moment," Trent replied, once again bracing himself as Dalton turned into the West property and nearly took out a wooden post as the truck spun out. "Don't second-guess yourself. That can make a man crazy."

Dalton's heart beat so fast it hurt. The snow had

stopped falling and a sliver of moonlight sliced through the clouds, faintly illuminating the wintry landscape.

He flew past his dad's place, his brain screaming a litany of pleas. Let her be okay. Please let her be safe. Over and over the words played in his mind. It was as if, if he thought it often enough, that would make it so.

His hands ached from his fierce grip on the steering wheel, but that pain was nothing compared to the one that pierced his heart as he thought of Janette and little Sammy being in danger.

He raced by Tanner's house, skidded around Clay's half-built place and toward the grove of evergreen trees that surrounded the little cabin. He turned through the small lane and pulled up in front. Horror swept through him as he saw that the old wooden front door had been crashed in. He was out of the truck, gun drawn, in a frantic heartbeat.

Trent was right behind him and together the two men approached the silent cabin. Dalton stepped through the doorway and crouched with his gun held in both hands in front of him.

There was nobody in the living room. "Clear," he called out, and Trent stepped inside. As Dalton moved toward the kitchen his biggest fear was that he'd find only Janette's body somewhere in the cabin. The smashed front door seemed to cry that he and Trent were too late.

Emotion pressed thick in Dalton's chest and he drew a steadying breath as he entered the kitchen. Nothing. No body, no signs of any struggle, nothing. "Clear," he called to Trent, who followed at his heels.

Trent checked the bathroom, then stepped back into the kitchen and both men looked at the bedroom door. It was closed, and a fear like he'd never known clawed at his insides.

Dalton moved to the door. His hand trembled, dread welling inside him as he reached for the knob. He flung open the door and the first thing he saw was the open window.

Relief shot through him as he easily realized the scenario. Sinclair had somehow found the cabin. He'd come in through the front door and Janette had escaped through the window. But the relief was short-lived as he realized it was possible he'd find her body in the snow.

"She's outside."

Together the two men hurried back to the front door. When they stepped outside the wind nearly stole Dalton's breath away. It cut sharp and deep, and frantic need welled up inside him. Even if Sinclair hadn't found her, the elements would be as deadly as the determined lawman.

They hurried around to the back of the cabin. Dalton stopped at his truck only long enough to retrieve a flashlight. Trent looked at Dalton. "Which way would she have run?"

Dalton stared out at the wide expanse of pasture that surrounded them. Janette was smart. She wouldn't have just taken off running without a plan of some kind.

She would have headed toward Tanner's house. Confirmation of his thoughts lay on the ground in faint footprints. However, it wasn't dainty small feet that had left the prints. It was big boot prints that filled his heart with a new sense of terror.

If he'd had any doubt of what had happened here tonight, those large footprints froze them away and also froze a part of his heart.

"Janette," he yelled, but the howl of the wind competed with his voice.

He and Trent trudged through the snow, following the barely discernible footprints as Dalton swept the flashlight in front of them. Dalton felt as if they were moving in slow motion as they systematically searched the area looking for Janette…or her body.

As they walked, the mistakes Dalton had made roared through his head. He should have gotten his family involved, but he'd been so busy isolating himself, so worried about giving any part of himself away, that he'd made what he hoped wouldn't prove to be a fatal mistake.

"Dalton!"

Dalton turned at the sound of his name and saw Zack running toward them. "What's going on?" he asked when he caught up to Dalton and Trent.

"Brandon Sinclair is trying to kill Janette," Dalton said. "He raped her, and now he's trying to kill her. We have proof." He could see that Zack was confused, but he couldn't take the time to go through everything. "I'll explain later. Right now we need to find Janette."

Find Janette.

Find Janette.

The words pounded in Dalton's head as it began to snow once again. He was relatively certain she was out here without a coat and possibly without shoes. She wouldn't have taken time to bundle up before escaping out the window.

If they didn't find her soon the icy cold and snow would do the job for Sinclair. Unless the sheriff had already found her. Unless it was already too late.

The gunshot exploded the night and the sound ripped through Dalton's heart. *Too late,* his brain screamed. *You're too late to save her.*

"It came from over there." Zack pointed to the right and they all took off running.

The cold air sliced at his lungs as he raced toward the direction where they thought the shot had come. The flashlight beam bobbed as he ran and fear made him feel as if he were dealing with an out-of-body experience.

As the flashlight beam fell on the old storage shed, Dalton's blood ran cold. Brandon Sinclair stood in front of the shed, and when he saw the beam of light he whirled around to face them. He had his gun drawn and wore a fierce look of determination.

"Sheriff West, I'm glad you're here," Sinclair said, ignoring both Dalton and Trent. "I have my suspect holed up in this shed. I need her out of there and placed in my custody."

Dalton started forward, but Zack grabbed his arm to hold him in check. "We heard a gunshot," Zack said.

"I fired a warning shot to let her know I meant business."

"Looks to me like you fired that warning shot right through the door," Zack observed.

"Look, I don't want any trouble here. I just want to get my prisoner into custody and get her back to Sandstone," Brandon said.

"You lying son of a bitch," Dalton exploded. This time it was Trent who grabbed hold of him as he tried to lunge forward. "If you've hurt them I'll kill you." He tried to escape Trent's firm grasp. He needed to get inside that shed.

Why didn't Janette come out? Was it possible that the single shot Brandon had fired through the door had found her and she was now lying bleeding—or worse—on the other side of the door?

"I suggest you get your brother under control, Sheriff," Sinclair said.

Zack narrowed his eyes. "I suggest you put your gun away and let me figure out just what the hell is going on here."

"I told you what's going on," Sinclair exclaimed, impatience obvious in his voice. "I just want to get my prisoner and go home." He must have seen something in Zack's eyes that made him holster his gun.

"I'm afraid that isn't going to be possible," Trent spoke for the first time. He looked at Zack. "I'm Trent Cummings, special prosecutor, and I want you to place Sheriff Brandon Sinclair under arrest."

"For what?" Brandon's hand moved down toward his gun.

"Don't do it," Zack warned as both he and Trent advanced on Sinclair.

"Rape. You're under arrest for the rape and attempted

murder of Janette Black," Trent said as Zack plucked the gun from Sinclair's holster then cuffed him.

Dalton could stand it no longer. He raced for the shed door and tried to push it open, but it refused to budge. "Janette, it's me. Open the door."

The silence that greeted him was deafening. A sob ripped from him as he shoved and pushed against the door, hoping...praying that it wasn't her dead body blocking the way.

Trent helped, putting his shoulder against the door next to Dalton and together they managed to get the door open. "Janette!" Dalton cried, his flashlight frantically scanning the area.

He found her crouched behind an old love seat, her knife held tightly in one hand. "Is he gone?" she asked, her blue lips trembling uncontrollably.

The relief that crashed through Dalton nearly brought him to his knees. "It's over, honey. He can't ever hurt you again." Dalton helped her to her feet, noting that her eyes were huge in her deathly pale face. He hurriedly took off his coat and wrapped it around her slender shoulders as she cuddled Sammy tightly against her chest.

As they stepped out of the shed he gripped her closer to him as she saw Sinclair. "Whatever she's told you, it's a lie," he yelled and twisted his shoulders as if trying to escape from his handcuffs. "I'll admit we had sex, but she wanted it. She begged me for it."

Dalton tightened his arm around Janette's shoulders. "That's funny. The night you pulled Janette over for a speeding ticket, she had a tape recorder running. We've got that entire night's events on tape. You're going to prison."

Sinclair looked stunned.

Janette raised her trembling chin and smiled. "Gotcha," she said.

The night seemed to last forever. Dalton wanted Janette and Sammy to be taken to the hospital, but she refused, insisting that all she needed to recover from her ordeal was warmth.

They left the cabin and drove into town, where Sinclair was locked in the jail. The rest of them went to Dalton's apartment, where Janette was questioned by both Zack and Trent.

As the night progressed, she felt Dalton distancing himself. He grew quiet, adding nothing to the conversation, and his green eyes seemed to stare at everything in the room except her.

Her worst fear had been realized. Brandon Sinclair had found her, but she'd survived. Sammy had survived. And now Janette's future stood directly in front of her.

It was almost four when the talk was finally finished. She promised Trent that no matter where she and Nana settled, she'd give him their address so he could let her know when Sinclair would go to trial.

She would be the prosecutor's star witness, and that fact held a certain poetic justice that sent a sense of peace through her.

After Trent and Zack left, she fell into Dalton's bed, exhausted by the trauma of the night. Sammy slept peacefully next to her and she fought the impulse to pull him close against her, to assure herself that they both truly had survived.

As she'd hidden in the shed, she'd believed she wouldn't leave it alive. She had thought she'd never see Sammy take his first step, say his first real word. She'd believed she would never hear Nana's voice or see Dalton's handsome face again.

Sleep, when it finally came, drifted over her like a soft, warm blanket and held no nightmares. She awakened to the sun shining through the window and a sense of peace she'd never known before.

The man who had forever changed her life would now face Lady Justice and have his freedom taken away for a very long time. She no longer had to be afraid. She would not live her life looking over her shoulder.

She frowned as she stared at the window. The cast of the sun shining through the window made her realize it was late morning. Why hadn't Sammy awakened her?

She turned over and found the bed empty. Panic sliced through her for a split second, but it quickly ebbed. She wasn't sure exactly where Sammy was, but she knew he was safe, because they were in Dalton's apartment and Dalton wouldn't let anything happen to them.

Getting out of bed she tried to shove away the aching sadness that found her heart, the sadness of knowing that today she would tell Dalton a final goodbye.

After a quick stop in the bathroom to brush her teeth and wash her face, she belted her robe around her waist and went in search of the two men in her life.

She found them in the kitchen, and for a moment she

stood just outside the door and peeked in. Dalton sat at the table with Sammy on his lap. He was trying to feed Sammy rice cereal, but it looked as if Dalton was wearing more than Sammy was eating.

A smile didn't make it to her lips, but it squeezed her heart as she watched the man she loved interact with her precious baby.

"Come on, buddy. We can do this," Dalton said. "Don't you want to grow up to be big and strong?" He held a spoonful of the cereal and Sammy laughed and waved his hand, striking the spoon and sending the cereal to the front of Dalton's shirt.

"Why don't I just lay you against my chest and let you graze off my clothes?" Dalton muttered.

"Problems?" Janette asked as she stepped into the room.

"If he makes this big of a mess with cereal I can't wait to see him with a bowl of spaghetti," he said.

Again an internal fist squeezed Janette's heart. They both knew he wouldn't be around to watch Sammy eat spaghetti. He wouldn't be around to see that Sammy grew big and strong.

"Coffee's made," he said, as if he sensed the awkward moment between them.

"Thanks." She moved to the counter and poured herself a cup. "Usually when he gets to the point that he's knocking it out of the spoon instead of eating it, I figure he's finished." She sat at the table.

"That works for me," he agreed easily. He stood with Sammy in his arms and carried the little boy over to the sink. "I'm not sure who needs to be hosed down first, you or me," he said to Sammy, who grinned and released a string of gibberish.

When he had Sammy clean she held out her hands and he placed the baby on her lap, then sat once again at the table across from her.

"You look well-rested. I figured you could use a little extra sleep this morning, so when I heard Sammy start to fuss I got him."

"I appreciate it." She took a sip of her coffee as he stared at a point just over her head.

A new silence descended and she guessed it was the awkward silence of the end of a relationship when there was nothing more to say. She finished her coffee, then carried her cup to the sink. "I'm going to go take a shower and pack up my things."

"I'll hang out with Sammy so you can get showered," he offered.

As he took her son from her, she wanted to say something to break the somber mood between them, but she didn't. She simply went into the bedroom to take her shower and pack her belongings in preparation for going to the motel to meet Nana.

It was as she stood beneath the hot spray of the shower that she recognized that she couldn't leave here without telling Dalton how she felt about him. If she kept her feelings inside, she'd always wonder what might have been different if she'd spoken them aloud.

As she thought of baring her heart, a touch of fear fluttered inside her stomach, and that seemed ridiculous given what she'd just gone through the night before.

She'd faced a man whose sole desire was to see her dead, yet her heart beat just as wildly as she thought of facing Dalton and telling him how she felt.

As she packed her suitcase she found herself revisiting each and every moment of the time she had spent with Dalton. Who knew that when she'd walked out of that bus station so alone, so afraid, that she'd walk into the arms of a man whom she'd want to hold her for the rest of her life?

And he didn't want a wife. He had no desire for a family. She knew she could do nothing to change that, that her words of love would probably fall on deaf ears. But that didn't mean she didn't intend to speak them, because she refused to live the rest of her life with regrets.

When she pulled her suitcase into the living room, Sammy was propped up in the corner of the sofa and Dalton was playing peekaboo with him.

It amazed her that this big strong man had a soft center he displayed with Sammy. He was meant to be a father. He was meant to be *Sammy's* father. But, no matter how much she wanted it, no matter how much she needed it, she couldn't make him be something he didn't want to be.

He caught sight of her and stood. "It's still early," he said. "I thought maybe you'd like to go to the café in town and have lunch."

"Actually, I have something I'd like to say to you before you take me to the motel." She felt the swell of emotion in her chest as she gazed into his beautiful green eyes.

"Is something wrong?" He sank back to the sofa and patted the cushion next to him.

She remained standing, afraid that if she sat beside him, she'd fall to pieces. She searched her mind, struggling to find the right place to begin. "I don't know how I would have survived without you, Dalton."

He frowned and his eyes darkened. "You would have probably been just fine on your own. I spent most of the night kicking myself for all the mistakes I made."

"Mistakes? What are you talking about?"

"I almost got you killed last night because I didn't want to allow anyone else in my life. I should have had somebody at the cabin with you every minute that you were there."

"I have to accept part of the responsibility for the decision you made," she countered. "I made you swear that you wouldn't tell anyone I was there."

"But he could have killed you because I didn't do my job."

For the first time that day, she realized the deep torment he felt and hope blossomed in her heart. Surely a man who didn't care wouldn't be so tortured. Surely a man who didn't love her wouldn't care as deeply as what she saw shining from his eyes.

With a new courage she walked over to the sofa and sank down beside him. "You saved my life, Dalton. Without you I would have been out in the snowstorm alone and afraid. Without you I would have never had the courage to face Brandon Sinclair."

He smiled then, a soft smile that pierced straight

through to her heart. "I have a feeling you would have been just fine on your own. You're an amazing woman, Janette Black."

"You're an amazing man. In fact, you're so amazing I've fallen in love with you." Her breath caught in her throat as the words hung in the air between them.

He stared at her, and she wasn't sure if he was stunned or horrified by her words. He got up from the sofa as if goosed by an invisible hand and stepped back from where she sat.

"Janette, I appreciate the idea that you think you're in love with me, but I'm sure once you get away from here, once you get away from me, you'll realize it's not really love."

She would have been able to deal with him telling her he didn't love her. She would have accepted him explaining that he didn't feel the same way about her. But his attempt to negate her feelings altogether shot an edge of anger through her.

"Don't try to tell me what I feel and what I don't feel," she exclaimed as she got up from the sofa.

Dalton swiped a hand through his hair and frowned at her. "Look, you've just come off a roller coaster of traumatic events. We've been cooped up together, and emotions got out of control." He cast his gaze away from her but not before she saw something in his eyes that encouraged her.

She stepped closer to him. "Dalton, I don't know a lot of things, but I know that I'm in love with you, and there have been times in the last couple of days that

I believed that you were falling in love with me and with my son."

He looked at her then, his expression dark and unfathomable. "I'm sorry if I gave you that impression. I thought I'd been clear about the fact that I'm not interested in any long-term relationship or in having a family."

Even though she'd suspected their relationship would end this way, it didn't stop the hot press of tears that burned at her eyes. How was it possible that his eyes told her one thing and his mouth said another?

It didn't matter. Now that she'd bared her soul, all she wanted to do was escape. She walked over to where Sammy was sitting on the sofa and picked him up, cradling him close to her breaking heart. "I'd like to go to the motel now."

There was no point in spending another minute with him. She needed to get away, to cry, to mourn, to once again find some way to heal herself and move on.

He didn't argue with her. Instead he got her coat and silently they prepared to leave. She felt numb. She hadn't realized how much she'd hoped that he would take her in his arms, confess that he loved her, too, until that hope had been stolen away.

She should have known better, she thought bitterly as she got into his truck. He was an educated man who enjoyed listening to jazz and reading thick tomes. Why would he want to bind himself to an uneducated woman with a baby?

She gasped when she saw the infant car seat in the

backseat of his big cab. The fact that he'd thought of Sammy's safety only broke her heart again.

The drive to the motel was silent except for Sammy's cooing talk. She kept her gaze averted out the passenger window, afraid that if she looked at Dalton she'd cry.

She'd endured a rape and being chased out in the snow by a man who wanted to kill her, and she'd survived. And she would survive Dalton West's rejection, as well. But it was going to take time.

Dalton pulled up in front of the motel office and parked, then turned to look at her. His eyes radiated a deep pain. "You'll be all right?"

"Of course we will," she replied, her voice sounding clipped, brittle to her own ears. "Nana will be here around three and we'll figure out where we go from here."

"If you ever need anything…"

"We'll be fine," she quickly interjected. "You've done more than enough for us already." She opened the truck door and took Sammy out of the car seat as Dalton got out of the vehicle.

He grabbed her suitcase from the back and carried it to the front door of the motel office as she followed just behind him. She'd known telling him goodbye would be difficult, she just hadn't imagined it would be this difficult.

"I can get it from here," she said.

He nodded and set the suitcase down. "Here's the key to the room." He told her the number. "I guess this is goodbye."

"Before I tell you goodbye, I just want to say one more thing." She searched his stern features, remembering how they had softened into something beautiful as they'd made love, how they'd transformed with laughter as he'd interacted with Sammy.

She drew a deep breath and consciously willed away the tears that threatened. "Even though you don't love us, I hope you'll eventually open yourself up to loving some woman. You'd make a wonderful husband, Dalton, and you'd be an awesome father." The tears she'd tried to hold in now splashed onto her cheeks. "I don't know what made you decide to live your life alone, but you're cheating some woman from finding happiness with you, and you're cheating yourself, as well."

She didn't wait for him to answer. She grabbed the handle on the suitcase, turned and hurried away, eager to get into a room where she could cry in private.

Minutes later, she sat on the edge of one of the two double beds in the room and tried to keep the tears from flowing. She was afraid that if she started to cry she wouldn't be able to stop, and she didn't want Nana to arrive and see the depths of her despair.

Besides, she had a future to plan, a life to live. She knew eventually her heart wouldn't hurt so much, but at the moment it ached with unrelenting sadness.

One man had raped her and the other had thrown away her love. Both had left indelible scars on her soul, but it was Dalton's kindness, his passion and laughter that would linger in her thoughts for a very long time to come.

She stretched out across the bed, grabbed one of the pillows and cried into it, not wanting her sobs to disturb her sleeping son.

Later she would figure out where her life went from here, but for now she'd give herself time to mourn what might have been.

Chapter 15

Dalton opened his apartment door, stepped inside and drew in a deep, weary breath. She was gone. All trace of her and Sammy were gone except the faint scent of honeysuckle that lingered in the air.

The silence felt odd, but he knew eventually it would feel familiar and safe. He shrugged out of his coat and hung it in the closet, then eased down in his chair and stared around the room.

The painter he'd hired hadn't even begun the job yet. The walls didn't really need to be painted, but Dalton wouldn't cancel the job. Maybe the smell of fresh paint would remove the last trace of her scent from the apartment.

He leaned back in the chair and closed his eyes, fighting against the emotion that pressed tight in his chest. He'd done the right thing. He knew how these things worked. He'd learned the hard way by his experience with Mary. He didn't believe in repeating past mistakes.

Janette would move on, build a life and realize that what she'd really felt for him was nothing more than gratitude. However, he wasn't confused about his feelings for her. He loved her. His feelings for Janette were far deeper, far more profound than anything he'd felt for Mary.

A solitary life. That's what he'd believed he wanted, but now he realized how selfish he'd become. He'd guarded himself from not only women and dating, but also from his family and life.

For the first time he thought about all the reasons he'd distanced himself from his family, and for the first time he realized the answer.

His brothers had all found love. They'd found the special women with whom they would spend the rest of their lives and build happy families. He'd been glad for their happiness, but their happiness had pointed out the utter emptiness of his own life.

He needed to go into the office. He needed to do something, anything to get away from his own thoughts. He'd have one more cup of coffee then head to the West Protective Services office and spend the rest of the day there taking care of boring paperwork.

As he entered the kitchen and headed for the coffeepot his gaze fell on the bowl in the sink. It was half-full of rice cereal, and the sight of it convulsed his heart so hard, so unexpectedly, it brought tears to his eyes.

Janette wasn't the only one he'd fallen in love with. Sammy had stolen his heart the first time he'd grinned at Dalton and cooed.

"I did the right thing," Dalton said aloud, but his voice lacked conviction. He just didn't understand how doing the right thing could feel so terribly wrong.

"You look peaked." Nana stared at Janette closely as she stepped into the motel room. "You aren't getting sick, are you?"

"No, I'm not getting sick," Janette replied. Definitely heartsick, but that didn't count. She gave her grandmother a fierce hug. Nana dropped her small overnight bag on the floor and beelined to Sammy, who had awakened and had somehow found his own toes with his hands.

"Look at you!" Nana picked him up and nuzzled his neck. "You look like you've grown a foot." She settled on the bed with Sammy in her arms. "So, where are we going from here?"

Janette sat on the opposite bed and frowned thoughtfully. "I don't know. It's a decision I didn't want to make without your input."

"I'll be honest, if I had my way we'd go back to Sandstone and get a new trailer. I've got my friends there, but I know that isn't what you want, so whatever you decide is fine with me." Nana's smile was filled with love and her expression was soft as she gazed first at Janette, then at Sammy. "I just want you and this little boy to be happy. That's all I really care about."

At the moment happiness seemed a distant state that

no bus ride could ever take her to, but she didn't tell that to Nana.

"We don't have to make a decision right this minute," Nana said. "What I want to hear right now is how you and this Dalton of yours got Brandon Sinclair arrested."

This Dalton of yours. How she wished it were so. For the next thirty minutes she related all that had happened to Nana.

She'd just finished her story when a knock sounded. Janette jumped off the bed and opened the door to see Dalton. She'd left something behind, that was the first thought that jumped into her head at the sight of him. He was here to deliver whatever item she'd forgotten to pack.

"We need to talk," he said without preamble. He started to step inside but she held the door to keep him out.

"I'm all talked out," she replied.

"Janette, please. It's important." His body vibrated with tension and a fierce intensity radiated from his eyes.

Janette looked over her shoulder at Nana seated on the bed holding Sammy, then back at Dalton. "We can't talk in here."

"In my truck, then."

She hesitated, wondering if she could handle any more from him. "Okay, I'll be out in just a minute." She closed the door and turned to face her grandmother. "It's Dalton. He says he needs to talk to me. It's probably about the case." She grabbed her coat and pulled it on. "I should be back in just a few minutes."

Nana stared at her for a long moment. "Follow your heart, honey," she said as if she knew everything that had happened between Janette and Dalton.

Janette slipped out of the door and headed for his truck, all the while telling herself that she'd followed her heart and it had led her into pain.

She opened the passenger truck door and slid inside. "What's up?" she asked.

For what seemed like an eternity he stared directly ahead, as if she wasn't seated next to him and waiting for him to speak.

What was he thinking? Why was he here?

"A year ago I was on assignment in Tulsa guarding a woman who'd been the victim of domestic abuse." He didn't look at her but continued to stare out the front window. "We both got caught up in each other, started making plans for our future together. When the assignment was over I came back here to Cotter Creek, certain that within a short period of time Mary and I would begin to build a life together. But before that happened, she realized that she'd mistaken gratitude for love, had gotten caught up in the fantasy we'd spun. It was a fantasy that had nothing to do with reality."

His words stunned her, and her heart swelled with grief for him, for the dreams of happiness he'd obviously had for himself, dreams that had never come to fruition.

He turned and looked at her then, and his eyes were as dark, as mysterious as a primal forest. "My feelings for you have made me realize Mary was right. Not only did she not love me, but I wasn't really in love with her.

I'm in love with you, Janette, but I can't go through it again. I don't want to bind myself to you heart and soul only to find out a month or two from now that what you feel for me really isn't love after all."

"Dalton, there are many things in my life at the moment that I'm uncertain about, but my love for you isn't one of them." She reached out and placed her hand on his forearm, needing to touch him.

"I don't love you because you gave me shelter from a snowstorm, and I don't love you because you saved me from Brandon Sinclair. I love you because when you look at me, I feel strong and beautiful. I love the sound of your laughter and that little wrinkle you get in your forehead when you frown."

Tears filled her eyes as she continued. "I love your strength but I also love your weaknesses. Oh, Dalton, don't you see? I'm a woman who has been able to separate my feelings about Sinclair and what he did to me and love the result of that horrible act. I'm certainly able to know the difference between my gratefulness to you and my love for you."

His eyes began to sparkle with a light that warmed her heart. "What weaknesses?"

She laughed, because she saw her future shining from his eyes. "Hopefully we'll have many years together for me to point out each and every one of them."

He leaned toward her and traced his finger down the side of her face, all trace of humor gone. "Stay, Janette. Stay in Cotter Creek with me. Let me be more than just a temporary bodyguard in your life. Let me be the man who stands beside you and Sammy for the rest of your life."

"Yes," she whispered. "I want that."

"And I want it, too." He dropped his hand from her face. "And now we need to get out of this truck so I can really hold you in my arms and kiss you hard enough, love you enough that you never doubt how much I love you."

"Dalton West, you take my breath away," she said as she opened the truck door. They met in front of the truck and he grabbed her in an embrace that left no room for doubts, no question that her future would be one filled with laughter and love.

Epilogue

"How soon can we get out of here?" Dalton leaned over and whispered in Janette's ear.

Here was a tent on the West property where Meredith West and Chase McCall had just exchanged their wedding vows. It had been a beautiful ceremony and the late March weather had cooperated with a day of sunshine and blue skies.

The band was playing and people not only danced on the wooden dance floor, but also helped themselves to the banquet that had been prepared for the big event.

"Why are you in such a big hurry, Mr. West?" she asked lightly. "It's a beautiful day and Nana is baby-sitting."

"That's exactly my point, Mrs. West." His eyes glittered. "We could be spending this entire afternoon in bed."

Mrs. West. She and Dalton had married in a quiet ceremony at city hall two weeks ago, and she still thrilled at the words that identified her as his wife.

"Nana is keeping Sammy overnight so there's plenty of time for us," she replied with a grin.

At that moment Red West stepped up in front of them. "I make it a habit despite my arthritis to dance with every one of my daughters-in-law, and I haven't had the pleasure of dancing with you yet." He held out a hand to her.

Janette smiled warmly. "I'd be delighted." She took his hand in hers and together they walked toward the dance floor.

"I understand congratulations are in order," Red said as they began to move to the slow music.

A burst of pride filled Janette. "Yes. It was a long time coming, but I finally got my GED."

"And Dalton tells me you've already signed up for college classes for this summer."

"I have. I'm really excited about it. I hope to get a teaching degree and I'd love to teach first or second grade."

"You'll do well." Red smiled down at her and Janette felt his affection radiating from his pale blue eyes.

Over the past two months, Dalton's family had embraced her with warmth. Nana had gotten settled into a brand-new trailer on the lot where her old one had burned down, and Janette and Dalton were house-hunting, as the apartment was too small for a family.

The biggest news over the past two months had been the eight women who had contacted Trent to tell him that they, too, had been raped by Brandon Sinclair. Much to Janette's surprise, she had found herself something of a local hero.

"I'm a happy man today," Red said, and she followed his gaze to the area where the family was congregated together. "Tanner has his Anna and their new little baby. Zack is happy with Katie. Clay and Libby and little Gracie are building a wonderful life together. Savannah was the best thing that ever happened to Joshua, and Meredith has finally married the man who makes her happy."

"Then there's you." Once again he smiled. "You and that little boy put a smile on my son's face and a lightness to his step. All my kids have found love, and I expect their mama is smiling down from heaven."

Janette looked up at the old man. "And she must be proud of you for raising her children to be wonderful adults."

"I expect she is," he agreed as the music ended.

As he led her off the dance floor Dalton stood, his eyes gleaming with wicked delight. "She's a keeper, son," Red said as they reached him.

"I know, Dad. Believe me, I know." As Red left, Dalton leaned down to Janette. "Now can we get out of here? All this wedding stuff has made me want to spend alone time with my wife."

"I'll race you to the truck," she said and whirled around and began to run.

She heard his burst of laughter just behind her and she slowed to let him catch her as love swelled inside her. The storm had passed and spring had come, and it had brought with it all her heart desired

* * * * *

THE COWBOY'S
SECRET TWINS

Chapter 1

Melissa Monroe couldn't help but wonder if she was making a huge mistake. A fierce case of déjà vu filled her as she drove the Texas road. The lonely highway, the snow coming down from the overcast sky and the Christmas carols playing on the car radio all evoked memories of the last time Melissa had driven on this particular road.

It had been just a little over a year ago, only at that time the snow hadn't been comprised of pretty little flakes lazily drifting down, but rather a blizzard white-out condition that had eventually forced her to pull over.

A sexy stranger in tight jeans and a cowboy hat had rescued her. He'd told her his name was James and they'd ridden out the storm together in a vacant farmhouse.

It had been a wild and crazy night and she'd acted completely out of character. The consequences of her actions that night were in two car seats in the back.

Joey and James, who were a little over four months old, had been completely unplanned and unexpected, but since the moment she'd realized she was pregnant, they had been desperately wanted and loved.

She glanced back now to check on them and smiled. Snug as bugs they were in their little blue coats and matching hats. They'd been sleeping for the better part of an hour and Melissa hoped to get where she was going before they woke up demanding another meal.

Thirty minutes ago she'd passed the place in the road where she'd had to pull over during the storm a year ago. It was just outside the small town of Rockport, Texas. She was now ten minutes from the Texas town of Dalhart and her final destination.

On that night a year ago she'd been on her way from her home in Amarillo to visit a friend in Oklahoma. Tonight she was on her way to someplace just on the other side of Dalhart.

Tightening her hands on the steering wheel, she hoped she wasn't on some kind of a wild-goose chase. Suddenly all kinds of doubts crashed through her mind. Maybe she was a fool to trust her cyber friend, a woman she'd never met in person but had bonded with over the past year in a chat room for single moms.

MysteryMom had been a source of support, information and friendship over the past year. She'd helped Melissa through the difficult pregnancy. Then once the twins were born she'd been a font of advice on everything from colic to diaper rash.

MysteryMom and Melissa's best friend, Caitlin, were the only two people on earth who knew about the circumstances of the twins' conception.

Melissa suspected that MysteryMom had given her directions to her place, that she was bringing Melissa to her home for a face-to-face meeting and to spend the holidays together.

For the past couple of weeks Melissa had been depressed. Christmas was only four days away—the twins' first Christmas—and she hadn't even had any extra cash to buy a tree or a single present.

She'd always dreamed of giving her children the kind of Christmas she'd never had, with family gathered close and laughter in the air. It wasn't all about a lack of money that had depressed her, but certainly financial worries played a role.

She'd been working at building her own interior design business when she'd found herself pregnant. The pregnancy had been difficult and the business had fallen by the wayside. Since the twins' birth Melissa had been living on her savings, which were dwindling fast.

It had been all she could handle to take care of newborns, but after the first of the year she was determined to somehow provide for them and delve back into her work.

She slowed as she reached the Dalhart city limits. According to the directions MysteryMom had sent her she was to turn off the main highway and onto a country road approximately ten miles from where she was now.

With a new burst of nervous tension kicking up inside her, she pulled into a restaurant parking lot and grabbed her cell phone from her purse and punched in Caitlin's number.

"Are you there yet?" Caitlin asked when she answered.

"According to the map I'm about fifteen minutes from the place," Melissa replied.

"How's the weather? I heard they were calling for snow."

"It's been spitting a bit, but nothing to worry me," Melissa replied.

"I don't know why you just didn't plan on coming to my place for Christmas instead of taking off on this adventure of yours."

Melissa smiled into the phone. "You're going to have so many fancy parties to attend, the last thing you need is me and the boys hanging around." Caitlin was single and gorgeous and working up the corporate ladder at blinding speed. "Besides, look what happened the last time I was on my way to visit you."

"It's not my fault you got stuck in a blizzard and then decided to kick it with some sexy stranger."

"True, it wasn't your fault. I've decided it was all Tom's fault," Melissa replied and tried to ignore the faint pang of her heart at the thought of her ex-boyfriend.

"Ah, don't even mention that snake's name," Caitlin replied. "I thought he was a creep when you first starting dating him and he definitely proved me right."

"Water under the bridge," Melissa replied. "Anyway,

I just wanted to check in with you and let you know I'm almost there."

"You'll call me when you arrive? Tell me all about this MysteryMom of yours?"

"Definitely."

"And, Melissa, I hope you have an amazing Christmas. You deserve it."

Melissa put her cell phone back in her purse and pulled her car back on the road. Dusk was falling and she was eager to get to her destination before dark.

As she drove her mind filled with thoughts of Tom Watters. She'd thought they'd marry and build a family together and after two years of dating she'd begun to press him about setting a wedding date. He'd finally told her there wasn't going to be a wedding, that for the past six months he'd been involved with another woman, one who was much sexier, much more a woman than Melissa.

Once again she clenched her hands on the steering wheel as she thought of that moment. She'd immediately made plans to visit Caitlin, needing to get away from her dismal apartment and all reminders of Tom.

Reeling not only with a broken heart, but also with a damaged ego, she'd been easy pickings for the handsome stranger who had come to her aid.

Her cheeks burned hot as she remembered that night of unexpected passion. James had looked at her with such desire. He'd made her feel so sexy, so wanted. She'd never before experienced that kind of wild abandon and suspected she'd never experience it again.

She cast all these thoughts aside as she drew nearer

to the road her directions told her to take. As she left the small town of Dalhart behind, she spied the highway sign where she needed to turn.

In approximately ten miles she should be at the destination that she suspected was MysteryMom's home. Excitement danced in her chest as she thought of finally coming face-to-face with the woman who had been not only a friend, but also a surrogate mom through the trials and tribulations of being a single new mother to twins.

If she didn't like the looks of the place she'd turn around and make the two-and-a-half-hour drive back home. If she got any bad vibes at all, she'd just drive away. There was no way she'd put her babies or herself at risk.

The first surprise was the enormous stone monuments that marked the entry to the address she sought. The second surprise was when she drove down the tree-lined narrow drive and got her first glimpse of the house. No, *house* was too plain a word for the mansion that rose into view.

The two-story home was as big as a hotel, with several equally impressive outbuildings. Lights spilled with a cheerful welcome from several of the windows as the evening had begun to thicken with night shadows.

"Oh, my goodness," she whispered to herself. The whole place breathed money.

As she drove up the circular driveway she saw that one of the outbuildings was a stable and she was more convinced than ever that this was MysteryMom's house. MysteryMom had mentioned that she loved working with horses.

She parked the car and glanced into the backseat where Joey was awake. Of the two boys, Joey was the most laid-back. He rarely fussed and seemed content to take life as it came at him.

On the other hand, James was a handful. Demanding and impatient, he was the first to set up a frustrated cry if he needed a diaper change or a meal or if she took away his beloved rattle. But, he also had begun to belly laugh when happy and the sound of it never failed to delight her.

She looked at Joey, who gazed at her with bright blue eyes. "Are you ready to go meet Mommy's new friend?" she asked. He waved his arms as if to show his excitement.

As she got out of the car she realized it had grown darker, as if night hadn't just stealthily approached but had rather slammed down without warning.

She opened the door to the backseat and first unbuckled Joey and pulled him up on her hip, then went to the other door and did the same with James. In the past four months she'd become quite adept at not only carrying both boys, but also her purse and a diaper bag all at the same time.

The cold air chased her to the front door, where she managed to use her toe to knock. Her heart hammered with excitement as she waited for MysteryMom to answer. When the door opened her excitement transformed to stunned surprise.

He filled the doorway with his broad shoulders and lean hips, and his blue eyes widened with the same shock that she felt. His gaze swept over the two babies in her arms and his face paled.

James.

For a moment her mind refused to accept what she saw. "Henry? Who's here?" a feminine voice called from somewhere in the house.

Two thoughts flew into Melissa's head. Apparently his name wasn't James and he must be married. Oh, God, this was all a mistake. A terrible mistake.

Before she could take a step backward, before she could even move a muscle, a ping sounded next to her and the wood of the doorjamb splintered apart.

Everything seemed to happen in slow motion. Another ping resounded and James or Henry or whatever his name was leaned forward, grabbed her and pulled her inside the house. He slammed the door behind them.

"Call the sheriff," he yelled. "Somebody is shooting at the house." He opened a drawer in the ornate sideboard in the entry, pulled out a gun, then without a backward glance at her, disappeared out the front door.

Melissa stood in the center of the entry, her heart banging frantically. Mistake. This was all some sort of horrible mistake.

What kind of a man was her babies' father that somebody shot at the house the minute he'd opened his door? Was he a drug dealer? A criminal of some kind?

As Joey and James began to cry, Melissa fought back tears of her own.

Henry Randolf clung to the shadows of the house as he tried to discern exactly where the shooter might be.

He thought the attack had come from the stand of trees directly in front of the house.

As he moved forward he tried not to think about the woman who had appeared on his doorstep. Melissa, that was her name. She'd crossed his thoughts often over the past year, but he couldn't think about her now or the two babies she held in her arms. He couldn't afford to get distracted while somebody with a gun was on his property.

One problem at a time, he told himself. The shooter first, then he'd have to figure out what to do about his unexpected visitor.

He clenched his gun tightly as he worked his way to the stand of trees, listening for a sound, seeking a shadow that would indicate where the attacker might be. As he thought of how close those bullets had come to Melissa and those babies, a slow seething rage built up inside him.

This wasn't the first time he'd been shot at in the past week. Three days ago he'd been riding his horse across the pasture and somebody had taken a potshot at him. His mount had reared and taken off for the stables as Henry had pulled his gun to defend himself from the unknown.

He was still outside checking the area when the sheriff's car pulled up. Sheriff Jimmy Harrick lumbered out of his patrol car like a sleepy bear exiting a favorite cave. He pulled his collar up against the cold night air as Henry approached him.

"I've checked the area. There's nobody around now. The shots came from that stand of trees over there but it's too dark to see if there's any shell casings or evidence."

He pointed toward the house. "Let's go inside and talk." Henry didn't wait for a reply but headed for the door. He hadn't felt the cold when he'd first burst outside, but now the damp December air seeped into his bones.

"Got company?" Jimmy asked as they passed the older model car in the driveway.

"Yeah, an old friend." Henry's stomach kicked with nerves as he thought of the woman who had stood on his doorstep carrying twins who looked remarkably like he had when he'd been a baby.

Damn, what mess had he gotten himself into? He had a feeling his life was about to get extremely complicated.

As he and the sheriff walked into the living room he saw Melissa seated next to his mother on the sofa, each of them with a baby in their arms.

Melissa's blue eyes were wide with fear. He couldn't blame her. There was nothing like a welcoming committee of bullets to put that expression in a woman's eyes.

Henry tore his gaze from Melissa and focused on the sheriff. "Something's got to be done, Jimmy. This is the second time somebody has taken potshots at me in the past week."

Jimmy shoved his meaty hands in his pockets and rocked back on his heels. "I'm not sure what to do about it, Henry. There's no question that you've made some enemies with your decision to run for mayor."

"And so it's okay for somebody to try to kill me? Because they don't like my politics?" Henry was acutely aware of Melissa listening to every word, watching him with those amazing eyes of hers.

Jimmy pulled his hands out of his pockets. "Now, you know that's not what I'm saying," he protested. "I'm going back out there with my flashlight and I'll take a look around, then I'll head back to town and start asking questions. I'll let you know if I find anything. If I don't then I'll give you a call sometime tomorrow."

"Fine," Henry said curtly. He knew nothing more could be done tonight and in any case he was having a difficult time thinking about anything but the woman who sat next to his mother.

He walked Jimmy to the door, then closed and locked it and drew a deep breath to steady himself. How had she found him? They'd only exchanged first names on that crazy night they'd shared a little over a year ago and he hadn't even given her his real first name.

And then there were those babies. Henry had decided he was never going to marry and he'd certainly never planned to be a father, but there was little question in his mind about the paternity of those twins. Now he had to figure out what he was going to do about it.

He returned to the living room, where the two women on the sofa didn't appear to have moved, although Melissa and the two little boys no longer wore their coats.

His mother had that look on her face she used to get when he was a kid and had done something he knew he shouldn't do. He definitely had some explaining to do.

She stood and walked over to him and thrust the

baby she held into his arms. "I'm retiring to my room. It appears you and Melissa have a lot to talk about."

The little boy smelled of baby powder and gazed up at him with curious blue eyes. As Henry stared down at him the little boy's lips curved up in a sweet smile.

"That's Joey," Melissa said. "And I have James." She said the name with forced emphasis and he remembered that the night they'd been together he'd told her his name was James.

That night he hadn't wanted to be the wealthy Henry James Randolf III. He'd just wanted to be an ordinary cowboy named James. "My name is Henry. Henry James Randolf," he said.

As he looked at her several things struck him. She was still as pretty as he'd remembered her with her long blond hair and those big blue eyes, but she seemed tired and stressed.

Her cheeks grew pink beneath his scrutiny. "I don't quite know what to say. I didn't expect you."

He frowned and tightened his grip on Joey, who wiggled like a little worm. "What do you mean, you didn't expect me? You came here. You knocked on my door. Who else would you be expecting?" He sat in a chair across from the sofa as Joey leaned his head against his chest. To Henry's surprise his heart knocked hard.

"I thought I was coming to spend the holiday with a woman I met last year on the computer." Once again her cheeks warmed with color. "We met in a chat room for single pregnant women and she's been a wonderful source of support through my pregnancy and single parenting. She goes by the name of MysteryMom. She gave me this address, emailed me directions and told me to come here."

He eyed her suspiciously. The story certainly didn't have any ring of truth to it. "And how did she find me?"

Melissa raised a hand that trembled slightly to tuck a strand of shiny hair behind her ear. "I don't know. When we first got close I told her about the blizzard in Rockport and you coming to my rescue. All I knew about you was that your name was James and that you drove a black pickup with a license plate number that started with tin."

TIN-MAN, that's what his plate read. An old girl-friend who had proclaimed that he had no heart had dared him to get the personalized plate, and he never backed down from a dare.

"When I first realized I was pregnant," she contin-ued, "I went back to Rockport and asked around about you, but nobody had any clue who you might be. Some-body tried to kill you."

He blinked at the unexpected change of topic. "I think it was a warning, not a real attempt on my life. Our current mayor was diagnosed with cancer and has decided to resign. The city council has called an emer-gency election to be held in two months. I decided to run for the position and somebody apparently doesn't like my politics."

James began to fuss, waving his fists in the air and kicking his legs. "They're hungry," Melissa said. "If you could just show me to the kitchen, I'll fix them bottles, then we'll be on our way."

"On your way? You can't leave now," he protested.

"It's dark and getting later by the minute and I don't know if the person who fired that gun earlier is really gone from the area." He stood with Joey in his arms. "You'll stay here tonight and we can discuss everything further in the morning."

She stood and gazed at him with somber eyes. "You haven't even questioned if they're yours or not."

For the first time since he'd opened his door to her, he offered her a smile. "They look just like me. They even have my cleft chin. And I know we used no protection that night."

"I'm not here to cause you any trouble," she replied.

Henry nodded, although he wasn't so sure about that. "Let's go into the kitchen and get those bottles ready," he said.

Time would tell if she had really been led to his doorstep by some mystery cyber friend or if she was just another woman who had recognized who he was on the night of the blizzard and had found a way to cash in on the Randolf fortune.

Chapter 2

Melissa snuggled down in the bed in a guest room fit for a princess. The twins were sound asleep in an old playpen that Henry had found in the attic. It had been dusted off and the padding covered with a crisp, clean sheet. The boys were clad in their pajamas and sleeping beneath a cashmere throw that was as soft as a cloud.

She'd called Caitlin just to let her friend know that everything was all right and that it hadn't been MysteryMom's home she'd come to, but rather the man who was the father of her boys. She'd promised to let Caitlin know everything that happened when she returned home in the morning.

She was exhausted now, but sleep refused to come. The night had been filled with far too many surprises. The first had certainly been the sight of Henry as he'd opened the door. The second had been the bullets that had come precariously close to both her and her babies.

Even after the trauma of the shooting had passed she hadn't been able to get a read on Henry. He'd said little as he'd helped her bottle-feed the boys. She knew he had to be as stunned to see her as she'd been to see him.

They hadn't spoken much, just attended to the boys' needs, then he'd shown her to her room for the night with the promise that they'd talk further in the morning.

She didn't know what would happen. She had no idea what to expect from him, if he intended to be part of the boys' lives or not.

She'd resigned herself at the time of their birth to the fact that Joey and James wouldn't know their real father. At least now she wouldn't have to tell them the humiliating story of how she'd gotten pregnant by a stranger in a vacant farmhouse during the middle of a snowstorm.

MysteryMom must have somehow traced him with the partial license plate letters Melissa had mentioned. She obviously had resources Melissa didn't have. If MysteryMom had hoped for some kind of happy ending for Melissa, she was functioning in the world of make-believe.

Despite the intimate night they'd shared, Melissa and Henry didn't know each other at all. He hadn't even given her his real name that night.

Certainly he was in a social position to date all kinds of sophisticated, successful women. And the last thing Melissa was looking for was a man in her life.

Tom's betrayal still burned bright in her heart and if that wasn't enough, she had two little boys to raise.

She didn't want a man. She didn't want anything from Henry, except for him to be a father for her boys.

She'd been hoping to spend Christmas someplace where the spirit of the holiday was everywhere. There was no sign of Christmas in the Randolf home and in any case she didn't belong here.

First thing in the morning she'd be on her way back home to her little apartment and maybe on the way home she'd stop at a discount store and buy one of those little metal trees in celebration of the twins' first Christmas.

She finally fell asleep and dreamed of that night with Henry in front of the fire he'd built to warm them through the snowy night. The heat of the flames had been nothing compared to the fire in his kisses, the warmth of his hands on her body.

When she woke up bright sunshine drifted through her bedroom window, not the faint light of dawn she was used to, but full sunlight that let her know it was late.

The boys!

She shot up and looked at the playpen. It was empty. She jumped out of bed and yanked on her robe. Henry had gotten her suitcase from the trunk of her car the night before despite her protests that the gunman might still be out there lying in wait for him. She'd held her breath until he was back in the house safe and sound.

Now her breath caught once again in her throat as she raced out of the bedroom and down the grand staircase to the lower level of the house.

She heard voices coming from the formal dining

room and headed there, her heart beating frantically as all kinds of irrational fears whirled through her head. She flew into the room and stopped short.

The boys were in their car seats on the polished mahogany wood of the huge table. Henry's mother, Mary, stood in front of them, shaking a rattle at first one, then at the other as they bubbled with laughter.

"Melissa," Mary said with a smile that faltered as Melissa sagged against the doorjamb. "Oh, dear, we frightened you, didn't we?"

"I woke up and they were gone. I wasn't sure what to think." Melissa's heart slowed its frantic pace.

"It was Henry's idea really," Mary said. "You looked so tired last night and he thought it would be nice if you got to sleep in a bit this morning. So we sneaked into your room around dawn and grabbed these two little bundles of love and brought them down here. We gave them each a bottle and then I gave them a little sponge bath and changed their clothes. I hope you don't mind."

Melissa wanted to be angry that they'd obviously riffled through the diaper bag and taken her boys from their bed. But the look on Mary's face as she gazed at the twins made it impossible for Melissa to maintain anger. Besides, if she were perfectly honest with herself the extra couple of hours of sleep had been glorious.

"You know, I never thought I'd live to see grandbabies. Henry is quite the confirmed bachelor so I'd resigned myself to the fact that there would probably never be grandchildren." She smiled at the twins. "But these two are like gifts from heaven."

Melissa smiled. "You haven't changed one of their

messy diapers yet. That might change your mind about gifts from heaven."

Mary laughed. "Oh good, you have a sense of humor. I'm so glad. And now if you'll get dressed I'll have Etta make you some breakfast. Henry and I have already eaten."

"Oh, that's not necessary," Melissa replied. "I'm not much of a breakfast person and besides, I'd like to get back on the road as soon as possible." She not only wanted to get back to Amarillo, but she was still determined to stop someplace on the way home and pick up a few things to bring Christmas to her tiny apartment.

At that moment Henry appeared in the opposite doorway. He seemed bigger than life, his presence sucking some of the oxygen out of the air.

He looked like the rugged, handsome cowboy she'd met on the road that night. Clad in a pair of fitted jeans and a flannel shirt that emphasized the width of his broad shoulders, he let his gaze sweep the length of her before he smiled and said good morning. Even though he smiled, his eyes remained shuttered, enigmatic.

Melissa was suddenly aware of the fact that her robe was tatty and frayed and her hair was probably sticking out in every direction. She hadn't even washed her face before hurrying down the stairs.

"I'm just going to run upstairs and shower. I'll be right back."

"When you come back down I'd like to have a talk with you," Henry said.

She nodded and backed out of the dining room then escaped back up the stairs. There had been an edge in

Henry's tone of voice when he'd said he wanted to talk to her that worried her.

This whole trip had been a nightmare. The unexpected presence of a man she'd never thought she'd see again, bullets splintering a door and now the promise of a conversation she had a feeling she didn't want to have.

He was probably going to tell her to take her babies and leave, that being a dad didn't fit into his lavish single lifestyle. And even though that was fine with her, it made her heart hurt just a little bit for her sons.

She knew what it was like to grow up without a father. She remembered the empty ache his absence had created inside her and she certainly hadn't consciously chosen that for her boys.

Minutes later, as she stood under a hot spray of water she found herself again wondering what MysteryMom had hoped to accomplish by leading her here. Of course it would be nice for the boys to have a father in their lives. She wanted that for them. But she wasn't in control of Henry's reaction to instant parenthood.

Mary had said he was a confirmed bachelor. It was definitely possible a bachelor wouldn't want to be saddled with two little boys who required a lot of time and attention.

By the time she'd finished her shower and dressed, nervous energy bounced around in her stomach. She certainly didn't know Henry well enough to second-guess what he might want to discuss with her, but it didn't take a rocket scientist to know that it had something to do with Joey and James.

Despite the night of desire they'd shared, since the

moment she'd arrived at this mansion Henry frightened her more than a little bit. Oh, she wasn't physically frightened of him. What scared her most was the fear of him rejecting his sons, sons that he'd never wanted and had never asked for.

When she returned downstairs Mary had the boys on their tummies on a blanket in the living room. She smiled at Melissa. "That James, he's a feisty one, isn't he? He reminds me of Henry when he was a baby. Demanding and impatient, there's going to be no holding him back when he starts to walk."

James arched his back, raised himself up and grinned at Melissa, as if relishing the very idea of being independent and mobile. Meanwhile, Joey rolled over onto his back, perfectly content to play with his fingers.

"It must be hard, being a single parent to twins," Mary said.

"I manage okay," Melissa replied with a touch of defensiveness.

"I'm sure you do, dear. Henry is waiting for you in the study," Mary said. "It's down the hall and the first door on your right."

Melissa nodded and with one last look at her contented boys, she went down the hall to the study. The door was closed and she knocked on it with a gentle tap.

She heard him tell her to come in and she opened the door. Henry sat behind a massive mahogany desk and although he smiled at her as she stepped into the room, it did nothing to alleviate her nervousness.

The study was as beautifully appointed as the other rooms in the house. A stone fireplace took up one wall and floor-to-ceiling bookcases filled another. "Melissa, please have a seat." He gestured to the chair in front of the desk. She sank down and tried not to be intimidated by the surroundings, by him.

"Mom said you were eager to get on the road and head home, but I wanted to talk to you about the possibility of you staying through Christmas," he said.

"Oh, I'm not sure…" She paused as he held up a hand to stop whatever she was about to say.

"We're forever linked now by those boys and despite the fact that we had that night together, I don't know anything about you."

Oh, but he did, she thought. He knew she liked to be kissed just below her ear, that if he stroked her breasts she moaned deep in the back of her throat. A whisper of longing swept through her as she remembered that night and him. She forced herself to focus on what he was saying.

"We stopped having anything to celebrate at Christmastime three years ago when my father unexpectedly died of a heart attack on Christmas Day. Since then Christmas each year has slid by with little celebration in this house. But this year we have something to celebrate. The twins. I'd like to give them a terrific first Christmas, so please tell me you'll stay."

Her first instinct was relief, that he wasn't casting the boys out and that he apparently wanted to get to know them better. Still, there was one thing that made her relief short-lived. "I have to be honest. I haven't forgotten those bullets that flew when I arrived here," she said. "I don't want to put Joey and James in harm's way." She fought against a shiver as she thought of the bullets that had come far too close to them the night before.

"I feel more comfortable with you here rather than going back outside," he replied. "Somebody is being a nuisance, obviously attempting to make me rethink my position in running for mayor, but I won't let any harm come to you or the children."

She considered his words thoughtfully and believed him. There was something solid about him, a strength in his eyes that let her know he wouldn't allow danger to come to her or her babies.

He was their father and all he was asking was for her to remain a couple more days. Surely there was no harm in that, in giving him and his mother the first Christmas with the boys.

"Okay," she finally replied. "We'll stay through the holiday." She had no idea if it were the right thing to do or if it was possible she was making a terrible mistake.

A wave of satisfaction swept through Henry at her reply. From the moment she'd stepped into the study he'd smelled her, a familiar scent of fresh flowers with a hint of vanilla. It was the same fragrance she'd worn the night they'd been snowbound together and it stirred all kinds of crazy memories inside him.

As she stood and tucked a strand of hair behind her ear he remembered how soft, how silky her hair had been beneath his touch. That wasn't all he remembered. There was the taste of her mouth open to his, the spill of her warm, full breasts into his palms and the moans that had escaped her at his every touch. Desire slammed into his stomach, hot and wild and completely unexpected.

He had no idea if he trusted her, hadn't spent enough time with her to know if he even liked her, but that didn't stop him from wanting a repeat of what they'd shared on that snowy night.

"Good. We'll make it a Christmas to remember," he said and stood.

She backed toward the doorway, as if eager to escape him. "I'm going to take the boys upstairs for their morning naps. I'll see you later."

"Melissa," he said, stopping her before she could disappear from the room. "I don't even know your last name."

She smiled, the first real smile he'd seen from her, and the gesture lit her up from the inside out. "Monroe. Melissa Monroe."

The minute Melissa left the study Henry leaned back in his chair and gazed thoughtfully out the window. From this vantage point he could see the carriage house in the distance. It was a two-bedroom self-contained cottage that was occasionally used as guest quarters.

Henry had been living there before his father's death. His heart constricted as he thought about his dad. Not a day went by that Henry didn't miss him. Big Henry, as he'd been called, had not only been father, but he'd also been friend and mentor to his only son. The two of them had worked side by side running Randolf Enterprises, which was comprised of not only the ranch but also oil wells and enormous financial holdings.

There were people in town who were threatened not

only by the financial power Henry possessed, but also by his decision to run for the position of mayor and clean up the corruption he knew ran rife through the city offices of Dalhart.

He had a couple suspicions of who might have taken those shots at him, but suspicions didn't work for an arrest. He also suspected that whoever had shot at him hadn't really tried to kill him but rather was just warning him, hoping he'd decide not to run for mayor.

Those gunshots didn't scare him half as much as the idea that Melissa might not allow him to be as big a part of the boys' lives as he wanted.

"Henry?" His mother entered the study, her features worried. "Is she going to stay?" She sat in front of him in the chair that Melissa had vacated.

"She didn't tell you?"

"I was in the kitchen speaking with Etta about dinner. Melissa took the babies and went upstairs before I got a chance to ask her."

"She's staying until after Christmas." He leaned forward. "I don't quite know what to make of her. The story she told me about some cyber friend giving her directions here sounded more than a little bit shady."

"You think she's after money?"

"It certainly looks like she could use it." He frowned as he thought of the rusted old car out front, the frayed robe that had hugged her curves that morning.

Mary leaned back in her chair and folded her hands in her lap. "You want to tell me how this happened?"

Henry grinned at her. "You need a lesson in biology?"

She scowled at him. "You know what I mean, Henry. I've never heard you mention this woman's name before and yet she shows up here with two babies who are obviously yours."

"Remember the blizzard we had at the beginning of December last year? The night I couldn't get home from Hilary's because of the whiteout conditions?"

"That was the night you broke up with that woman."

Henry nodded. "I was on my way home when the conditions got impossible to drive in. As I pulled over to the side of the road I saw another car there and Melissa was inside. I had no idea how bad the weather was going to get and I'd just passed the old Miller place and knew it was vacant, so I got her out of her car and we holed up there for the night."

Mary raised a hand. "That's all I need to know about the particulars. Is it possible she knew who you were?"

Henry pulled a hand down his lower jaw. "I don't know. I suppose anything is possible. I've always been so careful. I've always recognized how vulnerable I was to gold diggers."

Mary arched an eyebrow upward. "Need we mention Hilary's name?"

Henry smiled as he thought of the woman he'd been dating and had broken up with the afternoon of the blizzard that had brought him and Melissa together.

"Hilary might be a gold digger, but she never kept that fact a secret," he replied. Since the day of their breakup the attractive brunette hadn't stopped waging her battle to become Mrs. Henry Randolf III. She called him or came by at least once a week in an attempt to seduce him back into her arms.

Mary straightened her back and sniffed indignantly. "That woman couldn't wait to marry you and have me shut up in a nursing home someplace. The evil witch."

And that had been the very reason Henry had broken up with Hilary. It was at the moment she mentioned that she thought it would be uncomfortable living with Mary and that Hilary had been searching for a nice nursing home for the older woman when Henry had recognized there would never be a future with her and certainly not a marriage.

"You don't have to worry about that," he said to his mother. Once again he leaned back in his chair and cast his gaze out the window.

"I never really thought about having kids," he said softly. "But now that they exist I want them here with me. I want them to grow up here on the ranch and learn the family business. I want to teach them like Dad taught me."

"Aren't you forgetting one little thing? Melissa might not want to move here. She might have a perfectly fine life, perhaps with a boyfriend or family of her own."

Henry frowned thoughtfully. "I find that hard to believe. I mean, according to her story she took off from her home to meet some cyber friend and spend Christmas with her. If Melissa has family or a boyfriend, why didn't she stay home to spend Christmas with them?"

"I'm sure I don't know. You know her better than I do. But, Henry, you have to remember that just because you want something doesn't mean you can have it. You're talking about a woman here, not a business deal."

Mary stood. "All I know is that I intend to enjoy each and every minute of having those babies in this house. And now I'm going to go make a shopping list. There's only two shopping days left before Christmas and suddenly I'm in the mood to shop."

She practically floated out of the study. Henry hadn't seen his mother this happy since his father had been alive.

Even though he'd had the entire night to process the fact that he was now a father, he still wasn't sure how this was all going to work. The first thing he would have to do was get to know Melissa, find out if she'd come here looking for easy street or if the story she'd told him was true.

But before he could do that he had some phone calls to make. He'd promised Melissa a Christmas to remember and Henry never broke a promise.

His mother was wrong about one thing—this *was* a business deal. Melissa had what Henry wanted and all Henry had to figure out was what price he'd have to pay to get it.

Chapter 3

Melissa stood at the window and watched as a car pulled up out front and Mary got into the car's passenger side. When the vehicle pulled away Melissa wondered if she should be doing the same thing—driving out the main gates and heading for home.

Behind her in the playpen the two boys had just fallen asleep. They usually napped for about an hour in the morning and the same amount of time in the afternoon.

Restless energy coursed through Melissa and she moved to the window on the opposite side of the room to gaze out at the pastures, corrals and outbuildings on the land. In the distance she could see what appeared to be a carriage house.

The dusting of snow that had fallen the evening before had melted beneath the warmth of the sunshine. It was a beautiful day, cold but clear.

A whisper of noise whirled her around and she saw Henry standing just outside the room in the hallway. He motioned to her and she left the room. "I thought maybe while the boys napped you might want to have a cup of coffee with me. I'd like to get to know you, Melissa."

Once again nervous energy fluttered in her chest. Of course he wanted to know her better. She was the mother of his children. "And I'd like to get to know you better," she agreed. "Coffee sounds wonderful."

She checked on the boys to make sure they were still asleep, then followed him down the staircase to the dining room where Etta, the Randolf cook, carried in a tray laden with two cups of coffee, cream and sugar and two small plates with slices of cinnamon coffee cake.

Henry introduced the older woman to Melissa. "Etta has been keeping the Randolf family well fed for the past twenty years."

"And it's been a pleasure," Etta replied. Then with a friendly smile at Melissa she turned and left the dining room.

Melissa pulled a coffee cup before her and wrapped her fingers around it. As Henry watched her she felt ill at ease and wasn't sure what to say, where to begin.

"This is awkward, isn't it?" he finally said.

She flashed him a grateful smile. At least he felt it, too. "Terribly awkward," she agreed. "I know you have no reason to believe me, but it's important to me that you know that I don't just fall into bed with strangers I meet."

She couldn't hold his gaze and instead looked down at her coffee as she continued. "That morning the man I'd been dating for two years, the man I thought I was going to marry, let me know that he had found a new girlfriend, somebody sexier than me." She felt her cheeks warm with her confession. "That night I just… It all went more than a little crazy."

He laughed, a low chuckle that was both pleasant and surprising. She looked up at him sharply, wondering if he were laughing at her.

"It seems fate had a hand in our meeting that night. I was coming home after ending a relationship with a woman I'd been dating for over a year. Maybe we were both a little reckless that night."

"But that's not who I am," she replied. "I'm usually not reckless."

He took a sip of his coffee, eyeing her over the rim of his cup. "And yet you took off with an address to an unknown place given to you by a woman you've never met before."

"A calculated risk," she replied. "If I didn't like the looks of the place when I arrived, I wasn't going to stop." She tugged on a strand of her hair in frustration. "Okay, it wasn't the brightest thing in the world to do," she conceded.

She wasn't about to tell him that it was an aching loneliness that had driven her to meet MysteryMom. Although she loved her boys more than anything else on the face of the earth, she'd been hungry for adult conversation. The idea of spending the holiday alone had depressed her.

She reached for one of the plates and a fork. Whenever she was nervous she wanted to eat and it was impossible to ignore the heavenly scent of the cinnamon that wafted from the coffee cake.

"Okay, let's start with the basics," he said. "Henry James Randolf, thirty-five years old, rancher and oilman. I'm a Taurus. I like my steak rare and sunrise rides on my horse. I've been told that I'm stubborn but I don't necessarily see that as a fault. I'm not a big drinker but I do like a glass of scotch or brandy in the evenings. Now, your turn."

"Melissa Sue Monroe, thirty years old. I'm a Libra and I like my steak well-done. Before I got pregnant I was working to build my own interior design business. I've never been on a horse and my drink of choice is an occasional glass of wine. Oh, and I've been told I have a bit of a stubborn streak, too."

He smiled, although she noticed that the gesture didn't quite warm the blue of his eyes. "What about family?" he asked.

She shook her head and paused to take a bite of the cake. "I don't have any. My father left when I was five, told my mother he wasn't cut out for family life. I never saw him again. My mother passed away two years ago and since then it's just been me...and of course, the boys."

"You have friends who give you emotional support?"

"My best friend lives in Oklahoma, so I don't see her very often. As far as other friends, to be honest the birth of the twins has pretty much put an end to any social life for me."

"How's your interior design business?"

She considered lying. She thought about telling him that she was wildly successful, but he was obviously an intelligent man. He only had to take a glance at her car and note the worn condition of her clothing to know that the money wasn't rolling into her household.

"Nonexistent," she finally said. "The pregnancy was difficult and for the last three months of it, I couldn't work. Since then it's been just as difficult. The boys have required all my time and energy." She raised her chin. "But after the holidays I'm going to try to get back to work."

She took a sip of her coffee and wished he didn't smell exactly like she remembered from that snowy night, a scent of clean male and wintry air and a faint whisper of spicy cologne. It was a fragrance that stirred her with memories of warm hands and hot kisses.

"How have you been supporting yourself?" he asked.

"I had a small inheritance from my mother." She shifted positions beneath the intensity of his stare and took another bite of her coffee cake.

"You have a boyfriend? Somebody significant in your life?"

A small laugh burst from her. "Definitely not. The only males in my life wear diapers and drool."

This time the smile that curved his lips warmed the blue of his eyes. "At least they're cute when they drool." His smile faded. "I'm sorry I wasn't there to help through the pregnancy. I'm sorry you had to go through it all alone and I promise you won't be doing it all alone now."

She wasn't sure why his words, rather than comforting her, filled her with a new burst of apprehension. Maybe if she really knew him, knew what kind of a man he was, she wouldn't feel so worried about what he might have in mind for her and the boys.

"Having grown up without a father figure in my life, I understand how important the role of father is and will be to my boys. I want you to know that I'm open to a discussion about visitation for you," she said.

"There will be time to discuss the particulars of that over the next couple of days," he replied. He took a sip of his coffee and leaned back in his chair. "So, are you originally from Amarillo?"

She nodded. "Born and raised there." This was the kind of talk they might have had if they'd been on a date, the kind they should have had that night instead of falling on each other like two sex-starved teenagers.

"Do you have somebody special in your life? A woman you're seeing? I don't want my presence here to make any problems for you," she said.

"You don't have to worry. There's nobody special. I don't intend for there ever to be anyone special." There was a firm finality in his voice.

She took another sip of her coffee. God, the man was so good-looking she couldn't imagine the women in the area leaving him alone. "Your mother mentioned that you were a confirmed bachelor."

"I am. The only reason I might have entertained the idea of marriage would have been to have a son to pass the ranch to when I died. You've managed to give me two without the nuisance of a marriage."

Nuisance of marriage? Funny how different they were, Melissa thought. She'd wanted to be married for a very long time, had always thought that by the time she turned thirty she'd be part of a family like she'd never had growing up.

She still hoped for that someday. The only difference her dream had from reality was that in reality her boys would have their real daddy and then maybe eventually they'd have a loving, caring stepfather.

But at the moment, any kind of relationship with a man seemed impossible. She was just too tired to even think about romance. She'd been tired for months, not that she minded. The twins were more than worth any exhaustion they caused.

"You look tired, Melissa," he said as if he'd read her thoughts. "I hope you'll take your time here and allow my mother and me to help so that you can get some extra rest. It can't be easy dealing with twins all by yourself."

"I'm fine," she assured him. "It's gotten easier since they sleep through the night most of the time now."

"Still, I hope you'll let us take some of the burden for the next couple of days."

"They aren't a burden. They're my joy," she exclaimed a bit more vehemently than the situation warranted.

He leaned forward and reached out and brushed the corner of her mouth. "You had a little cinnamon," he said as he pulled his hand back.

She grabbed a napkin and wiped her mouth and tried to ignore the electric jolt his touch had shot through her body. *He just swiped your mouth,* she told herself. A simple, casual touch and yet she felt it from head to toe.

A loud knock sounded on the front door and he pushed back from the table. "You might want to come with me to answer it," he said. "I think it's for you."

"For me? Who would be here for me?" She got up from the table and followed him to the front door.

He looked outside, then smiled and this time his smile warmed her completely. "It's Christmas, Melissa. Christmas has officially arrived at the Randolf house."

Henry opened the door to allow in the four ranch hands who maneuvered a huge evergreen tree through the door. The boughs were tied down and Hank and Tim, the ranch hands bringing up the rear, carried between them a huge pot to stand the tree in.

"It was the biggest one old man Keller had on his lot," Charlie said as they carried the tree into the living room.

"Melissa, can you help me move the coffee table?" Henry asked.

She quickly grabbed one side and he grabbed the other. They moved the table out of the men's way. "Just set it up in the corner," he instructed.

"That's the biggest tree I've ever seen," Melissa said, her eyes round with wonder.

Henry smiled. "I told them to get the biggest one they could find. We'll decorate it this evening after dinner."

"We could string popcorn and cranberries." She flushed and shook her head as if irritated with herself.

"That was silly of me. I'm sure you have lovely expensive ornaments."

He could tell she was embarrassed and he found that oddly endearing. "Actually, I've always wanted to do a tree the old-fashioned way. I think it would be fun to string popcorn and cranberries."

The look she gave him was so sweet, so grateful, that he once again felt a stir of desire deep in the pit of his stomach. When he'd brushed the trace of cinnamon from her lip moments earlier, he'd wanted to kiss it off.

He focused on watching his men wrestle the tree into the stand. Something about Melissa touched him, a vulnerability, a wistfulness in her eyes that he hadn't seen in a woman's eyes for a very long time.

He still didn't trust her. The only woman Henry really trusted was his mother, who had no ulterior motive for loving him. Any other woman he'd ever allowed close had ultimately shown herself to be more interested in the Randolf fortune than in whatever Henry could offer her as a man.

He didn't know if perhaps Melissa was just smarter than them all and had managed to trap him like none of the other women had managed to do.

Once the men had the tree up and the ropes off, Henry introduced Melissa to them. "These are some of the best ranch hands in the state of Texas," he said. "That's Hank and Tim, Ben and Mike and Jacob and that rascal with the black hat is Charlie, my right-hand man."

Melissa's eyes had glazed over and he smiled at her. "Don't worry, there won't be a test later," he said.

She laughed and the sound of her musical laughter shot a rivulet of warmth through him. "Good, because you lost me at Hank." She smiled at all the men. "But it's nice to meet you all."

"I'll be right back," Henry said to her as the men began to head for the front door.

In the entry he touched Charlie's shoulder and motioned for Charlie to stay behind while the rest of them got back to their work.

"You heard about the shots fired last night?" he asked.

Charlie nodded. "Jimmy talked to a couple of us late yesterday evening."

"I want all of you armed while on the property until we know what's going on," Henry said. "And I'd like to work a couple of you in shifts so that somebody is always working the house. Talk to the men and see what kind of schedule you can arrange."

Charlie's eyes narrowed. "You looking for more trouble?"

Henry released a small sigh of frustration. "To be honest, I'm not sure what I'm looking for, but twice now somebody has taken potshots at me and I don't like the idea of anyone on my property attacking me or mine."

"We'll work out a schedule and I'll get it to you this afternoon," Charlie replied.

"Thanks, Charlie. I really appreciate it," Henry replied.

"It's no problem. We can't let the boss get hurt." With these words he stepped out the door.

Henry watched him catch up to the other men. Charlie was a good worker, always pitching in for even the dirtiest jobs. When Henry had broken up with Hilary he'd worried that he was going to lose Charlie. Hilary was Charlie's sister and Henry had feared that Charlie might feel compelled to stop working for him because of sibling loyalty. But Charlie had assured him that he wasn't going anywhere and that he didn't get involved in his sister's affairs.

Henry had gotten the impression that there was no love lost between the two. In any case, he was grateful that he hadn't lost Charlie. Good workers were hard to find.

In fact, he was going to have to let Hank go. He'd noticed the tall, thin man had smelled like a brewery despite the fact it wasn't even lunchtime. Henry had already warned him twice about drinking on the job. There wouldn't be any more warnings.

He closed the front door and returned to the living room to find Melissa gone. She'd apparently gone upstairs to check on the twins. He walked over to the large floor-to-ceiling windows and gazed out to the outbuildings in the distance. The tree was only the first of the deliveries that would take place over the next two days.

The brief conversation he'd had with her over coffee had told him exactly what he needed to know. She had no family and he suspected she had few friends. That would make what he had in mind much easier. All he had to do was convince Melissa that his plan was in the best interest of them all.

He looked up as he heard the sound of her coming

274 The Cowboy's Secret Twins

down the stairs, a baby on each hip. He hurried to meet her halfway and took one of the boys from her.

As he scooped the little one from her arms he tried not to notice the warmth of her body, that scent of her that half dizzied him with memories.

"Which one do I have?" he asked.

"Joey," she replied.

"How can you tell the difference?" The little boy snuggled against Henry's chest, as if aware that he was held in loving arms. Once again the heart that Henry didn't know he possessed filled with a strange wonder and a fierce sense of protectiveness.

"Once you get to know them better, it's easy to tell them apart by their personalities," she said as they hit the landing. "But the quickest way is that Joey has a tiny scar in his right eyebrow. He was reluctant to be born and the doctor had to use forceps."

Henry looked at the little boy in his arms and noticed the tiny scar at the corner of his eyebrow. Joey grinned up at him and reached for his nose. Henry laughed as he dodged the little hand.

James kicked his feet and wailed, his face turning red as Melissa wrestled with him. "He's hungry and he has no manners," she said.

"Ah, a boy after my own heart," Henry replied. "Let's go to the kitchen and get them some lunch."

The kitchen was a huge room although Henry and Mary rarely took meals there. This was Etta's space but it was also the easiest place to feed two hungry little boys.

Etta was in the process of preparing lunch, but

smiled with welcome as they all entered. Henry got the car seats that were serving as high chairs and placed them in the center of the large oak table, Once the boys were settled he watched Melissa prepare two small bowls of cereal.

As she approached the table he held out his hand for one of the bowls.

"You might want to put on a hazmat suit," she warned as she gave him one of the bowls and a small baby spoon. "They not only like to eat cereal, they also like to blow it and spit it and play in it."

Feeding Joey was a pleasure like Henry had never known before. The kitchen filled with laughter as he and Melissa spooned cereal into their waiting mouths, off the front of their shirts and themselves.

"Well, this sounds like fun," Mary exclaimed as she came into the kitchen.

"Ah, the shopper is home," Henry said as he wiped off Joey's face then handed him his bottle.

"Randy is putting my purchases upstairs in my room." She smiled at Melissa. "It's been far too long since this house had such laughter in it. And the tree, it's going to be just lovely."

"Melissa thought it would be fun to string popcorn and cranberries for the tree," Henry said.

Mary clapped her hands together. "What a lovely idea. We'll have a real old-fashioned tree trimming. I'll make hot cocoa and we'll play Christmas music and have such fun."

Melissa looked from Mary to Henry. "You both are

so kind," she said and once again he saw a touch of vulnerability in the depths of her eyes.

"Nonsense, you're family now," Mary replied.

But she wasn't family, Henry thought. She was still a stranger. And she would never really be family, he mentally added. Sure, he had a strong physical attraction to her and she was the mother of his boys, but she would never be anything more than that to him.

His father had spent a lot of years warning Henry about the women who would want him for his money, women like Hilary who would turn themselves into whatever he wanted or needed to access the kind of lifestyle he could provide for them. As far as his father was concerned, aside from his wife, Mary, women were cunning creatures to avoid except for the occasional physical release, and then only if protection was used.

"I was lucky, boy," his father would often say. "I was poor as a church mouse when I met your mother. I never had to worry about if she loved me for my money or for myself. You won't have that luxury. You'll never really know if a woman loves you or your money."

He knew without a doubt that Melissa hadn't set out to seduce him that night. There was no way she could have orchestrated the blizzard and the two of them being on the road at the same time in the same place.

What he didn't know was that once fate had placed them in that position, had she recognized him and taken a calculated risk of getting pregnant? It had been a mutual seduction that night. She'd been as willing a participant as he had been.

He frowned thoughtfully as he watched her coo and

sweet-talk the two little boys. But if that was the case, if she'd recognized him that night before she'd slept with him, why hadn't she contacted him the minute she realized she was pregnant? Maybe she'd been afraid he'd talk her into an abortion.

One thing was clear. Henry wanted his boys living here with him and he would achieve that goal with or without Melissa's help.

Chapter 4

The afternoon seemed to fly by. Melissa was shocked
when two baby cribs were delivered and Henry had
them set up in the room across from hers. And the beds
weren't all. High chairs were also delivered, fancy high
chairs that seated infants then changed to accommodate
toddlers, along with boxes and packages in all shapes
and sizes.

"This isn't necessary," she'd protested. "We're only
going to be here a couple of days."

"Then things will be more comfortable for the couple
of days that you're here," Henry had replied.

Dinner was a pleasant meal with the boys happily
seated in their new high chairs and most of the conversation between Mary and Melissa. Henry had been
quiet, watching Melissa with an enigmatic gaze that

made her overly self-conscious and more than a little bit nervous.

After dinner they all gathered in the living room for the tree-trimming party. Mary supplied thick thread and needles to string the popcorn and cranberries that Etta provided, and Henry carried the two high chairs into the room and placed the boys in the seats.

"Why don't I put the lights on while you two make the garland?" Henry asked.

Mary smiled at Melissa. "He'd do anything to get out of using a needle and thread."

"Sewing is a woman's work," Henry replied.

"Stubborn and a male chauvinist, what a surprise," Melissa exclaimed.

"I'm not a male chauvinist," he protested. "I just don't like needles."

"Okay, then stubborn and a bit of a wuss," Melissa replied teasingly.

Mary laughed in delight. "Finally, a woman who can put you in your place, Henry."

Henry looked at Melissa and in the depths of his eyes she saw a flicker of heat that stirred something wild and hot inside her.

"Ouch!" she exclaimed as she pricked her finger with the needle. She instantly put her finger in her mouth and Henry's eyes flamed brighter.

"And that's why I don't like needles," he finally said and turned his attention to the string of Christmas lights.

There was definitely something between them, she thought. Something hot and hungry. She wasn't in love with him, didn't know him well enough to gauge exactly what she thought of him. But there was no denying the strong physical attraction that existed between them.

"I always wanted to do a tree like this," Mary said. "Old-fashioned and simple. Big Henry was into flash and gaudy." A soft smile curved her lips. "That man wouldn't know simple if it tapped him on the head."

"You miss him," Melissa said.

Mary leaned back against the sofa cushion, the smile still lingering on her lips. "He was stubborn as a mule, ridiculously opinionated and could make a saint weep with frustration, but yes, I miss him each and every day." She tapped her heart with a finger. "But he's still with me in here."

That's what Melissa wanted, what Mary and Big Henry had apparently shared, a love that would last through eternity. "I'm so sorry for your loss," she said and covered Mary's hand with hers.

Mary smiled and gave her hand a squeeze and then released it and began to string popcorn once again. "Thank you. I'm just sorry he's not here now to meet his grandsons. He would have been so pleased to know that there will be another generation."

"I'm going into town tomorrow and thought you might like to take the ride with me, Melissa," Henry said. "Mom can babysit the boys for an hour or so."

"I'd be happy to do that," Mary agreed.

"Oh, I don't know," Melissa said hesitantly. She'd never left the boys for a minute since their births.

"I promise I won't beat them or chain them to their beds," Mary said gently.

Melissa laughed. "That never entered my mind." She looked at Henry. "Aren't you afraid to go out? I mean it was just last night that somebody shot at you…at us."

"I won't be a prisoner in my own house," he said with a tone of steel in his voice. "Besides, I've got my men watching the grounds and we'll be safe in town. Nobody would risk trying to hurt me with so many other people around."

Melissa was torn. She was reluctant to leave the boys for any amount of time, yet there was a tiny simmer of excitement as she thought of an hour or two without them. The idea of a trip into town was appealing, but she was surprised by how cavalier he was about somebody trying to hurt him.

"I keep telling you that I don't believe my life is really in danger, that I think somebody is just trying to aggravate me, trying to manipulate me into throwing in the towel on my plans to be mayor," he said.

"Okay, I'll go with you," she finally said, unsure if it was just another reckless decision on her part.

"Good. We'll plan on going after breakfast and we'll be home before lunchtime," he replied.

"It will be fine, dear." Mary reached over and patted Melissa's hand. "I remember the first time I left Henry with somebody. He was just about the twins' age and Big Henry had decided I needed a night out. I must have called home a dozen times to check on Henry in the two hours we were gone. Big Henry finally decided to bring me home."

Melissa smiled. "They're getting to the age where if you blink you feel like you've missed a first."

"I've already missed too many firsts," Henry said with a touch of vehemence.

He would make a good father, Melissa thought. Whenever he looked at the boys she saw a fierce love shining from his eyes. As crazy as it sounded, there was a tiny part of her that wished that same expression were in his eyes whenever he gazed at her.

She recognized the foolishness of such a wish. He was a confirmed bachelor and in any case he was the kind of man who could choose from a harem of successful, beautiful women if he ever did decide to end his bachelorhood.

She'd be a fool to entertain any kind of happily-ever-after ideas where Henry was concerned. He was right in that they were forever bound because of the boys, but the ties that bound them would be dual parenting and nothing more.

When the phone rang Henry went to answer, leaving Mary and Melissa alone. Melissa looked at the woman who had been so kind to her.

"I can't imagine what you must think of me," she said.

Mary smiled. "I certainly wouldn't want anyone to look at some of the things I've done in my life and make a judgment. I'm not about to do that to you."

"I appreciate that," Melissa replied gratefully.

As Melissa thought about all the ways coming here could have been so terrible, she was even more grateful to Mary and to Henry for their welcome, for embracing the boys and her into their home.

As Henry came back into the room James exploded

in one of his rich belly laughs. Henry froze, the look on his face one of sheer wonder and delight.

"What's so funny, little man?" he asked as he leaned down and picked up the rattle James had dropped. He handed the rattle back to James, and James promptly threw it on the floor once again and looked at Henry and laughed. Henry laughed as well and picked up the rattle and once again gave it to James, who tossed it over the edge of the high chair tray yet again.

Melissa laughed. "That's his new game and he'll play as long as you will."

Henry's eyes sparkled with a new warmth she hadn't seen there before. "They're amazing, aren't they? It's obvious already that they're smart."

Melissa smiled. It was fun to see him being a proud daddy, certain that his boys were more intelligent and cuter than any other babies on the face of the earth.

The rest of the evening passed quickly. They drank hot cocoa and strung the popcorn and cranberry garlands on the tree, then added tinsel and ornaments that had been in the Randolf family for years.

Mary knew the history of each and every ornament and Melissa was entranced by the stories she told.

"I picked these up while I was out today," Mary said as she grabbed a box from the bookcase that Melissa hadn't noticed. She took the lid off the box and pulled out two ornaments and handed them to Melissa.

The ornaments were little cowboys and each sported the words *Baby's First Christmas*. For a moment as Melissa gazed at them her heart was too full to attempt speech. "I don't know what to say," she finally managed to sputter. A sudden mist fell in front of her eyes. She quickly blinked them away. "Once again, thank you for your kindness."

"Pick a good spot and hang them on the tree," Mary said. "It's the beginning of a new tradition. There will be an ornament every year for each of the boys to add to the collection. When they leave home and have their own trees, they can take them with them."

Melissa got up from the sofa and approached the tree, vividly aware of Henry's eyes on her. She'd felt him watching her all evening long, an intense, almost predatory gaze that had kept her in a state of anticipation.

It was still there between them, that crazy, wild attraction, that white-hot desire that had exploded out of control on the night of the snowstorm. She saw it in the depths of his eyes, felt the electricity in the air whenever he was near.

She hung the ornaments and then James began to fuss. "It's past their bedtime," she said as she unbuckled James from his high chair and pulled him up into his arms.

"I'll get this one," Henry said and picked up Joey.

"I think I'm going to call it a night as well," Melissa said to Mary. "Thank you for a wonderful evening and I'll see you in the morning."

Mary kissed each of the boys on their foreheads and smiled at Melissa. "Sleep well, Melissa."

As Melissa went up the stairs she was conscious of Henry just behind her. She could smell the scent of him, felt a stir in the pit of her stomach. It was easier to be around him with Mary in the room. Being alone with him made her think of how his lips had felt on hers, how his eyes had burned electric-blue as he'd taken her that cold, wintry night.

She carried James into the bedroom across from where she'd slept the night before, where the two new cribs awaited. The boys were already dressed in their sleepers, but each needed a diaper change before going to sleep.

"You can just put him in that bed," she said. "And I'll take it from here."

"What else needs to be done?" he asked.

She smiled and unsnapped James's sleeper bottom. "Diaper duty."

"Toss me one of those diapers and I'll take care of Joey," he replied. She looked at him in surprise. "I wrestle cattle. I think I can handle wrestling a diaper on a little bottom," he said with a smile.

Within minutes the boys were changed and half-asleep. Melissa kissed their downy heads then walked to the doorway and turned out the light. A night-light glowed from a socket in the corner as she and Henry stepped back out into the hallway.

"That's it? Now they'll just go to sleep?" Henry asked.

"If we're lucky. If it's a good night," she replied.

"And if it's a bad night?"

He stood so close to her she could feel the heat from his body radiating to her. Memories of the night they'd shared shot through her mind. She remembered the feel of his hand around hers as they'd raced through the blinding snow to the abandoned farmhouse, his gentleness as he helped her pull off her wet shoes and socks.

He'd rubbed her feet between his hands, then had gotten a roaring fire started using a stack of wood that had been left by the fireplace.

As crazy as it sounded, that night in the arms of a stranger she'd felt more loved, more cared for than she'd ever felt in her life. It was a pathetic statement on how lonely her life had been up until now. She suddenly realized that even with Tom she had felt lonely.

She also realized he was looking at her expectantly, that he'd asked her a question she hadn't yet answered.

"If it's a bad night then I usually walk them or rock them until they finally go to sleep," she said. "Hopefully they won't have a bad night while we're here so they won't wake up you or your mother."

"You don't have to worry about them waking up Mom. Her rooms are on the other side of the house. And I don't mind if they wake me up. I'd be happy to walk or rock a baby back to sleep."

She was quickly developing a crush on her babies' daddy and she found it appalling. "Then I guess I'll just say good-night," she said as she backed away from him.

"Good night, Melissa," he replied then turned his attention back to the bedroom where the boys slept.

It wasn't until Melissa was in her nightgown and had slid beneath the blankets on the bed that the first stir of uneasiness filtered through her.

The new cribs, the high chairs, even the ornaments on the tree suddenly took on an ominous meaning. She'd worried that Henry wouldn't want to be a part of

Joey's and James's lives but now her worry was exactly the opposite.

What if those things hadn't been bought to make her visit more pleasant? What if they'd been bought as the beginning to creating a permanent place here for the boys?

Henry certainly had the money and the power to make a play for custody of the boys and Melissa was in no financial position to be able to fight him.

Don't jump to conclusions, she told herself, but she couldn't stop the burning fear that somehow, someway, Henry intended to take her babies away from her.

Chapter 5

"Are we ready to take off?" Henry asked Melissa the next morning when they'd all finished breakfast. She looked so pretty in a bright pink sweater and worn jeans that hugged her hips, but she'd been unusually quiet since she'd gotten up that morning.

She glanced at the boys still seated in their high chairs. "Go on, Melissa. I can take it from here," Mary assured her. "Go enjoy a little shopping or whatever. It's a beautiful day and we won't see many more of them."

"I just need to get my coat," Melissa said.

As she ran up the stairs, Henry walked to the entry hall and retrieved his gun and shoulder holster from the drawer. He quickly put them on and then pulled on his winter coat.

He didn't want the presence of the gun to frighten

Melissa, but he also didn't intend to go out the door without it. Although he anticipated no trouble, he intended to be prepared if trouble found him.

As she came back down the stairs he felt a tiny fluttering heat in the pit of his stomach. He was looking forward to spending some time with her, without the boys, without his mother as a buffer between them.

She intrigued him. He couldn't get a handle on her. He didn't know if she was really what she seemed— a nice woman who had acted uncharacteristically the night she'd been with him, a loving mother who had come here to find a friend, or a schemer who was like so many of the other women who had drifted through Henry's life.

"Ready," she said as she reached the landing.

He'd already had Charlie bring his truck to the driveway and as he stepped out the door he was on alert. As Charlie got out of the driver's seat, Henry helped Melissa into the passenger side.

Once she was in he met Charlie at the driver door. "Thanks, Charlie," he said.

"No problem. You watch your back in town."

Henry nodded. "I'm sure we'll be fine. You keep an eye on things here while I'm gone. Oh, and Charlie, tell Hank I'm giving him three weeks' severance pay, but he's fired. I warned him about his drinking, but he didn't take my warning to heart."

Charlie's expression didn't change. "I'll tell him, boss."

Within minutes Henry was in the truck and they

were pulling out of the ranch entrance and onto the main highway that led into Dalhart.

He cast her a sideways glance. "You've been rather quiet this morning."

She looked out the side window, making it impossible for him to see her face. "I was up most of the night. The boys were restless and fussy." She paused a moment and then continued, "You know it's not all fun and games, dealing with the boys. You've seen them on their best behavior, but they can be so difficult. They cry and fuss and keep you up all night. They spit out their food and make a big mess."

He frowned, wondering where she was going, what had brought on this little diatribe. "I'm aware that parenting isn't all fun and games," he replied.

She turned to look at him. "How could you possibly be aware of that? You've only been around them for a day and a half." Her eyes were wide and her lower lip trembled slightly.

"Only a fool thinks it's easy to raise kids, and I'm not a fool," he replied.

Once again she cast her gaze out the side window. She appeared at ease, but he could feel the tension wafting from her. Something had put a burr on her butt and he couldn't imagine what had caused it. Maybe she was just one of those moody women who got mad at the world without any provocation. Maybe this was a negative character trait that he would have seen if they'd dated for any length of time.

He figured eventually he'd know what had set her

off. "Are you warm enough?" he asked as he turned the heater fan up a notch.

"I'm fine," she replied. She turned her head and he felt her steady gaze on him.

They rode in silence for only a few moments, then she sighed, an audible release that sounded weary. "You're obviously a man who is accustomed to getting what you want in life."

"I do all right," he replied cautiously. They had entered the town and he pulled into a parking space in front of Nathan's General Store. He unbuckled his seat belt and turned to look at his passenger. "Melissa, something is obviously bothering you. You want to tell me what's going on?"

Her eyes were filled with anxiety as she studied him. She raised a hand that trembled slightly to shove a strand of her long, pale hair behind her ear. "You scare me, Henry. Your power and your money scares me."

He looked at her in surprise. "It's been my experience that most women find my power and my money exciting—even intoxicating."

"Then I'm not most women," she replied. "Maybe those women had nothing to lose, but I do." Her voice thickened. "I need to know if you intend to take the boys away from me."

"What makes you think I'd do that?" he countered.

"Because you can," she replied and her eyes flashed with a touch of anger. "Because it's obvious you've already taken them into your life. You've bought cribs and high chairs and heaven knows what else and don't tell me you bought those things in order to make my visit with you more pleasant."

"I have no intention of taking the boys away from you," he said.

For a long moment their gazes remained locked. He saw the internal battle going on in her eyes, knew she was trying to decide if she could trust him or not.

"Melissa, I'm not going to lie to you. I want those boys living at the ranch. I want them to grow up here. I don't want to just be a weekend dad. I want to teach them to love the land, to be a part of Randolf Enterprises, which will one day be their legacy."

Her eyes narrowed with each of his words and he watched her stiffen in protest. She was a mother bear, sensing danger to her cubs and he liked that she looked as if she were about to rake his eyes out.

"I have a suggestion so that the boys will remain with you, but I also get what I want," he said.

"And what suggestion is that?" she asked dubiously.

"There's a carriage house behind the main house. It's a two-bedroom fully functional unit. I'd like you to consider moving there with the boys."

"That's a crazy idea," she said immediately. "I have a life in Amarillo."

He raised an eyebrow. "A full life? From what little you've told me, it sounds like a lonely life."

"But it's mine," she replied fervently. "It's my life, not yours."

Henry stifled a sigh of frustration. She'd said she was stubborn and at the moment that stubbornness lifted her chin and flashed in her eyes. "Look, I'd just like you to consider making the move. It would be great for the boys to have not just me, but my mother in their lives on a full-time basis. Just think about it. That's all I'm asking of you."

Once again those beautiful eyes of hers studied him thoughtfully. "And you promise that you won't try to take the boys from me. You won't use your money to try to get custody of them from me?"

"I promise," he replied.

"How do I know you aren't lying?"

He opened his truck door. "I guess you're just going to have to trust me, just like I'm trusting that the story you told me about some mystery woman bringing you to my house is true. Now, let's do a little shopping and let me show you the charms of Dalhart."

In all honesty, he hadn't really seriously considered going to court to take the boys away from her. They were babies, not some company he could buy or sell.

Besides, he knew how important a mother was to children. He had a wonderful relationship with his own mother and would never deprive his children in that way. He hoped Melissa could put away her fears at least for the duration of their outing and she appeared to as she got out of the truck and offered him a tentative smile.

"I'd like to pick up something for your mother while we're out," she said.

"You don't have to do that," he protested. He knew that money was tight for her.

"It's something I want to do," she replied, her chin once again lifted in that stubborn thrust. "She always smells like roses so I was thinking maybe some rose-scented soap or lotion."

He was surprised both by her observation about his mother and by her thoughtfulness. "Okay, I'm sure we can find something like that in one of the stores. I've got some things to pick up, too."

He gestured her toward the door of the store. Shopping at Nathan's General Store was kind of like delving into a treasure hunt.

The floor-to-ceiling shelves were stuffed full of items with no rhyme or reason for their placement there. Candles sat next to disposable diapers, jars of peanut butter next to boxes of cereal.

"Wow," Melissa exclaimed as they entered the store. "It looks like you could find whatever you need in this one store."

"If you can find what you need," Henry said dryly. "Nathan has an unusual way of arranging things."

"I can see that," she replied. "But that's just going to make this fun." As she drifted toward a shelf, he watched her and wondered what it was that so drew him to her.

Granted, she was pretty, but it wasn't the heart-stopping beauty that could make a man yearn. She was pretty in a girl-next-door kind of way. But she wasn't a girl. She was a woman with lush curves that he remembered intimately. She also had an intriguing aura of a combination of strength and vulnerability. Certainly she had to be strong to take on the job of raising twins alone. But there were times when he saw a wistfulness in her eyes, a yearning for something that he had an idea had nothing to do with his money or his lifestyle.

A blue sweater, he thought suddenly. That's what she needed. A sweater the exact color of her eyes. He'd like to buy her several things, but he wasn't sure if his gifts would please her or make her angry.

He'd like to buy her a new robe to replace the one she'd been wearing yesterday morning. He'd like to buy her a new car to replace the junk on wheels that she'd driven to his house. But besides her strength and stubbornness he sensed more than a little bit of pride.

He liked that about her and yet knew it was that very trait that might make it difficult for him to get what he wanted.

Although he wouldn't mind another night of pleasure with her, he certainly didn't want to marry her. He didn't even want a romantic relationship with her. All he had to figure out was a way to convince her that it was in everyone's best interest for her to move into the carriage house. That's what he wanted more than anything and he would stop at nothing to get what he wanted.

Despite the anxiety that had weighed heavy in Melissa's heart from the moment she'd opened her eyes that morning, she was enjoying the unexpected shopping time with Henry. The talk in the truck had helped ease some of her fear. He'd promised he wouldn't try to take custody of the boys and she only hoped that she could trust that promise. She'd steadfastly refused to think about his offer of the carriage house. She might think about it later, but she didn't want her ambivalence to ruin a perfectly good day out.

They'd wandered in and out of stores and she'd been successful in buying rose-scented lotion and body soap for Mary.

Dalhart was a charming little city that Henry explained got an influx of tourists each summer.

In August there was a three-day celebration that included the largest free barbecue in the United States, a rodeo and three nights of live music and fun.

"See that building over there?" He pointed to a four-story brick structure on the corner. "That's the Randolf Hotel. I bought it six months ago and it is currently undergoing massive renovations. I'm going to need an interior designer when the renovations are done. I'd hire you if you were living here."

"Sounds suspiciously like a bribe," she replied lightly.

He grinned. "Maybe a little one. But I have to hire somebody and it might as well be you."

"You don't even know if I'm good at it," she exclaimed.

"I have a feeling you're good at whatever you put your mind to," he replied.

As they continued to walk the sidewalks Henry pointed out other places of interest and eventually led her to a café where he insisted they go inside and have a cup of coffee before heading back to the ranch.

She agreed. Although she was eager to get back to the kids, she was also reluctant for this time with Henry to end. He'd been charming, making her laugh with a surprising sense of humor and making her feel as if she were the most important person on the face of the earth.

He'd introduced her to people that greeted them and she'd seen the respect, the genuine admiration Henry's friends and neighbors had for him.

In the café they were led to a table in the back where they sat and ordered coffee. "I thought you said you had things to buy," she said once the waitress had poured their coffee and departed from the table.

"I got them," he replied.

"But you don't have any packages." She reached for the sugar to add to her coffee.

"I always have my purchases delivered to the house."

"I guess that's one of the perks about being you," she said dryly.

He grinned and the charm in that gesture kicked her in the heart. "I'm not going to lie. There are definitely perks to being wealthy. For instance, I never go to bed at night and worry about how I'm going to pay the rent. You'd have that same luxury if you'd move into the carriage house."

"That's not true. I would never expect to live someplace free of charge. I pay my way, Henry." She wrapped her hands around her coffee mug. It was one thing to be independent, but it was another to make the boys suffer from her independence.

"There are two things I'd ask of you," she said after a moment of hesitation.

"What's that?"

She realized this close that his eyes were really more gray than blue. Almost silver, they were the kind of eyes a woman could fall into, eyes a woman could lose herself in.

"I haven't been able to afford to get them health insurance," she said. "Maybe it would be nice if you could put them on your policy."

"Done," he answered without hesitation.

"The other thing is that maybe you could help me with a college fund for them. I didn't have the opportunity to go to college, but I'd like my sons to."

"You didn't have to ask for that. I'd want to make sure they go to college," he replied. "Why didn't you go?"

"There were several reasons. Financially it was impossible, but even with a full scholarship I couldn't have gone." She paused to take a sip of her coffee and then continued. "When I was a junior in high school my mother developed health complications due to diabetes. She lost most of her eyesight and they had to take one of her legs. There was no way I could leave her to go to college. She had nobody but me to take care of her."

"Quite a sacrifice on your part," he observed.

Melissa smiled. "I never considered it a sacrifice. I considered it a privilege to take care of the woman who had always taken care of me."

"One of the reasons I broke up with the woman I'd been dating for a while was because she thought it was time to put my mother into a nursing home."

Melissa looked at him in stunned surprise. "What was she thinking? Your mother certainly doesn't belong in a nursing home."

"My sentiments, exactly," he replied. "And you don't

even need me to tell you what Mom thought of the idea. Needless to say Mom wasn't upset when I broke it off with Hilary. Now, tell me how you got involved with interior decorating."

As Melissa told him about working in a furniture store and finding her calling in arranging rooms and décor, she once again remembered the thrill of his mouth on hers, the way his arms had felt holding her tight.

"Shouldn't we be getting home?" she asked when she'd finished telling him about her struggling business. "It's been a couple of hours and I don't want to take advantage of your mother."

"We'll head back," he agreed. "But I can promise you my mother wouldn't feel taken advantage of if we were gone all day. She's absolutely crazy over those boys."

Melissa smiled. "I can't tell you how wonderful it is that the boys not only have a father like you, but also a grandmother like Mary. I'm well aware of the fact that James the cowboy could have been a man who wanted nothing to do with them."

He looked at her sheepishly. "I want you to know that night was the first and only time I've lied about my name." He motioned for the waitress to bring their tab. "To be honest, that night I just wanted to be James the cowboy, not Henry Randolf III."

The café had grown busy with the approach of the noon hour and Melissa was aware of several people looking at her with curiosity as she and Henry left their table and headed for the door.

They were just about to reach the door when a tall,

willowy brunette walked in. "Henry!" she cried in obvious delight, then her gaze swept to Melissa and her smile faltered slightly.

"Hilary, this is Melissa Monroe, a friend visiting from Amarillo. Melissa, this is Hilary Grant," Henry said.

"Nice to meet you," Hilary said to Melissa, then turned her attention back to Henry. "I was going to stop by your place this evening. I made a batch of that fudge you love and was going to bring it to you."

"That's not necessary," Henry protested.

"Well, of course it isn't necessary, but it's something I want to do. Will you be home this evening?"

"We'll be home, but it's Christmas Eve. It's really not a good time," he replied.

Her lush red lips pursed with a hint of irritation. "Then I'll give the fudge to Charlie to give to you tomorrow," she said. "I made it especially for you, Henry."

He smiled at the beautiful Hilary. "That was very nice, Hilary, and now we'd better get out of here. We're blocking the entrance."

"Nice to meet you, Hilary," Melissa said.

She nodded and returned Melissa's smile but there was nothing warm or inviting in the dark centers of her eyes. She swept past them toward a table where another woman sat as Melissa and Henry stepped out into the cold late morning air.

"Hilary knows Charlie?" Melissa asked.

"They're brother and sister," Henry replied.

She glanced up at him. "That must have been a bit awkward when you broke up with her."

"Actually, it was fine. Charlie doesn't seem to get involved with his sister's life. I get the feeling that they aren't real close."

They had gone only a few steps down the sidewalk when they came face-to-face with a short, squat man. Melissa felt Henry's instant tension. "Tom," he said and gave the man a curt nod.

"Henry. Heard you had some excitement out at your place the other night."

"And you wouldn't know anything about that," Henry replied. His eyes were cool, steely in a way Melissa hadn't seen before.

"Just what I hear through the grapevine. Sounds like there are some folks who aren't too happy about your decision to run for mayor."

"Just a handful, mostly the people who have something to lose if I get into office. You wouldn't be one of those people, would you, Tom?"

"Taking potshots at a man with a rifle isn't my style. You'll see me coming if I come after you." Tom gave Melissa a curt nod, then stepped around them and walked by.

"Who was that?" Melissa asked as they arrived at Henry's truck.

"Tom Burke, city manager and the man who definitely doesn't want me to become mayor." Henry opened her car door and she slid in and watched as he walked around the front of his truck to get into the driver's side.

She could tell he was irritated. A muscle ticked in his strong jaw and his shoulders looked more rigid than usual.

"You don't like Tom Burke?" she asked as he got into the car.

"I think he's a criminal masquerading as an upstanding citizen," Henry replied as he started the truck. "He knows that if I get into office I'm going to do everything in my power to see that he loses his job."

"So, you think he's behind the attacks on you?"

He backed out of the parking space before replying. When he was on the road that led back to the ranch he visibly relaxed. "Yeah, Tom Burke is definitely at the top of my list of suspects. He knows I believe that he's been taking kickbacks from inferior contractors doing work for the city and he knows that if I succeed in being elected, his days are numbered."

"Have you told the sheriff this?"

He nodded, his dark hair gleaming in the sunshine that danced into the truck window. "Jimmy knows. Unfortunately Tom isn't the only councilman who I think is on the take. The corruption in this town runs deep and I'm determined to do some housecleaning."

"And what do the townspeople think?"

"I think they're behind me, but nobody has been brave enough to speak up. I'm hoping they'll speak by voting for me."

Melissa admired what he wanted to do. Like an old Wild West hero he was riding into town filled with outlaws with the intention of cleaning it up.

"She's very beautiful," she said.

He didn't pretend not to know who she was talking about. "She's okay."

She'd been more than okay, Melissa thought. Hilary Grant was stunning. Tall and slender, with lush long dark hair and exotic olive eyes, she'd looked like a model in her long, fashionable coat and boots.

"What does she do?" she asked curiously.

"She's a beautician and she does some local modeling gigs. She and Charlie had a pretty rough life and mostly Hilary is looking for somebody to change all that rather than figuring out how she can change it herself."

"She's in love with you, you know," she said.

"She was never in love with me," he scoffed. "She was always in love with my money."

"Were you in love with her?" Melissa was surprised to realize that his answer mattered. It mattered much more than it should to her.

"No, but there was a weak moment when I considered marrying her."

"You'd marry somebody you weren't in love with?" Melissa asked with surprise.

"I considered it a business deal," he replied with an easiness that astounded her. "Hilary would have made a good wife when it came to giving parties and acting as hostess for social affairs. In return she would have been able to live the lifestyle she desperately wants."

"And you'd do that? You'd marry as a business arrangement instead of for love?" Melissa asked.

"As far as I'm concerned love is overrated." He cast her a wry look. "I suppose you're one of those hopeless romantics?"

"Absolutely," she exclaimed. "I'll only marry for love. I want to marry somebody who loves me mindlessly, desperately, and I want to love him the same way.

I want somebody to laugh with, to love, somebody to grow old with and love through eternity. And I won't settle for less."

As if to punctuate her sentence there was a loud pop. The truck careened wildly to the right side of the highway as Henry muttered a curse.

Melissa saw the deep ditch in front of them and knew they were going to hit it—hard. She squeezed her eyes closed and screamed as she felt the truck go airborne.

Chapter 6

Henry fought the steering wheel hard, trying to keep the truck on the road, but he lost the battle as the vehicle flew far right, hit the lip of the ditch and flew with all four tires off the ground. It came down with a crunch and a hiss, jarring the teeth in his head as it finally came to rest.

His heart raced and he quickly looked at Melissa. "Are you all right?"

She opened her eyes and gave a slow nod, but her face was chalky pale. "I'm okay." She drew in a deep breath and her hand shook as she shoved her hair away from her face. "I hope you have a spare," she said.

He pulled his gun from his holster with one hand and reached for his cell phone with the other. Melissa's eyes widened at the sight of his weapon. But he didn't have time to deal with her fear.

He handed her the cell phone. "Call Jimmy." He rattled off Jimmy's cell phone number. "Tell him we're three miles from my place on the highway and somebody just shot out my tire."

As she made the phone call, Henry kept his gaze on the wooded area on the right side of the highway. He was ninety-nine percent certain that a mere second before the tire had blown he'd heard the unmistakable faint crack of a rifle.

"Jimmy said he's on his way," she said, her voice higher than normal in tone.

He felt her fear radiating across the seat, but he didn't look at her. Instead he kept focused on the area where he thought danger might come. He didn't know now if the attack was over or if the blown tire was just the beginning. Was somebody approaching the truck now, knowing it was disabled and that he and Melissa were sitting ducks?

Minutes ticked by—tense minutes of silence. He was grateful that Melissa understood his need for focus, for complete concentration, and didn't attempt to engage him in any way.

His heart continued to bang unusually fast, but as the fear began to recede, anger took its place. Who was behind these attacks? Dammit, there had to be something he and Jimmy could do to figure out who was responsible and get them behind bars.

Henry didn't relax until he saw Jimmy's patrol car pull up on the side of the road. Henry lowered his gun and opened his window as Jimmy got out of his car, gun drawn and headed across the ditch toward them.

"You're becoming a full-time job, Henry," Jimmy said as he reached the driver side of the truck. "You both okay?" He bent down to look at Melissa. "Ma'am?"

"I'm fine," she replied, her voice a little stronger than it had been moments before.

"You sure the tire was shot out?"

"I heard a crack right before the tire blew. I think it was a rifle shot."

Jimmy scanned the area. "You have any idea where the shot came from?"

"Somewhere in those trees, about a quarter of a mile back," Henry replied. "I'm sure whoever it was is gone now. If the intention was to do more harm, then he would have come after us while we were sitting here waiting for you."

"Any ideas on who might have taken the shot?" Jimmy asked.

"The usual suspects," Henry replied dryly. "Oh, and I have a new one to add. I fired Hank Carroll this morning before we left for town. You might want to check him out. Can you get somebody out here to take us home?"

Jimmy nodded. "I'll radio for Gordon to come out and give you a ride. Meanwhile I'll check out the woods and see if I find anything. You armed?"

Henry showed his gun. "Nobody is going to sneak up on us. You see what you can find and we'll wait here for Gordon."

Jimmy nodded, hitched up his pants, then turned to walk back to his patrol car.

Henry shot Melissa a quick glance, pleased to see some of the color had returned to her cheeks. "I don't think we're in any danger," he said softly. "And I appreciate the fact that you haven't fallen into hysterics."

She offered him a faint smile, although her lips trembled slightly. "I'm really not the hysterical kind of woman. You fired Hank?"

He nodded and returned his gaze to the outside. "I'd warned him twice about drinking on the job, but he was half-lit when he carried in the tree yesterday."

"I noticed," she replied. "Would he do something like this?"

Henry frowned thoughtfully. "To tell the truth, I don't know. He hasn't been working for me very long. I hope this doesn't change your mind about living in the carriage house."

"I haven't made up my mind about living in the carriage house," she replied. "And I'd say now is definitely not a good time to ask me how I feel about living here."

At that moment a deputy car pulled up and Gordon Hunter got out. Jimmy returned as Henry and Melissa were getting into the backseat of Gordon's car.

"I couldn't find anything. I don't suppose you'd do me a favor and stay inside that secure castle of yours until I can figure out who's after you? I mean, tomorrow is Christmas, surely you don't have to be out anywhere."

"I won't be out and about for the next couple of days, but, Jimmy, I'm not going to become a prisoner in my own home," Henry replied.

Jimmy frowned. "I know, Henry. I'm doing the best I can but these drive-by shootings, so to speak, aren't giving me much to work with."

Henry clapped his hand on Jimmy's shoulder. He knew Jimmy was as frustrated as he was by these sneak attacks. He also knew Jimmy was a good man who took his job seriously.

"I'll arrange for Willie at the garage to pick up your car," Jimmy said. "And I'll be in touch in the next day or two. In the meantime, try to have a merry Christmas."

Henry nodded and got into the back of Gordon's car next to Melissa. "Okay?" he asked her.

"Never a dull moment with you, is there?" she said.

There was still a tiny flicker of fear still in the depths of her eyes and he reached over and took one of her hands in his. She immediately curled her cold fingers with his as if she'd desperately needed the contact with him.

He was surprised by the sudden surge of protectiveness that filled him holding her small, slender hand in his. He wanted to keep her from harm. Surely it was only because she was the mother of his children and nothing more.

Still, he was equally surprised to realize that he had no desire to release her hand until Gordon deposited them at the front door of his house.

Melissa grabbed her shopping bags and Henry ushered her into the house, where Mary met them at the door. "What happened?" she asked, worry thick in her voice.

"Nothing serious, just a blowout," Henry said quickly

before Melissa could reply. "The spare was flat and Gordon just happened to be driving by so we hitched a ride home with him."

The last thing he wanted to do was worry his mother, but he wasn't sure if Melissa would play along with his story.

She did, not countering his story to his mother. "How were the boys?" Melissa asked. "Did they behave for you?"

Mary's face lit up. "They were absolute angels," Mary said as Henry flashed Melissa a grateful smile.

As Melissa and his mother disappeared into the house Henry headed for his office. He needed to call the garage about his truck and he needed to talk to Charlie to see how things had gone with Hank.

The main thing he needed was some distance from Melissa. Even with the concern that somebody had shot out his tire, he couldn't stop thinking about how nice her hand had felt in his, how the scent of her had dizzied his senses all morning long.

He wanted her. He wanted her naked in his arms, gasping beneath him as she'd been on the night they'd shared. But she'd made it clear what she was looking for—that happily-ever-after and love forevermore nonsense. That definitely wasn't what he'd be offering to her.

Would she be interested in a night of passion with him with no strings attached, no promise of love or commitment? It was possible.

He knew she wasn't immune to the sparks that snapped in the air between them. He'd seen an awareness in her eyes when he got too close to her, noticed the way her gaze lingered on him when she thought he wasn't looking.

He sank down at his desk and realized it was much easier to speculate on how to get Melissa into bed than trying to figure out who in the hell was trying to kill him.

"You're perfectly safe here," Henry said later that evening to Melissa. "The house has a state-of-the-art security system. Nobody can get in here without me knowing about it."

Melissa nodded and took a sip of her wine. Mary had just gone to bed, the boys were also down for the night, and Henry and Melissa were sitting in the living room with the glow of the Christmas tree lights the only illumination in the room.

There was no question that the safety of her sons had been on her mind all afternoon and evening. How could she even consider moving here knowing that somebody wanted to do harm to Henry? Knowing that it was possible she or her boys could be casualties in whatever war was being waged?

"I can't seriously consider moving here until the issue is resolved, not that I'm seriously considering it anyway," she said, giving voice to her thoughts.

"But I want you to consider it seriously," Henry said. He paused to take a sip of his scotch. "The special election is in February. Certainly by then I'm confident that Jimmy will be able to figure out who is hassling me. It would probably take you that long to make the move anyway."

"Hassling you?" She raised one of her eyebrows at him. "Honestly, that's a pretty weak description for what's happened just since I've been here. That tire blowout could have killed us both. The truck could have rolled and we wouldn't be sitting here right now."

"I swear I won't do anything to put you or the boys in danger," he replied.

She shrugged. "It doesn't matter now. I plan on going home tomorrow afternoon."

"But it will be Christmas Day," he protested. "You can't leave tomorrow. You'll break Mom's heart."

She smiled at him. "Ah, first you try to bribe me with a job offer and now you're using your mother to manipulate me. You should be ashamed of yourself."

He laughed and that familiar warmth shot through her at the pleasant sound. "I refuse to feel guilty if it forces you to stay a little longer. Besides, Etta will be making a traditional Christmas feast for lunch tomorrow and what difference does another day or two make?"

"You just want more time to try to talk me into moving here," she said.

He nodded, his eyes teasing her. "There is that," he agreed.

"Okay, I won't leave tomorrow. But the next morning we've got to get back home."

He finished his scotch and set the glass down on the coffee table. "And what then?" The teasing light in his eyes vanished. "When will I see the boys again?"

Melissa realized that her life was about to get more complicated. She'd been thrilled that Henry wanted to be a part of the boys' lives, but now she was faced with the logistics of how they would make it all work.

"I guess I can commit to twice a month driving here for a weekend visit," she said. "I know it isn't ideal, that you'd like to see the twins every day," she added as she saw the dismay on his face. "But, Henry, you have to work with me here."

"I know." He leaned back against the sofa and frowned thoughtfully. "I never knew how kids would make me feel, how much they'd make me want to be there for them, to protect them and teach them. I never dreamed that thoughts of them would be so all-consuming."

She smiled, finding him even more attractive than ever with love for his children—for her children—shining from his eyes. "Welcome to parenthood."

He shook his head and smiled. "I never knew it would be like this." His features were soft in the glow from the Christmas lights and Melissa found herself wishing for things that could never be.

She wished she and Henry were married and tonight after checking on their children they'd get into bed together and make love all night long. She wished they'd share breakfast the next morning and talk about their shared dreams, laugh over secret jokes and know that they would face each other over their first cup of coffee every morning for the rest of their lives.

Foolish wishes, she knew. Wishes brought on by the glow of the Christmas tree and the warmth of family that permeated this house. She was slowly being seduced by Henry and his mother and she knew she'd be a fool to hope for anything except weekend visits for the boys and nothing more.

Still, she'd allowed him to talk her into staying another day because she'd been reluctant to leave this house of warmth, reluctant to leave him.

"Are there twins in your family?" he asked, pulling her from her wayward thoughts.

"Not that I know of. What about yours?"

"I think there were twins on my father's side of the family," he replied.

The doorbell rang and Henry checked his watch with a frown. "Who could that be?" Melissa watched as he rose from the sofa with a masculine grace.

When he disappeared from her sight, she leaned back in her chair and released a sigh. She'd enjoyed the day with him far too much.

His ideas about marriage had shocked her. Was he so afraid a woman would take his money? Did he not believe that he was worth anything simply as a man? What good was it to have money if all it made you do was worry about who might take it away from you?

She wondered what had made Henry so cynical about love. Had some woman hurt him in the past? Certainly Tom had hurt her, but even the pain of his rejection hadn't made her belief in true love waver.

When he returned he carried his car keys with him. "That was Willie from the garage. He delivered my truck." He pocketed the keys and sat back down on the sofa.

"Henry, do you have a computer?" she asked. She knew he had never really embraced her story about MysteryMom and more than anything she wanted him to believe that she had no interest in any of his money for herself.

"Sure, in my study. Why?"

"I was wondering if maybe you could let me use it to see if I can connect with MysteryMom. This is the time of the evening when I normally could find her in the chat room. It's important to me that you believe what it was that brought me here to you."

"You haven't given me a reason not to believe you."

She heard the faint edge of doubt in his voice and the *yet* that had remained unspoken. What he meant was that she hadn't given him a reason not to believe her *yet*.

"Maybe not, but for my own peace of mind I'd like to show you."

Once again he got up from the sofa. She finished her wine and then followed him down the hallway to the study. The room had seemed enormous the first time she'd been in here, but as he gestured her into the chair behind the desk and he stood immediately behind her, the room seemed to shrink.

They waited for the computer to boot up, and she was intensely aware of his scent, that provocative scent of clean male and spicy cologne. She could feel his warm breath on the nape of her neck and she fought a shiver of pleasure and hoped he didn't notice that she was suddenly breathless.

"There you go," he said. "You're Internet connected and can go wherever you want to go."

She placed her hand on the mouse and began to maneuver her way to the chat room where night after night for months she had talked to MysteryMom and other single mothers and mothers-to-be. But when she tried to find the room where she had spent so much of her time, bared so much of her soul, it was gone.

"I don't understand," she muttered softly as she clicked and whirled the mouse in an effort to locate the chat room. "It's not here." She felt a sick frustration welling up inside her.

"Melissa, it's Christmas Eve, that's probably why nobody is there." He placed his hand on her shoulder.

"No, you don't understand. The room always had a virtual sign welcoming single mothers and it's gone. The room itself isn't there anymore."

She looked up at him, surprised to feel thick emotion rising up inside her. She'd wanted to prove to him that it had been MysteryMom who had brought her here and not his money or the lure of a life on easy street.

"Do you have an email address for this Mystery-Mom?"

She shook her head negatively. "We always just talked in the room. If we wanted to talk privately we instant messaged each other. I only got one email from her and that was the directions here, but when I tried to answer her back my reply bounced back to me." She covered his hand with one of hers. "You have to believe me, Henry. It's so important to me."

He gazed at her for a long moment. It was a piercing gaze, as if he were looking into her very soul. "I believe you, Melissa. You don't have to prove anything to me."

He pulled his hand from her shoulder and turned off the computer. "Come on, it's getting late and Santa will come early in the morning."

She was ready to get out of the study, ready to get away from him. His scent, the gentle touch of his hand and the way he'd gazed at her had all combined to make her feel more than a little weak in the knees.

They left the study and as they walked back through the living room Henry turned out the Christmas tree lights, then turned on a switch that illuminated the stairs. They climbed up the stairs side by side and again Melissa was struck with a wistfulness that things were different between her and Henry. Everything would have been much less complicated if they'd dated for a long time, fallen in love and then she'd gotten pregnant.

And if wishes were horses, I'd have a whole herd, she thought. When they reached the top of the stairs she went into the boys' room and Henry followed right behind her.

She went to Joey's crib first and her heart expanded in her chest as she saw him sleeping peacefully. He had a little smile on his lips, as if his dreams were happy.

She then checked on James, unsurprised to see that he'd managed to wiggle himself sideways in the crib and had worked the blanket off him. She didn't attempt to move him from his position, but covered him again with the blanket, then backed away from the crib and into the hallway.

"James is a restless sleeper. He's more easily awakened than Joey and never keeps his blankets on," she said softly as she moved across the hall to her bedroom doorway. "I guess then I'll just say good-night."

"Melissa, I enjoyed spending the morning with you." He took a step toward her and stood so close she could feel the radiating warmth of his body.

"I had a nice time with you, too," she replied as her heart drummed a little faster.

There was a heat in his eyes that excited her and when he reached up to smooth a strand of her hair back from her face his simple touch electrified her.

"I thought about you often after that night," he said, his voice a husky whisper that stirred a simmering fire inside her. "I wondered if you'd gotten where you were going okay, if somehow, someway, our paths would ever cross again. I can't believe how little we shared and yet how much we shared."

"It was a crazy night," she replied half-breathlessly.

"I'm feeling a little crazy right now." He didn't give her time to think, time to process what he'd just said. He pulled her into his arms and his lips claimed hers.

It never occurred to her to step back from him, to deny him and herself the pleasure of kissing him. Just as she remembered, his lips were a combination of tenderness and command, of controlled hunger.

She opened her mouth to allow him to deepen the kiss. His body was rock-hard against hers as his hands slid down her back and pulled her closer to him.

Their tongues swirled and danced and Melissa felt herself falling into a sensual haze of instant desire. No man had ever been able to stir her like Henry. No man had ever made her feel as alive as she felt in his arms, with his mouth on hers.

He released her suddenly and stepped back, his eyes hooded and dark. Melissa fought for composure when all she really wanted was to grab him by the arm and pull him into the bedroom with her. Then she was struck by a thought that dashed all desire away.

"You've tried bribery and manipulation to get me to agree to move here. Is seduction your next weapon to use?" she asked.

A slow grin curved the edges of his mouth upward. "I promise you I will never seduce you in order to get you to move into the carriage house. The only reason I would seduce you is strictly for my own personal pleasure and nothing more."

He reached out and touched her lower lip with his index finger. "And I do intend to seduce you, Melissa. But, for tonight, sleep well and I'll see you in the morning."

Chapter 7

Henry awakened the next morning with a sense of excitement he hadn't felt since he'd been a very young boy. The air smelled of Christmas, of baking cinnamon rolls and fresh evergreen boughs and the cranberry-scented candles his mother loved to burn.

For a moment he remained in bed, thinking about the day ahead and the night before. Kissing Melissa had been an early Christmas present to himself. He'd wanted to kiss her all day.

As he watched her wander through the stores, her lips pursed thoughtfully as she considered her purchases, all he could think about was capturing that lush mouth with his own. Even in those moments immediately after the blowout he'd wanted to cover her trembling mouth with his and kiss her until the fear in her eyes transformed to something else.

Kissing her had been just like he remembered. Her lips had been soft and hot and welcoming and he hadn't wanted to stop. He'd wanted to take her by the hand and lead her to his bed.

Afterward he'd told her good-night and he'd gone back downstairs and spent the next several hours wrapping presents and placing everything he'd bought and the items that had been delivered over the past twenty-four hours under the tree.

By the time he'd finished it looked like toy land had come to the Randolf home. As pleased as he was about what he'd bought the twins, he couldn't wait for Melissa to open her presents from him.

It had been a long time since Henry had been excited about giving to somebody else. Sure, he was a generous contributor to a variety of charities, but buying for Melissa had given him a special kind of pleasure.

He pulled himself from bed and after a shower left the master suite. It was just after six when he passed Melissa's door and glanced inside to see her still in bed.

She was nothing more than a short, lean lump beneath the blankets, her hair the only thing visible. He wanted to crawl beneath the blankets with her, pull her into his arms and make love to her as the sun crested the horizon. That would definitely make it a Christmas to remember.

Instead he backed away from the doorway and checked on the boys, who were still sleeping soundly. He drew in a deep breath of their baby scent and felt a piercing ache at the thought of having to tell them good-bye even for a brief time.

He continued down the stairs. The tree was lit up, candles burned on the mantel and two stockings were hung, each with one of the boy's names in big glittery letters. His mother had been busy already.

He found her in the dining room, sipping a cup of coffee. She stood as he entered and gave him a kiss on the cheek. "Merry Christmas, Henry," she said, her eyes twinkling as brightly as the lights on the tree.

He hugged her and returned the greeting. "You're up early," he said as he poured himself a cup of coffee from the silver coffeepot in the center of the table.

"I couldn't stay in bed another minute. I can't wait for Melissa to see everything we've bought for the boys. I can't wait to see them in the little outfits I bought for them." She smiled and shook her head. "Christmases are going to be wonderful from now on."

"When Melissa and I sit down to discuss the visitation, I'll insist that the twins are here at Christmastime," he replied, although the words certainly brought him no comfort.

He wanted the boys here all the time. He wanted to see their first steps, he wanted to hear the first time they said da-da. He didn't want to wait days or weeks at a time between visits.

"You haven't managed to talk her into moving here? Staying in the carriage house?" Mary asked.

"Not yet. But I still have until tomorrow to make my case," he replied.

"She's leaving tomorrow?" Mary's dismay showed on her features.

"That's what she says."

"It would be nice if we could talk her into staying until after New Year's Eve."

Henry grinned knowingly at his mother. "Then we could try to convince her to stay until after Valentine's Day, or maybe Easter."

Mary laughed and nodded. "I don't have a problem with that." Her smile grew thoughtful. "It's not just the boys. I like Melissa. She's the kind of girl I once dreamed that you'd marry and build a family with."

Henry scowled. "You know that's not happening so don't even start." Most of the time Mary seemed to respect his decision to remain single, but occasionally she launched a sneak attack in an attempt to get him to change his mind.

"If not Melissa, then surely you can find some nice woman to fall in love with," she continued as if he hadn't spoken. "I hate the idea of you growing old alone. I want you to have what your father and I shared."

He paused to take a sip of his coffee. "I have sons who will keep me company as I grow old and that's all I need."

"I'm just saying it would be nice if they all could be here full-time."

Henry leaned back in his chair. "I have a feeling she isn't going to make a decision about moving here until I can assure her that it's safe. The greeting committee of bullets flying has to play a role in her not even considering it right now."

"Jimmy still doesn't have any idea who is responsible?" she asked with concern.

Henry shook his head. "He's coming over tomorrow and we're going to sit down and discuss the whole thing."

At that moment Melissa appeared in the doorway, a twin on each hip. Both Mary and Henry jumped up to take the boys from her.

"Merry Christmas," she said, her eyes sparkling brightly. She looked beautiful in a cheerful red sweater and jeans. Her cheeks were flushed with color and her hair was shiny and smooth to her shoulders.

"And the same to you," Mary said as she took Joey from Melissa's arm.

Henry took James, who offered him a half-cranky smile, then fussed and kicked his feet. "They're hungry," Melissa said. "I'll just go make them some cereal and I'll be right back."

Henry watched her disappear while he put James into his high chair. The fussing stopped, as if James knew he was about to get what he wanted. Within seconds Mary had both boys giggling as she made funny faces and silly noises. The sound of their laughter welled up inside Henry, filling him with such love it brought unexpected tears to his eyes.

Sons.

His sons.

He still couldn't quite wrap his mind around it and he was thankful for the blizzard that had brought him and Melissa together for that single night that had resulted in Joey and James.

There was no way he wanted a long-distance relationship with them. What if Melissa tired of the drive back and forth from Amarillo to here? What if eventually she fell in love and married a man who resented sharing the boys?

Fear clutched his heart at the very thought. He had to convince Melissa to move into the carriage house. It was the only way Henry could get what he wanted—a full-time position in his sons' lives.

He smiled as she came back into the room carrying two cereal bowls. "You sit back and enjoy your coffee. Mom and I will do the honors," he said as he took the bowls from her. "Did you sleep well?"

"Like a log," she replied. She poured herself a cup of coffee and sat in the chair next to Henry. Instantly he could smell the scent of her, clean and floral and intoxicating.

"Etta should have breakfast ready in about fifteen minutes," Mary said as she spooned cereal into Joey's mouth. "And after that we'll go in and see what Santa left for us."

"Santa has already given me more than enough," Melissa said. Her eyes were filled with warmth as she looked first at Mary, then at him. "The welcome you've both given me is more than I ever expected to find this Christmas."

"Maybe later today you would let Henry show you the carriage house," Mary said, surprising Henry with her forwardness. "Just have a peek at it before you definitely make up your mind one way or the other."

"I guess I could do that," Melissa agreed slowly, but

she lifted her chin in the gesture Henry had come to know as stubborn pride.

At that moment Etta entered the dining room carrying a tray of fist-size biscuits, a bowl of gravy and a platter of scrambled eggs.

Breakfast was pleasant with he and his mother telling tales of Christmases past and Melissa sharing some of her fond childhood memories of the holiday when her mother had been alive. Henry found his gaze drawn to her again and again. She looked so soft, so inviting and it was more than memories of the sex they'd shared that attracted him to her.

He loved the sound of her laughter. He liked the habit she had of shifting that shiny strand of hair behind her ears when she was thinking or when she was nervous.

He felt a little like he had in seventh grade when he'd had a crush on a girl named Angela. She'd been blond-haired and blue-eyed like Melissa and it had taken him months to work up his nerve to ask her to a school dance. The experience had been his first taste of how materialistic women, even very young women, could be.

He shoved the ancient painful memory away as he focused on the conversation and the musical ring of Melissa's laughter.

When they were all finished eating they adjourned into the living room, where the first thing his mother insisted they do was dress the boys in the little Santa suits she'd bought for them.

As the women dressed the little ones, Henry moved the high chairs into the room, as excited as a kid to distribute the presents to everyone. When the boys were in their little Santa suits, Mary took dozens of pictures and Henry knew she'd be sporting those photos all around town, bragging about her grandbabies.

Henry donned a Santa hat that James found incredibly funny. As the little boy laughed that rich burst of joy, Henry knew this was definitely going to be a Christmas to remember.

Melissa sat on the sofa next to Mary as Henry began to unveil the bigger presents hidden under sheets. Rocking horses and walkers and stuffed animals as big as Henry himself were just the beginning. There were boxes of clothes and diapers and educational toys. Of course, the boys liked the shiny wrapping paper best of all.

Mary opened her gift of the lotion and soap from Melissa and exclaimed that it was the brand and scent that she loved.

Melissa was already feeling overwhelmed when Henry gave her a present. "You shouldn't have," she said to him.

He smiled. "Open it, Melissa. I picked it out just for you. It's the exact color of your eyes."

Melissa couldn't help the way her heart fluttered at his words. She carefully removed the wrapping paper and opened the box to display the most beautiful blue sweater she'd ever seen in her life. It was soft as a whisper and she was touched by his thoughtfulness.

"Oh, Henry. It's beautiful." She felt the ridiculous burn of tears at her eyes.

"That's not all." He handed her a larger package. "I

hope you won't be offended by the more personal nature of this gift, but I couldn't resist it."

She frowned at him, wondering just how personal the gift might be, aware that his mother was seated right next to her. It was a robe, a beautiful long burgundy robe with a satin collar and belt. He must have noticed the worn condition of her robe.

One of the things she was grateful for was that although he had been extravagant with the things he'd bought for the boys, the things he'd bought for her had been ordinary presents, as if he'd known she'd be displeased if he went overboard for her.

"I have something for you, Henry." Melissa got up from the sofa and grabbed the small present she'd slipped under the tree when she'd come downstairs that morning. He looked at her in surprise, took the gift and sat in one of the chairs to open it.

"There's not much I can buy for a man who appears to have everything," Melissa said. "But I know it's something you don't have, something I think you'll want to have."

He looked at her curiously, then ripped the paper off to expose two small frames. Inside the frames were the newborn pictures of the boys and two cigars with bands that exclaimed, "It's a Boy."

His eyes filled with emotion as he gazed at the gifts, then back at her. "It's the most perfect present you could have given me." He stood and kissed her on the cheek. "Thank you."

Her skin burned with the press of his lips and once again she felt overwhelmed by the warmth, by the feel of family and by the gifts he and Mary had bought for her sons.

By ten o'clock most of the mess from the morning had been cleaned up and the doorbell rang to announce a guest. Henry went to answer as Melissa finished placing the last of the wrapping paper into a large garbage bag.

She tensed as she heard the familiar female voice. Hilary. The sharp pang of jealousy that roared through Melissa stunned her. She shouldn't feel jealous of any woman Henry might have in his life. She had no right to feel that kind of emotion.

As Hilary walked into the living room she stopped short at the sight of the twins in their chairs. She looked at the boys, then at Henry, and her pretty features tightened with stunned surprise.

"Hello, Hilary," Melissa said. The woman was exceptionally beautiful and sophisticated in a gold sweater and tight black slacks. Her dark hair was pulled up and gold earrings danced at her dainty ears. She carried in her hands a platter that Melissa assumed was the famous fudge she'd promised Henry the day before.

"Merry Christmas, Mary and Melinda," Hilary replied.

"Melissa. My name is Melissa."

"Of course," Hilary said, then turned her attention to Henry. "Could I speak to you privately for a moment?"

"Okay. Let's go into my study." Henry gestured her down the hallway.

"I can't imagine what he ever saw in that woman," Mary said the minute they had disappeared.

"She's very beautiful," Melissa said as she put the last of the wrapping paper into the trash.

"Maybe on the outside, but it's inner beauty that really matters. Now, if you'll excuse me, I'm going to go help Etta with the lunch preparations."

"And I'm going to put the boys down for their nap," Melissa replied.

Minutes later Melissa stood in the doorway of the room she now thought of as the nursery. Joey had fallen asleep almost immediately and James was almost there, fussing a bit as he fought sleep.

As he finally gave up the battle, Melissa turned from the door and gasped in surprise at the sight of Hilary in front of her.

"He won't marry you, you know," she said softly.

"I don't expect him to marry me," Melissa replied.

Hilary smiled. "He's not going to marry me, either. I'd hoped that eventually I could wear him down, but Henry has no interest in being married. You seem like a nice woman and it would be a shame for you to get hurt."

"I appreciate your concern, but trust me, Henry has made it clear to me a hundred different ways that he's not the marrying kind. Besides, what makes you think I would want to marry him?"

Hilary looked at her and released a dry laugh. "You're kidding, right? I mean, he's good-looking and nice and wealthy. Why wouldn't you want to marry him?"

Melissa couldn't believe she was having this conversation with a woman who had been Henry's lover.

"My life is in Amarillo. I'll be going home tomorrow to my life."

"Well, in any case I just came up here to tell you that it was nice to meet you and I hope you have a safe trip home." With a curt nod, Hilary turned around and walked down the stairs.

Melissa drew a deep breath and went into her bedroom. While the morning had been one of the happiest she could ever remember, she felt a sudden burn of tears in her eyes.

There was no way she'd ever to be able to provide for the twins like Henry could. Would she be denying her sons by choosing not to move here? She didn't want to do the wrong thing, but she didn't know what was the right thing. Maybe she should just take a look at the carriage house and keep an open mind.

Still, she couldn't ignore the fact that somebody was trying to hurt Henry and it was possible she and the boys might become accidental victims.

"Melissa?"

She whirled around to see Henry standing in the doorway. "Everything all right?" he asked.

"Everything is fine," she replied.

"I know Hilary came up here. She didn't say anything to upset you, did she?" He gazed at her worriedly.

Melissa smiled. "Not at all. She simply told me that it was nice to meet me and she hoped I had a safe trip home."

He seemed relieved. "Hilary tends to have a bit of a sharp tongue."

"Don't worry, Henry. I'm a big girl and I can take care of myself."

He nodded. "I was wondering if while the twins are napping if now would be a good time to take you to see the carriage house." He smiled, that slow sexy grin that heated every ounce of blood in her body. "I was also wondering when I was going to get to see that blue sweater on you."

"Why don't you give me five minutes and I'll meet you downstairs and we can take a look."

"Great. I'll meet you downstairs."

The minute he left the room she closed the door and pulled the sweater out of the box. It fit perfectly and was exactly the color of her eyes. The fact that he'd even thought about her eyes made her heart flutter just a little bit.

It was only as she was walking down the stairs that she realized the terrible truth—she was more than a little bit in love with Henry Randolf III.

Chapter 8

The morning had gone far better than Henry had hoped. The living room had been filled with laughter, warmth and a feeling of family that had been missing from the house since his father's death.

Melissa had teased him as if they'd known each other forever, and in many ways that's the way he was beginning to feel about her. She was comfortable, and yet made him simmer with expectancy. He couldn't remember a woman who had done both for him.

He pulled on his holster and his gun and then covered it with his winter coat. Despite the fact that it was a holiday and the season of peace and joy, Henry couldn't let down his guard. He was eager to have a sit-down meeting with Jimmy the next day to see if the lawman had come up with any evidence as to who might be after him. They needed to come up with a plan to force the person out into the open.

He turned as Melissa came down the stairs, clad in the blue sweater and the jeans that did amazing things for her legs and curvy butt. Something about her stole his breath away.

Lust, he told himself. That was it. Lust and nothing more. If he slept with her again he was certain these crazy feelings would go away.

Her plans were to leave in the morning and short of locking her up in a tower, there was no way he could stop her. He pulled her coat from the closet and held it out to her. "Ready?"

She nodded. "Ready."

"I've got to say, you look sexy as hell in that sweater."

"I'll bet you say that to all the girls," she replied lightly but her cheeks flushed as she pulled on her coat.

They stepped out the door, and Henry threw an arm around her shoulder. He told himself it was because he wanted to protect her if somebody came at them, but the truth was he'd been dying to touch her all day.

She didn't pull away but instead snuggled into him as the cold wind whipped her hair against his face. They walked briskly, not speaking. Henry kept his gaze bouncing left and right, relaxing as he saw Charlie and several of his men in the distance.

When they reached the carriage house he unlocked the door and ushered her into the foyer. "You might want to keep your coat on. We just have the minimal heat running in here right now."

She nodded, stepped into the living room and caught

her breath. "Oh, my gosh. This is four times the size of my apartment."

It was an open floor plan, the living room flowing into the kitchen. The living-room flooring was a soft beige carpeting and the kitchen had an attractive tile in Southwest colors. The furnishings were simple but tasteful and the kitchen was fully equipped with every pot and pan that a chef might need.

"If you wanted to bring in your own furniture we could store all of this," he said, unable to read the expression on her face. "Let me show you the bedrooms." He led her down a short hallway to the first bedroom. It was definitely large enough to accommodate two cribs and later two twin beds for the boys. From the window the stables and corral were in view, perfect for two little cowboys.

From there he led her into the master bedroom, which was huge, with an adjoining bathroom complete with a Jacuzzi tub. For a moment his head filled with a vision of how she'd look in that tub with her shiny hair piled up on her head and her body surrounded by scented bubbles. He tried desperately to shove the provocative vision out of his mind.

She wandered around the room and when she finally turned to look at him, tears glimmered in her eyes. Instead of looking pleased, she looked achingly miserable.

"What's wrong?" he asked.

The tears spilled from her eyes onto her cheeks. "I don't know what to do. I'm so confused. I'm so overwhelmed by everything."

Henry realized at that moment he didn't like to

see her cry. He walked over to her and captured her pretty face between his palms. The look in her eyes was slightly wild, as if she wanted to escape him and the entire situation.

"Melissa, don't cry," he said gently. "Tell me what's wrong."

She jerked away from him and took several steps backward. "You don't understand. This place is so wonderful and all the things you bought for the boys were unbelievable. I know they could have a wonderful life here, but they could have a wonderful life with me in Amarillo, too."

She raised her chin and swiped angrily at her tears. "Lots of children just see their father on the weekends and they survive just fine. People get divorced or never marry and visitation is worked out okay."

He stared at her for a long moment. "But that's not what I want," he said. He shoved his hands into his coat pockets and leaned against the wall. "I don't want to be a weekend dad. What can I do to make this work for you? Of course I'd take care of all your moving expenses and if you have a lease that needs to be broken, I'll take care of that, too. If you're worried about work, I'm sure I can find you some clients for your interior decorating and there's always the hotel that you could be contracted to do. I can take care of all your needs, Melissa. We can make this work."

As he'd spoken, her tears had dried and she gazed at him with an inscrutable expression. When he finished she shook her head and offered him a small, somehow sad smile.

"Henry, there are some things your money just can't buy. You can't buy me. I don't care about money or things. My mother and I didn't have money, but we were happy." She paused and frowned.

"So, this is a no?" he asked flatly.

"It's an I don't know," she replied with obvious frustration. "I've known you and your mother for a couple of days. I refuse to make a life-altering decision that quickly. What I suggest is that I go home tomorrow and think things through without your influence. I want to do what's best for everybody, Henry, and that includes what's best for me."

Although he was disappointed with her decision, he couldn't help but admire her strength in not succumbing to an easier life than the one he thought she was currently living.

"You know I won't stop trying to change your mind," he said lightly, hoping to dispel some of the tension that sparked in the air between them.

She offered him a smile. "Why am I not surprised by that?" She walked out of the bedroom and he followed just behind her.

"I told you I was stubborn," he said.

"Just be aware that you might have met your match," she replied.

As they stepped out of the carriage house he noticed that the sun had disappeared beneath a thick layer of clouds and the air felt colder than it had before.

What he needed was a good old-fashioned blizzard that would make Melissa stay long enough for him to get her to agree to what he wanted.

But Henry knew there were two things he couldn't control. The weather was the first and apparently Melissa was the second.

It began to snow at nine o'clock that evening. Melissa stood at her bedroom window and stared out in dismay. If this kept up there was no way she could leave after breakfast in the morning like she'd planned.

She checked on the boys, who were sleeping soundly, then went back down the stairs where she knew Henry was probably having a glass of scotch. Funny, after such a brief time she'd begun to know his habits. He usually sat in the living room to unwind after his mother excused herself for bed.

Sure enough, he was seated in his chair, a glass of scotch at his side as he stared at the lights still twinkling on the Christmas tree. He smiled when she appeared in the doorway. "How about a glass of wine?"

"That sounds nice," she agreed and sat on the sofa while he went to the bar and poured her drink.

It was odd, anytime she was near him a sizzle of anticipation raced through her and yet she was also comfortable with him. He was an easy man to be around, easy to talk to and share things with.

As he handed her the glass of wine, she again wondered if somehow somebody had hurt him in the past. Had somebody made him believe that he had nothing to offer a woman except for his bank account and a lavish lifestyle? His money seemed to be the only bargaining chip he knew how to use to get the things he wanted in life.

"Looks like your plans to take off tomorrow morning might have to be postponed," he said as he returned to his chair.

"Don't look so smug about it," she replied teasingly. "Actually, I'm hoping it stops soon and the roads will be all right for travel by morning."

"And I'm hoping it snows until March and you're forced to stay here and I'll have all that time to convince you to move into the carriage house."

She laughed. "You're positively relentless." She took a sip of her wine and eyed him curiously. "Tell me why you're such a cynic when it comes to love. Haven't you ever been in love before?"

"The last time I was in love I was in seventh grade. Her name was Angela and I was absolutely crazy about her." He took a drink of his scotch and then continued. "It took me months to get up the nerve to ask her to a school dance that was coming up."

Melissa sensed a sad tale ahead and there was nothing worse than young love scorned. "Did she go to the dance with you?"

He smiled, and she saw a hint of sadness, a whisper of loneliness in the depths of his eyes. "She did. She told me she knew I was rich and if I'd buy her a gold bracelet she'd go with me."

"So you bought her the bracelet?" A tiny pang pieced Melissa's heart, a pain for the boy he'd been who had learned early that his worth was in his wallet.

He nodded. "Bought her the bracelet, took her to the dance and thought it was the beginning of a wonderful love match. Then when I took her home that night she told me that she'd only gone out with me for the bracelet and that I shouldn't bother her anymore." He smiled again and this time it was the smile of the cynic he'd become. "That was my first and only experience with love."

"That's horrible," she exclaimed.

He shrugged. "It was a long time ago. Tell me about the man you were dating before we met that night. Were you in love with him?"

"I believed I was at the time." She thought of Tom, who she'd once thought she would marry. There had been a time when any thought of him brought pain, but all she felt now was relief that she hadn't married a man who had cheated on her, a man who hadn't valued her.

"I loved what I thought we had. I loved the idea of getting married and building a family. I loved the idea of waking up with the same man I went to bed with day after day, year after year. We'd dated for over two years and it had become comfortable. I just assumed we'd take the next step and get married but now I'm glad we didn't. He didn't love me the way I wanted to be loved."

"Mindlessly, desperately," Henry said.

"Exactly," she replied, surprised that he'd remembered she'd said that before.

They fell silent, but it was a comfortable quiet. Melissa sipped her wine and found her gaze going again and again to him.

He was such an attractive man with sharp, bold features and that sexy cleft in his chin. But it wasn't his physical qualities that drew her. She loved the teasing light that so often lit his eyes. She loved the respect and caring he showed to his mother. He was a good man and he would make a wonderful role model for her children.

"I think I'll call it a night," she finally said. "I'm still hoping to be able to get home in the morning." She stood and finished the last of her wine, then headed for the kitchen to place her glass in the sink.

"I think I'll call it a night, too," he said and followed behind her into the kitchen. "Jimmy is coming over tomorrow and we're going to sit down and discuss what's been going on and what we're going to do about it." He placed his glass in the sink next to hers.

"What can you do about it? You don't know who is after you." She looked at him worriedly. "Even if the person is just trying to scare you, there's nothing that says he won't make a mistake and actually manage to shoot you." She was shocked by the fear that rocketed through her, fear for him.

"Yeah, that thought has entered my mind, too," he said dryly. "I'm sure Jimmy and I can put our heads together and come up with a plan to figure out who is responsible and get them behind bars. Don't you worry about it. I'll get it all taken care of."

"I can't help but worry about it," she replied. "You're now a part of my life." Emotion began to well up inside her. "I mean, I don't want my boys to grow up without their father," she said hurriedly.

As they left the kitchen and headed for the stairs, Melissa tried to get her emotions under control. It was true, she didn't want anything to happen to him for the twins' sake. But it was also true that as a woman she'd be devastated if anything happened to him.

He turned off the Christmas tree lights then together they climbed the stairs. As always, the first thing Melissa did when she reached the top of the stairs was go into the boys' bedroom to make sure they were still peacefully sleeping.

Henry followed her in and a soft smile played on his face as he looked first at Joey and then at James. That smile, filled with such love, with such tenderness, created a warmth inside her.

She would never have to worry about her sons being loved. If anything ever happened to her, Henry would make sure they not only had what they needed to survive, but he'd make sure their world had the love he refused to believe in for himself.

"Melissa." He grabbed her hand as they left the room.

She knew immediately what he wanted, what she wanted from him. For months after that night of the blizzard she'd thought about the pleasure she'd found in his arms.

She wanted it again. She wanted him again and she could tell by the heat in his eyes that he wanted the same.

She stepped closer to him and raised her face to him and he took the unspoken invitation by crashing his mouth down on hers.

His mouth was hot hunger against hers and she felt as if she'd been waiting for this since the moment he'd first opened the door to her.

Allowing him to deepen the kiss, she leaned into him, wanting him to have no question in his mind that she wanted him.

His tongue danced with hers as his hands slid down her back and pulled her hips into his. His arousal was evident and fed the flames of desire inside her.

The kiss seemed to last forever before he finally dropped his hands from around her and stepped back. "You look beautiful in that blue sweater, but I remember how beautiful you looked naked. I want you, Melissa. This has nothing to do with anything but you and me."

"I want you, too," she said, her voice a husky whisper.

"You know I'm not making any promises. I need you to understand that there's no future with me. I'm not the man to give you your happily ever after."

"As far as I'm concerned, tonight you're a handsome cowboy keeping me warm on a wintery night and nothing more," she replied. His eyes flamed as he pulled her into the bedroom and back into his arms.

Chapter 9

This time his kiss left her breathless and aching. When he pulled her sweater over her head she was more than ready for him. There was no embarrassment as she stood before him in her wispy bra. The light from her bathroom spilled into the bedroom and she could see the flames that lit his eyes while he gazed at her.

Every bone in her body weakened and she reached out to unfasten the buttons on his shirt. The heat from his body radiated to her, urging her to unbutton his shirt and sweep it off his broad shoulders.

He was beautiful, with his chiseled chest and flat abdomen. He pulled her back into his arms and as he kissed her he reached around her to unfasten her bra. He tugged the straps off her shoulders and when it fell away he embraced her again and she delighted in the feel of his bare skin against hers.

"I've wanted this since the moment you arrived," he said, his breath hot against her throat.

"I've wanted it, too," she confessed.

Within minutes they were both naked and beneath the blankets in bed. Even though she'd only made love with him once, his skin felt just the way she remembered, warm and firm as he pulled her against him. The familiar scent of him filled her head and she knew any other man who ever wore that particular brand of cologne would always evoke memories of Henry.

As his kisses made her mindless, his hands cupped her breasts and a low moan escaped her lips. He pulled his mouth from hers and looked down at her. "You are so beautiful," he whispered.

She felt beautiful beneath his gaze. That was part of Henry's gift. He'd made her feel beautiful and desirous that night of the blizzard, and he made her feel that way now.

He lowered his mouth to capture the erect tip of one of her breasts and she tangled her fingers in his rich, dark hair. Sweet sensations sizzled through her.

He teased her nipple, swirling his tongue and using his teeth to lightly nip. Melissa closed her eyes as all concerns about the future melted away beneath the heat of his caresses. She couldn't think about anything but him and the magic of his touch.

She ran her hands down the length of his broad back, loving the play of muscle beneath her fingertips. She felt safe with him, not just physically protected, but emotionally as well. She felt as if she could say anything to him, tell him her deepest, darkest secrets and he'd keep those secrets safe.

The love she'd tried not to feel for him welled up inside her, a love she knew would never be reciprocated. But at the moment that didn't matter. She had this night with him and she knew it had to be enough for her. She wouldn't allow this to happen again but she intended to enjoy every moment of it.

"This is much nicer than a hardwood floor beneath the scratchy blanket from my truck," he said, his voice thick with desire.

"I have very fond memories of that scratchy blanket and the hardwood floor." She could speak no more as his mouth once again claimed hers.

Every inch of her skin was electrified, for each and every place he touched, he kissed, sizzled in response.

His heartbeat was strong and quick against hers, the heart that didn't believe in love, the one that refused to believe that anyone could love him for himself.

She slid her lips down his neck, wanting him to feel loved, to feel as desired as he made her feel. Her mouth moved down his chest and she licked first one of his nipples, then the other.

He gasped, a quick intake of breath that made her even bolder. He rolled over on his back as she moved down the length of his body, kissing and nipping and teasing his fevered skin with her lips.

Tangling his hands in her hair, his entire body tensed as she kissed his inner thigh. He was fully erect and although this was something she'd rarely done for Tom, she wanted the utter intimacy with Henry.

As she took him into her mouth she let out a low groan and every muscle in his body tensed. "Melissa," he moaned as his hands tightened in her hair.

She loved the strained sound of her name on his lips, loved the pleasure she knew she was giving to him. But it didn't take long for him to push her away and roll to his side.

"Now, it's my turn," he said, his eyes gleaming with promise. He ran his hand down her body and rubbed against her. "I want you gasping for air and crying out my name."

As he moved his fingers against the very center of her, a rising tide of pleasure began to build inside her. She arched her hips up to meet his touch, needing release, wanting the wave to consume her.

And then it did, crashing through her as she cried his name over and over again. She shuddered with the force of it and tears filled her eyes. But he wasn't finished yet. He rolled over and grabbed a condom from the nightstand and while she was still weak and gasping, he moved between her legs and entered her.

For a moment neither of them moved. The pleasure of him filling her up was so intense she feared if she moved she'd lose it again.

He froze, his arms holding him up from her chest. From the light shining in from her bathroom she could see his features. His eyes were closed, his neck muscles corded as if he were under enormous strain.

He opened his eyes and looked down at her, then

slowly slid his hips back and thrust forward. That single slow movement broke everything loose between them.

Fast and furious, he stroked into her and she encouraged him by clutching his buttocks and pulling him into her.

Lost. She was lost in him and once again she felt the wild tide rushing in. As it washed over her she felt him tense and moan against her, knowing it had claimed him, too.

He collapsed on her and she wrapped her arms around his back, wishing she could hold him there forever. But all too quickly he got up and padded into the adjoining bathroom.

Melissa turned her head to one side and fought a sudden rush of tears. Of all the foolish, reckless things she'd ever done in her life, this was probably the worst. She'd chosen to make love to a man who apparently wasn't capable of loving her back.

MysteryMom couldn't have known that she was sending Melissa into a new heartbreak. The woman had probably simply wanted to unite a man with his sons, ease the burden of single parenting for Melissa. She'd accomplished that. Melissa would no longer be alone in the task of raising her sons. She knew in her heart, in her soul, that Henry would always be a support and help in the parenting process.

But MysteryMom couldn't have known that Melissa would fall mindlessly, desperately in love with Henry. She couldn't have known that Melissa would repeat the same mistake that she'd made on that snowy night over a year ago. At least he'd used a condom and there wouldn't be another accidental pregnancy.

As he came out of the bathroom she assumed he'd leave to go to his bedroom, but instead he surprised her by sliding back beneath the sheets and taking her in his arms. He kissed her on the temple, a sweet, soft kiss that touched her more than anything that had occurred between them.

"Definitely better in a bed," he said. He lay on his back and pulled her into his side. His hand stroked her hair as she placed her head on his chest. "I really hate to see you take off tomorrow."

"It's time, Henry. It's been a wonderful holiday but now it's over and I have to get back to my real life." It was more important than ever that she leave here as soon as possible. Her heart had gotten involved in a way that already would ache when she left. More time here would only make the ache sharper when she did go home.

She raised her head to look at him. "You know I'll do whatever I can to make it easy on you to see the boys."

"I know that." He raised his hand and trailed a finger down the side of her cheek, across her lower lip. "I can't think of a better woman to be the mother of my boys."

The tears that had hovered just under the surface sprang to her eyes at his words. "You're just saying that now because you have me naked in bed with you," she replied with a choked little laugh.

"You know that's not true," he chided. "You have the values I want the boys to have. I know you'll teach them to have integrity, to have strong but gentle hearts."

She ran her hand across his chest and placed it on his heart. Her last thought before she fell asleep was that the one thing she would teach her boys was to believe in the power and wonder of love, something apparently nobody had ever taught Henry.

Henry stood at the window in his study and watched the snow swirling in the air. It had snowed about two inches overnight, effectively postponing Melissa's plans to leave first thing that morning.

He was now waiting for Jimmy to arrive. Jimmy had called earlier to tell Henry that the snow wouldn't keep him from his appointment.

Staring at the carriage house in the distance, Henry thought of the night before. Making love to Melissa had been amazing and he'd been in no hurry to leave her bed.

Henry couldn't remember the last time he'd slept with a woman in his arms. He'd never stayed the night with Hilary, had always preferred the comfort of being alone in his own bed. But sleeping with Melissa had been not just comfortable, but comforting in a way he'd never imagined. It had been nice to feel the warmth of her next to him as he'd drifted off to sleep. And it had been equally as nice to wake up with her curled in his arms.

Surely these crazy feelings he was developing for her were nothing more than gratitude. After all, she'd given him the greatest gift a man could get—children.

He wasn't going to mention the carriage house solution to her again. He recognized that over the past two days he'd become a bore and bordered on becoming a bully in trying to get her to do what he wanted.

Whatever she decided, they'd make it work because it had to work. Even though they weren't married, he knew they'd do whatever was in the best interest of the twins.

At the moment Melissa and his mother and the twins were all in the kitchen. It was Etta's day off and they were in the process of making dinner.

As he'd walked to his study he'd heard the sound of laughter and merriment coming from the kitchen. The house would feel empty once Melissa and the boys were gone.

Actually, the house had felt empty for a long time. And if he thought about it long enough he'd admit that his life had been fairly empty for a very long time. He frowned, irritated with the direction his thoughts were taking. Maybe it was a good thing Melissa was leaving soon. She was messing with his mind in a way that was distinctly uncomfortable.

He turned away from the window as a knock fell on his door. The door opened and Jimmy poked his head in. "Your mom told me to come on in," he said.

Henry motioned him inside. "How are the roads?" he asked as he gestured his friend into the chair in front of the desk.

"A little nasty but not too bad. The road crews are out working so if we don't get any more accumulation we should have everything under control." He eased into the chair. "You got any of that good scotch hidden away in here?"

Henry walked to the minibar in the corner and poured himself and Jimmy a drink, then handed Jimmy his and sat at the desk with his own.

Jimmy took a deep swallow and sighed. "I don't know if Willie told you or not, but he found the bullet that shot out your tire still in the rubber that was left on the truck. It was a .22 caliber. I know it wasn't Hank. At the time your truck was fired on, Hank was down at Lazy Ed's, completely sauced."

Lazy Ed's was a popular tavern for the ranch hands in the area. "I'm not surprised. His drinking is what caused him to get fired in the first place," Henry said.

"Before we get into all this, I want to know about those twin boys that your mother introduced me to in the kitchen. They sure do have the Randolf chin. You been holding out on me about your love life?"

Henry smiled and knew in an instant he wasn't about to tell Jimmy the truth about how the twins were conceived. Although Henry certainly wasn't a prude, he didn't want to give anyone in town a reason to think less of Melissa.

"Melissa is a friend from Amarillo. She's a terrific woman and we've been close for some time. When she got pregnant we agreed that we'd share the parenting of the boys and remain friends."

"I never even knew you wanted kids," Jimmy said.

Henry smiled. "I didn't know I wanted them until they were here. I got to tell you, Jimmy. They change your life. They make you want to be a better man. That's why it's so important we get this mess cleaned up, these attacks that are happening on me. I can't have them around if it's not safe."

Henry leaned back in his chair. "You know who is at the top of my suspect list."

Jimmy nodded. "Tom Burke. You scare him, Henry."

"He should be scared," Henry said with a scowl. "You and I both know he's a criminal."

Jimmy nodded. "I've been in contact with the FBI and I'm hoping they're going to look into his actions as city manager. The problem is we both know he's a likely suspect. What we don't have is any proof."

"Did you question him about his whereabouts at the time my tire was shot out?"

Jimmy nodded. "According to his wife, he was at home with her."

Once again Henry frowned. "You know damn good and well she'd lie for him."

Jimmy nodded. "I've put a couple of my men on Tom. Full-time surveillance as long as I have the manpower. If he tries anything we'll be on top of him. It's the best I can do, Henry."

Henry nodded. He knew Jimmy was as frustrated as he was by what had been happening. He took a drink of his scotch.

"If this had all started the night that Melissa showed up here with those babies, I would ask you if you thought Hilary might be playing a woman scorned," Jimmy said.

Henry laughed at the very idea of Hilary hiding out in the woods with a gun. "No way. I'll grant you she wasn't too happy to discover I had two babies, but Hilary knew the score where I was concerned. Besides, she'd never risk breaking a nail to do anything like this."

"And the first attack happened to you before Melissa arrived on the scene," Jimmy said.

Henry nodded. "I'm telling you it's Tom Burke or it's somebody he's hired. He's the only person who has a hell of a lot to lose if I become mayor."

Jimmy tilted his glass up for another drink of the scotch. "I just wanted to come out here and tell you that I'm doing the best I can."

"What about a ballistics test on the bullet Willie dug out of my tire?" Henry asked.

"Unfortunately the bullet hit your rim and was pretty mangled. Besides, in order to do a ballistics test you have to have a weapon to compare it to and Tom Burke insists he doesn't have a rifle."

Henry snorted in disbelief. "I don't know a man in this entire county who doesn't own a rifle. This is Texas, for God's sake."

"You're preaching to the choir, Henry."

For the next thirty minutes the men spoke about other potential suspects. There were only two that Henry could think of, both council members and friends of Tom Burke.

"You definitely have the support of the people," Jimmy said. "People like you, they admire your integrity and they trust you. If you can stay alive until February there is no doubt in my mind that you'll be voted in as mayor."

"That's nice to hear," Henry replied.

Jimmy glanced toward the window. "I've got to head back into town." He stood.

"I appreciate you coming out on such a crummy day." Henry stood as well.

"I swear I'm going to get to the bottom of this, Henry," Jimmy said as they left the study.

"I just hope you do before this mysterious shooter gets lucky," Henry said dryly.

The two men walked to the front door, where they said their goodbyes. The snow had begun to fall again and as Henry closed the door he realized that he was more worried now about whoever was trying to hurt him than he'd been before Melissa had arrived in the house.

Before, he'd just been irritated by the whole thing. But now all he could think about was if anything happened to him the boys wouldn't have their father. He had every reason in the world to want to stay alive.., for them and for Melissa.

The laughter coming from the kitchen pulled him away from the front door and to the source of the sound. Once there he found his mother and Melissa finishing up dinner preparations.

As he walked into the room, the twins flashed him smiles that as always filled him with warmth. "Something smells wonderful," he said.

"Melissa can cook," Mary exclaimed.

"It's just spaghetti with meat sauce," Melissa replied as she took a pot of boiling pasta off the stove top.

Henry took a seat at the table and watched as she dumped the spaghetti noodles into an awaiting colander. "You don't understand. Mom would think you were amazing if you could just boil an egg. She's the worst cook in the entire state of Texas."

Melissa shot a quick glance to Mary. "Don't worry," Mary said with a laugh. "He's quite right. It's one of the reasons Big Henry hired Etta. He knew if we tried to live on my cooking we'd all starve. Henry, why don't you set the table and I'll get the salad."

As always, dinner was a pleasant time. They chatted about favorite foods and Mary regaled Melissa with some of her war stories at the stove. The boys kept up their end of the conversation by babbling and cooing.

At one point James blew a raspberry. He looked startled and as they all laughed, he grinned and blew another one.

Henry smiled at Melissa. "You might have gotten his very first smile, but at least I didn't miss out on his very first raspberry."

After they'd finished eating Mary took the boys into the living room while Henry and Melissa cleaned up. "Dinner was terrific," he said as he stacked the dishes she rinsed into the dishwasher. "Do you like to cook?"

She nodded. "I do, but most of the time it seems like a lot of trouble to cook for one. When my mother was alive I did a lot of cooking, but not so much since she passed."

"You miss her."

She smiled with a touch of sadness. "Every day. Unfortunately diabetes is a ruthless disease and I think she was tired of fighting. It's some comfort to know she's not in pain anymore."

"I miss my father, too. He and I weren't just father and son, we were friends." Henry smiled at thoughts of his dad. "He was bigger than life, one of those colorful characters that people didn't forget after meeting him."

Melissa handed him the last plate. "And he taught you everything you need to know about being a wonderful father."

Henry smiled. "Yeah, I hadn't thought about it before, but he was a wonderful role model." He took the towel she offered him and dried his hands.

"It worried me that I was all alone," she said, her expression somber. "I worried about what would happen to the boys if I got hit by a car or had a sudden heart attack. Now I don't have to worry anymore. I know if anything happens to me you'll love them and take care of them."

"Nothing is going to happen to you," he assured her. "You and I are going to parent those boys until they're hulking adults and we're old and gray."

She smiled. "I like that plan, and speaking of the boys, I think it's probably time for a diaper change."

The rest of the evening passed and by nine o'clock it was time to put the boys down for the night. Mary said her good-night and retired to her wing of the house while Melissa carried Joey and Henry carried James up the stairs to their room.

Once the boys were settled into their beds, Melissa motioned Henry into her room. "Do you think I'm going to be able to head home tomorrow?" she asked.

Henry walked over to her window and peered outside. A light snow was still falling. He turned to look at her. "Why don't you make a decision in the morning?

It's snowing now but maybe it will stop before too long. I can call Jimmy in the morning and ask him about the condition of the roads."

What he really wanted to do was have a repeat of the night before. But something in the way she stood with her arms crossed in front of her chest made him think she wouldn't be open to the idea.

"You want to go back down and have a glass of wine or something?" he asked.

She shook her head. "No, I think I'll just call it a night now. I really am hoping that we'll be able to travel in the morning. Besides, it's been a long day and I'm exhausted."

He realized she was already distancing herself, preparing for the goodbye. He was surprised at the edge of sadness that took hold of him. It wasn't like it was going to be goodbye forever, he told himself. Most likely one way or another he'd be seeing her every weekend. If she didn't want to drive here, then he'd drive to Amarillo. But somehow he knew that once she left here things would never be the same between them again.

"Then I guess I'll just say good night," he said. He couldn't help himself. He stepped closer to her with the intention to deliver a kiss to her forehead, but instead found his mouth claiming hers.

The minute their lips connected the window where Henry had stood moments before shattered. As Henry saw the device that lay on the floor in the bedroom fear screamed inside him.

He shoved Melissa toward the door and they fell into the hallway as the bomb went off.

Chapter 10

One moment Henry had been kissing her and the next Melissa found herself on the hallway floor with Henry on top of her. The back of her head had connected hard with the floor in the fall and she was dazed and confused.

The loud explosion still rang in Melissa's ears, making her momentarily deaf. As Henry got off her, her hearing began to return. Above the din of the house alarm ringing she could hear the cries of her babies and her heart slammed into her chest with enough force to steal what little breath she had left.

"Check on the boys," Henry yelled as he pulled her up off the floor. He raced back into the bedroom and tore down the curtains that had caught on fire. As he stamped out the flames, she ran across the hall to the boys' room. They were safe, but scared by the noise.

She took them into her arms, and her heart beat so fast it felt as if it were trying to burst out of her chest. She stood in the center of the room, afraid to move, unsure what might happen next. She tried to calm the boys but with the alarm ringing discordantly it was impossible. Tears raced down Melissa's cheeks as she tried to still her own fear.

Somebody had thrown a bomb of some kind into the window of the bedroom where she'd slept, at the window where Henry had been standing only moments earlier. Her head couldn't wrap around it.

The blast could have killed him. It could have killed her. Had Henry not reacted as quickly as he had, they both could have been seriously hurt or worse.

She hugged the boys even closer to her chest and breathed a sigh of relief as the alarm suddenly stopped ringing. Now what? Had the danger passed? Was there more to come? Too afraid to move, she remained in the center of the room.

A moment later both Henry and Mary rushed into the room.

"You okay?" Henry asked her, his features taut with tension.

"We're fine," she said and felt a new press of tears as Mary put an arm around her shoulder.

"Jimmy is on his way," Henry said as he took Joey from her arms. "Let's go downstairs to wait for him."

By the time they got down the stairs several of Henry's ranch hands were at the front door. Henry opened the door to allow them inside and they all gathered in the living room.

"We heard the explosion," Charlie said, his features grim. "Then we saw the fire at the window. I'm just glad to see you're all okay."

"You didn't see anyone?" Henry asked as he shifted Joey from one arm to the other.

Both Charlie and Randy shook their heads. "Didn't hear a car, didn't see a soul," Charlie said. "Dammit, it's like it's a phantom."

"It wasn't a phantom that threw a bomb through the window," Henry said, his anger rife in his voice. He handed Joey to his mother. "I want to go out and take a look around. With the snow there should be some footprints that can be tracked."

Charlie frowned. "Unfortunately, Randy and I might have messed up any prints," he admitted. "When we heard the blast we both ran to that side of the house. I didn't even think about footprints."

"There still might be some prints that don't belong to the two of you," Henry said.

"Please, Henry, wait for Jimmy before you go out," Melissa said. She had no idea what other danger might await him if he ventured outside and she couldn't stand the thought of anything happening to him.

"Yes, Henry," Mary spoke up, her voice filled with a mother's worry. "Please wait for Jimmy. I don't want you out there."

Melissa could tell by Henry's expression that he was chomping at the bit, needing to do something, anything that might find the guilty party.

"If you want, Randy and I can go back out and take another look around," Charlie offered.

"Trust me, if there's anyone around I'd be happy to tie him up and beat his ass until Jimmy shows up," Randy exclaimed.

Henry clapped him on the back. "I appreciate the sentiment, Randy, but the last thing I want is for anyone to get hurt. Why don't we all sit tight until Jimmy gets here?"

Charlie and Randy sat on the two chairs while Melissa and Mary sat on the sofa with the twins. Henry paced the room, looking like he wanted nothing more than to punch something or someone.

There was no question that somehow, someway, Melissa had to leave here as soon as possible. She couldn't place her children at risk. The idea that the pipe bomb could have easily been thrown through the window of the bedroom where the twins slept filled her with a kind of terror she'd never felt before.

"Randy, what I'd like you to do is see if you can find a piece of plywood in the shed to put over the broken window after Jimmy takes a look around." Henry turned to look at Melissa and his eyes were dark as midnight. "Melissa, I want you to pack a bag for you and the boys."

She looked at him in surprise. "But where are we going?" She knew the roads were snow-packed and her tires weren't in the best shape. There was no way she'd take off at this time of night for home.

"I'm going to have Charlie check you in to a motel until the roads are safe enough for you to travel home."

Henry looked at his mother. "You might want to pack a bag, too."

"Nonsense," Mary scoffed. "I agree with you that Melissa should take the twins and go but nobody is chasing me out of my home."

Henry nodded, as if unsurprised by his mother's decision to stay put. He returned his attention to Melissa. "The latest weather report I heard said that the snow is going to stick around for at least another twenty-four to forty-eight hours, so pack enough things to last you and the boys for a couple of days."

"But what about you?" Melissa asked. She wanted him to come with them, to leave this place of danger and hide out with her someplace where she knew he'd be safe.

"I'll be fine as long as I know you and the twins are safe." He took James from her arms. "Come on, I'll go up and help you get your things together."

"I'm going to head out to the shed," Randy said. "It's been long enough now I imagine whoever threw that bomb is long gone."

"And I'll wait here with Mrs. Randolf," Charlie added.

Henry said nothing as they climbed the stairs back to the room where the blast had occurred. The scent of smoke and gasoline lingered in the air.

"It must have been loaded with fuel," he said as he surveyed the damage. "At least it wasn't filled with any kind of shrapnel."

Melissa shuddered at the thought. She pulled her suitcase from the closet and quickly packed what little

364   *The Cowboy's Secret Twins*

she'd brought with her. They then moved into the boys'
room, where she packed their clothes and diapers.

"I'll have Charlie get you settled in at one of the mo-
tels and I'll call you first thing in the morning," he said.
She turned to face him and saw the worry in his eyes,
a worry coupled with rage.

He stepped up to her and placed his palm against
her cheek. She turned her face into the warmth of his
hand. "He could have hurt you tonight. He could have
hurt you and the boys."

"But that didn't happen," she said softly.

"Not this time, but I can't take another chance. I
thought you were safe here, but I now realize I can't
guarantee your safety. You'll be safe in a motel until
the roads are clean enough for you to go home."

"Henry?" Jimmy's voice drifted up the stairs.

Henry dropped his hand from her face and stepped
back from her. "Come on up, Jimmy."

Melissa and Henry met the lawman in the hallway.
"You can have a look around. I'm sending Melissa with
Charlie to a motel for the rest of the night. I'll be back
up here as soon as I get those arrangements made."

Henry didn't say a word as they went back downstairs. Once there, as Melissa and Mary began to put
the coats on the boys, he disappeared into his study.

Minutes later he came out. "I've got you set up in
a room at Ed's Motel. It's clean and comfortable and
the owner is a friend of mine. The room is registered
in the name of Hank James. Nobody will know you're
there and the key will be waiting for you in the office."

A muscle knotted in his jaw. "Charlie will get you

there safe and sound and I'll call you in the morning."
He shoved a wad of cash into her hand. "There's a diner
right next door to the motel. They'll deliver whatever
you need to your motel-room door."

It was crazy, but as Melissa pulled on her coat and
Charlie grabbed her bags, she had a sudden terrible
fear for Henry.

"Please, stay safe," she said as she held the twins
in her arms.

He kissed Joey and James on the forehead and then
gently shoved a strand of her hair behind her ear. "Get
out of here and let me do what I need to do."

It took only minutes for her and the boys to be loaded
into Charlie's four-wheel-drive vehicle. While they
pulled away from the house Melissa looked back to
see Henry silhouetted in the front door.

Once again she was struck with the strong, inex-
plicable fear—the fear that she was never going to see
him again.

"Henry, where are you going?" Jimmy asked as
Henry pulled on his winter coat. They had just spent
the last hour picking through the rubble in the bedroom.

Jimmy had collected the pieces of the device to use
as evidence and now Randy was hanging the plywood
over the broken window.

Charlie had returned to the ranch after dropping Melissa and the children at Ed's Motel. At least Henry had
the comfort of knowing she and the babies would be
safe there until she could leave town.

With each moment that had ticked by a rage had

grown in Henry, a seething sick rage that begged to be released. And he knew exactly where to vent it.

"I'm going to Burke's house." Henry buttoned his coat but didn't reach for his gun in the drawer. He knew if he had it on him he might use it and as much as he wanted to hurt the man he believed was responsible for the pipe bomb, he didn't want to kill him. He was a father now, a man who had too much too lose by letting his rage get the best of him.

"Dammit, Henry, you can't go off half-cocked," Jimmy exclaimed in frustration.

"Trust me, I'm not half-cocked, I'm fully loaded," Henry replied dryly.

"Just stay put," Jimmy said. "I'll go talk to Burke."

"Then I'm coming with you." Henry didn't give Jimmy another opportunity to talk him out of it, but instead slammed out the door and walked into the snowy night.

Minutes later he and Jimmy were in Jimmy's patrol car navigating the slick roads as they headed into town. All Henry could think about was how devastating the results might have been had that bomb been thrown into the boys' room. The thought of such a tragedy stoked the flames of his rage even hotter.

"He could have killed my kids, Jimmy. He could have killed Melissa," Henry said, breaking the silence in the car.

"I know," Jimmy said. He grunted as the back of the car threatened to fishtail out. He steered into the slide and straightened the car. "We'll check out Tom's alibi for the time that the bomb was thrown through the window."

"It's possible he didn't personally throw it, but instead hired somebody." Henry frowned. "I've got to put an end to this." He stared out into the dark night. "Maybe I should withdraw from the election."

Jimmy shot him a stunned look. "You'd do that?"

"If I just had myself to worry about then I'd never quit. But it's not just me anymore, Jimmy. I've got kids and Melissa and they are going to need me."

"So they win and the corruption in Dalhart continues." Jimmy released an audible sigh. "Just give me a few more days before you make a decision. You're running on pure emotion right now. Give yourself time to calm down and let me sort this out."

Henry didn't reply. He knew Jimmy was right. He was definitely running on emotion, but as he thought of Melissa and Joey and James, he couldn't help but be filled with emotion.

He'd wanted to be a hero to the town, to clean up the mess that had been allowed to go on for far too long. But he now wondered if the stakes were too high. He'd rather be a father than a hero.

He sat up straighter in the seat as they approached town. The only other vehicles they'd passed were snow trucks laying down salt and pushing snow.

Tom Burke lived well above his means and salary in a five-bedroom luxury home on a three-acre lot. The first thing Henry noticed was that Tom's car was parked in the driveway. Not only was the car relatively clean of snow, but tire tracks showed that it had recently been driven.

The rage that had slowly begun to wane during the drive now roared back to life inside Henry. He was out of the car before it had come to a complete halt.

"Henry, dammit, wait for me," Jimmy cried as he parked the car and got out.

Henry didn't wait. He headed for the front door with a single-mindedness and once he got there he banged on the door with his fist.

By the time the door was opened by Tom, Jimmy had reached the porch. Henry didn't say a word, but rather grabbed the short man by the front of his pristine white shirt and dragged him out the door.

"Hey, get your hands off me," Tom yelled and jerked out of Henry's grasp. "What the hell is wrong with you, man?"

"Have you been out to my place tonight, Tom? I see your car has been driven. Did you come to pay me a little visit?" Henry glared at him and became aware of Deputy Gordon Hunter joining them on the porch.

"I don't know what you're talking about," Tom exclaimed, his beefy face red. "I haven't been anywhere near your place tonight."

"Then you hired somebody to throw that pipe bomb through my window." Henry took a menacing step toward him. "I had babies in the house, you bastard."

Tom looked from Henry to Jimmy. "A pipe bomb? I don't know a damn thing about a pipe bomb."

"Then where did you go tonight?" Henry demanded. "Your car has been driven recently. Where did you go?"

"To the damned grocery store," Tom exclaimed in frustration. "We're supposed to get more snow. I needed to get a gallon of milk. Is that a crime now?"

"It's true," Gordon said. "I've been watching him, tailing him all evening. The only place he went is to the grocery store."

Henry stared at Gordon, then back at Tom. "I'm warning you right now, Tom. If anything happens to anyone I care about, I'll be back here to see you and I'll beat your ass to a pulp."

Tom looked at Jimmy in outrage. "Did you hear that? He threatened me with bodily harm."

Jimmy shook his head. "Nah, he didn't threaten you. He promised you." Jimmy clapped his hand on Henry's back. "Come on, Henry, nothing more can be done here for now."

Henry shot Tom another killer glare, then stalked back to Jimmy's car and got into the passenger seat. As Jimmy and Gordon spoke to Tom for another few minutes, Henry steamed.

How were they ever going to get to the bottom of this? Whoever was responsible was smart enough to leave no clues behind, to do the kind of sneak attacks that made it impossible to investigate.

One thing was clear. He couldn't allow Melissa and the boys back into his home until the situation was resolved and that angered him more than anything.

It was a tension-filled ride back home. Jimmy talked the whole way, detailing his plan to investigate what had happened.

"We might be able to find fingerprints on the pieces

of the bomb that survived the blast. There might be specific traceable material that was used. Don't you worry, Henry. I'm going to get to the bottom of this."

As he babbled on, Henry stared out the window, his mind drifting to Melissa and the boys. What were they doing at this moment? He glanced at his watch and realized his sons would be sound asleep and tonight he wouldn't be able to stand in the doorway and smell their scent, watch their little faces as they dreamed. Tonight he and Melissa wouldn't be able to sit together in the living room, enjoying quiet conversation after his mother had gone to bed.

The fact that some nut had taken these particular pleasures away from him reignited the fire of his anger. But by the time they finally reached the house the anger had burned itself out and he was simply exhausted.

Randy and Charlie sat with his mother in the living room and he quickly told them what had happened with Tom, then Charlie and Randy left.

"Are you all right?" his mother asked as he walked to the bar and poured himself a healthy dose of scotch.

"No. I'm angry and frustrated and I'm wondering if I shouldn't just pull out of the election." He sat on the sofa next to her.

"Is that what you want to do?"

"I don't want anything to happen to Melissa and the boys."

Mary smiled at him. "That didn't answer my question. Besides, as soon as the roads clear Melissa and the boys will return to Amarillo. You still have to live here with any decision you make."

Henry released a sigh and dropped his head back against the cushion. "I've never really been scared in my life, but the thought of how close danger came to Melissa and the boys put a fear in my heart I never want to feel again."

"Parenthood brings with it a multitude of fears." Mary patted his hand. "The first time those boys get on a bicycle your heart is going to race with fear. The day you put them on a bus to go to school you're going to be filled with a terror as you think of all the things that can go wrong. But you'll also know a joy greater than anything you've ever experienced with them."

Henry nodded.

"And then there's Melissa," Mary said softly. "You light up in her presence, Henry."

"She's the mother of my children," he replied.

"I think she could be more than that to you if you'd just open up that heart of yours," Mary said.

"I don't want her to be any more than that," he replied with forced lightness.

Mary sighed. "Your father was a wonderful man, Henry, but he was obsessed about some woman stealing your money. I worry that instead of making you careful, which was his intention, he made you incapable of allowing anyone close to you."

He was in no mood for one of his mother's attempts to get him to change his mind about love and marriage. He tipped his glass up and drained his drink, welcoming the hot burn down his throat. "Mom, it's been a long day and I'm exhausted. I have a lot of things to think about and I don't want to have a conversation about my decision to stay single."

"You're right. I'm sorry." She got up from the sofa. "I'm going to bed. I'll see you in the morning and hopefully by then Jimmy will have this all figured out and we can get back to a normal life."

"Good night, Mom." He watched her disappear up the stairs, then once again leaned his head back and released a long sigh.

He hoped Jimmy had some answers in the morning, but he didn't expect him to have any. He looked over at the phone. What he'd like to do is call Melissa, just hear her voice before he called it a night. But it was late and he didn't want to wake the boys. Besides, he'd told her he'd call her first thing in the morning.

He got up from the sofa and walked to the window. It was snowing again. Yesterday he'd hoped for snow so that he could keep Melissa and the boys here longer. Now he prayed for it to end so she could take the boys back to Amarillo where they would be safe from the madness that had become his life.

Chapter 11

It was the longest night of Melissa's life. The motel room was typical of motel rooms all around the country, equipped with a king-size bed, a television in a cabinet and a desk. It was spotlessly clean and once she'd placed the desk chair and a barricade of pillows along one side of the bed, the boys fell asleep almost immediately.

Unfortunately sleep remained elusive for her. She took a fast shower and changed into her nightgown, then got into bed and tried not to relive the events of the night.

What was happening at the house? Were Henry and Mary all right? If anything happened who would come to tell Melissa that something had gone wrong? Surely somebody would keep her informed.

She tossed and turned with worry and fear and it

was during those long hours of sleeplessness that she realized the depth of her love for Henry James Randolf III. And in that realization she knew she would never be able to give him what he wanted.

The idea of making her home in the carriage house, so close, yet not a part of his life, was physically painful to consider. She could easily imagine the kind of routine they'd fall into over time.

The twins would spend a lot of their time in the big house with Henry and Mary and occasionally the desire Henry and Melissa felt for each other would rear up and explode and they'd make love. There would be no commitment, no love, just an arrangement. She couldn't do it. She couldn't sacrifice her own dreams of a marriage and love forever just so that Henry could get what he wanted—full-time access to the boys and an occasional release of sexual tension with her.

As soon as possible she was heading home and she and Henry would work out a viable visitation plan, one that didn't involve her living in his backyard.

She finally fell asleep around dawn and awakened around eight with a sliver of sunshine drifting in around the edges of the curtains. The boys were still asleep. The disruption from the night before had apparently exhausted them.

She got out of bed and pulled on the luxurious burgundy robe Henry had bought her and moved to the window to peer outside. Although it had snowed another inch or so overnight, the sun was a welcome sight. Surely by late evening or first thing in the morning the roads would be cleared enough that she and the babies could go home.

She needed the reality of her little apartment, away from Henry, where she could think clearly. Being with Henry definitely muddied her mind.

The ring of the telephone on the desk pulled her from the window. She grabbed up the receiver and said a soft hello.

"You okay?" Henry's deep voice filled her ear.

"I am now that I know you're okay," she replied. "I couldn't sleep last night. I've been worried about you."

"I almost called you last night to tell you that everything was fine, but I was afraid I'd wake the boys. I've got a glass company coming out first thing this morning to replace the broken window in the bedroom. Jimmy and his men went over it with a fine-tooth comb looking for anything that might be evidentiary. How are the boys?"

She glanced over to the bed. "Still sleeping. What happened after I left last night?" She listened as he told her about going to Tom Burke's home and confronting the man he thought responsible.

"You didn't really expect him to confess, did you?" she asked when he was finished.

"No, but it would have been nice if we could have settled all this last night. I'm hoping Jimmy will be able to get something from the pieces of the device he collected last night, something that will be enough evidence for an arrest."

"You know I can't come back to the house," she said, her heart heavy as the words left her mouth.

"I don't want you and the boys back here," he replied. "Not until this is all resolved. Last night was too close for comfort and I'd never forgive myself if anything happened to you or Joey or James."

Melissa squeezed the receiver closer to her ear as she heard the passion in his voice. He cared about her. She knew he did, but it wasn't enough for him to invite her fully into his life.

"You have everything you need there? The roads are still pretty bad but you should be able to get home sometime tomorrow."

"That's what I thought when I looked outside the window a minute ago, and yes, I have everything I need—we need."

"I'll have Charlie or one of the other men deliver your car later today or first thing in the morning. I don't want to be seen there with you." He paused a moment. "So I won't be able to tell you or the boys a personal goodbye."

She could hear the regret, a true longing in his voice, but she was almost glad that there wouldn't be a personal goodbye. There were going to be enough goodbyes in their future and she had a feeling she'd find each and every one of them difficult. "You'll let me know if anything changes?"

"Of course," he replied. "I'll call you later this evening in any case. And, Melissa, I'm so sorry about all this."

"You don't have to apologize. Just take care of yourself, Henry. My boys need their daddy."

"And I need them," he replied softly, then with a

murmured goodbye he hung up. By that time the boys were awakening and she changed diapers and fixed them each a bottle of formula.

While they ate their breakfast she made a pot of coffee in the coffeemaker provided, then studied the menu she found on the desk from the diner next door.

She was starving and she knew part of it was probably stress-related. She picked up the phone and called in an order for an omelet and toast. While she waited for the food to be delivered she got dressed for the day.

The boys had just finished their bottles when her food was delivered. She sat at the desk to eat and kept one eye on the twins, who entertained themselves by playing with their fingers and toes and gurgling to each other as if sharing a secret language.

The omelet was excellent and after she'd cleaned up the mess she stretched out on the bed and played with her sons.

Maybe it had just been the spirit of Christmas that had her feeling so strongly about Henry. The days she had spent in his home had been like a fantasy of everything she'd ever wanted in her life. She didn't care about the lavish gifts or the fancy mansion; she didn't care about personal cooks and sterling silverware. She didn't need any of that.

It had been the warmth of family that had seduced her, the caring both Mary and Henry had offered to her and her children. It had been the shared laughter and the comfortable small talk.

Henry was going to make a tremendous father, but he'd warned her all along that he wasn't interested in becoming a husband. Still, somehow he'd made her want to be his wife.

Instead of thinking of what would never be, she tried to focus on what she intended to do when she got home. She was more determined than ever to jump back into her decorating business. She'd contact old clients, solicit for new ones and hopefully the business would grow.

Somehow she and Henry would work out a solution to the visitation issue, one that would allow each of them the independence to continue their own lives. Eventually perhaps she would find a man who would love her like she wanted to be loved, a man who would bind his life with hers. Although at the moment the idea of any man other than Henry filled her with repugnance.

What she'd once felt for Tom was a pale imitation of her feelings for Henry. She realized now that she hadn't loved Tom. She'd never loved like she loved Henry.

The day passed achingly slow. When the boys fell asleep for their naps, she turned on the television and watched two soap operas that she'd never seen before.

Around four o'clock she placed another order at the diner, deciding that an early meal and early bedtime would be the best thing.

The sun had continued to shine throughout the day and she'd heard the rumble of street plows working, letting her know that she should be able to leave first thing in the morning.

By five-thirty she'd eaten her dinner, fed the boys and the sun had gone down. She was considering changing back into her nightgown when a knock fell on her door.

With the chain on the door she cracked it open a mere inch to see who was on the other side. "Charlie," she said and quickly unfastened the chain to open the door. "Henry said you might come by to bring my car."

"Actually, Henry sent me here to take you and the boys back to the house," Charlie replied as he stepped inside the room.

"What?" She looked at him in surprise. "Has something happened?"

Charlie nodded. "Tom Burke has been arrested and the danger is over. Henry wants you all back at the ranch."

"When did all this happen?" she asked, a wave of happiness sweeping through her.

"Just a little while ago. I don't have any real details. Henry just told me to come here and collect you and the boys and bring you home."

Melissa looked around the room. "It's going to take a few minutes for me to pack everything up again."

Charlie smiled. "Take your time. I just know Henry doesn't want you here another night since it's safe now for you to be back at the house."

Melissa was thrilled by the news that Tom had been arrested and Henry was no longer in danger. Charlie entertained the twins with silly faces while Melissa scurried around and quickly packed her things.

She was going to have to say goodbye in person. The thought broke her heart just a little bit. It would have been easier to take off in the morning without any long goodbyes to Henry. But she knew Henry probably wanted to spend time with the twins one last time before she left for home the next day.

Tonight she would have to tell him about her decision not to move into the carriage house. It would be difficult but she was firm in her decision and he was just going to have to accept it.

Finally she had her things ready to go. While Charlie carried her suitcase back to his SUV, she got the boys into their coats. "You're going to see Daddy again," she said, buttoning Joey's coat.

"I'll carry this little guy," Charlie said as he came back into the room and picked up James. "I've still got the car seats so everyone will ride safely."

Within minutes they were all packed in the car and Charlie started the engine. "Do I need to check out or anything?" she asked.

"Nah, Henry will take care of it." He put the vehicle in Reverse and backed out of the parking space.

"So you don't know what kind of charges have been pressed again Tom?" she asked.

"No, but I'm assuming it's attempted murder or something serious like that," Charlie replied.

"I'm so happy that it's finally been resolved, that Henry is safe and can get on with his life." She stared out the window and frowned. "Shouldn't we be going the opposite direction?"

"No, I'm going exactly where I need to go." Charlie turned and smiled at her, but in the depths of his eyes she saw something cold, something calculating and the first whisper of fear edged through her.

Her throat went dry. "Do you have an errand to run before you take us home?"

"Yeah, an errand that's going to change my life." He reached into his coat pocket and pulled out a gun. "And I suggest you sit back and enjoy the ride."

Melissa stared at him with a rising sense of horror. Charlie? Why was Charlie holding a gun on her and where was he taking her?

Fear screamed inside her head, a fear for herself, but more important, a fear for the two babies who were in the backseat.

It had been a busy day but no matter what Henry did his thoughts were on Melissa and the boys. It ached in him that he wouldn't be able to give the boys a final kiss on their sweet cheeks before sending them back home, that he wouldn't be able to fill his lungs with the sweet baby scent of them.

He would have liked the opportunity to tell Melissa goodbye in person, too. One last look at that shine in her eyes, one more of her lovely smiles to end the holidays would have been nice.

But he reminded himself that this wasn't a permanent goodbye. Whether they liked it or not they were in each other's lives for at least the next eighteen years.

Etta hadn't made it in because of the snow so at dinnertime he and his mother had a quiet meal of ham and cheese sandwiches. In fact, throughout the day the house had been far too quiet.

He hadn't realized how much Melissa and the boys had filled it up and brightened every dark corner. He told himself this was just temporary, that eventually they'd be back and the house would come alive once again.

It was almost six o'clock when he sat down in his study and picked up the phone to call her. The phone rang at the motel room once…twice…three times. Henry frowned as it rang a fourth and fifth time.

He finally hung up but stared at the phone with confusion. Surely she wouldn't have taken the boys out anywhere. She didn't have a car and it was frigid outside. *Maybe she's in the shower,* he thought.

Picking up a pen, he tapped the end of it on his desk as a vision of Melissa in the shower filled his head. He could easily imagine her slender body beneath a steaming spray of water, visualize the slide of the soap across her full breasts.

He threw the pen down, irritated with these kinds of thoughts. He'd believed that if he made love to her one more time she'd be out of his system. He thought that the crazy physical attraction he felt for her would wane, but instead of diminishing, it seemed to have grown stronger.

He picked up the phone and tried her number again. It rang and rang and still there was no answer. How long did a woman spend in the shower?

He got up from the desk and paced the room, a thrum of anxiety inside his chest. Moving to the window, he stared out in the direction of the carriage house. He still hoped to talk her into moving in there. It would make everything so much less complicated.

They were going to work well together as a team in

raising the boys. He was incredibly lucky that a woman like Melissa was the mother of his children.

He returned to the desk and tried to call her once again. When there was still no answer, the anxiety that had whispered through him screamed with alarm. Racing out of the study, he headed for the coat closet in the foyer and yanked out his coat. He grabbed his gun from the drawer and stuck it in his pocket.

"Henry? Where are you going?" Mary appeared in the foyer.

"I can't get hold of Melissa on the phone. Nobody answers and I've got a bad feeling."

Mary's hand flew up to her heart. "Maybe she was in the bathroom, or stepped outside for a moment. Maybe she went to the office for something?"

"Maybe," he replied grimly. "But I won't be satisfied until I go there and check it out."

"Should I call Jimmy?" she asked worriedly.

"No, I'll call him if I need him. It's possible there's a perfectly logical explanation for her not answering the phone." He leaned over and kissed his mother on the cheek. "Don't worry."

"You'll call me?"

"The minute I get there and know that everything is all right." He didn't wait for her reply, but instead braced himself and hurried out into the cold evening air.

Minutes later as he pointed his truck toward town, he thought of all the logical explanations for the unanswered calls. Maybe she'd gone to get ice. Maybe one of the boys had been crying and she hadn't heard the ring of the phone.

There could be a dozen innocent reasons, but the possibility of those wasn't what made his heart bang in his chest. And his heart was banging fast and furious. He felt as if a wild beast had been let loose in his chest.

Fear. Rich and raw, it clawed at his guts, made him sick with worry. He'd never felt like this before. He'd never known this kind of fear.

The going was slow as the roads were slick and nasty. His hands clenched the steering wheel tightly as he prayed that nothing was wrong, that nothing bad had happened.

A lump lodged in the back of his throat. Had one of the boys gotten ill and Melissa had somehow taken them to a doctor? Surely if that had happened, she would have called him.

By the time he reached the city limits he was almost nauseous with worry. Ed's Motel was on the south side of town along the main highway. It was a typical one-story building with connecting rooms that faced the parking lot. The office was in the center, but Henry went past it. He knew Melissa was in Room 112 and it was in front of that unit that he pulled up and parked.

He cut the engine and jumped out, his heart banging faster than he could ever remember it beating before. "Melissa?" He banged on the door. "Melissa, it's Henry. Open the door."

Nothing. No answer, no door opening. Absolutely nothing. He hammered on the door with his fist, then tried the door. It opened into a dark room.

He flipped on the light. The bedspread was wrinkled with pillows lined up against one side, but there was no suitcase, no babies and no Melissa anywhere in the room.

Maybe he got the room number wrong, he thought, but even as he grabbed onto that idea, he smelled the faint familiar scent of Melissa lingering in the air. She'd been here. Oh, God, so, where was she now?

He wouldn't have thought his heart could beat any faster, but it did, thundering in his chest with painful intensity.

He left the room and ran across the parking lot to the diner. Maybe she'd decided to take the boys there for dinner. Although he couldn't imagine her packing them up and carrying them across the way when the diner would deliver whatever she needed, he clung to the hope that this was the explanation for her absence.

Although on a normal evening at this time the diner would be packed, the weather conditions had the place nearly deserted. Henry took two steps inside the door and instantly knew she wasn't there.

His heart crashed to the floor. He stepped back outside and pulled his cell phone from his pocket. His fingers trembled as he punched in Jimmy's phone number.

"Jimmy, it's me," he said when the sheriff answered. "I need you to meet me at Ed's Motel. Something has happened to Melissa and the boys."

With Jimmy's assurance that he'd be right over, Henry walked back to the motel and into the office. Maybe he'd gotten the room number wrong. Maybe he'd only imagined the scent of Melissa in the room.

The owner, Ed Warren, was at the front desk and greeted Henry with a friendly smile.

"Henry, didn't expect to see you tonight," he said.

"Ed, that room I rented from you by phone. What room number was it?"

"112," Ed replied without hesitation. "I know because it's the only room I've rented in the past couple of days. This damned weather has practically closed me down. Why? Is there a problem?"

"Have you noticed anybody around the room? Have you seen a car or anything parked in front of it?"

"No, to be honest I haven't moved from behind this desk all day. I know a pretty lady came in for the key last night and that's all."

"The pretty lady isn't there now and she had a couple of babies with her. You haven't seen them this evening?"

Ed shook his head. "Sorry, Henry. I can't help you."

Henry reeled back out the door, almost blinded by the sickness that welled up inside him. Where were his babies? And where was Melissa?

Chapter 12

Melissa had never known such terror. There was no escape. She couldn't open the car door and jump out, not leaving Joey and James still in the car with Charlie. She was trapped and she had no idea why this was happening, what Charlie had planned for them.

As they left the city limits and began to travel on dark, lonely country roads, the terror clawed up the back of her throat and twisted her insides.

Joey and James had fallen asleep, unaware of the drama taking place. "Where are you taking us?" she finally asked, her voice reed thin.

"Don't you worry about it," Charlie replied. "If you do what I tell you to do then there's no reason anybody has to get hurt and you and your kids will be fine."

"What do you want, Charlie? Why are you doing

this?" She needed to make sense of it. "Is this because of your sister? Because Henry didn't want to marry her?"

Charlie laughed, the sound not pleasant. "I don't give a damn about Hilary. That stupid bitch dated Henry for over a year and couldn't close the deal. If she'd gotten Henry to marry her then I would have been on easy street. As Henry's brother-in-law I wouldn't have been shoveling horse crap anymore. I could have worked a respectable job with all the perks. Now I have to take matters into my own hands."

Henry had believed that somebody on the town council was responsible for the attacks on him. But he'd been wrong. "You were trying to kill Henry?" she asked.

Charlie glanced at her and laughed once again. "Trust me, if I'd wanted Henry dead, he'd be dead. I just wanted to disrupt his perfect little life, make him go to bed at night a little nervous."

"But why? What's he ever done to you?"

"I hate him!" Charlie exclaimed with vehemence. "I should be living his life. I should have his money. All he did to earn it was be born. I've been working my ass off for all my life. I came from nothing, but those babies in the backseat are my ticket to something."

It all crystallized in Melissa's mind. Kidnapped. Charlie was kidnapping her and the boys and was going to demand a ransom.

Henry had spent his entire life worrying that some woman might try to take his money from him and now because of her and the boys his fear was coming true, except it wasn't a woman about to take him, but a madman.

What if he didn't pay? Even as the possibility entered her mind she dismissed it. She'd only spent a couple of days with Henry, but she knew the man he was, she knew what was in his heart. He'd turn his bank account inside out to assure the safety of his children.

But what if something went terribly wrong? What if Charlie snapped or things didn't go as he planned? There was no question that to Charlie she and the boys were expendable. Nobody knew where they were, nobody would suspect Charlie of wanting to hurt Henry or having anything to do with her disappearance.

They were in mortal danger and at the moment she saw no way out of it. Maybe when they arrived to wherever he was taking them she'd be able to do something—anything—to get away. She grabbed on to that hope, that somehow, someway, she'd be able to figure out a plan.

She glanced at her wristwatch. It was just after six. Henry had said he'd call her sometime this evening. Had he tried to call? Did he even know they were missing yet?

It seemed like they drove forever before Charlie finally pulled to a stop. In the glare of the headlights stood a small shanty. It was dark and isolated, surrounded by trees laden with snow. There wasn't a light from a neighbor or a sign of civilization anywhere.

A shudder worked through Melissa, a shiver that had nothing to do with the cold as Charlie opened his car door. "Get the kids and don't try anything stupid. You're worth nothing to him or to me and I won't hesitate to kill you if you give me any trouble."

She believed him. The coldness in his eyes, the hardness in his voice let her know he meant what he said. Charlie knew Henry would pay whatever the demand to get his children back, but she was definitely expendable. Henry didn't love her.

She was grateful that the boys didn't awaken as she unfastened them and pulled them from the car seats. She held them tight as Charlie motioned her into the shanty with the barrel of his gun. Once inside he turned on a light that illuminated the dismal interior.

There was a sink, a small refrigerator, a two-burner hot plate, a microwave and a small table along one wall. On the other side of the small room was a single-size cot and a door she assumed led to a bathroom. A small electric heater blew warm air, but not enough to heat the entire room.

"Put the kids on the bed," he commanded.

On trembling legs she moved to the cot and gently placed the sleeping twins in the center of the small area. Tears blurred her vision as she straightened up and turned to face her captor.

"Unfortunately this is going to be your home away from home for the next day or two," he said. "Sit down." He pointed to one of the chairs at the table.

With one backward glance at the sleeping twins Melissa did as he asked. "You threw that bomb through the window, didn't you?" she asked and was appalled by the quiver in her voice.

Charlie opened the cabinet beneath the sink and pulled out a heavy chain. The sight of it shot a new wave of fear through her. "Yeah, it's amazing how easy it is to build a little pipe bomb. I shot out the tire on Henry's car, too. My original plan was to waylay you as you left town, but Henry's decision to move you into the motel made it all so easy."

He straightened and locked one end of the chain on a metal hook that had been driven into the wall and then approached her with the other end.

"Please, you don't have to do this," she said, the tears not only blurring her vision but running hot down her cheeks. "I can talk to Henry. I'm sure he'll give you whatever you want. Just please, let me and my babies go."

"Shut up," he said. He bent down and grabbed her ankle. She instinctively kicked at him, the survival instinct roaring to life.

He stepped back from her, the gun pointed at her head. "Don't make this difficult. I told you that if you cooperate, you won't get hurt. But I won't hesitate to put a bullet through your head if you give me any trouble. You understand?"

She drew a deep breath, gulped back a sob and nodded. She didn't want to give him a reason to kill her. She had to stay alive. She had to figure out a way out of this and save her boys.

"Now, I'm going to put this chain on your ankle. There's enough length for you to move around the room, take care of the kids and use the bathroom. There's some grub in the refrigerator and you should be fine until I get back here."

He fastened the chain around her ankle and she shuddered at the cold bite of steel against her skin. "I'll bring in your things so you should have everything you need."

With that he disappeared out the door. Instantly Melissa grabbed the chain in her hands and began to attempt to pull it out of the wall. She yanked and pulled, but there was no give at all.

She quickly dropped the chain as Charlie came back in carrying her suitcase and the diaper bag. The one thing he didn't have was her purse with her cell phone inside.

"Don't look so worried. You should only be here a couple of days, however long it takes him to get the cash for me. I'm not even going to make a ransom demand until tomorrow. I'll give him a night to worry. It will put him in a better mood to deal with me and my demands."

"Please, Charlie," she said one last time. "If you let us go now I won't tell anyone what you did."

"If and when you get a chance to tell anyone I'll be long gone. I'll be a rich man on some tropical beach living under a new name."

"Henry will never stop looking for you," she insisted. "He'll hunt you down wherever you go. You'll live your life looking over your shoulder."

He smiled, obviously not concerned by her words. "But what a great life it's going to be. I'll be back later." He dropped the suitcase and diaper bag to the floor, then left the shanty. She heard him lock the door from the outside and then she was alone with just her sleeping babies to keep her company.

* * *

"Henry, there's no sign of a struggle or forced entry," Jimmy said. He'd arrived at the motel room with two of his deputies. "There's nothing to indicate that anything bad happened her. Maybe she just went home."

"Without her car?" The urgent burn in Henry's gut had only intensified over the past half an hour.

"Maybe she had somebody pick her up," Ben Whitfield, one of the deputies, said.

Henry shook his head. "She wouldn't have done that. She wouldn't have left without telling me goodbye."

"Maybe the scene at your house last night scared her more than she let on. Maybe she was afraid to tell you she was going home because she was afraid you'd try to change her mind," Jimmy said.

A new sick feeling swept through Henry. Had he been pushing her so hard the past couple of days that she might have taken off without telling him? Afraid that he'd push her to do something she didn't want to do? Even though their time together had been relatively brief, he believed he knew the kind of woman Melissa was and he was convinced that wasn't the case.

"I'm telling you, Jimmy, something's happened. We've got to find her." He looked at the sheriff. "She's in trouble. I know it. I feel it."

"Ben, you and Jake hit the streets, see if you can find anyone who might have seen something," Jimmy said.

"What about Tom Burke?" Henry asked.

"I already checked with Gordon. Tom is home with his family and can't have had anything to do with Melissa or your boys."

Henry grabbed Jimmy by the shoulder. "We have to do something, man. We have to find them." The emotions that filled Henry left him weak, a combination of the worst fear he'd ever known in his life.

"We'll find them, Henry. Why don't you go home and wait. Maybe she'll call."

"I can't go home. I need to do something," he said in frustration.

"Henry, take a deep breath. We don't even know that something bad has happened," Jimmy repeated.

But Henry knew. He felt it in his gut. There was no way that Melissa would have left town without speaking to him, no way she would have left her car at his house and taken off with somebody.

Something was wrong.

Something was horribly wrong.

"I'm going to drive around and see if anyone has seen her," Henry said. He couldn't go home and tell his mother that Melissa and the boys were missing.

Telling Jimmy he'd be in touch, Henry got into his truck and started to drive down the street, looking for anyone who might have seen Melissa and the boys. For the next hour he stopped at each and every business that was open and questioned anyone he found in the place.

Where could they be? What had happened in that motel room? Jimmy was right, there had been no sign of a struggle. Whoever she left with, she'd apparently gone willingly.

Surely if she'd planned on having somebody pick her up and take her back to Amarillo she would have said something to him when they'd spoken earlier on the phone. She would have made arrangements to get her car.

It was almost nine when he finally headed back to the ranch. He didn't know what else to do, where else to look. He only knew the terror that filled his heart.

The drive back to his place was the longest he'd ever made. Tears burned behind his eyes but he refused to let them fall. Tears implied sadness, grief and he absolutely refused to grieve for Melissa and the boys. He needed to stay strong.

His mother met him at the door. "What's going on?"

"They're gone." The words fell from his lips and suddenly the tears that he'd fought so hard to control spilled from him.

"Melissa and the boys aren't at the motel. We can't find them, Mom. We don't know where they are."

Mary reached for him and wrapped her arms around him, attempting to comfort him like she had when he'd been a little boy and had skinned his knee. But he wasn't a little boy and this was far worse than a bruised knee.

He stuffed back his tears and straightened. "I don't know what to do. I don't know what's happened. I've never felt so helpless in my life."

He allowed his mother to lead him into the living room, where they both sagged down to the sofa. "Jimmy and a couple of his men are out looking. I drove up and down the streets and asked everyone I saw, but nobody had seen them."

"Maybe she called a friend," Mary said, but Henry could tell by her tone that she didn't believe her own words.

"You and I both know she wouldn't have left town without telling us goodbye. That's not who Melissa is." He leaned his head back and closed his eyes and prayed that somehow this nightmare would end.

Both he and Mary jumped as the doorbell rang. Henry shot up off the sofa and raced to the door. He opened it to see Charlie.

"I just heard," Charlie said. "Is there anything I can do to help?"

Henry motioned him inside the foyer. "Last night when you dropped Melissa off at the motel did you see anybody around?"

Charlie frowned. "Not that I noticed. I made sure we weren't followed when we left here. I can't be a hundred percent certain that nobody saw her when I let her and the boys out of the car. God, man. What can I do?"

Henry raked a hand through his hair. "I don't think there's anything anyone can do at the moment. Jimmy and his men are out searching in town and I don't know what else to do."

"I'm heading home. You'll call me if I can do anything?"

"Thanks, Charlie. I will." Henry watched as the man left the house and walked to his vehicle in the driveway.

The night was dark and cold and Melissa was out there with his babies. "Maybe we scared her away," his mother spoke from behind him.

He turned to look at her.

"Maybe we came on too strong. We bought so many things, made it look as if we were making a home here for the twins." Mary wrung her hands together. "Maybe she's afraid you'll take those babies from her and so she ran away."

"No, she wouldn't do that." He knew in his heart, in the depths of his very soul, that she wouldn't just disappear. He turned back to the door and stared outside. "I think somebody has them. I think somebody took them from the motel room."

"But why?" Mary cried.

Once again he turned to face her. "Maybe as a final attempt to make me pull out of the election. I don't know. We won't know for sure until whoever has them contacts us."

"Surely whoever has them wouldn't hurt them." Mary's voice trembled with her fear.

He didn't attempt to give her false pacification. "I don't know, Mom."

"So, what do we do now?" she asked.

Henry's stomach clenched. "We wait."

Melissa wasted no time the minute Charlie left the shanty. First she worked to try to get the chain off her ankle. He'd secured it with a padlock and she was hoping maybe she could use something to pick it open. But a search of the two drawers in the kitchen area yielded nothing more than two spoons. Even the handle of the spoon was no good in trying to pick the lock.

The boys remained sleeping soundly. She was grateful for their silence. She needed to think. Even if she did manage to get herself free from the chain, then what? She had no idea where they were, no idea how far she'd have to walk with the twins in her arms to get help.

But she figured her odds were better braving the elements than staying here until Charlie returned. Henry had said that his breakup with Hilary hadn't seemed to matter to Charlie. Apparently, it had.

Charlie had seen Hilary and Henry's marriage as a ticket for him off the ranch. When that had fallen apart, she'd made the mistake of coming here and giving Charlie a new bargaining chip. She glanced at the twins. No, two bargaining chips, she thought.

What scared her more than anything was that she didn't think Charlie intended to let her live. The twins couldn't identify their kidnappers, but she could. If she died then Charlie would be safe. He'd never have to look over his shoulder to see if somebody was after him.

For the next hour she pulled on the place where the chain was connected to the wall, hoping to break it loose. She finally sat on the floor, exhausted by her efforts and overwhelmed with defeat.

Silently she began to weep. She would never see her babies grow up. She'd never see their first step or hear them say Mommy. She wouldn't be there to put them on the bus for their first day of school, to straighten a tie when they went to their first school dance.

Pain flooded her as she stuffed a hand against her mouth to keep the sobs from ripping out of her. She wept until there were no more tears to weep and then she prayed. She prayed that no matter what happened to her, the boys would be safe. She prayed that they would live a long and happy life with Henry and Mary.

Thoughts of Henry brought more tears. She'd never see him again. She'd never see that slow slide of a sexy grin across his lips, the simmering sparkle of pleasure in his eyes.

Surely by now he knew they were missing. She looked at her watch. Almost ten. He would have called the room and gotten worried when she hadn't answered. He was probably looking for her now. Unfortunately there was no way he'd ever suspect his right-hand man on the ranch, the worker he depended on. The last person he'd suspect would be Charlie.

She pulled herself up and looked in the cabinets, seeking something that could be used as a weapon. He might intend to kill her, but she'd like to be able to hurt him before he did. She'd like to be able to mark him in a way that might bring up some questions.

Her fingernails were kept too short to do damage to his face. But surely she could use something in the cabinets.

She searched every nook and cranny on the room and found nothing. The cabinets held only a handful of canned goods, some soup and pork and beans and corn. The refrigerator had a gallon of milk, a loaf of bread, a package of bologna and a small jar of mayo. The freezer contained five frozen dinners.

She had a feeling the food had been brought in specifically for her and there was just enough for a couple of days. This hadn't been a spur-of-the-moment decision on Charlie's part. He'd planned this and that depressed her even more.

Finally, she sat next to the bed where the twins slept and laid her head back. She could smell her babies, the sweet scent of innocence and love.

She closed her eyes with the weary knowledge that at least she knew they'd be loved by Henry for the rest of their lives, even if she wasn't around to share it.

Chapter 13

"Henry, Hilary is on the phone," Mary said.

Henry frowned. "I don't have time to talk to her now. Tell her I'll call her back later." He returned his attention to Jimmy, who sat on the chair opposite the sofa where Henry was seated.

"We're treating the motel room as a crime scene," Jimmy said. "Even though we don't know if a crime has occurred. I've got a couple of my boys lifting prints to see what we find."

"It's a motel room. You're probably going to find the prints of people who stayed there ten years ago," Henry said with a weary sigh.

"Ed's place is pretty clean. It's possible we'll lift fresh prints."

"And then what? Unless you have a matching set on file the prints won't tell us anything."

"Henry, we're doing the best we can," Jimmy replied patiently.

"I know, I know. You tell Tom Burke that if he had anything to do with this, then he wins. If he'll let them go unharmed, I'll leave him alone. I'll pull out of the race for mayor and he can continue his business practices as he sees fit."

"Henry, I don't think it's Tom," Jimmy said. "Or anyone he's hired. I've known Tom for most of my life. Sure, he's a scoundrel, he's a white-color criminal but this isn't something he's capable of."

"Would you stake Melissa's life on that? Stake the lives of my boys on it?" Henry replied.

"Of course not. I'm just telling you what my gut is telling me and that's that Tom isn't responsible."

"Then who is?" Henry asked as a hollowness threatened to swallow him whole. "Jesus, Jimmy, who is responsible? Who could hate me this much?"

Jimmy swiped his broad hand down the length of his face. "I don't know. It might not be about hate. It might be about greed. If this is some kind of kidnapping then I'm guessing that you'll hear from the kidnapper."

Henry looked at his watch. It was after ten. "We don't even know how long they've been missing. I spoke to her this morning but didn't speak to her after that."

"I checked with the diner. Dinner was delivered to the room at around four-thirty so we know she and the boys were there then," Jimmy said.

"I've made coffee," Mary said as she stepped into the living room.

Jimmy stood. "Come on, Henry, let's go have some coffee. It looks like it's going to be a long night."

The last thing Henry wanted was to sit around and drink coffee while Melissa and his boys were out there somewhere. He wanted to beat on every door in the town of Dalhart until he found the place where Melissa and the twins were being held.

But he followed Jimmy into the kitchen, where the two men sat at the table while his mother poured them each a cup of the fresh brew.

"Shouldn't we call the FBI or something?" Mary asked. She looked as if she'd aged ten years in the past couple of hours.

Jimmy shook his head. "They won't be interested until I have evidence that a crime has occurred. She's only been missing for five or six hours and we don't know if she made the decision to go missing of her own free will."

Henry frowned and wrapped his hands around his coffee cup, seeking the warmth to banish the icy chill that had taken possession of his body the moment he'd entered the empty motel room.

"If this is a kidnapping for ransom I wish to hell somebody would call me," Henry said.

They all froze as Jimmy's cell phone rang. Henry's stomach clenched as Jimmy answered. He listened for a moment. "Just keep me posted," he finally said then hung up. "That was Jake. He and Ben have questioned everyone in the block surrounding the motel and nobody has seen Melissa."

"Why doesn't he call?" Henry cried. "If somebody has them why in the hell haven't they called to tell me what he wants?"

The frustration, the fear and the rage that had been building throughout the night exploded and Henry slammed his hands down on the table. "If anybody hurts them I'll kill them. I swear, Jimmy. I'll kill the bastard responsible for this."

At that moment the doorbell rang. Henry leaped up from the table and hurried to the door, his heart thundering in the hope that it would be Melissa.

It wasn't. It was Hilary.

"Henry, I heard about Melissa and the babies missing. I need to talk to you." There was a trembling urgency in her voice.

"Hilary, this really isn't a good time," he said, unable to stop the crashing waves of pain that coursed through him.

She reached out and placed her hand on his shoulder. "Please, Henry, I think maybe I know who is responsible."

He stared at her, wondering if this was some crazy ploy to get close to him. "What are you talking about?"

He was aware of Jimmy and his mother stepping into the foyer.

"Charlie was real upset when we broke up. He thought if you and I got married then you'd get him a job that paid well, a job in a fancy office somewhere. A couple of days ago he told me he had plans to get enough money to blow this town and live the easy life. When I pressed him for details he refused to say anything more."

The words exploded out of her in a rush, along with a torrent of tears. "I might be a lot of things, Henry, but I saw the way you looked at Melissa, I saw the look in your eyes when you saw those babies and I can't condone this. I think Charlie has done something terrible and I just had to tell you."

Henry stared at her in confusion. Charlie? Henry's mind buzzed. Charlie knew where she was staying. Melissa would have trusted Charlie. She would have gone with him without questions. Still, he was reluctant to believe it. "But he was here just a little while ago. He offered his help."

"I'm just telling you what I think, Henry, and I think he has Melissa and the boys," Hilary said.

Henry pulled his cell phone from his pocket and punched in Charlie's phone number. His heart crawled into his throat as he heard it ring and ring. "There's no answer," he said as he clicked off.

"I know where Charlie lives," Jimmy said with a frown. "There's no way he could have Melissa and the twins stashed in that tiny little apartment of his. Somebody would hear the boys crying or would have seen him bring them all inside."

Henry was processing everything in the span of seconds. Charlie could have easily taken the shot at him when he'd been out riding in the pasture. Charlie would have known that Henry and Melissa had gone to town and would have known about when they would be returning home. Charlie, who then tramped through the snow to obscure his own footprints, could have easily tossed the pipe bomb through the window.

Charlie. He still had trouble wrapping his mind around it. Charlie had been his right-hand man, his go-to guy for everything around the ranch.

"Charlie has a little shack, a place he goes hunting. Maybe he has them there," Hilary said.

"Why? I trusted him. I've always treated him fairly," Henry said.

"I think he hates you, Henry. He envies you your money, your life and I think he knew how much you cared about Melissa and the boys, cared enough to pay whatever ransom he might come up with."

The slow simmering rage that had been building in Henry throughout the night once again rose to the surface. "Where's the shack?" he asked.

Hilary wiped her tears with the back of her hand. "I hope I'm not sending you on a wild-goose chase. I don't want anything to happen to Melissa or those precious babies."

"Where's the shack, Hilary?" he demanded. He suddenly felt like too much time had been wasted.

As Hilary gave them directions to the shack, Henry was already pulling on his coat. He grabbed his gun and looked at Jimmy expectantly.

"Let's go," Jimmy said with a nod. He looked at Hilary. "If Charlie contacts you, don't tell him you spoke to us. Don't say anything to warn him or I'll see you behind bars for obstruction of justice."

"Please be careful. I honestly don't know what he's capable of," she said.

As Henry stepped out into the cold dark night he had a last glance of Hilary reaching for his mother's hand. He hoped to hell she was telling the truth and he prayed that they wouldn't be too late.

Melissa was cold. She didn't know if it was because the little heater simply couldn't warm the interior of the cabin or if it was fear that had her freezing.

Waiting. Wondering what happened next, that was what had her blood icy in her veins.

She certainly couldn't sleep, although she was grateful that the boys slumbered soundly. Seeking internal warmth, she finally opened a can of tomato soup and emptied it into a pan, then set it on the hot plate to warm.

As she waited for it to heat she wondered if Charlie had contacted Henry, if he'd already demanded a king's ransom for the return of the boys. He'd said he'd wait until morning, but maybe he'd gotten impatient. She just wanted this over.

She winced as she stood to stir the soup. She'd worked so long at trying to get the chain off her ankle she'd made it bleed.

Maybe she should be sleeping. Maybe Charlie didn't intend to return tonight and she should be getting what little rest she could. But even as she thought that, she knew there was no way she could sleep. She wanted to hold her boys. She wanted to squeeze them to her heart. She wanted to hear James's belly laugh one last time, see Joey's sweet smile. She stirred the soup as tears began to course down her cheeks once again.

Henry, her heart cried. She would never see him again. The only thing she could hope was that he would tell the boys about her, about how much she'd loved them, about what a good mom she'd wanted to be.

She froze as she heard the sound of a vehicle approach. Headlight beams flashed into the window. Sheer terror leaped into her throat. Had the deal gone down? Had Charlie come back to kill her?

The footsteps on the porch sounded loud, like gunshots, and when the door opened Charlie came inside. "Hi, honey, I'm home." He snickered, as if finding the joke amusing.

Melissa turned away from the hot plate. "Have you contacted Henry?"

"Not yet. I told you I was going to give him a little time to worry. I just figured I needed to stop back here and check on my investment." He leaned against the door and looked down at her ankle. "Looks like you worked hard to get out of that. Short of chewing off your foot, you aren't going anywhere."

Melissa had never hated anyone as much as she hated him. She'd never believed herself capable of killing anyone, but she'd kill for her children and if she got the chance, she'd kill Charlie without a blink of her eyes.

He kicked out a chair and sat at the small table and she backed up against the cabinet. "You're going to kill me, aren't you?" She didn't wait for him to answer. "I won't tell that it was you. I'll say that I don't know who took us, that he wore a mask and I didn't recognize him."

She hated that she was begging for her life, but she wanted to live. She had all the reasons in the world to want to stay alive.

"Lady, I wouldn't trust you as far as I could throw you," he replied.

With those words Melissa knew that he had no intention of letting her live and a new wave of grief crashed through her.

She turned back to the soup at the same time the front door crashed in. She whirled back around and everything seemed to go in slow motion.

Henry stood at the door, bigger than life, his eyes wild and dangerous. At the same time Charlie jumped up and drew his gun and lifted it to point at him.

In an instant Melissa knew Henry was about to die. Without thinking, she picked up the pan of hot soup and threw it at Charlie. As it splashed across the back of his head, he yelled and his gun dropped to the floor. The twins began to cry as Henry let loose a thunderous roar and tackled Charlie to the floor.

Melissa kicked Charlie's gun under the bed, then ran to the twins as Henry and Charlie wrestled with each other. Her heart pounded as she pulled the screaming boys into her arms and watched the life-and-death battle between the man she loved and the man who would kill her.

A sob escaped her when Henry pressed his gun barrel into Charlie's temple, halting the fight. At that moment Jimmy burst into the room.

"I got it, Henry. Drop your gun," he said.

Henry didn't move. His handsome features were twisted into a mask of rage. His entire body trembled and it was obvious how badly he wanted to put a bullet through Charlie's head.

"Henry, don't do it," Jimmy said and touched Henry's shoulder. "Come on, man. Let him go. I'll take it from here."

Henry squeezed his eyes closed, the internal battle he was waging bringing a new fear to Melissa. She knew if he shot Charlie his life would never be the same. It might feel good at the moment but eventually it would destroy him.

"Henry." She spoke his name softly. He opened his eyes and met her gaze. In the depths of his eyes she saw the torture he'd suffered over the past couple of hours. "Let Jimmy take him away. Please, I need your help with the boys."

With a strangled sob, he lowered his gun and rolled off Charlie. Jimmy immediately handcuffed Charlie and hauled him to his feet.

Henry rushed over to her and knelt in front of her. He cupped her face between his palms, his gaze intense. "Did he hurt you? Oh, God, did he hurt you or the boys?"

"No, I'm okay. We're all okay." The boys had begun to calm.

He glanced down at the chain around her ankle and as he tensed as if to spring up again, she grabbed his arm. "It's okay."

Henry turned to look at Charlie and Jimmy. "Search him, Jimmy. I need a key to get this chain off her."

A moment later he unlocked the chain and removed it from her ankle. As he gently rubbed her skin, she remembered how he'd rubbed her cold feet on the night that they had been snowbound together.

Then she was in his arms, weeping in the aftermath, and he held her tight, as if afraid to ever let her go again. Eventually he did let her go. Gordon arrived along with several other deputies who would process what was now part of a crime scene.

Jimmy left to take Charlie to jail and Melissa and Henry and the boys got into Gordon's patrol car so he could take them home.

The car seats were shifted from Charlie's vehicle to the back of Gordon's car and once the boys were settled in they immediately fell back asleep. Melissa sat between them, happy yet exhausted by the turmoil and the lateness of the hour.

As they drove home Henry told Melissa about Hilary telling them that she thought Charlie might be involved. When they got back to the house Mary and Hilary stepped out on the porch to greet them.

Henry carried the twins and when Melissa reached the porch Mary pulled her into a bone-crunching hug. "Thank God," she said. "Thank God you're all okay."

As Mary released her, Melissa grabbed Hilary's hands. "Thank you," she said to the beautiful woman. "You saved my life."

Tears shone in Hilary's eyes. "I'm so sorry. I can't believe he did this. I always knew Charlie had a mean streak, but I never knew he was capable of something like this." She pulled her hands from Melissa's. "I'm going home now. I'm sure you all need some time alone."

An hour later the twins were asleep in their beds upstairs and Jimmy arrived to take a statement from Melissa.

It was near dawn when Jimmy left and Mary led Melissa to one of the spare bedrooms. As they passed the boys' room she saw Henry sitting in a chair just inside the door, as if guarding the king's treasure. Daddy on duty, she thought, and knew he'd probably be in that chair until dawn.

Minutes later as she lay in bed, even though she was exhausted she couldn't shut off her mind. Not only did her brain whirl with all the events and emotions of the night, but thoughts of Henry also filled her head and her heart.

She needed to get home. She couldn't stay here any longer. She'd allowed him into her heart in a way no other man had ever been. Each and every moment she spent with him only deepened her love for him.

It was time to go.

Chapter 14

Henry felt sick.

She was leaving. They were leaving. Even though he'd known this time would come, he wasn't ready to tell them goodbye, even if it was just a temporary goodbye.

It was midafternoon and the sun shone through the window as she finished the last of her packing. "I hate to see you go," he said.

"I know, but it's not like this is a final goodbye." She shut her suitcase and smiled at him, but her smile looked forced. The sunshine found her hair and sparkled in it and a press of emotion rose up in Henry's chest. He swallowed against it, unsure why this was so difficult.

She pulled her suitcase off the bed and set it on the floor. "I need some time at home, Henry." Her eyes weren't as bright as they usually were. "I need some time to process everything that's happened."

He nodded. "I know. At least we know now that there's no more danger here. The next time you come back things will be completely different. You'll have no reason to be afraid."

She gazed at him with an enigmatic expression on her face. "I'm just glad it's all over for you…for us."

"I'm sorry, Melissa. I'm so sorry that you and the boys were put in any danger."

She held up a hand to stop him. "Don't apologize. It wasn't your fault. You couldn't have known about Charlie. You have nothing to be sorry for." She glanced at her watch. "And now, I really need to get on the road."

He nodded and reluctantly picked up her suitcase. Together they went down the stairs, where Mary and the twins were in the living room.

"You'll come back, won't you?" Mary asked worriedly.

"Of course," Melissa replied. "And anytime you want you're welcome to come to Amarillo for a visit."

Mary smiled. "I might just surprise you."

"I'd love a visit from you," Melissa replied. She leaned down and picked up James from the blanket on the floor where they had been lying.

"I'll get Joey," Mary said. As she picked up the smiling little boy tears filled her eyes. She looked at Melissa and gave her a teary smile. "I don't know what's worse, saying goodbye to these precious boys or saying goodbye to you."

"I packed up some of the Christmas presents in the

trunk," Henry said as they all left the house and walked to Melissa's car, and Mary put Joey in his car seat. "If you need or want anything else, just give me a call."

"We'll be fine," Melissa said, then leaned into the backseat to buckle James into his seat. When she straightened, her gaze held Henry's for a long moment.

In the blue depths of her eyes Henry saw words unspoken and a shine of emotion that momentarily stole his breath away. It was there only a moment, then gone.

"Thank you. Thank you both for your generosity," she said. Once again her gaze met Henry's and he thought she was going to say something more, but instead she slid into the driver's seat and waved goodbye.

As he watched her car disappear down the driveway, he was struck with the fiercest wave of loneliness he'd ever felt.

"You're a fool, Henry James Randolf," his mother exclaimed and started back into the house.

"What are you talking about? I didn't do anything," he said.

"That's right. And that's why you're a fool." She went into the front door and slammed it behind her.

Henry swiped a hand through his hair and sighed. Women. He'd never understand them. His mother was probably upset with him because he hadn't managed to talk Melissa into moving into the carriage house. But after the trauma she'd suffered the night before, he hadn't wanted to pressure her anymore about it.

There might be a time in the future to bring up the subject again. In the meantime he had some things to take care of that would hopefully take his mind off the empty ache inside his chest.

For the next three days Henry stayed as busy as he could. Everyone in town was stunned to hear what Charlie had done and Henry was shocked and warmed by the amount of support he received from friends and neighbors.

He also made a difficult apology to Tom Burke, who surprised him by saying he was resigning his position as city manager and he and his wife were moving to Florida.

It was each evening after his mother had gone to bed and he sat in his chair with a glass of scotch when thoughts of Melissa and the boys filled his head.

It was amazing how much they had imbued the house with warmth, with joy. He missed seeing her smile and hearing that musical laugh of hers as she teased him. He missed talking to her, just sharing moments of time that could never be recaptured again.

She was a wonderful woman and someday she'd make some man a wonderful wife. He couldn't help it that he wasn't the man to fill that role in her life.

He would be the best father that he could be, but that's all he had to offer her. He hadn't pretended to be anything else but what he was—a confirmed bachelor.

The time with Henry at his house had taken on the quality of a wonderful dream as Melissa threw herself back into her real life. The boys settled back into their normal routine as if they'd never been away from home and Melissa tried to do the same.

It was Thursday morning when she sat at her computer in her living room working to build a brand-new slick webpage to advertise her business.

The twins were on the living-room floor, babbling happily to her and to each other. At least they didn't appear any worse for the drama that had taken place in that little shanty. Even Melissa was surprised by how easily she'd managed to put it all behind her. She had a life to build and couldn't dwell on that night with Charlie and how close she'd come to losing everything.

She tried not to think too much about Henry. She was in his life by accident and she couldn't forget that. It hurt to think of him, to love him and know that she would always be the mother of his children but never the woman of his heart.

For the past four nights she'd spent hours on the internet trying to reconnect with MysteryMom but she hadn't been able to find the woman in any of the chat rooms she'd visited or anywhere else. It was as if she'd been a figment of Melissa's imagination.

Melissa would have liked to tell her that she'd successfully united Joey and James with their daddy and in that respect the story had a happy ending.

And someday maybe Melissa would find her happy ending with a man who would love her, a man who wouldn't be able to wait to marry her. At the moment the idea of romance with anyone left a bad taste in her mouth. It would take her a while to heal, to get over the heartbreak of loving Henry.

At least he hadn't spoken again about her moving into the carriage house. If he brought it up again she was afraid she would confess that the reason she didn't want to live there was because she was in love with him. She didn't want to burden him with her love. The last thing she wanted to do was complicate their relationship.

It was important for the boys' sake that Henry and Melissa's relationship remain calm and pleasant, not filled with stress or tension.

She stopped working on the webpage at six and fed the boys a bottle, then snuggled with them on the sofa. This was the time of the evening when loneliness struck her the hardest.

As the twins got sleepy and fell silent, the quiet of the apartment pressed in on her. She couldn't help but remember those nights with Henry when they'd sat and talked and just shared little pieces of each other.

She had to make sure in the future she maintained an emotional distance from him. She was going to have to see him on a regular basis but somehow, someway, she had to uninvolve her heart where he was concerned.

When the boys had fallen asleep she carried them one at a time to the cribs in their small bedroom then returned to the living room. She sat back down at the computer, but her thoughts were still consumed by Henry. He'd called every day since she'd been home, short chats about the twins that had only made it more difficult for her to gain the emotional distance she needed from him.

He'd wanted her to drive back to Dalhart this weekend, but she'd told him that she wasn't ready to make the drive again. He'd been disappointed but seemed to understand and they'd made plans for him to come to her apartment the following weekend.

There was a motel nearby and he could stay there and when she went back to Dalhart she would stay at a motel and he could visit the twins there. It was important that she set boundaries when it came to the visitation. He was her weakness and it would be far too easy for her to fall into his bed if he wanted her every time they were together for visitation.

Even now as she thought about being with him, kissing him and making love with him, she was filled with a longing that knew no bounds.

She was just about to stop working on the webpage and turn on the television when a knock fell on her door. She opened the door and her breath caught in her throat.

Henry. He stood before her as if conjured up by her thought, by her deep longing for him. "Surprise," he said with a smile that looked distinctly uncomfortable.

"Henry... What are you doing here?" She opened the door to allow him inside and as he swept by her she caught the sweet familiar scent that belonged to him alone. She closed the door and turned to face him.

He looked wonderful in a pair of worn jeans and a flannel plaid shirt and his winter coat. He looked just like the sexy, handsome cowboy who had rescued her on that snowy night over a year ago.

"I couldn't wait until next weekend or the weekend after that," he said.

She frowned. "But you've come so late. The boys are already asleep for the night. You should have called and let me know you were coming."

He shrugged out of his coat and laid it across the back of the sofa. "I would have called, but I didn't know

I was coming until I was in the car and on my way." He stared at her for a long moment, his gaze inscrutable. "We need to talk."

He seemed nervous and ill at ease and suddenly she was afraid. Had he come to tell her that he'd changed his mind, that he'd decided he was going to fight her for custody of the twins? Had being away from them made him decide he'd do anything to keep them with him?

"Talk about what?" She sank down on the sofa, afraid that her trembling legs wouldn't hold her up any longer. She motioned him into the chair opposite the sofa but he remained standing with his back against the door, as if he might escape at any moment.

"I want to talk to you about the carriage house," he said.

"Henry, I…"

He held up a hand to stop her from saying anything more. "Please, just listen to me for a minute. I've never offered something to somebody and then taken it back, but that's what I'm doing now. I don't want you to live in the carriage house."

Even though she hadn't intended to move in there, his words shot a sliver of pain through her. He didn't want her there. He didn't want her that close to him.

She nodded and told herself it was for the best. It hadn't been something she wanted to do anyway. "Okay," she replied.

"No, it's not okay. Nothing has been okay since you and the boys left." He shoved off from the door and walked the width of the room to stand in front of her. He stared at her, his expression impossible to read.

He finally drew a deep breath. "I thought I had my life all figured out, then you arrived with the boys and everything got all screwed up."

"I'm sorry. It was never my intention to mess up your life," she replied. Could this get more horrible? She fought back the sting of tears, refusing to allow him to see the depth of emotion inside her where he was concerned.

With one smooth movement he sat next to her. "My mother told me that my father might have done me a disservice in pounding into my head that all any woman would ever want from me was my money. Certainly my relationship with Hilary proved him right."

"But he was wrong, Henry," Melissa exclaimed fervently. "You're a wonderful man and you'd be a wonderful man with or without your money."

He smiled then, that slow sexy grin that would always have the capacity to warm her. "Last night I was sitting in the living room alone and thinking about the boys and what the future might hold. When I thought about them mounting a horse for the very first time, you were there in my vision. When I visualized putting them on the bus for their first day of school, in my vision you were standing beside me and holding my hand. Each and every fantasy of the future I imagined had you in it."

He frowned and his gaze never left hers. "And it wasn't just the boys' future that I fantasized about. I thought about your laughter and the way your eyes light up when you're happy. I thought about sleeping next to you, making love to you and I realized there was no way

I wanted you living a separate life in the carriage house. I don't want you dating. I don't want you to be alone."

She didn't say a word. She was afraid she was misinterpreting what he was telling her. She remained frozen, her gaze locked with his.

"I realize now why it's been so easy for me to be a confirmed bachelor," he continued. "It's because I'd never met a woman I wanted to share my life with, a woman I loved mindlessly, desperately, until I met you."

Melissa's heart soared. "I wasn't going to move into the carriage house because I'm in love with you and I couldn't live there and see you every day and not be a real part of your life."

Her words seemed to break something loose in Henry. His eyes flared bright and he reached out and placed his palm against her cheek. "God, I was hoping you'd say something like that."

"I love you, Henry, but are you sure your feelings for me aren't because of the boys?"

"Melissa, I love you as the mother of my children, but my love doesn't begin and end there. I love you because you're strong and beautiful. I love you because you make me feel like I've never felt before in my life. I want to spend my life with you. Marry me, Melissa. Marry me and move into my house. Let us be a real family together."

His mouth took hers in a kiss that tasted of desire, but more it tasted of the future, of promises made and kept and the family she'd always wanted.

"You haven't answered me," he said when he finally

pulled his mouth from hers. "Will you marry me? Will you share the rest of your life with me?"

"Yes," she replied breathlessly. "Yes! Yes!"

He pulled her into his arms and she leaned her head against his chest, listening to the strong beat of his heart.

"I wonder if MysteryMom has any idea what she's managed to accomplish?" she said.

"I have a feeling she knows," he replied. "I'll give you the world, Melissa. Whatever you want, whatever you need to be happy."

"I don't need or want anything but you and the boys," she replied.

"There is one thing you can eventually give me, if you're willing."

She rose up and looked at him. "What on earth could I possibly give you that you don't already have?"

He smiled, his eyes lit with love. "Twin daughters."

Melissa's heart swelled inside her. She was filled with such love, such joy, that she couldn't find her voice. She could only nod as he once again claimed her mouth with his.

She would forever be grateful for the blizzard that had brought them together on that night so long ago and to a woman named MysteryMom who had led her to happiness that she knew was going to last a lifetime.

Epilogue

She sat in front of her computer and stared at the email she'd just written, but hesitated in hitting the button that would send the message on its way.

MysteryMom picked up the cup of coffee sitting next to her at the desk and took a sip, her mind whirling with the words she'd just typed.

It was amazing what kind of information could be gained when money was no object and you had contacts everywhere in the world. For the past year she'd used those contacts and her money for a mission—the mission of uniting people for the sake of their children.

It had begun when she'd started dropping in on various chat rooms and began to hear stories about women who didn't know where the father of their children were or how to get in touch with them to let them know they were fathers.

The stories had torn at her heart until finally she'd decided to try to do something—use her resources to bring some sort of reunion to the men and women who had parented children.

So far she'd been successful with several couples, but this one worried her. She reread the email she'd composed and thought of the man and woman involved.

A terrible fate had pulled Emily Grainger and Jagger Holtz apart after a single night together. The result of that night had been a daughter named Michelle.

MysteryMom now had the pieces of the puzzle that could potentially bring together Emily and Jagger. She knew the information contained in the email could save a man's life, but might also bring extreme danger to both him and Emily.

He's already in danger, she thought to herself. And if the -mail wasn't sent then in all probability he would die.

She owed it to Jagger Holtz to send the email and she prayed that when she did Emily Grainger would survive whatever consequences might come.

Drawing in a deep breath, the woman who called herself MysteryMom hit the send button.

* * * * *

We hope you enjoyed reading this
special collection from Harlequin® books.

If you liked reading these stories,
then you will love
Harlequin® Romantic Suspense books!

You want sparks to fly!
Harlequin Romantic Suspense stories
deliver strong and adventurous women, brave
and powerful men and the life-and-death
situations that bring them together.

Enjoy four *new* stories from
Harlequin Romantic Suspense
every month!

Available wherever books and
ebooks are sold.

Calvin Sweet knew he was taking some big chances, but
taking risks always invigorated him. Coming back to his
home in Conard County was the first of the new risks. Five
years ago he'd left for the big city because the law was closing in on him.

Returning to the site where he had hung his trophies was
a huge risk, too, although he could claim he was out for a
hike in the spring mountains. There was nothing left, anyway. The law had taken it all, and the sight filled him with
both sorrow and bitterness. Anger, too. They had no right
to take away his hard work, his triumphs, his mementos.

But they had. After five years all that was left were some
remnants of cargo netting rotting in the tree limbs and the
remains of a few sawed-off nooses.

He could close his eyes and remember, and remembering
filled him with joy and a sense of his own huge power, the
power of life and death. The power to take it all away. The
power to enlighten those whose existence was so shallow.

They took it for granted. Calvin never did.

From earliest childhood he had been fascinated by spiders and their webs. He had spent hours watching as insect after insect fell victim to those silken strands, struggling mightily until they were stung and then wrapped up helplessly to await their fate. Each corpse on the web had been a trophy marking the spider's victory. No one ever escaped.

No one had escaped him, either.

He was chosen, just like a spider, to be exactly what he was. Chosen. He liked that word. It fit both him and his victims. They were all chosen to perform the dance of death together, to plumb the reaches of human endurance. To sacrifice the ordinary for the extraordinary. So he quashed his growing need to act and focused his attention on another part of his life. He had a job now, one he needed to report to every evening. He was whistling now as he walked back down to his small ranch.

A spiderweb was beginning to take shape in his mind, one for his barn loft that no one would see, ever. It was enough that he could admire it and savor the gifts there. The impulse to hunt eased, and soon he was in control again. He liked control. He liked controlling himself and others, even as he fulfilled his purpose.

Like the spider, he was not hasty to act. It would have to be the right person at the right time, and the time was not yet right. First he had to build his web.

**Don't miss UNDERCOVER HUNTER
by *New York Times* bestselling author
Rachel Lee, available January 2015 wherever
Harlequin® Romantic Suspense books and
ebooks are sold.**

ROMANTIC suspense

Heart-racing romance, high-stakes suspense!

BAYOU HERO
by *USA TODAY* bestselling author
Marilyn Pappano

Available January 2015

One family's scandal is responsible for a rising body count in New Orleans's Garden District...

Even for an experienced NCIS agent like Alia Kingsley, the murder scene is particularly gruesome. A man killed in a fit of rage. Being the long-estranged son of the deceased, Landry Jackson quickly becomes a person of interest. But does Landry loathe his father as much as the feds suspect?

It's clear to Alia that Landry Jackson has secrets, but his hatred for his father isn't one of them. Alia feels sure Landry isn't the killer, but once more family members start dying, she's forced to question herself. What if the fierce attraction she has developed toward Landry has compromised Alia's instincts?

Don't miss other exciting titles from
USA TODAY bestselling author Marilyn Pappano:

UNDERCOVER IN COPPER LAKE
COPPER LAKE ENCOUNTER
COPPER LAKE CONFIDENTIAL

Available wherever Harlequin® Romantic Suspense
books and ebooks are sold.

ROMANTIC suspense

Heart-racing romance, high-stakes suspense!

HIGH-STAKES PLAYBOY
by *New York Times* bestselling author
Cindy Dees

Available January 2015

Who will get this Prescott bachelor first— the girl or the killer?

To help his brothers, marine pilot Archer Prescott goes undercover to find out who's sabotaging their movie set. But the die-hard bachelor isn't ready for what he finds in the High Sierras: his doe-eyed girl-next-door camerawoman is the prime suspect.

Marley Stringer isn't as innocent as she seems. As Marley turns irresistible and the aerial "accidents" turn deadly, Archer begins to wonder who's more dangerous—the perfect woman who threatens his heart...or the desperate killer who threatens his life.

Don't miss the first exciting installment from Cindy Dees's *The Prescott Bachelors* series:

HIGH-STAKES BACHELOR

Available wherever Harlequin® Romantic Suspense books and ebooks are sold.

www.Harlequin.com

HRS27903

HARLEQUIN®

A Romance FOR EVERY MOOD™

Stay up-to-date on all your
romance-reading news with the
Harlequin Shopping Guide,
featuring bestselling authors, exciting new
miniseries, books to watch and more!

The newest issue will be delivered right to you
with our compliments! There are 4 each year.

Signing up is easy.

EMAIL

ShoppingGuide@Harlequin.ca

WRITE TO US

HARLEQUIN BOOKS
Attention: Customer Service Department
P.O. Box 9057, Buffalo, NY 14269-9057

OR PHONE

1-800-873-8635 in the United States
1-888-343-9777 in Canada

Please allow 4-6 weeks for delivery of the first issue by mail.